ROB BROWNELL

ALLIGOR

This story is entirely a work of fiction. The characters or incidents portrayed in it arose in the author's fevered imagination or from his hazy impressions of ancient history and religion. Any resemblance to any actual living person, tribe, event, organisation, place or contemporary global superpower must therefore be assumed to be entirely coincidental.

For more information see www.alligor.co.uk

One

Who knows how the winds arise? Some say there is an immortal being to whom the gods have entrusted a sack that contains the winds: others that the winds are themselves gods. Benign Zefir or boisterous old Borea leave their mountain caves in due season and move over the earth according to their characters. But what of those winds that come out of their proper season, unnatural movements of the air which because of their nature are usually ascribed to evil djinni or daemons? These are winds of enormous power and are sometimes spoken of as winds of prophecy, or chastisement, or even of moral change. And who is to say that when the order of the world of men is overturned by evil, that this outrage should not be reflected in the order of nature? After all, are we not creatures of the wind? We breathe the moving air and speak by shaping the wind in our throats. It is a remarkable thing therefore that by writing words it is as if you seize the wind in your hand and make visible that which is invisible and impossible to grasp. To read therefore is sometimes to let loose that which has been imprisoned. (Johannes Petrafluvius: *Uvae Irae* cap.i)

Afterwards they would say that it began with a sunset. Clouds soared upwards, luminous and beautiful like celestial palaces, but their bright rosy glow soon darkened into livid tints of corruption and decay. Late travellers looked at the evening sky and imagined the dust of clashing armies or the smoke of burning cities. They glanced uneasily over their shoulders and hurried to their night's refuge. The darkness was humid and close. Most slept restlessly with half-dreams of hoofbeats and armed strangers who passed in the night.

The people of the plain awoke to a dawn of preternatural stillness. Not a leaf or blade of grass stirred. The birds were silent. The sky was brightening in the east, but in the west the mountains were hidden by a thick orange haze. Early workers in the fields exchanged worried looks as the sulphurous clouds climbed up the sky. Soon the entire western horizon was obscured. All work stopped as the people became aware of a distant noise: a constant roar like a fever headache. It grew louder. All faces turned west. They saw the landscape vanishing under a wind-blown tidal wave of torn leaves, snapped twigs and choking pink dust. As one they turned and fled.

The wind stripped the roofs from houses, barns and byres. The villagers clung to each other as the snug fastnesses of their homes were opened to the racing sky. Buildings that had stood for a hundred seasons swayed and fell. The soft emerging leaves were blasted and blackened by the wind. The nostrils of the nursling lambs were choked with dust. Everything good and new and fresh had to be sheltered or it would perish. Everything loved for its age and its permanence seemed to be the special quarry of this fearful gale. Here the age-silvered barn door, its wrought iron hinges grown like ivy into the planks, had survived for generations by careful handling and fond usage. The wind tore it from its pinions and spread its bones across the farmyard. There the ancient bell-tower had held evil spirits at bay for centuries, but now it was rudely pushed over into the nave, shattering the marble pavement and cracking the altar stone. This was no ordinary storm of air. The tumult did not cease. There was no healing deluge. The sun did not return to warm the earth. The people sensed a vicious, punishing force at work: vindictive without reason; vengeful without cause.

The wind raced onwards across the plain. With no more natural barriers to overcome, it became lewd, cruel and mocking. It lifted the veils of young maidens and, as the matrons stooped to work the soil, it hoisted their skirts over their backs. When the workers left the fields, the new seedlings were torn from the ground and flung against the field walls. The wind stole the tilth from the land of the honest husbandman and piled it in drifts against the doors of the idle. It whirled the straw from the peasant's stack. It ripped the silken clothes from the merchant's drying wall and draped them on thorn bushes. Roaring soundlessly with sadistic pleasure the great gale tore over land which became ever less fertile, ever more arid and sparsely populated. Still it sought out what was fresh and young or vulnerable through age.

Daylight faded and the storm still raged. A sleepless night, a red-eyed dawn, and still the sky roared across the plain. The brawling wind was not softened by the grinding poverty of the lands it scourged. Here the ancient carpentry could not be replaced because the woods and trees had all long since been cut down. A wind-blighted field meant starvation for the family who depended on it. A well of water choked by wind-blown dust could not be re-dug in time. Day followed day without any respite. The weight of the wind slowly tipped the scales of survival, sending whole communities into perilous flight as refugees. Even on the road the dispossessed poor were harried; their tents torn from their huddled forms and flung away to the horizon. The whole land shrank from the blast. Blinded by the whirling, stinging dust; buffeted by its bullying force, the people had to bow their heads in deference to its power.

Only in one place did the wind meet an obstacle against which it was powerless: a barrier beyond which it could not press. In the midmost point of the barren plain it came against mighty windowless walls which stopped its vicious career. For five days the wind beat futilely against the book-city of Alligor, then, its force spent, it fled out of the land and across the gulf of waters, bending the spars of the heeling dhows and galleys which cut across the sparkling ocean.

Alligor still stood, but though the wind had not loosened a tile or turned back the lead on the roof; though not even the slightest breath had penetrated its silent halls; though not a mote of its dust of ages had been stirred: its fate was sealed.

Two

The library was the city and the city was the library. It was old, old past memories, past histories, past dreaming. Once it had been close to the heart of a mighty empire but the empire had passed away. Now no-one knew which state had conquered, which states had succumbed. Through the millennia, kingdoms had grown, flourished, spread, absorbing lesser states, then decayed, lost their territories, their very identities. Languages had changed. Religions which had swept the world lost their grip on the souls of nation after nation. New prophets promised new paradises, until they too were forgotten. Even the colours of the peoples' skins had changed as the shifting balance of powers dappled the face of the great plains like the shadows of summer clouds. Whilst cities rose in splendour and crumbled into dust, only Alligor, the City of the Book, still stood: an eternal monument to the enlightened despotism of a forgotten emperor. In a world of tumult and destruction, the Book City seemed to have a charmed existence. Even passing armies had treated it with superstitious reverence. Whether they swept by in the full panoply of successful conquest or straggled back in ignominious rout: Alligor was not touched.

For thousands of years the wisdom of the world had been accumulating in the great library. Nearly everything of value which had ever been written had somehow found its way to the leagues of shelves. From the sweat-stained manuscripts of humble scholars: a life's work bound up with hide thongs and carried barefoot across continents; to the bejewelled volumes of monarchs bequeathed by the camel-load; all had been accepted. Alligor had no gate-keepers, for who could say that one book was more worth saving than another? Mere mortals might express preference from amongst many, but judgement was for the gods. The number of books increased until there were too many for a scholar to read in one lifetime. Still the library accepted everything it was given, no matter the language, just so long as it was written down in words. Gradually the library filled itself with words: words scratched on soft stone, incised in wax, pressed into copper, painted onto silk; then in ink on papyrus, parchment or paper; words on tablets, on rolls and bundles of leaves, all bagged, bound up or boxed. As more books arrived, more and more books remained unread. Without constant attention they gathered dust. Beneath the sift of ages, in the silence of neglected rooms, the millions of books waited patiently for their chance to speak. Everything was collated and arranged, but whether according to subject, or age, or beauty or rarity was not clear. The hundreds of librarians had all had their part to play in the great inscrutable task of arrangement, but none could say if there was a great master plan, for in such an abundance they could only know their own small parts.

Scholars who consulted the great archive often found that one book led to another in a disconcerting way. Many believed the place to be enchanted. A two-day visit to consult a rare volume often extended into weeks, into months, into years. The call of the books was strong. For some it was irresistible. The mythology of Alligor included stories of young men who entered the library and never came out again, of old men who came out and who no-one remembered having gone in. Some, they said, came out with the light of the other world already shining in their eyes, too weak to manage more than a score of steps beyond the great gate. They were buried where they fell, all their wisdom reduced to a heap of stones.

The original architect of the city had built for eternity and planned for a virtually unlimited accumulation of literature. Sheer walls of dressed red sandstone rose a hundred feet above the plain and enclosed an area of almost a square mile. According to legend there had once been room for a thousand tents inside the great courtyard of the Book City but, through the centuries, as the collection grew, the courtyard had been quarried for stone and gradually built over to create new galleries and storerooms. Every structure above ground meant more space under the surface for granaries and cisterns.

All the windows looked onto internal courtyards or light wells. The only opening in the outer walls was the great gateway. The mighty bronze and steel doors could open to let a fully laden war elephant pass inside. When they were closed they would repulse an army. These gates bore an inscription in several ancient classical scripts. The original words had such a multiplicity of meanings as to render any literal translation inadequate, but they were usually roughly translated as: 'The fruit of the tree of knowledge is sweet in the mouths of the pure in heart, but poison in the mouths of the faithless'. The inscription was popularly assumed to refer to a powerful spell which had been laid upon the library at the time of its foundation.

Beside the gateway, the smooth sandstone walls had been defaced by the scratchings of thousands of scholars and passers-by. Some were touchingly human: 'I AM ALI THE MERCHANT AND I BROUGHT MY WIFE YEAR 640'. Others were tinged with historical irony: 'KURIS SOLDIER IN THE ARMIES OF THE MIGHTY KAISER DIMIAN PASSED BY ON THE CONQUEST OF THE WORLD YEAR 1666' . Two years later Dimian's whole army had perished in a nightmarish month long battle against disease and Greek fire in the swamps of Zandria. Nearly all the greatest thinkers and scholars of the past had scratched their autograph on the wall: 'CLATON SEEKER FOR TRUTH YEAR 369' was the best known. The great philosopher's name had been almost worn away by the fingers of visitors tracing the letters in near religious devotion. Scholars would nod sagely at the tiny autograph of: 'PHILOKARPUS OF TYRO' slashed through by a great diagonal forming a letter of 'SARDON KING OF KINGS'. Philokarpus had conquered the world with his ideas whilst both King Sardon and his empire had vanished without trace. All that was known of Sardon was that he was arrogant enough to proclaim himself in letters as big as a man and ignorant enough to deface the name of the author of 'The Wisdom of Kings'. One name remained untouched and unapproached by any other hand in a clear patch of wall: that of 'GROPIUS' the black archimage. It was a name to frighten children and cause even the godless to touch their amulets in dread.

Down the ages visitors had gazed at names upon names upon names which stretched for hundreds of yards on either side of the gateway. At eye level were the foot travellers, higher up came the horsemen and above them the rulers and their elephant drivers. Now, for the first time ever, the names were hidden from view. The wind had driven the dust of the plains before it and pushed huge drifts of it against the massive walls. The giant doors were blocked by tons of sand. The mouth of the Book City was stopped.

Three

No-one inside Alligor knew about the wind. But Small knew. He knew because he had tried to get out on the roofs, had felt the stinging blast and had been forced to cover his face and retreat. He knew by his rumbling intestines just how long he had been prevented from foraging for birds' eggs and wild strawberries in amongst the acres of valleys, gables, gutters and sinks which formed the roof landscape. Alligor raised a great roof plateau above the surrounding plain. Metalled domes of every variation of form and size alternated with terraces of lead, copper or bitumen. Hillsides of riven stone tiles were patterned with thick encrustations of lichens and deep beds of mosses. Vertical cliffs of dressed stone reared above deep valleys, the bottoms of which ran like rivers when the rains came. The rainwater filled gutters and channels, each ending in a dark overgrown cavern and a deep shaft down which the torrents tumbled into the underground cisterns. Down the ages, every nook and hollow which wasn't scoured by wind and water had silted up with airborne dust. The silt held moisture. Sometimes this was the merest hint of damp, jealously guarded by cacti and speargrass. But often, particularly where gutters had become blocked, quite extensive meres and flashes formed. Round these fragile oases grew stunted figs and tamarinds, vines and tiny wild strawberries, seeded by the flocks of brightly coloured birds of passage which rested on the roofs in their migrations. Even large trees grew on the roof, sometimes in surprising places. One massive stone gable was cracked and riven by the roots of an enormous cedar of Lebanon whose strange horizontal foliage shaded a whole valley of exotic ferns. The roof was Small's private domain. Only Small and the old man knew about the secret ways into the upper levels of the galleries. The old man seemed to know a lot, but even he didn't know how to get onto the roofs. Only Small knew that, and as far as he knew, there was only the one way up.

The roof was not just a playground for Small. It was his health and strength. Without the natural harvest of his roof-Eden, both Small and the old man would have been reduced to the same state of shambling lethargy as the other librarians. Their monotonous and meagre diet of old grains and rancid oil from the book-city's store sapped their vital spirits, numbed their brains, and made them curiously prone to bouts of hallucinatory vision. Sometimes Small felt guilty about his secret food supply but there never seemed to be enough even for himself. He was always hungry.

The great gale shocked Small. He had never before been prevented from foraging by natural violence of this sort. He was not just hungry, he was frightened. He had to tell the old man. He was Old. He would know about these things. Even though Small knew the parts of the library where the old man was most likely to be found, it was no simple task to seek him out. The library had grown organically according to the interests of book-donors or of librarians. Consequently, rooms opened into rooms, smaller rooms into larger rooms or larger into smaller. Some suites of rooms ended in blank walls, others led into other suites. Sometimes long winding gallery corridors linked distant architectural masses together. They might be airy and spacious, carried on bridges thrown over the lightwells and courtyards, or they might be dim passages contained within the thickness of the massive walls. Stairways of every shape and style linked the levels in a similar unsystematic fashion.

To reach a point directly below you on a lower floor might be a simple matter of going to the stairway in the corner of the room. On the other hand, that stairway might only go up - or it might go down five floors without any access doorways. To get where you wanted to go could take several days of horizontal and vertical meandering through many levels of the library and every solar orientation. But then, no-one in Alligor ever travelled simply in order to find a geographical location - unless of course it was the refectory. Travel was from book to book. Readers were impelled by ideas, and the most interesting and imaginative linkages could sometimes be arrived at only by circuitous routes. Alligor was a labyrinth in which even a Minotaur might lose itself. The Ariadne in its echoing corridors was wisdom - her clew unwinding from the beginning of the world guiding her lovers through the maze of human affairs.

The history of every ancient and beautiful city is embodied in its street plan. Alligor was no exception. But the book-city had no trade routes, no commercial districts, no military barracks, no religious foundations as such. Alligor had been shaped by the history of ideas. The pattern of communications in the library had been formed by rivers of thought, broad pathways of common understanding, blind alleys of delusion, ambulatories of error, intricate labyrinths of subtle logic. Whole avenues of investigation had been opened up by religious enthusiasm. Heretical thought simmered behind bricked-up doorways. Stairways spiralled down into bare limewashed cells shaped by ascetic zeal, or upwards into high and shadowy chambers of mystical proportions. The galleries had been built according to the spirit of their ages, whether religious or enquiring, mechanical or mythical. Each room had its mood. It was as if the thoughts of the authors hung in the air. Small could scamper through most of the library galleries, but certain rooms seemed to command decorum: a measured stride through a chamber of Law, a military tramp through the galleries of stratagem. Above all, certain rooms containing clusters of occult works could only be traversed on tiptoe, with frequent glances over the shoulder and a final sprint for the door.

It was a day and a half before Small found the old man. He was huddled in a window niche on the fourth level on the East side, dozing. Spots of tinted light from the coloured window glass spilled over his face, beard and ragged robes.

"Greetings, Old"

"Greetings, Small. Have you food for me?"

"No, Old. There was a great wind. I was nearly blown off the roof. It threw sand in my face. I could not see or breathe."

There was a silence as the old man digested this news.

"No doves' eggs?"

"No."

"No wild fruit or tender plants?"

"Nothing at all, Old."

Another silence.

"A great wind you say? I think I felt it." The old man's hand floated around his face and upper body brushing cobwebs away. "I had a dream. I dreamed of a dark unholy beast that bellowed in wild triumph over the bones of broken temples. It turned towards me, towards Alligor. Its foul breath buffeted me."

"What does the dream mean? What is this Beast, Old?"

"That is difficult to say." The old man spoke slowly and deliberately. "It may be nothing. The sport of the Great Author. But sometimes great spiritual movements have their effect on the material world. This gale is perhaps no ordinary movement of the airs. Great immorality can cause an unbalancing of Nature. It may be quite literally a breath of evil on the land, the material counterpart of a ripple which passed through the world of dreams. It could even be that there is a demonic power loose in the world..."

Old stopped suddenly. He seemed to be trying to recall something long forgotten.

"The wind is very bad, Old." said Small after another long silence.

After yet another long pause in which the only sound was Small's hard foot rhythmically scuffing the pavement, a curious change seemed to come over the old man. With a visible effort he raised himself to his feet clutching at Small's shoulder to stop himself tottering. His face seemed to have hardened into an expression of weary resolve.

"It is time, Small. I almost fear I have left everything too late. I am stupid, old and tired, but we must begin straight away."

"Begin what, Old? What do you mean?" Small followed as the old man shuffled painfully through the galleries past the endless shelves of books and manuscripts.

"Do you know who I am, Small?"

"You are Old."

He smiled. "Yes, I am Old. But I was not always Old. Once upon a time I was Small like you. I was Quicksilver, I was Youngstrong, and then my name changed again. I was known as Clever, then Wise, then Allwise. You see, I did not have the roofs to play on. The books were my world and I read constantly. I read so much that I had to seek through the galleries for the sort of books I liked. I learned many things about the Library. I began to discover its secrets. The paths through the Book-Maze began to open to me. I began to see patterns in the arrangement of the books. I began, as you have, with fantastical fairy stories and magical adventures in imaginary kingdoms - believing everything, lost in wonder. How the older readers laughed at me when I asked them if those places I read about were far away!" He paused whilst the young boy opened the heavy oak door into the next gallery. The noise of the latch echoed hollowly.

"Slowly I realized that some kingdoms existed only in the mind. That there was history and there was faerie. For a while I blushed with shame at my childish gullibility. Then I determined to separate truth from falsehood. History became my study. One kingdom in particular fascinated me. Its history seemed to be the embodiment of all the adventure stories I had read. It seemed a wonderful place and I could not read enough about it. Above all else it was a real place. It existed in the world. I read how noble its citizens were, how beautiful its maidens, how wise its rulers, how cunning its generals. I read how their armies had freed many other states from tyrannical rulers. How those other peoples must have rejoiced when they were freed! I started to search for the books and poems of these liberated folk and found - nothing. Only when I looked outside these 'liberated' lands did I begin to find other accounts of my wonderful kingdom. At first I did not recognize it, so darkly was it painted. An evil satanic empire ruled by selfishness, greed and lust, its people little more than slaves to their desires and fears. It invaded its neighbours without reason, profaned their ancient sacred places, suppressed their books, drained the wealth of the cities and corrupted youth. Any who spoke out disappeared. Its armies waded in the blood of innocents. I was greatly perplexed. How could the truth ever be discovered if every historian told a different story? But then I remembered..."

"The Mirror of Almeira!" Small's sudden exclamation echoed down the galleries.

The old man was genuinely surprised. "You are even quicker witted than I thought, Small! How did you know that was the book?"

"Because that book taught me too that there can be great truth in poetry and great lies in history. I read it first as a faerie story and only much later saw that there is great wisdom hidden in its foolish plot."

"Just so, my small friend! Little did I suspect how important that book was to be. I read it many times before I saw my path open before me. When I knew which book I was seeking, I was able to reason where it would be found. When I got to the place, I found an old man sitting by a window with the book I wanted in his hands ..."

"But Old! That's just how it happened with me and you!"

"So it was, Small. So it was."

Small puzzled over this curious coincidence and what it might mean.

"I don't understand. How did he know? How did *you* know? What are these paths you speak of? What is the Book-Maze?"

"The old man was to be my teacher, my guide, as I must be yours Small. He was waiting for me because he had been watching me. As you will have noticed, not all the infants abandoned at the great door of the Book-City grow up to love books. Of those who become readers, many lose their way. They wander off the paths seeking power in knowledge of the Black Arts, magic, Mantik, alchemy. Some pursue the futilities of the politic art, and others slump into moral degradation, reading only books concerning lust and sensuality. Of all the orphan babes we take in to raise in the ways of the Books, only a handful have the moral character to seek persistently for truth. Of these just one in a generation might have the sharpness of intellect to find his way. The hidden passages of the upper levels were created so that those who had mastered the patterns of the library could find others who had the wit to do the same. Through the secret spy-holes in the upper levels, the old man had been reading over the shoulders of all the readers in the Eastern Galleries. He knew every book I had ever read."

"Spy-holes! Did you spy on me, Old?"

"Of course, small one, that was my task."

"Why was it your task?"

13

"The library must be looked after. Only those who know its true value can really care for it. My task has been to seek them out."

Small was not sure where this strange tale was leading. "Are you going to show me the secret paths? Are they like the secret stairs to the upper levels? And this Book-Maze, are you going to lead me through it?"

The old man gave a dry chuckle. "No Small, you misunderstand. And yet in a metaphorical sense you are right. The secret paths can lead you up out of the ordinary world and onto a higher plane of understanding. My task was to help you to understand the nature of the Maze of Knowledge, and, as far as I was able, to prevent you losing your way. But now...What to do now? What to do?"

Small was struggling to open the door which led from the gallery into the Great Eastern Stairwell. Like many of the library doors it had sagged on its worn hinges and was cutting a wide arc into the stone threshold. Small held the massive wrought latch with both hands and braced his feet against the wall. With all his strength he was just able to jerk the door open, a few fingers' widths at a time.

"You see Small, the doors of knowledge do not open easily. To find the paths, to know the Library, can take a whole lifetime. In the past, when the library was rich, scholars came from all corners of the earth. There were many librarians and many masters. All were well fed and looked after. But now, the world has forgotten us. Even the caravans no longer pass our door. The lands around have grown poor and arid. The tithes which used to fill our granaries are worthless. For many years no-one has had proper food. What grain we have is old and dry. The oil is bad. The Library is mortally sick."

"What will the Masters do, Old?"

"Know this, small one, there are no more Masters. There is only me. Know also that in twenty years you are the only foundling left at the Great Door. You may well be the last librarian. So you see, there is only you and me to save the Library and all it contains. I am Old. I have not much time left. Soon there will only be you."

The two figures spiralled down into the gloom of the giant stairwell. Small felt threatened and uneasy. In his short life he had only ever known the Book-City. He had no experience of the world beyond the Great Door. Suddenly everything familiar and solid seemed about to topple off its shelf. The Library had seemed eternal - it had been there so long. Everything about it spoke of age and permanence. It seemed impossible that it could end. The old man too. Had he not always been old? He was the nearest thing to a father that Small had ever had. Small had never considered that Old might be mortal. Even Mother Nature herself seemed suddenly hostile and dangerously unstable. What had Old called it? An 'unbalancing of Nature', and what about the 'dark unholy beast' that crushed sacred shrines, was it coming to crush the Library too?

"Old you frighten me." Small's voice echoed hollowly. "The Library has been here for so long. Could it really be no more? Who would want to see such a thing happen? And why? Can't we find someone to give us food? Will no-one help us? What can we do?"

The old man stopped. He leaned against the curve of the wall. His breathing was rapid and harsh. A slight sheen of sweat gleamed upon his nose and cheeks. Wisps of dirty grey hair clung wetly to his forehead. After a while his breathing became quieter. "How well did you read the *Mirror of Almeira*? Can you remember the lion hunt? When a wounded animal shouts for help it is already dead. The others of its kind flee from it. The predators hear an invitation to dine."

"What are we going to do, Old?"

"Do? Well first we're going to get something to eat."

Despite the gnawing emptiness of his stomach, Small was not sure this was a good idea. There was always an element of risk involved in eating from the library store. Everything had a tang of mildew and the after effects could range from vomiting and diahorrea to hallucinations and even death. Though the kitchen staff had learned not to use the grains tainted by the blue ergot mould, there were plenty of other less obvious poisons in the store. As the levels of the granaries got lower and lower, more and more ancient corruptions were being uncovered.

The refectory flanked the Great Gate. It was one of the oldest parts of Alligor. As well as feeding the librarians and readers, it had in times gone by also functioned as part of a caravanserai where the camel and mule trains from the east could rest in safety and relative comfort. The shadowy vastness of its high vaulted interior was still impressive. The present emptiness of the building spoke eloquently of past glories and present decline. At the foot of a slanting shaft of daylight, a knot of seven or eight diners huddled by the kitchen entrance. Small and the old man headed towards them.

"Don't worry," the old man said, with a wink to reassure him, "these other folk have eaten already and they seem healthy enough."

The group of diners included some familiar faces. Small recognized the large square form of Dim. The big man beamed with delight.

"It's Thmall! It's Thmall! Look, look! Thmall's coming to eat!"

God had touched Dim at birth. He had that strange simplicity of mind which excludes all guile. His colossal strength had never ever been used in anger. No matter what cruel tricks had been played on him, no matter what hurtful words had been heaped on his head, his reaction was always the same puzzled smile. Dim could not be devious, or lie. He didn't seem able to reason out the advantages of such actions. In the end, even his worst tormentors grew strangely fond of this great guileless child-man.

"Thmall! Thit here! Thit by me!" Dim shuffled sideways along the bench to make a space. This sudden movement caused the angular figure at the end of the bench to descend abruptly onto the stone pavement. Violent cursing arose from the flailing heap of bony limbs and raggy robes on the floor. Dim reached down a massive fist, grabbed the cursing bundle and set it, not quite the right way up, back on the seat. The enraged features of Tentpole reared above the edge of the table.

"Thorry Tentpole." Dim mumbled. His crestfallen expression was genuine, but momentary. Before Tentpole had drawn breath for a new outburst, Dim turned back to face Small, his face beaming, and totally oblivious of the blows which the outraged Tentpole began to rain on his back.

"My friend Thmall!" he announced proprietarily to the whole table.

The titters and snorts of laughter at Tentpole's discomfiture were drowned in the fit of coughing which overtook that poor man after he inhaled some part of the great cloud of dust which his blows had detached from Dim's robe. The table subsided into expectancy. Old picked up a slab of hard bread and put a handful of wet grains upon it from the communal bowl. After nodding to the other diners he began to eat noisily and messily. Their curiosity being thwarted, they shifted their attention onto Small. Small smiled widely at them and then became suddenly engrossed in his own slab of bread.

It was Sly who spoke first. He had the hollow cheeks and unhealthy complexion which marked all those who ate in the refectory. "So, small one, it is a long while since we last saw you in our humble dining room."

Through a mouthful of food, Small mumbled what might have been agreement.

"It is a great wonder of Nature," continued Sly, "how small boys manage to survive without visiting the Refectory. All the kitchen helpers find it very unusual, almost supernatural, And yet you seem to thrive on your fasting. Won't you let us in on your secret?"

Small adopted what he hoped was an open and innocent expression, shrugged his shoulders and stuffed more bread into his mouth in order to avoid answering. He felt deep and secret guilt about the food from the roof. The other diners noticed his face reddening.

16

Tentpole sensed that the hunt was up.

"Yes, Small, what is your secret? Where do you eat if not here?"

"Tell them Thmall!" said Dim, sensing the boy's discomfiture and having every confidence in his ability to explain.

In desperation Small reached for another piece of bread. His hand was suddenly gripped by Sly.

"Not so fast, boy, you'll do yourself harm."

Small began to feel the first intimations of panic.

Old spoke without looking up from his food.

"Let the boy eat, Sly, he must be half-starved." His tone was disinterested and yet he too was alarmed at the directness of the conversation. Sly had obviously been brooding upon the subject for some time. It might be difficult to throw dust in his eyes this time. Old had however succeeded in diverting attention away from the boy. Sly shifted his intense gaze onto the old man.

"Perhaps you might be able to solve our riddle, since it seems to me that you too can do without the sustenance provided by our hard working kitchen staff?"

"How's that Sly? I'm eating now aren't I? Perhaps you and I have simply visited the Refectory at different times from each other?"

The answer might have satisfied the lethargic logic of the other diners, but Sly had not come by his name without reason. He had expected such a simple ploy.

"But Old, I missed your stimulating conversation. I asked the kitchen staff to watch out for you. They could not remember having seen you at all."

"Oho!" Old guffawed loudly, "Forgive me Sly, but I shouldn't arrange any shelves by that! The kitchen staff are not famous for their feats of memory – that's why they are here instead of in the Library. Alligor is full of old men with irregular eating habits!"

Sly was about to speak but checked himself momentarily as he cast around for a response to this setback. It was enough. Old clapped Tentpole on the shoulder.

"How are your knees, old friend?" Tentpole was obsessed with his painful knees and could talk endlessly about the noises they made, the excruciating pain he felt, the effects of temperature on them and above all the unjustness of Fate which had inflicted such knees upon such a godfearing and blameless character as himself. Several of the diners were all too familiar with Tentpole's endless monologues. Not even the great food mystery would induce them to sit through another. As Tentpole drew in his breath to begin his customary plaint there was a general scramble to leave the table.

It was then that something outside in the sunlit yard caught the attention of those who had stood up and they remained standing by the table. Small too stopped eating and stared out through the arched doorway. Some sort of struggle or dispute was taking place at the foot of the Great Gate. Soon all the diners had turned to see what was happening. The kitchen slaveys with their enormous bronze cauldron of slops seemed to be having some difficulty opening the Gate. There were shouts, and dust was being raised. Small saw his chance of escape. After detaching his hand from Sly's bony grip he stood up and wandered out into the bright sunshine to see what was going on.

The Great Gate was a fine piece of ancient engineering. The locking bar, which was said to weigh as much as an elephant, was mounted on rollers. Usually it slid easily in and out of its groove in the wall. Today it was immovable. The kitchen slaveys strained and heaved till the veins bulged on their necks and foreheads but the bar would not budge. They stood back baffled and panting as the librarians ambled over from the refectory to join Small.

"Come on Dim, show them how it's done." This from Spoon, the flabby head cook. Smiling broadly, Dim gripped the serpent handle of the bar and braced himself.

"Save your strength, Dim." Old ran his hand along the locking bar. "The bar is bending. Somehow the doors are being forced inwards. Open the squint and see what is on the outside."

The small square peep-hole was unlatched and a murmur of astonishment arose from the crowd around the Gate when, instead of the expected shaft of sunlight, a steady cascade of fine red dust streamed between the iron bars and fell to the ground. Almost immediately a perfect cone began to form.

"Sand!"

"There must have been a sandstorm, I have read of them happening in the South."

"But here! It has never been known."

Small stared incredulously at the growing heap of sand as it climbed up the face of the Gate. The evil wind had done it. He instinctively looked up at the ragged clouds which raced across the sky. For an instant it seemed that it was the sky which was still and the book city hurtling to its doom. He felt dizzy and the hairs on the back of his neck began to rise. There was a tug on his sleeve. Old was standing behind him. With a barely perceptible twitch of his eye, Old indicated that they should slip away. The extraordinary event at the Gate had caused such general amazement that even Sly did not notice them leave the gate-yard.

The gloom of the refectory was like a pressure on the eyes after the bright sunlight. As they passed the deserted table, Old took the remaining bread and pushed it into his book-pouch. Small was still numbed with the implications of what he had just seen at the Gate.

"Old."

"Yes."

"The wind has blown sand against the gates."

"Yes."

"How much sand will be there?"

"Well, enough to bend the bar, which means too much for us to move from the inside."

"But Old, that means we are trapped in here - perhaps for ever."

"Were you thinking of leaving then?"

"No..." Small checked himself. He had never thought of leaving Alligor, but if Old was right about the Library dying. "But what you told me - about the food and no new librarians - something has to be done."

"Listen boy, I was a doddering old fool and I nearly went to sleep at my post. Now I am still doddering, still old, but wide awake. Do not fret about the food or the Book-Warders. The end of the Library is not to starve to death or mumble into dotage and extinction. If I am right, and now I am almost certain, the final days of the Book-City may well be upon us. Come with me. Make sure we are not followed. I will tell you of the founding of the Library, its purpose and the prophecy of its end. So was it told to me by my Master, and he by his, and so back in an unbroken line to the first Librarian.

"Where are we going, Old?" asked Small, glancing furtively over his shoulder as they entered the stairwell.

"We are going to a place where you have never been. Indeed I am possibly the only person left who knows of its existence. Were I to end my life on these damnable stairs, the secret of the Library would be lost forever."

Old tottered against the wall of the stairwell. "Ha! Don't worry small one," he said, seeing the sudden expression of alarm in the boy's face, "I'm only pausing for breath."

When he had recovered, Old started to climb the stairs again. In a low voice he began his tale.

"Once upon a time, many ages before this time of the world, all things were new, all thoughts were being thought for the first time, all things were being tried out with no sure knowledge of their consequences. The world itself was new, fresh and abundant. There were great forests filled with beasts and birds that had never seen a hunter or his tools. The rivers teemed with fishes. The people of that time were just ordinary people, no better nor worse than today. They fought amongst themselves. They sought power, riches, dominion, but for the main part they did what they knew was right as far as they could. In that time a person's good name was his most important possession. Everywhere it was seen as right that the old were cared for and respected, that the very young were nurtured and set on the right path, that women were treated with respect, that wrongdoers were dealt with. People looked after their own kind and they were fiercely proud of what made them different from other clans, tribes or races. Hospitality was a point of honour, almost a sacred duty. An unarmed traveller could expect food, drink and shelter wherever he was benighted. Though every race had different gods, the existence of a divine ordering power was unquestioned. Above all else there was a reverence for Wisdom and for Beauty. Philosophers and skilful makers of beautiful things were treated as the possessors of divine gifts and regarded as a boon to the whole world. To have killed or abused one of them would have been like casting gold into the sea.'

'It was a rough and ready world, but it was a world in which everybody had an accepted place. Yes, there was evil in that time, but of only two kinds. There was the evil of ignorance and the evil of passion. Some people did evil because of want of knowledge; some people did evil because they could not control their anger, their jealousy and so on. These were evils indeed, but they were evils of weakness and part of shared human experience - for both the cure was greater wisdom. But then a third form of evil entered the world which was to destroy that original world for ever. It was evil done with full knowledge of both the deed and its consequences. It was evil done in cold blood and without passion. It was thus an evil which fed on wisdom, an evil of strength and not of weakness. This was the so-called evil of knowledge.'

'Here is the story of how it came about. A mighty and noble king ruled in the west. Not only was he famous in feats of arms, but he was also a strategist and diplomat of rare merit. Needless to say his name was held in high esteem. He was called Holman. Before he had passed the prime of his life he had become the head of a great empire between the mountains and the sea. But as his youth waned, so did his lust for conquest, and although his generals urged him to cross the mountains and seek fresh dominions, this time he did not send for his war palanquin. Instead he sent out a summons for all the philosophers and poets of the Empire to attend the spring court in the high country by the mountains. His empire was larger than any other before it, and it seemed that all the wisdom of the world was assembled in that exquisite palace amongst the melting snows. In the great hall warmed by log fires that were fed night and day, the King addressed his guests.

'A King is but a keeper of a kingdom - his treasure the treasure of the whole nation held in trust. Yet I have conquered kingdoms where the king sat on vaults of treasure, room upon room filled with gold, silver, gems - without the wit to do anything other than run the coins through his fingers or watch the candlelight sparkle on the gems. Outside his palace gates the people dwelt in rags and ignorance. Never did a city fall so quickly to my armies. Most truly is it said, 'judge a man by the condition of his servants'. I too have rooms full of treasure, held in trust. But my real treasure is here in this room. You are my treasure and I want to put you to work. I am the most powerful King the world has ever seen. If I give my armies the order to march, I could become the ruler of the whole world. And yet I am uneasy. I do not know if this would be a good thing or a bad thing. When I was a child my father took me to visit the city of the blue men. They were so unique, so different from other peoples. Besides wearing blue clothes, they had ebony skins and throughout all their history had never learned to read or write. They did not ride horses, nor had they knowledge of the wheel. They never built any architecture of stone but lived in dwellings of straw, leaves and wood. Despite all this they were the happiest and bravest of men. They had the whitest of teeth and the broadest of smiles. They beat drums and sang and danced all day and night. They had story tellers who could hold their audiences spellbound. My father did not conquer these people. He only sent troops to protect their lands during the imperial wars. It was enough. When I revisited their city their culture had been destroyed. They had discarded their blue robes and aped the fashions of the empire; they married our women and neglected their own. They learned to read and write and to build in stone. Today they are almost indistinguishable from all other peoples of the Empire. Is this a good thing? All of you will help me to decide. Each evening we will meet in this place. Those with ideas can speak, others can agree or disagree. Thus will I use my treasure and come to my decision.'

'The debate began. Spring turned to summer, summer turned to autumn, autumn to winter and the whole court moved to the South. Still the arguments multiplied and sub-divided. The King could have called an end to the debate at any time, but it seemed that he wanted every subtle avenue to be explored. The simple argument whether a man should do a thing simply because he could, eventually extended into debates about the nature of free will, duty, honour, morality, religion, history, destiny and a thousand other concepts. Schools of philosophers and even religious sects grew out of the great debate. Whole new codes of law were devised. Novel political systems were proposed. Even the way in which objects of great skill and beauty were made became the subject of differing opinion.'

'Time passed and both factions adopted ever more extreme views in the case. All original causes forgotten, there began a great intellectual war in which, increasingly, the only important thing became winning the argument. The daily debates grew fiercer and more adversarial. As is always the way in such matters, the debaters eventually divided into two opposite parties each led by a powerful and subtle thinker. On the one hand there was Gropius the Swart, a southerner. Gropius argued not just for conquest, but for immediate and total conquest. Conquest without quarter. Conquest in which not only opposing armies would be annihilated but where no focus of opposition would be tolerated. All this in pursuit of a stable empire - one world, one religion, one army, one philosophy - a world society ruled by those who had proved themselves worthy by right of conquest. On the other hand, there was John of the Red Coat, a northern poet. John Redcoat did not only deny the right to conquer but argued for self-rule for all those already conquered. The treasure of the world, according to the northern poet, was its variety, its diversity, its sheer redundance of kinds and sorts.'

'The King made no comment or judgement as year by year the debate grew fiercer. The whole empire divided into reds and blacks. The great debate led to religious pogroms and political assassinations as the factions struggled for power. Finally, realising that things were getting out of hand, the King ordered his scribes to take down summaries of the rival philosophies. After he had read them through and deliberated long and hard, the King delivered his verdict. He chose not to conquer the world, but neither would he relinquish his empire. If he had thought thereby to end the controversy, the King was to be disappointed. Of the two rivals it was Gropius who felt most aggrieved by the decision. Through a variety of means, not all either honourable or legal, Gropius had contrived to make his party the larger, more powerful group. By this time the Black concept of total conquest decreed that every possible element of superiority should be turned to the party's advantage. Hence a 'natural law' was proposed that the majority were always right. The more people who believed in an idea, the more 'right' that idea became ...''

"But that is absurd! What can number have to do with it?" Small was genuinely astonished.

"Too true! But it was all part of his belief in total conquest." Old paused. Leaning against the staircase wall he mustered his strength for the last part of the climb.

"Gropius became convinced that the King was not worthy of the power of the imperial throne. Now he believed that the Empire itself must be purged and conquered anew by the Blacks before the armies could cross the mountains. What the Empire needed was a strong hand, and whose better than his own? He knew that he could not compete with the King in popularity. Holman was held in high esteem for his honour and his courage. But when the King married and a female heir was born, Gropius began to see a way in which he could manipulate the people and take the throne for himself.'

'Many years before, when the King was young and lusty, he had conceived an illegitimate son upon a young and noble lady from one of the very highest Imperial families. By the time of the Great Debate the whole episode was a half-forgotten rumour. With characteristic thoroughness Gropius uncovered the facts. It had been the King's one momentary lapse in an otherwise unblemished reign. At the time he was the all-conquering hero - young, strong, handsome - in the first flush of success. She was a remarkable beauty, although very young, wild and headstrong. She was called Almah, which means daughter of the moon. Her family had taken no interest in her upbringing - indeed the occasion on which she was conceived seems to have been the only time her parents occupied the same building, let alone the same bed! As it was she had been allowed to run wild, her wet-nurse was a woman who was rumoured to be of the Wicc'a - as you would say, a witch. Had the young lady been properly brought up and chaperoned she would not have been alone with the King after the Victory Feast and would not have suffered the consequences. When it was discovered what had happened, the King's counsellors investigated her background and the King was advised to have nothing more to do with her - for the good of the state.'

'For his part although King Holman felt honour bound to marry the young lady, it was clear to him that he had made a dreadful mistake. His protestations were half-hearted and when some days later a rebellion occurred in the South, he led his army out of the city relieved at being able to leave the whole problem behind him. The wild and beautiful young woman, far from regretting her rash and promiscuous behaviour, felt shamed and humiliated when the King deserted her. She had lost her reputation. Her suitors shunned her and she became an outcast of the court. When later she realised that she was with child, she withdrew herself to a large country estate. The child was raised in an atmosphere of obsessive resentment, bitterness and anger directed against the whole Imperial Court, but against the King in particular.'

'It was a simple task for Gropius to find the Lady and rekindle her hatreds. When he then persuaded her that her son had a prior claim to the crown, Gropius had the lever he needed to topple Holman from his pedestal. The King's dishonourable behaviour was trumpeted throughout the Empire, the Blacks backed the Pretender's claim and to cut a long story short the Empire plunged into civil war. Such a war had never been seen before. By appealing to his philosophy of total conquest Gropius persuaded his armies to do things which they knew to be evil. If an advantage were to be gained neither age nor youth nor sex were respected. Whole cities were poisoned. Sacred temples burned to the ground. Children tortured to extract information from their parents. Honour, mercy, sentiment, respect, all became signs of weakness. The Empire became a charnel house.'

'Gropius was a formidable enemy. He seemed to have diabolical powers. Armies sent against him were decimated by plague: city strongholds torn apart by bursting fire. The rumour spread that he had sold his soul to Sa'than Lord of Darkness in return for the powers of a sorcerer. Gropius took to wearing black robes. Black became the livery of his armies. It was thought that they became invisible at night. Before long the mere sight of his black war palanquin would send whole provinces onto the roads in panic stricken flight. It seemed to be in many places at once."

Small found that they had reached the top of the great stairwell. Old paused in his tale and cocked his head on one side, listening. A dark and neglected corridor led off to their right. Old motioned the boy to follow him.

"You see, Gropius fed the worst instincts in his followers, because he believed that greed, lust and cruelty were stronger in most men than honour and vision. The reward for ferocity in battle was slaves and loot. His campaigns were driven by rapine and pillage. But as the war dragged on, this strategy proved to be his undoing. Against a lesser opponent than King Holman he might have prevailed more quickly, but the loyalty and courage which the King inspired led to increasingly strong resistance. Front line cities were evacuated of all non-combatants and all portable wealth. If they fell Gropius had only an empty barracks to reward men who had been promised harems and palaces. The land being fought over became increasingly barren. Life under Gropius became unpleasant, violent and often short. A rumour spread that Almah and her son the pretender had been put to death.

The population began to drift across to the King's realms in search of law and stability. The longer the war continued, the stronger the King became because the people realised what life would be like under the Dark Lord. The courtly virtues which the Imperial Monarchy represented and promoted were no longer mere abstractions. The people saw them as vital pillars of the social fortress which allowed them to sleep safe in their beds at night.'

'Gropius was not stupid. He saw quite clearly the way things were developing. The war had to be ended quickly or his own men might turn on him. He decided to risk everything on a final gamble. Summoning all his generals he held up before them a mighty bauble, the Imperial capital itself, to be taken by surprise, by moving at night, whilst the Imperial armies were drawn away to the south by a feint attack. Everything went according to plan at first. The Imperial armies marched off to the South. For three nights the Dark Horde slipped through the sparsely populated northern realms in darkness and without being detected. Arriving at the capital city, they camped where only a shallow and easily fordable stream lay between them and their goal. But Fortuna the fickle goddess snatched their triumph away from them. Before day broke, heavy rains in the mountains had turned the stream into a raging flood impossible to cross. As the sun rose Gropius watched impotently as despatch riders streamed out of the city gates alerting the whole empire to his predicament. The surprise attackers were now themselves trapped. The armies would return from the south and within days they would be surrounded. With everything to lose and everything to gain, he had no choice but to stand and fight.'

'Even tied to a stake Gropius was a dangerous opponent. Battle was joined with grim ferocity on both sides and continued day and night. The slaughter was appalling. With the battle at its height, scores of nobles, the flower of the Empire, perished when the Imperial cavalry was lured over ground mined with bursting fire created by alchemists working with the Dark Horde. At this crucial moment the entire population of the city, well aware of what would be their fate should the dark forces prevail, streamed out of the city and over the battlefield. Old men, women, children, even cripples and beggars stripped weapons from the fallen and launched themselves in desperate frenzy upon the enemy. The tide of battle turned for the last time. The rebels were checked, thrown back, routed and scattered."

"What happened to Gropius?" Small asked.

"He vanished without a trace and was never seen again. But his black war palanquin was captured by northern soldiers some miles from the battlefield. They swore that he had been in it minutes before. The pillows were still warm, and there was something else."

"What was it Old?" Small's eyes widened with excitement.

"A manuscript."

"What was written on the manuscript, Old?"

"No-one knows, small one. Some say it was a prophecy of great evils which would befall the world: others that it was a book of spells and curses to bring them about. Certainly it was cursed since everybody who read it seems to have been struck dumb. It must have been a terrible thing."

"What happened to it?" said Small.

"The King placed the manuscript in a sealed room under guard whilst he decided what to do with it. You see they never did find Gropius and though the manuscript seems to have been a source of evil power, no-one could be sure that it had not been copied or even re-written by Gropius himself. Otherwise they could have simply burnt the thing. It was too dangerous to exist but it might be equally dangerous to destroy it. The King sent for John Redcoat who by this time was an old and very wise man. Redcoat told him that the Evil of Knowledge had entered the world. He told the King that once knowledge of a thing had entered the world it could never be unlearned or driven out. That henceforth the world would be changed for ever. The King must make sure that as few people as possible knew that this new form of knowledge had entered the world, but it was important that somebody somewhere knew about it in case the evil power revived. The manuscript seems to have been regarded as one of those poisons which can cure as well as kill. It was both the spell and its antidote. The King decided that the manuscript was so dangerous that it had to be hidden, but hidden in such a way as to be discoverable if a similar evil power ever rose again."

At this point the old man stopped abruptly and peered around him with narrowed eyes. "Tell me, Small, with your sharp young eyes and ears, is there anyone else in this corridor?" They were in a very old part of the book-city. The low vaulted corridor curved out of sight in both directions. There were very few windows in these parts. Small strained his senses in the gloom. The silence was heavy and oppressive. When he could hold his breath no longer he re-filled his lungs and answered. "We are the only ones here."

"Good, good." Old lifted the skirts of his robe and, to Small's embarrassment; he began fumbling with a curious undergarment. Eventually, and not without a good deal of struggle he drew out a large key of a very antique form. Small had not really noticed the small pointed door in the wall until the old man turned to it and inserted the key in its lock. There were ancient doorways everywhere in Alligor. Many were locked, veiled with cobwebs, their hinges seized with corrosion, their secrets lost with their keys in the mists of time. As Old rubbed away the swags of spindrift from the door, Small saw that the handle was fashioned in the form of a paw with talons. This belonged to a ramping griffin which had been formed in luxuriant coils and turns of bronze strapwork from the hinges of the door.

Old inserted the key into the lock, turned it, reversed the key and inserted its other end. Another turn and the bolt of the lock cleared its shackle. Small pressed the taloned paw and shouldered the door open. They both passed through it. Old carefully re-locked the door from the inside. In the faint grey light which filtered down from above them, Small saw stone steps rising in front of him. He started forward but Old held him back by the elbow. From the cobwebs beside the door Old retrieved a corroded metal rod which he proceeded to insert in an all but invisible socket in the riser of the first step.

"Help me to move this over", Old whispered. Small lent his weight to the lever. With a soft grating sound a section of the stone staircase swung back and down, risers becoming treads, treads risers. The stairway which had led upwards now descended into inky darkness. Small gripped the old man's sleeve as they went down the steps. At the bottom of the short flight, the old man used the bar again and the staircase rose to its original position. In the total darkness Small heard the old man fumbling and scratching at something. To his horror a series of sparks lit the vault. Fire of any kind was expressly forbidden in the Library. Old eventually succeeded in lighting the wick of a small oil lamp with flint and tinder. This he lifted out of its niche in the wall. Its wavering yellow light revealed a steeply descending passage without windows. Carefully shielding the flame of the lamp, Old led the way down into the bowels of Alligor.

"This passage is cut into one of the four original city walls. It was cut after the wall was built. See the marks of the miner's tools on the walls. They would have been foreigners brought from some distant province. Even the builders could not be trusted with all the secrets of Alligor."

After a long descent they arrived at another door. Even Small could see that this one was much older than the first. It was of such cunning workmanship as to baffle any forced entry. The bronze valve fitted so tightly into the frame that even the slimmest dagger point would have been useless. No hinges or locks or handles were visible on its surface. Only an embossed copper gryphon cast its baleful gaze upon them.

Old seemed to be taking great pains to place his lamp in a niche by the door. Small was baffled.

"If you put your lamp so deep in the hole we will have hardly any light."

"If I don't put it in exactly the right place, small one, we will not get past this door ... There!" The old man stood expectantly by the door which to Small's great surprise began to move slowly forward on its concealed hinges. "The lamp is the key - somehow it withdraws the bolt."

Even though Small thought that this seemed suspiciously like sorcery he moved to help the old man. Together they pulled open the door and entered the room beyond.

Four

The room was pitch black but Small could sense that he was in a very large space. Once again Old struck sparks from his flint until his body was silhouetted against a steady glow. As the old man turned to face him, Small gasped. The lamp had revealed a great hall carved from the living rock. The walls below the vaulted ceiling were ablaze with colour. Hundreds of painted human figures, many dressed in blazing gold leaf, flashed their jewelled eyes in the lamplight. Only at the far end of the vault were the bright colours overpowered by a darker palette. Small knew instantly that he was looking at the great battle between the forces of good and evil. The sable clad armies of Gropius the archimage swarmed out of the gloom in their dark armour. With their pale faces and purple flashing eyes they spread across the vault like a foul mildew. Beneath them their feet trod a highway of mutilated bodies of all ages and sexes, broken images, trampled crops, ruined cities, and everywhere torn and damaged manuscripts with fragments of virtuous wisdom clearly written on them.

Small gazed in open-mouthed wonder as Old lit more and more lamps from the first. More of the painting became visible. Down one side of the hall, the forces of evil held sway over a shattered and ruined landscape. Their armies exulted over defeated enemies and revelled in slaughter and rapine. On the other side they fled like darkness before the sunrise as a gilded horde issued from city with walls, towered and turreted. He saw the river, choked with corpses black and gold: and the citizens stripping weapons from the dead and joining in the attack.

At opposite ends of the hall, Virtue and Vice sat on their respective thrones. Somehow Small was certain that he was looking at likenesses of King Holman and Gropius. The archimage lounged on his throne looking relaxed and confident. A mocking sneer curled the lip on a fine, intelligent, almost handsome face. Around him, more like a harem than a court, were vices portrayed as female figures. Gluttony, Lust, Greed, Anger, Hypocrisy and Vanity held elegant serpentine poses. Gropius stared directly at his adversary. King Holman was leaning slightly forwards from his throne looking alert but concerned. How cleverly the artist had caught that hint of human weakness, that shadow of doubt in his otherwise manly features. Holman's right hand gripped the arm of his throne and was itself covered by the hand of a tall female figure who stood beside him wearing a crown of green stones. His queen was a formidable allied power; her face calm, determined and strong. The King's other hand rested upon the hilt of his sword, to which was attached a chain of gold. The chain passed from the hand of one lady virtue to the hand of the next in a circle which ended with the queen. The effect was curiously harmonious and rhythmic, like a temple ritual. The virtues wore calm and dignified expressions as they paced the measure of their mysterious dance.

"There!" Old had finished lighting the lamps. Small looked around him. Down each side of the chamber was a single row of elaborately carved and painted seats or stalls. A continuous canopy ran above them, also intricately carved to resemble roofs, towers and pinnacles. The centre of the room was empty of furniture and the floor was of a black polished stone with tiny white inclusions in it. The effect was of looking into a midnight pool at the reflections of stars. An illusion enhanced by the uneven, rippling surface of the stone. Curiously the vault above had been coloured deepest indigo and powdered with golden stars which glowed strongly in the lamplight. Among the stars, Small saw Orion with Diana and a Centaur hunting zodiacal beasts, whilst other familiar figures prepared a feast.

With a loud groan, Old sat down on one of the seats.

"Come here lad and I'll try and finish the tale."

Small inserted himself into a neighbouring stall and pulled his legs up under him. "Did the King hide the manuscript in here, Old?" he asked.

"No, no, not quite," Old replied. "You see it had to be well hidden, but not locked away in the power of a small group. The One who needed to read the manuscript had to have access to it at all times. No-one knew who he might be or when he might come. The key to its secret hiding place could not be a piece of metal like my key here, or even a cunning contrivance like the lamp lock. The level of intelligence needed to operate such toys is rather low, and besides, machines can break or wear out, keys can be lost, key bearers can be corrupted, secrets can be betrayed. You see John Redcoat and the King did not know whether the Seeker would come the next day or in a thousand years time."

Small was puzzled. "But how would they know who the Seeker was? Lots of people would be curious about such a manuscript."

"Precisely! They had to be sure that the manuscript was not going to be discovered by someone motivated by mere curiosity, prurience...or worse. The Seeker would have to be a real Lover of Truth, but he must also be a subtle thinker. That is why they decided that intellect and imagination were to be the keys to the hiding place." Old smiled at the boy's baffled expression. "Now, my small but very clever friend, think hard. Where is the best place to hide a manuscript? Try remembering your *Mirror of Almeira...*"

Small thought for a long time.

"Ah! I see! When Amatis is being sought by the Great Khan, he joins the Great Khan's army! He says, 'the best place to hide an ear of corn is in a corn field'. The manuscript is hidden where there are thousands of other manuscripts. It is hidden in a library."

Old wrinkled with pleasure. "Just so, small one. You have such a sharp young mind. I am proud to be your Guide! But it could not be just any library. It had to be a great library. The biggest library in the whole world. Because then, not only would the manuscript be difficult to find amongst all the other books, but then also all the great seekers of truth would feel duty bound to visit the great library, even if it was only once in their lives. The king had only one problem. There was no such library. He had to set about building one. Perhaps no one else in all history could have attempted such a task. As it was he died before the building was finished. His queen oversaw the completion of the fourth wall and she too lived only to see the last block of stone lifted into place. Since that time there have been many builders with many motives, but all have been unconsciously helping to hide the secret of the library. During their lifetimes the King and Queen sent out agents to all the kingdoms of the world. They bought as many books as they could, but also spread the idea that the library would accept, and keep, each and every book that was donated. Writers and patrons quickly realised that the Great Library was their opportunity for eternal life. Once they were on the shelves their books would be looked after, preserved and hopefully read for as long as the Library stood. Throughout the ages the thousands of books became millions, the millions of books became so many that their number did not have a name. Every book which arrived was another ear of wheat in the field."

Small's laughter echoed around the hall. "What an idea! So tell me, where is it? Where is the manuscript?"

Old snorted and shook his head. "Do you not see yet? It is here in Alligor and that is as much as anyone knows. In my life I have read thousands of books. No-one knows the library better than I do. I have discovered many secrets. I might even have read the manuscript itself. But how could I tell? I have no idea what it contains. No-one does."

"But that is impossible!" burst out Small indignantly, "It would be difficult enough to find the book in Alligor. It would be a labour of Hercules; but without even knowing what it is ..."

31

"When the time is right: when the Evil of Knowledge rises in the world once more: the Seeker will know of it. He, or she, or they, will come to Alligor to find the antidote."

"But Old, you say that no-one outside this library knows about the manuscript. Why would they come here? How would they begin to search? You have spent a lifetime in the library and not found it."

"There is a prophecy, small one. Back in those ancient days they had far-seers who could see the way things would be. There it is, carved above the door." The old man did not need to read the ancient script, but summoned it from memory.

When the breath of the beast is on the land
And the mouth of the library is stopped
The One will light the world
And the hour that gave birth to the dragon
Will also bring forth the man
So shall the library find its end.

'You must know that there are more mysterious forces in this ordinary world of ours than we admit. We see them in dreams, we feel them in waking. There is communication in emotion. Sometimes much more than words pass between people when they talk. Memories can pass from generation to generation without a sentence being uttered. When many people believe, faith hangs in the air like incense smoke and sweetens every breath. When Evil triumphs then the whole world wishes for a saviour. That is why some man may well find himself compelled, even against his desires, to act the part. He knows not why or wherefore. Often he will believe himself to be carrying out the will of God. Certainly his whole soul commands him to act. Thus he really does become a supernatural being, capable of superhuman feats. As you so rightly say, that is the sort of person the library was built to receive. Ever since you told me about the wind; ever since I saw the great door blocked by the driven sand; I have felt certain that we should expect this person to arrive."

Small's shoulders drooped. "It will need a demigod to move the sand from the gate, never mind finding the manuscript."

"Unfortunately there is more. There is another legend of Alligor not so happily formed as the other one. Amongst the thousands of names graven in the wall outside the gate there is a name which should not be there. That name is Gropius."

"But you said he vanished!"

"So he did. But one day that name appeared outside our gate. In those early days of many readers and few librarians it was impossible to say if he had entered Alligor or not. The legend says he entered the library, found his manuscript, and marked it out for any who would follow in his footsteps."

Small was perplexed. "I don't understand. Why did he not take the manuscript with him, or destroy it."

"I have often thought about that myself. He did not need to take the manuscript because he already knew its contents. As for destroying it: he was its author. The library guaranteed its survival in a way that he could not. Other copies might be lost or destroyed but this one in Alligor would survive as long as the Book-city itself. All he had to do was to mark out a path through the book stacks that would lead those of like mind to the manuscript. The Masters have always believed in the existence of two paths through the library: the Path of Light and the Path of Darkness."

The silence in the chamber was absolute.

Old sighed. "In the old days your initiation into the secrets of the library would have been an altogether more magnificent affair. All these seats would have been filled with Book Masters. There would have been ritual. A sword would have been held against your chest whilst you were charged with the onerous nature of your duties. You would have been threatened with instant death should you ever reveal the secrets to any other. But now, there is only me, and I would not know how to go about killing anybody, even if I had the strength. Even so Small, you must make the promise to me. I have to put my trust in you - I feel that you will not let me down. But think carefully and long before you swear the oath. Be aware that if you break your word then the Omnipotent Author may change the plot of your life for something much less pleasant. You are young. The task is life-long. The secret is a heavy load which can never be laid down. The responsibilities are very great. The fate of the world could well be in your hands. Can you swear never to give up the task?"

"What would my task be?"

"You must keep and never reveal the secret. You must do all in your power to preserve the library. You must watch out for anyone following the Dark Path and stop him ... by any means necessary. You must await the arrival of the Seeker."

"And then?"

Old gave a helpless shrug.

"But how will I know him?"

"I don't know. He could be almost anyone. He might come and go without you realizing who he was."

"But Old, he might already have been and gone."

"I think not, small one. Had the Evil of Knowledge risen again in the world we would have known about it. In any case, the prophecy clearly links the arrival of the Seeker with the end of the library. Besides I feel it, Small, I feel in my bones that the end is coming soon. I feel the library calling out for the One. We must be ready. Will you take the oath?"

Small could sense that the old man was speaking from his heart. It was strange but even Small had felt a change in the atmosphere of the library. It was as if Alligor was waking from a long dream; roused by the evil wind which had tried to suffocate the book city while it slept. It was like the sudden silence after the hum of a long summer day. Birdsong ceases and the air fills with the premonitory tang of rain on parched earth as evening thunderstorms take to the sky. Small found that he was staring at the face of Gropius on the end wall. The archimage seemed to be mocking him.

Small had a sudden desire to be out of the bowels of Alligor and up on the roof.

"I swear, Old, before the Divine Author I swear the Oath! We will await the One together."

Small's hand gripped the arm of his seat. Old reached over and squeezed it reassuringly. "I know you won't let me down."

"Can we go now?"

Old struggled out of his seat, "Yes, yes." he said.

Climbing up out of the depths of the city was a long and tedious process. The old man had to stop more and more frequently to catch his breath. By the time the key was turned in the griffin door, Old had passed the limits of his failing strength and Small was all but carrying him. In the first gallery they entered, Small found the librarian's cubby-hole and lowered Old onto the hard wooden cot. A quick search turned up some scraps of threadbare fabric that might once have been blankets. The boy arranged them over the frail body as best he could. As he left the gallery the old man was already snoring faintly.

Despite the long climb Small felt curiously elated and gave in to a sudden urge to run as fast as ever he could down the long curving corridor. Deliberately making as much noise as he could with his feet, he ran until the dust he had raised shimmered in the air behind him. He ran and ran until his legs gave way and his breath failed. When he could run no more he doubled over and laughed loudly, enjoying the echoes which ran away from him down the corridor. As the ghostly laughter died, he became aware of a change in the sound of the library.

At first there was a faint buzz, a murmur as of many low voices in a far distant room. As he strained his ears, the sound became louder and smoothed itself out into a more constant hum. It might have been the wind moaning in the roofs but it had a strange animal quality. It seemed to be louder a little way ahead of him. He ran to the corner. The sound was louder but still seemed to be some way off. He was in a very long and broad room filled with book stacks. Ornate windows cast their light onto reading desks down one side of the room, but the room was gloomy on account of the thick webs of spider spin which hung in drifts against the greenish panes and festooned the furniture. No librarians had visited this gallery for a very long time. The noise had now resolved itself into a sound not unlike a very large choir of voices singing a complex and long drawn out chord. He ran into the next room. It was narrow and crowded. The shelves and cabinets were crammed with rolls of parchment, papyrus and leather. Some were bagged or boxed but all seemed extremely ancient. The next room was circular and lit from an eye in the roof. He could not locate the noise; it seemed to be inside his head. As he tried to clear his mind, he had a disturbing vision of the hundreds of parchment rolls around him as open mouths. The sound fell away and was consumed by its own echoes.

Small's head was ringing. More than ever he wanted to get out into the fresh air, but first he had to find the keeper of these galleries and ask him about the noise. Small's whole day had been of an hallucinatory strangeness. Perhaps the grains he had eaten had been tainted after all. He looked around. The whole district must have been part of the original library building. Ceilings and walls, doors and shelf-ends were all heavily carved and painted. The stacks were mostly filled with manuscript rolls. There were few of the more familiar bound books of leaves. He found the librarian's bell in the large cobweb swathed gallery and gave it a good drubbing. Cobwebs, dust and insect remains floated to the ground. There was no response. "Probably deaf as a post," he mumbled to himself, "or fast asleep."

Small began to walk through the gallery. In one corner the festoons of spun web seemed to radiate out from a whitish hump on the desk. As he got closer a deadly feeling at the pit of his stomach forewarned him that he had found the keeper of the galleries. There, cocooned in layer upon layer of whitish-grey spider web was the slight frame of an old man. Small reached out a hand to shake the form by its shoulder. Scores of small spiders shifted suddenly at the movement and then froze. They looked like black drops of blood. Small's hand withdrew instinctively. There were rumours of spiders in Alligor that killed with a bite. His skin crawled. Small ran for the door and this time he did not stop running until he found himself in familiar territory.

Five

Dim enjoyed pulling the book-sled. He loved the grating, sleering sound it made as he dragged it across the stone flags. He enjoyed shattering the customary silence of the Eastern Galleries. Strapped into the crude leather harness of the sled, Dim became the focus of the only regular social event to relieve the monotony of library existence. In the distant past, the bindery menials had been in constant employment. They brought in newly donated books, removed damaged books for repair and returned displaced books to their galleries. In these latter days the passage of the book-sled was a rare event. Increasingly it had become the only form of social contact between the various parts of the book city. Few, if any, readers disturbed the books on the shelves. Wear and tear had given way to quiet decay in the dark and neglected corners of the mighty library. Mildew and fungus scrawled their own poetry across the antique parchments. The incessant champing of insect larvae quietly censored the exquisite volumes of love allegory, before devouring them completely.

Dim did not labour alone at the book-sled. Two ancient menials from the bindery pushed on the sled handles from behind. Their efforts were largely symbolic compared to Dim's, but he enjoyed their company, even though they insisted on stopping to catch their breath in every gallery they passed through. As Small ran into the familiar gallery, the two menials were lounging in an alcove talking in undertones. Dim was standing in harness.

"Thmall! I'm pulling the book-sled." he boomed, his pride in his role easily overcoming his sense of the self-evident. He *always* pulled the book-sled.

"I can see you are, Dim," Small answered without any trace of irony, "a grand job."

Dim beamed with pleasure. Small greeted the menials by opening his palms bookwise to them. They responded politely.

"I've just come from the Old Quarter. Have you been there recently?"

With faded smiles the two men exchanged conspiratorial glances. One shook his head slowly from side to side.

"When was the last time you were there?"

"Well...," the man looked guilty. He was trying to think what to say. "...it all depends which part of the Old Quarter you mean."

"Oh no Thmall, we never go there!" Dim wanted to be helpful. "It'th a bad plathe."

A sense of foreboding began to envelope Small. "Aren't you supposed to visit every librarian in the eastern city at least every six weeks? Do you still do the full circuit?"

The other man spoke this time, "It's not always possible. There's only us. There used to be more helpers, more sleds..."

"There used to be more librarians...How many are left?"

Again, the guilty pause, the furtive glance. First the one man, then the other shrugged helplessly.

Small was bewildered. "Don't you ever go to the Old Quarter?" Downcast eyes gave him his answer. "A librarian has died. You must bring him out" Small saw in their eyes that this would not happen.

"We cannot do that Small." The first man again.

"Why not?" Small asked. "If it's the body you are afraid of, Dim will lift him onto the sled."

"No. It's not that. We just don't want to go into the Old Quarter. There's ... things."

"Things? You mean the spiders?"

"No. There's other things as well. Things have happened."

Small was mystified. "What kind of things?"

"Bad things."

"Bad things? Why haven't the librarians reported any of these things?"

"That's just it Small, there aren't any librarians left in there. Not leastwise any live ones. There's only footsteps, and whispers ... and spiders everywhere."

"There are spiders everywhere in Alligor. Are the ones in the Old Quarter different? Are they dangerous?

"You've been there...what do you think?"

Small nodded. He understood about the spiders at least. He had felt the same primeval intuition of danger in himself.

Small thought deeply about this unexpected situation. Seven days ago he would have accepted the whole thing as just another part of growing up in Alligor, like the rotting staircase in the Red Loggia, something to be remembered and avoided. He would have skipped away down the gallery and lost himself in a new book or climbed onto the roof to try his luck with wild birds. But now..., now he had duties. He had sworn the oath. The Library had to be looked after. Perhaps the menials had hallucinated their fears. They did eat in the refectory after all. There might be a simple explanation.

"Perhaps the librarians fell ill," he suggested hopefully, "perhaps they were carried out on a book-sled from the other side."

The first menial answered again. "I wouldn't know about that."

There was something ominous in the way the words hung in the air. "When was the last time you spoke to anyone from the other parts of the city?" Small asked.

The man screwed up his eyes in concentrated recall. The other man tugged his sleeve. "It was the year of the drought. You remember - that really ancient bag of bones with his beard tucked into his belt."

"Yes, that's it - that must've been the last one."

Small was horrified. "The drought was five years ago!"

"No doubt about it. That was the last one. We found him wandering in the Shambles by the old Well. Claimed he'd been walking for three days without seeing a living soul. Right off his shelf he was."

"Who was he? What was he doing there?"

"Well he was on his way to the next world, that's for sure. As far as we could gather his name was Master Noal or Noel and he was from the Rotunda in the North Galleries. He'd got the idea that he was the last Librarian. Most agitated he was. Going on about this book he'd written. Clutched it to his chest as tight as life. Some kind of Faery story. Kept talking about a Dark Lord, dragons and lamps, all that sword and sorcery stuff. He calmed down though when he found that the Eastern galleries were fully staffed, librarians, menials and all. We put him on the sled - it still had two wheels then - and started back to the infirmary. It couldn't have taken more'n half a day, but he never made it, poor old soul."

Small's heart was beating faster. "And the book?"

"Odd that. I thought the least we could do for him was shelve it somewhere, it being so important to him and him being dead and all. We searched everywhere for it. We even went back the way we came. Asked everybody. No sign of it. The crafty old sod must've shelved it himself somewhere along the way. Funny thing though. After all these years I still remember the title he'd written on the wrapper. 'Shining Path', that's what it was, 'The Shining Path'."

A sense of hopelessness washed over Small. He badly needed to think things out. He also needed to eat. He decided to try the roof again. A low late afternoon sun suddenly slanted in through the gallery windows. "I have to go." he said.

Dim's face fell. "Don't go Thmall. . . You can ride on the thled!"

Small remembered many happy hours spent on the sled being pulled at breakneck speed through the galleries. Those carefree days seemed a world away from him now.

"Sorry Dim, I've got things to do."

As the gallery door closed behind him, Small heard the sled start to move across the flagstones. He waited until the thud of the door closing at the other end of the gallery sent its dull echo fleeing through the hollow space before he re-entered. He stood in silence, making sure no-one was approaching.

The Eastern Galleries were panelled in ancient faded red wainscoting which went right up to the top of the shelves. The wooden panels were often elaborately carved. Up above the shelves the walls were frescoed with imagery that ranged from the everyday to the impenetrably esoteric. It was from these frescoes that this gallery derived its name, the gallery of the Horses. Finely painted horses raced around the walls. On the opposite wall several of their riders were passing torches from hand to hand in a kind of relay. The race ended in the corner behind the door where Small was now standing. Above his head, nine elegant maidens reached down from their balcony handing laurel crowns to the victors. Small lowered his eyes. A tiny carved figure on the wainscoting leered at him with its finger to its lips. Small reached out his hand, gripped and twisted the figure's face. The panel swung back on its concealed hinges and Small passed through. Climbing the dark stairs behind the panel, he remembered the first time he had pushed and twisted that mocking little face, so like the grown-up librarians, always telling him to be quiet. He still remembered the excitement of discovering the upper levels; of being able to roam unseen around the whole Eastern Quarter.

He walked the length of the gallery of the Horses in its secret upper level. On his right hand he could just make out the curving tops of the vaults and the circular bungs of the spy holes. In all the times he'd walked here how could he have missed them? Of course, they had been above his head when he first came here. The trapdoor in the dark angle of the gable though, that was another matter. That had been beneath the notice of the aged masters. Only a child would have found that little low nook interesting. For weeks after he discovered the tiny door, Small had really believed that beyond that door was a special world for children. Why else would the door be so small? The door had resisted all his puny efforts to force it open, but one day he had found it miraculously ajar. The hidden catch had simply corroded away.

Nowadays it was getting more and more difficult for Small to wriggle through the tiny door and the passage beyond. His shoulders were broadening with adolescence and his limbs were too long to flex properly in the confined space. More than once he had felt the onset of panic as his body jammed in the masonry. Now as he eased himself slowly through, he realised that there would soon come a time when he would be too big to pass through into his childhood domain. Not today though. Not just yet.

Small stood up. He was inside what must have been the largest and most awesome roof-space in Alligor. Before him in the impenetrable darkness, he could see in his mind's eye the seven colossal cedar roof trees which lifted and braced the massive rafters and purlins. The cunning prehistoric joinery seemed to set more snugly and more solidly the longer it bore its titanic burden. The forest felled to create this hollow mountain of a roof must have been seeded at the dawn of time and taken thousands of years to grow trees to such prodigious dimensions. The timber was so impregnated with perfumed resin that a hot summer day could still release the scent of the primeval forest.

A narrow catwalk carried Small over the massive joists. In the darkness beneath him the upper surfaces of the stone vaulted ceilings heaved, humped and dimpled like a bay of whales. The catwalk ended at a round arch in the thick gable wall. Beneath the arch was a door. Small braced the door against the wind as he lifted the latch, but it was not necessary. The door swung easily on its hinges. The great gale had ceased. The fierce cinnamon light of a sun setting under hurrying clouds shone full into his face. It was painfully bright. The cold clear air filled him with a sense of exhilaration. Although the high clouds still raced towards the gathering dusk, here on the roof the leaves of the creepers around the door rustled in the lightest of breezes. Small whooped for joy and ran up the great pyramid of riven stone tiles which rose before him. At the pinnacle of the roof a gigantic gilded weathercock crowed defiance to the wind from the west. Small grasped it round the neck and swung his leg over its broad back. From this fantastical mount he surveyed his kingdom.

His sense of release was short-lived. Even with the sun and the breeze on his face, Small could not find the soul's ease he was seeking. The view before him was subtly altered. Great drifts of red sand filled the roof valleys. Pinnacles and vanes leaned at strange angles. The crowns of familiar trees which had landscaped the roofs of the book city had vanished. There was no birdsong; no butterflies. Beyond Alligor and to the horizon, the whole pale landscape was unnaturally streaked with a red which made violent the contrast with the deep blue of advancing evening and the first pale stars. For a moment he gave himself up to the weirdness of it all. His heart beat faster. It had been a very strange day. His whole universe had irrevocably altered. He had thought to find refuge on the roof, but even up here, his own special realm reflected the supernatural tide which had passed over the land.

At the rim of the world the sun dimmed and disappeared. The warmth left his cheeks. A brown smoky cloud was rising out of the plain. Small stared in disbelief. Far in the distance a dark form was snaking slowly towards Alligor out of the gathering dusk. It seemed that the dragon had arrived.

Six

Small woke in a state of confused recollection. The sun lanced into the architectural nook where he had spent a restless night. There had been brown smoke on the horizon the evening before, now white smoke rose against the crystal blue morning sky. Its source was at the gates of Alligor itself. The smell of roasted flesh which drifted across the roofs was not familiar to him, but he knew that what he could hear was not the sound of a dragon, but the noises made by horses which neighed stamped and snorted. And then, quite clearly, a man laughed, carelessly. The laughter rang against the high walls of the book city and rose distinct in the thin clear air. And there! No mistaking it, a rhythmic chant in a curious ululating high voice. Curiosity overpowered Small's feeling of apprehension. He rose and began to walk the hundred or so paces to the western parapet. The noises became clearer and more varied. Distractedly he beat the red dust from his clothes as he walked.

Slowly and carefully he raised his eyes above the parapet. The first things he saw were two heavy covered wagons and between them a line of about twenty horses tethered to a picket line. Even Small could see that these were fine, muscular, glossy coated beasts. Horses fit to carry the heroes in his favourite story books. It was difficult to imagine anything less like the bony, spiritless nags that occasionally shambled past Alligor. Small put his palms to the stone and craned forward. There were gaily-coloured tents pitched in the purple shadow which the book city cast upon the red dust before the gate. Figures moved purposefully. They wore brightly coloured clothes which rippled and shone. Small guessed they were made from silk. One man poked at a cooking fire which sent up the column of blue smoke that turned white against the sky. This then was his dragon. A caravan snaking out of the west. The dust it had raised had been the smoke against the sun.

And then he saw. A slight figure with a grace of movement totally unfamiliar to him shook out her dark ebony hair until it dropped to her waist. She began to comb it rhythmically. A woman. Suddenly he noticed there were several more amongst the tents. Their long dresses sparkled with gold and silver. They were the first women he had ever seen outside a book. He thought that they were the most beautiful creatures in the world, more beautiful even than the cheetahs which once had passed like ghosts across the moonlit plain. Some of the men cooked food and some groomed the horses. Small stared in disbelief at several of the others who had stripped to the waist and were actually splashing water onto their heads and upper bodies. Small had never heard of such a strange ritual. The men had tanned skins and their bodies were muscular and well-formed. He could see one man scraping the hairs from his chin with a curved blade. Most were dark haired and clean shaven but one of the strangers had extraordinary yellow-white hair and a moustache of the same colour. All the men seemed larger and healthier than any Small had ever seen before. Even their teeth flashed white when they grinned. Convinced that this was a band of heroes, Small could not take his eyes from the scene. The gay colours, the well-knit bodies, the way the men moved with easy grace. Even the women seemed to bear themselves like athletes.

After a while he observed that two figures stood out from the rest by their appearance and demeanour: an old crone squatted in the dust by a black tent, sorting through packs of what looked like dried plants and herbs; and one of the men strode through the camp smiling, jesting, interested in everything but taking part in nothing. Activity in the camp seemed to radiate out from this man in white. No doubt but that he was their captain. Once he spoke sharply to a woman who seemed about to splash water on herself like the men. She immediately carried her basin back inside her tent. Another time he called to a man who was chanting an obscene poem in the common tongue whilst grooming his horse. The man changed his lyric in mid stanza, to the loud derision of his neighbours.

Vague notions swam into Small's mind. If the true seeker were indeed to come, then surely he would be a man like this. The leader of a band of handsome heroes. Small suppressed the thought. Having solemnly sworn to wait faithfully for the One, it just seemed ridiculous that he would arrive the very next morning. Small would not have thought very highly of an author who put such an improbable event in a story.

A shout came from the foot of the wall just below where Small was hiding. The man in white spun round. Small ducked down, not sure if he had been seen. As a precaution he moved further along the roof before peering over the parapet again. The man had disappeared. His seemed to be one of the loud voices coming from the sand drift against the gate. Orders were shouted across to the camp. Horses were unhitched and brought to the foot of the wall. The blond haired man strode over from the camp carrying a heavy coil of rope. Two others brought the large wooden tailgate from one of the carts. Small could not see what was happening until one of the horses cantered back into sight, haltered to the rope which had been doubled. The rope tautened and lifted into the air as the horse was urged forward by its rider. After about twenty paces the tailgate was dragged into view, angled and guided by the blond giant. More than a man's weight of red dust had been scooped up by it to be spilled out across the plain. Judging by the speed at which the tailgate was pulled back out of sight, the second horse was harnessed to the other ends of the rope which ran back towards the gate. After a few moments another load of dust followed the first. Small was impressed. The heap of dust blocking the gate would soon be cleared. It seemed that the strangers were not only heroes, but engineers too.

Small's curiosity kept him at the parapet until the sun had lifted itself high into a cloudless blue sky. The men took turns at shifting the sand, whilst the women had moved as far away as possible from the swirling pink dust cloud raised by the men and horses at the gate. Small was now certain that these men would continue until they had cleared the gate and entered the city. For some reason this made him anxious. He had never known anyone to arrive at the gate from the outside world. He had heard rumours of readers who came from time to time but he never seemed to meet up with them. Many of the librarians were so old and confused that they spoke of things a lifetime ago as if they had happened yesterday. It was almost as if the Library digested its readers and turned them into books.

The work at the gate had slipped into a steady rhythm which was beginning to bore him. The dust clouds made it difficult to see the camp. He decided that he must find Old and tell him what was happening. Making his way across the roof he paused to drink at a small sheltered pool. The water had a strange earthy, brackish taste. On impulse he splashed some water onto his face just as he had seen the men do. The shock of the cold water took his breath away. Icy rivulets coursed down his neck and sleeves. It was a decidedly unpleasant sensation. Heroes had strange customs. Near the pool he discovered some windfalls under a fig tree. He stuffed as many of the half-ripe fruit into his mouth as he could and then filled his book pouch. Old would be very pleased.

Of course, Old was not where he had left him the previous afternoon. The scuff marks in the dust led Small out of the Old quarter, but once back in the galleries where people still moved to and fro, he lost the trail. Angry with Old for wandering off, Small did not notice the hunched figure which glided towards him from amongst the stacks.

"You have some books for me?" Sly gestured towards the bulging book pouch.

"No. No, Sly, not today."

Sly was looking at him with a curiously attentive gaze. Small began to feel uneasy.

"I'm looking for Old."

"Yes," said Sly, "you would be. Well I haven't seen him. Not since his historic visit to our humble dining room."

Sly held the boy with a serpent's unblinking gaze. He sidled closer.

"Curious, very curious."

Small gripped his book pouch with both hands and slowly pushed it behind him. Sly however, did not seem at all interested in the pouch. Before Small could move Sly darted forward and touched him on the cheek with his bony forefinger. Small was baffled. For a moment he thought that Sly had gone mad, but then the tip of the bony finger was thrust close to his face.

"Red! See? Red dust made all streaky with water." Sly paused to see the effect of his words. "Where in Alligor does a boy get red dust on his face?"

Sly was genuinely baffled, but his devious mind was already as busy as a nest of ants. He would not give up until he had solved the puzzle. "Where, eh? Where do you go to?"

Small had been caught off guard. He did not trust himself as a dissembler with Sly. Sudden panic made him break away from the snake-like gaze which held him and run for the door. Sly's thin wavering voice pursued him from the gallery.

"I'll find out! You know I will. You can't fool me. I'll find out!"

Small found Old sunning himself in the gate-yard several hours later but not before Splint, the lame librarian from the crypt galleries had sent Small on a wild goose chase. He was furious with himself for believing the doddering old fool. When Splint said that he had just seen Old, it might have been Old, or somebody else, today or twenty years ago, or not. It might have been a story he had read, or a dream he had, or he might have just thought that Small would be pleased by what he said. In the Library it was as well to assume that everything was fiction.

Small spoke sharply, "I have been looking for you, Old."

The ancient librarian slowly opened one eye, "What? No greetings today?"

"Greetings Old. I could not find you anywhere."

"You are not yourself, boy. Usually you are more thoughtful. That you could not find me is something that may well have irritated you, but for which you cannot reproach me. I did not know where you were or that you had news for me."

Small was surprised to find that he was annoyed at being so transparent to the old man. "How did you know that I had news for you?"

Old smiled. "I cannot think of anything else in Alligor which would require my urgent attention."

"What about food? I have figs for you". Small patted the book-pouch.

The smile on the old man's face broadened. "Ah! Good. I can eat them while you tell me your news."

Small closed his eyes and inhaled sharply. To be so anticipated was insufferable. He tossed the figs at Old whose ancient reflexes were inadequate. The fruit scattered around the old man in the dust. For a moment Old looked hurt and puzzled but then his face softened in understanding. "Not Small for much longer I fear! Tell me young man, what is your news. I am all ears". Old gathered up the figs and began to rub them clean on his robe.

"There are people at the gate. Heroes with beautiful women. They are moving the dust. It might be the One."

Old was eating the figs. Small was disturbed at the feelings of anger which had welled up inside him. Why did Old suddenly seem so pathetic and pitiable?

Old ate for a long time before he spoke. "My son, once I was like you. People older and wiser than I was gave me advice. I ignored them, despised them even. They were old fools who had only lived in the past. Many years later I found that they had spoken wisely. Such is the way of the world. Soon you will be a man. You are beginning to chafe at the bonds of childhood. You feel your growing strength, your independent will. Like all young men you will listen impatiently to what I have to say and then go your own way. You become a man by making your own mistakes and learning wisdom that way. But here in Alligor, this is not the time or the place for errors of judgement. Too much is at stake. I say this to you. Appearances can be deceptive. Whosoever is called hero, whosoever is called villain, that depends upon the tale and who lives to tell it. What makes you think that these men are heroes?"

"Their skins are like untarnished copper and shine with reflections of the sky. Their teeth are white like frost. They laugh and are careless. They have strength and great cunning. Their horses are fine and well kept. They wear rich coloured silks. The women move with the grace of desert leopards. They are here, now. They will open the gate and set us free!"

Old nodded sagely, his eyes half closed. "You speak as if you are imprisoned. Is it not the nature of all strongholds, of all fortresses, that security has its price? Does not the safest building have the fewest windows? Is fear not your jailer? Are you so sure of these people and their motives that you have no fear of them at all?"

Small tried to be objective, but his thoughts were in turmoil. "I am not sure. I want to save the Library and the books. But I cannot see any harm in welcoming readers. If I fear the end of Alligor it is only because I fear what I do not know."

"That," said Old, "is what most men fear. But the end of Alligor itself would not hold any personal danger for you. It would be like the end of childhood. Fraught but not fatal. Rather should you fear the world without Alligor. Fear a world in which the Evil of Knowledge is once more abroad."

Small did not respond. Having lived his entire life with the ancient librarians he was used to having his enthusiasms quashed almost out of hand. Even so, Old's words had raised a doubt which skulked around the fringes of his excited mind like a stray dog at a wedding feast. He would try to keep an open mind.

The hours passed. Old dozed in the sunlight. At long intervals he rose painfully and shuffled about in the dusty courtyard, forcing the life back into his deadened limbs. Small had long since exhausted his fund of activities for passing the time and had settled into a repetitive checking of the locking bar on the gate to see if it had yet straightened. Who were they? Was it the Seeker? How could he be certain? What if they gave up and went away?

Small's obsessive interest in the gate had not gone unnoticed. High above him, through a small casement, a pale face, distorted by the uneven glazing, watched intently as the boy moved to and fro. Sly was fascinated. Why this sudden interest in the gate? What did the boy and the old man know that he didn't?

As the evening shadows climbed the courtyard walls, Small finally heard the muffled thumpings and scrapings at the top of the door. Shouts, and then silence. The day's work was ended.

Next morning the sun was high in the sky when the dust which trickled through the squint was finally replaced by a shaft of light and the grinning face of one of the newcomers. The news spread quickly. The yard began to fill as librarians and menials alike waited anxiously for the gate to open.

When Spoon and his greasy kitchen crew aided by Dim and the book menials finally pulled back the locking bar, an avalanche of red dust pushed the great gates aside. As the dust settled, the inhabitants of Alligor found themselves face to face with their liberators.

Curious as a child, Small pushed through the murmuring groups of old men and walked up to the open gates. Four or five of the heroes were positioned around the gateway. Two others were freeing the horses from their makeshift excavating gear. Small had intended to walk straight up to the men and greet them, but something in the way in which they gave their polite salutation caused him to stop on the threshold. Without his even being aware of it, a primeval intuition of their body language told him that despite their friendly smiles they would rather he stayed where he was and he felt more comfortable when he did so.

It soon became clear that they were waiting for the man in white to come from the camp. He arrived shortly afterwards at great speed on a superb horse, athletically sliding from the saddle before the horse had stopped and landing lightly in a puff of pink dust. As he strode towards the gates, the five others formed up around him. Without knowing why, Small found himself slowly backing away from the gates until he had re-joined the press of curious Alligorites in the yard. He found the newcomers so interesting with their handsome faces and their broad smiles. He noticed their ornate silver belt buckles and their soft leather boots. He was impressed by the precision of their movements, and how their flicking eyes had checked every possibility of ambush and attack as they entered. Without even a sign being given, a man was positioned at each side of the gate. It was a textbook entry; a chapter from a military manual such as Mungara's *The Virgin City*. Alligor had been entered by experts.

Seven

Like almost all the strangers, the man in white was beardless. He had a square-shaped face with a broad mouth. His dark hair was pulled back from his face and gathered into a short horse tail at the back. He stood arms akimbo and legs apart whilst his eyes roved amongst the crowd.

"Greetings to you all!" His voice was rich and full. He used the common speech, but with an alien accent, a slow drawl. "Is there one here who I should be talking to? A leader? An elder perhaps?"

Several of the librarians looked round for Old as the one to consult on such a question, but the old man had not roused himself from his position by the wall. He seemed to be asleep. After a short silence it was Sly who spoke.

"We have no leaders here. We are all merely servants of the books. But I will bid you welcome on behalf of us all. The Library is open to all comers. As ye seek, so shall ye find."

Whilst Sly was speaking, Small felt a hand grip his arm. Unnoticed, Old had joined the crowd. He looked intently as the man in white strode towards Sly with his hand outstretched. The stranger gave a broad friendly smile. Small blinked in surprise. Just before the smile had appeared, one side of the stranger's upper lip had momentarily curled into an unmistakable sneer which vanished as quickly as it came. Such was the power of the stranger's personality however, that Small found himself smiling too and warming to the man.

Old spun round, his face a mask of horror. Small was startled.

"What is it Old? What's the matter?"

"*Murgans*! May God help us. They are Murgans." Old spat out the words in a forceful whisper."

"What are you talking about? What is a Murgan?"

Old's hand was trembling. "Didn't you see it?" he hissed.

"See what? What are you talking about?"

"The *ulvis*!"

"What's that?"

"The curl of the lip! The sneer before the smile. It is the mark of the high-born Murgan!"

"And...?" Small was bemused. Old struggled to regain self-control.

"Not now. Ask me later. Act naturally. Act as if you don't know who they are."

Small almost laughed. "That won't be difficult. I have no idea what you are talking about."

He could see that the old man was genuinely shocked, but the strangers were far too wonderful and interesting for Small to decide whether or not they posed any kind of threat. In fact, when he compared them to the aged, filthy and badly nourished librarians, he began to feel slightly ashamed of belonging to such a ragged rabble. In his mind's eye he toyed with the image of himself dressed in silk, his pale skinny arms swelled into sunburned muscularity.

Still wearing his broad smile, the man in white was by this time shaking Sly vigorously by the hand. For his part Sly was trying to smile but seemed in some discomfort at the rough physicality of the greeting.

"My name is Puttfark!" The stranger spoke loudly enough for everyone to hear. "These are my partners, Lubrik and Kunig." Two of the men held up their left hands and smiled around at the gathering. "We are traders from the West, beyond the mountains," he continued, "We would like to rest here for a few days before we move on. We can pay for our keep."

Sly narrowed his eyes slightly, as he always did when exercising his scheming brain. He detached his hand from the stranger's before replying. "Our hospitality would be meagre enough for such wealthy travellers as yourselves. Such as it is you have well earned already by clearing the dust from our gate. Money is of no use to us here: we do not hoard it, nor can we spend it. The Library and its contents belong to no-one, but are the common heritage of all people. Alligor grew and persists only through charity and benevolence. Sad to relate our store of food is all but exhausted. Should you be able to provide any food for the common pot we would be glad for you to share our refectory".

A murmur of approval rose from the massed ranks of skin and bone. For his part the word 'charity' seemed to have caused some puzzlement to Puttfark. He consulted briefly with Lubrik as to its meaning. An expression of frank disbelief crossed his face, then the momentary sneer, before the affable smile was turned once again to the crowd. "Mr. Sly, I think we can do business!"

It was Sly's turn to be baffled. He looked over his shoulder at the blank uncomprehending faces of the librarians. 'Business? *Business*?' He recognized the root of the word in preoccupation and activity, but not the sense in which it was being used. It was not however in his nature to admit ignorance, especially in public, and so he smiled and nodded agreement at Puttfark, Lubrik and Kunig. If the truth were to be told Sly was enjoying himself more than he would have thought possible. He had always had a higher opinion of himself than others did. Secretly he despised the other librarians for their bovine stupidity in not recognizing his superiority. Well now they would see who he really was. All those years of reading the words of Viziers, of courtiers and diplomats would not be in vain. He would render himself invaluable to the strangers. He, Sly, was now acknowledged spokesman and representative of Alligor. He was light-headed with the sudden realization of personal power and when Puttfark placed his muscular and silk-clad arm around his bony shoulders; when he heard the chink of the golden bracelet on the sunburned wrist next to his ear; when he inhaled the heady but subtle perfume with which Puttfark anointed himself; when he saw the awed gaze of the librarians as the two men walked together into the refectory entrance; no first-born son accompanied by his proud father ever felt so rightful.

Small almost laughed out loud when he saw how seriously Sly was taking himself. He looked round to see if Old was sharing his amusement, but Old was nowhere to be seen. Small had been waiting for the formalities to end because he wanted to explore the strangers' camp. Now he skipped quickly to the Gate. The two strangers at the Gate stiffened imperceptibly as he approached. The Gate had not only been closed, but the bar had been pulled across it. Small laid hold of the serpent handle. A large hand was laid on his. The other man stood close behind him, his hand inside the front of his robe at the waistband. Small glimpsed the pommel of a dagger.

"I want to go outside." said Small gaily. "I want to see your camp, the horses ... the wagons. We don't often have visitors."

When the men did not reply, he attempted to pull the bar. He found himself being lifted in the air. His robe tore. When next he touched ground the two men were shoulder to shoulder between him and the Gate. He was baffled and shocked. There was never any physical contact between the librarians.

"Why did you do that?" he asked. They didn't seem to understand. Perhaps that was it. They did not speak the common tongue. He tried a number of the languages he knew: Assyr, Zumer, Gypsian, Minot, varying the pronunciation in case his text-based knowledge was slightly adrift from the spoken dialect. The men did not respond. He racked his brains for ever more obscure tongues. A hand was placed on his shoulder. It belonged to Lubrik.

"They don't understand you," he said. "Their orders are to secure the Gate. Until that order is countermanded, that is what they will do." He was smiling as he spoke, but his smile did not have the charm of his leader's. He had thick, black, curly hair atop square coarse features that masked an active intelligence, only visible in his eyes, which scanned rapidly from side to side as he spoke. "Let's go see the man who can help you."

Lubrik turned Small firmly away from the Gate.

"That's quite a skill you have there. How many languages do you know?"

Small was flattered. "I can read in about five. Old says that it is a gift. Speaking is more difficult because I never hear native speakers."

Lubrik's eyes began to flick to and fro more rapidly. "Who is this 'Old'?" he asked, "Why amongst so many old men does he bear that name?"

"Old is ..." Small hesitated, realizing that he was being interrogated and not feeling at ease. "He's just ... Old. Have you come far?"

Lubrik did not press the point. "From way beyond the mountains to the West. We have been doing business in many places."

Again that strange word.

Puttfark, the man in white, was seated at a refectory table with Sly. A dish of water and some dark and dubious bread had been set before him as the only hospitality that Alligor could offer. Small noticed that although he often raised the dish to his mouth, he never drank from it, just as he lifted the bread but it remained unbitten. Small wondered if this was from courtesy, contempt, or even caution.

Puttfark lifted his eyes in acknowledgement as Lubrik approached. "Lubrik!" he said, "Mr. Sly is telling me all about the Library. A fascinating account."

Lubrik nodded at Small. "This young man here is someone you should know about. He reads five languages and speaks in several although he's never spoken with the natives. I think he could be very useful to us."

"Five languages! A valuable talent indeed for such a young man."

Small glowed with pleasure. Praise from a hero was praise indeed, but he was still irritated by the happening at the Gate. "I wanted to see your camp. The men at the Gate prevented me. They did not seem impressed by my skills."

There was an exchange of eloquent eye contact between Lubrik and Puttfark, before Puttfark spoke again. "They were following my orders. They can be too loyal. Come, I'll show you the camp myself. Excuse us Mr. Sly. We will talk again later."

It was Small's turn to experience the man in white's charm at close quarters. Sly, left alone in the dim light of the refectory stared dejectedly at Small's retreating figure.

A wave of Puttfark's hand was all it took for the men to draw the bar and open the Gate. This impressed Small greatly. The two guards even smiled at him as he passed through. Although he was still quite upset by the physical encounter, he began to suspect that it had perhaps been a misunderstanding after all. He was so ignorant of the ways of the world. Outside the Gate the red dust was still heaped up into a substantial bank. From the top Small could see one of the Murgans was holding the bridle of Puttfark's horse. The horse whinnied in recognition as Puttfark approached it. The man in white caressed the beast's neck. Small had never been so close to an animal of this size. On impulse he reached out to touch its hind quarters. Instantly the horse shied away, rolling its eye backwards at him. Puttfark was startled.

"Goddinhell, boy! Don't you know better than to make sudden movements around the back end of a war horse? You might have been kicked into tomorrow."

Small was mortified. "I'm sorry. I've never been close to a horse before. I just didn't know."

"Never been close to a horse? Just how do they bring boys up around here? Where I come from boys learn to ride before they can walk. Have you never been on horseback?"

Small shook his head miserably. It looked like his bid to be a hero was going to fail at the first obstacle. Puttfark had adopted an expression of deep concern. "That is something we have to do something about," he said. "Come here and get to know Captal. The finest horse this side of the mountains. Captal, meet ...what are you called?"

"Small."

"Small?" Puttfark spoke the word slowly as if he might not have heard rightly and was concerned about giving offence. "What kind of name is that for a young man?"

"I am the youngest here. I was a baby left at the Gate. The name was given to me then and it was never changed."

"Something else we might have to do something about. Captal, meet ... Small. Let him see you and catch your, er, scent in his nostrils, then he will know you." He gave an order in his own language to the Murgan who stood nearby. The Murgan repeated the order as if he did not believe his ears. Puttfark held Captal's head. "Banco will help you get onto the horse's back."

Small was certain that he was being granted an extraordinary privilege. He moved as if he was in a dream. Seated on the horse's back he felt insecure, even when Banco shortened the stirrup loops. But when Puttfark began to lead the horse towards the Murgan camp, Small instinctively gripped the horse with his knees. For the first time in his short life he began to realise what it might be like to be a hero. He sat up stiff and straight, putting his nose as high in the air as he could. Puttfark looked over his shoulder and laughed silently. Small inhaled deeply, savouring the wind off the plain. Sometimes when he had been up on the roofs of Alligor he had felt exhilarated like this. There had been times when the wind had acted like a drug; times when he thought that he caught a whiff of adventure on the breeze. But he had never felt such a promise of life before. He sensed the wheels of Destiny turning his way. By the time they reached the camp he was ready to lay down his life for the man in white. If only the Murgans would let him ride with them into the sunset.

Small's arrival on Captal caused a stirring in the Murgan camp. All the Murgans were soon gathering around him, pressing just close enough for him to hear snatches of their strange drawling dialect. He strained his senses. There was something tantalisingly familiar about the Murgan Speech. Puttfark seemed to be explaining about Small to his people. Small's name caused general, if politely suppressed, amusement, but Small himself was scarcely aware of it. The youngster's entire attention was focused upon two young Murgan women who had appeared directly in front of him on the fringe of the crowd. The one had her arm around the waist of the other and, whilst gazing at Small with frank curiosity, gently laid her head on the other's shoulder. One glance from their dark flashing eyes and he was lost to the world. As the women became aware that Small was staring at them, they instinctively and provocatively adjusted their poses. Any man would have been stirred by that mixture of promise, challenge and dare. Small's senses were overwhelmed. It was then that one of the women spoke to the other. Small lip-read, and suddenly he understood. Blushing to the roots of his hair at the indelicacy of the joke the woman had made about his name, he realized that it was only the spoken language he did not know. He had seen it written many times. It was not a language he knew well, but as he listened to Puttfark, he began to pick out odd words and phrases. The Murgans spoke Babel.

Banco was tugging at his sleeve. It was time to dismount. Puttfark and Small strolled through the camp.

"So," said Puttfark. "Welcome to our home from home. For a boy who has just ridden his first horse, looking at people and wagons will be sort of ordinary."

"Oh, no. Everything is new and interesting for me: the tents, the people, everything. I have only ever known Alligor and those who live here. In books I have travelled the world and met its people. In books I have shared their adventures. I have even ridden with the cavalry of the Great Khan across the endless plain to where the sun rises - in books. But just now I realized that all I really know about is books, the stories that are in them and the words that they are made from. I don't know the first thing about horses."

"That, young man, can be easily fixed. Any farmer can learn to ride a horse, just as any peasant can swing a sword about. But knowing about books, and the languages of words, that is something not easily picked up. Very few folk have that kind of skill. It needs a sharp mind and years of work. For you it seems like nothing compared with having a horse to ride. It's the same with me and my Captal. I have always had fine horses to ride. I don't think of how I learned the art of making the money to buy them, how I learned to ride them or even the skills I use to stop anybody killing me and stealing them. I ride a fine horse and I know how to keep it. You know about books and words and you want to ride. Maybe I am curious about books. What say we teach each other what we know?"

Small's face lit up. "You would teach me to ride your horse?"

"Nothing simpler."

"But what can I tell you about books? There are millions of them. Which ones would you want to know about?"

Puttfark stroked his chin. "Young man." he said, "When you have become an expert horse rider, where will you ride to? There are millions of places to go."

Small grinned in pleasant confusion. Puttfark smiled back. Small scarcely noticed the *ulvis* this time. The man in white slapped him on the back "Do we have a bargain? Is it a deal?" Puttfark saw that Small did not understand him. He tried again, "Can we help each other?" Small grasped the outstretched hand, hardly daring to believe what he had heard.

The other Murgans had gathered around them as they spoke. Small was not sure how to feel about being the centre of so much attention. He would have much preferred to have roamed around the camp alone. The Murgans seemed friendly enough, and kept their distance - all but one. The old crone he had spotted from the roof shuffled towards him from her tent. She had such a malevolent expression that his instinct was to run away. But he told himself that heroes were made of sterner stuff and stood firm as she thrust her crinkled face close to his. The hideous face sniffed deeply. The crone did not like what her nostrils were telling her and demonstrated this by spitting on the ground. She harangued Puttfark and then the other Murgans for a good while before shuffling back to her tent.

She had a thick accent but Small thought he understood some at least of what she said. Puttfark confirmed his suspicions.

"She is our physician. She says you are dirty and smell as if you have never been near water in your life. You have vermin in your hair: your clothes are so infested and threadbare that if you took them off they would walk by themselves. She thinks you will bring diseases to her girls. She is very *Wicc'd*, as you would say 'wise' in such things and usually knows what she is talking about. Before you come back tomorrow, try and clean yourself if you can, and we will do the rest."

Small knew that he was being sent away. As he made his way back to Alligor he realized that after all he had not seen much of the Murgans or their camp. Even so, it had been an exciting day. He had to pound with his fist on the gate to get the guards to let him pass inside. As he ran off to look for Old, he did not notice Sly in the shadowy doorway of the refectory, deep in conversation with Lubrik and Kunig. Sly gave the boy a suspicious glance as he passed. Sly had already decided that these strangers were not ordinary traders, nor were they merely passing by. They had come to Alligor on purpose. What purpose he did not yet know. But everything he heard from Lubrik and his partner made him sure that it was the books that had drawn them here and not trade. And if that was so then they would need a guide. He would be that guide. In return, the strangers would divert food into Alligor and he, Sly, would control that supply. He did not yet know which books they wanted, but he was sure that he could make the search last at least until they stopped bringing in food. That was, as the strangers put it, the deal.

Eight

"I rode on a great white horse. His name is Captal. I went to their camp."

Small had not had to search for Old this time. The old man had installed himself on a windowsill inside the great staircase so that he could see the comings and goings in the courtyard below.

"What did you promise them?"

Small reddened. "How did you know?"

Old snorted with disgust. "They are Murgans, they never give anything for nothing, - not even a ride on a horse. They would not even have let you out of the gate unless you had something they wanted."

"Puttfark wants to know about the books. He says in return he will teach me to ride." Small began to feel uneasy about his triumph.

Old nodded slowly. "And what are you going to tell him?"

Small shrugged. "I don't know. I'm not sure what he wants."

"Don't trust them, Small." The old man grasped him by the arm as he spoke. "Murgans despise all cultures but their own, such as it is. Their own society is of such a twisted shape that they can never produce any real poets or makers. They have no real interest in books. Whatever they have come here for, you can be certain that it is not to acquire any proper wisdom."

Small did not want to hear his heroes brought low in this way and leaped to their defence. "You don't know that for certain. You only know from books. They have come here by chance. They are traders passing through."

"Traders!" Old's voice was hoarse with scorn. "The caravan routes are fifty leagues north of here. They are no more traders than I am. You've been to their camp. How many camels do they have with them?"

"None." Small replied in a low voice. "But they have two wagons."

"Think on, boy, how much room is left in those wagons after all their tents, their bedding, clothing, cooking pots, food and horse fodder, spare harness and weapons have been packed away? Just what is it that they are trading in?"

Small was irritated by the Old man's difficult questions. "They might be buying and not selling and if this is the first time they have been this far east they might not know the routes. I like them. Puttfark is kind to me. I will help him. They look to me like heroes, and ..."

"Heroes! What do you know about heroes?" Old was more agitated than Small had ever seen him. Even so, when Small opened his mouth, the words just tumbled out. "They look more like heroes than we do. Look at us. We are dirty and verminous; we dress in rags; we are starving; we know nothing of the real world. When I see the Murgans I am ashamed to be what I am."

There was a long silence as they both thought about what had been said. Old spoke first. "Know this much boy. We owe our lives to the Library and the people who cared for it. The heroic sacrifices of many quiet lifetimes have gone into making and preserving this great place. If it is now at last to achieve its purpose, then all those dirty ragged orphans would be heroes. You have sworn the oath. If you fail in your duty now, those same lives will all have been sacrificed in vain."

"But Old, you cannot be sure that he is not the One." said Small.

"No more than you can be sure that he is!" retorted the old man.

Small was defiant. "He wants to teach me to ride a horse. He says that all young boys learn to ride horses."

"He is a Murgan. He is using you."

"What do you know about Murgans?" Small replied, "You only know about books and books can't be trusted, you told me so yourself! The Murgans write about themselves as heroes: their enemies describe them as devils. How can you tell which account is true?" Small had never before challenged the old man's advice in this way, but now, having ridden a horse he felt that his superior knowledge of the real world entitled him to an opinion.

For his part, Old was unsettled by the boy's sharp logic. Age was beginning to creep up on the old man. His memory was becoming temperamental and sometimes he just could not summon up the mental energy he needed to think clearly. He was genuinely fond of the lad. He did not want to deny him his youthful pleasures. After all, had he not looked after the boy since the day he had been found at the gate? Why had he taken on such a task? He still could not rightly explain. Something in the babe's pitiful cries had touched his heart. He could not say that he had ever regretted the many hours he had spent feeding, cleaning, amusing and then educating the child. Even with all the wisdom of the world sitting on the shelves of his life, there had been an emptiness at the heart of Old's being. The boy had given purpose to his existence. Old wondered if perhaps he was more afraid of losing the boy's company than of the end of Alligor. He dismissed the idea. All his instincts warned him against the strangers. But could the boy be right? The real world might indeed be different from the world of books. Heroes were after all usually military men following a career of violence. Perhaps an aura of subterfuge, danger and threat was merely the mark of their calling.

Small was used to waiting for the old man to gather his thoughts. Eventually Old spoke.

"Neither of us knows anything of the world outside Alligor, except what the authors have told us. But the authors also say that the beginning of wisdom is to know that you know nothing. Let it be your task to learn all you can about these strangers. Observe them carefully. If they are otherwise than they seem then they will not be able to disguise their real character at all times. Enjoy your horse riding but remember your oath. Do not be the one who betrays Alligor. For my part, I put my faith in the authors. Art and Truth hold hands. The Murgans have no real poets or painters to plead their case for them. That alone is proof enough for me."

Small had heard enough. The old man was not completely sure about the intentions of the Murgans. He turned to leave but then remembered something else he wanted to tell. "The other day," he began, "I was in the old city. There didn't seem to be anyone there at all. I found a dead librarian. The menials were too frightened even to go there."

Old nodded sadly before he spoke. "Yes. The master died several years ago. His name was Know-all. A very wise man in his day, but a little too arrogant for his own good. I always meant to try and find out what happened to his librarians but nobody seemed to be in the mood for expeditions. A dead librarian you say? We are none of us getting any younger. No matter what the story, each book must have its end."

Small was not in the mood for such morbid thoughts. He left Old to his mumblings and musings and set off on more important business. "Try and clean yourself," Puttfark had said. Heroes did it with water. He had read about bathing and swimming but had never thought of it as a way of getting clean. Now he decided to try it. No point in making the long journey to the roof, the red dust was everywhere; it would have to be the cisterns.

The entrance to the subterranean parts of Alligor was through the kitchen. In this vast sooty cave, Spoon and his greasy minions were in the throes of preparing a cauldron of foetid greenish-grey gruel. A violent debate was taking place as to whose turn it was to taste the foul mixture. Today it seemed that nobody wanted to take the risk. The door to the cellars was ajar and the steep stairway was lit by cresset lamps cut into the wall. The lamps were burning rancid oil which gave off an acrid black smoke.

Beneath Alligor there was a vast underworld, all of it hollowed from the living rock. It was strange to think that all the stones of the library had once filled these cavernous spaces before being quarried and lifted up into the light. Casual readers could come and go without ever realising how much of Alligor lay beneath the plain. Spoon would often brag that his subterranean kingdom was not only the largest and most important part of the Book City, but that he, Spoon the Magnificent, was the greatest philosopher in the whole Library. From time to time, unwary or forgetful librarians would challenge this assertion. Whilst the Kitchen menials held their breath expectantly, a great beaming smile would spread across Spoon's greasy countenance as he anticipated his coup. In a voice that seethed and hissed like a cooking pot Spoon would say, "Don't I provide more food for thought than any other man in Alligor? And how much thinking would there be here without that food?" Small could not help smiling as he pictured the menials hooting and jeering the triumph of foolishness over wisdom.

Small did not like being underground. It was eerie and frightening even though the cavernous undercroft which lay beneath kitchen and refectory was now lit by the cresset lamps which sputtered and flickered in the gloom. Normally the only illumination in this vast space took the form of three spectral columns of light which came down the rainwater shafts all the way from the roof. The light penetrated the great arched ceiling and reflected from the surface of the water in the cisterns, sometimes in patterns that danced all over the vaults.

Down either side of the hall loomed the great stone grain silos. Between them squat pillars of enormous girth carried the arches of the vaults. These arches framed the inky mouths of side galleries which led off into the utter dark. Out there, somewhere in the blackness was the catacomb where, until about a century before, all Alligor's dead had been laid to rest. Over the millennia, thousands of corpses had been interred so that the tunnels and chambers were choked with their remains. Old claimed to have been there when he was a young man, but would not talk about his experience unless it was to say that the librarians left the world as they had entered it, naked as babes: no shrouds, no coffins, no cairns. Alligor itself was their only monument. Whenever Small came down here into the underworld, he always experienced a strange sense that these crowds of the dead were there in the shadows silently watching him. He felt it very strongly now as he stood at the lip of one of the water cisterns which had been cut into the floor. Steps had been cut into the side wall of the cistern. They led down into the greenish-yellow water. No-one knew how deep the water in the cisterns was. Even in the drought year only six steps had been uncovered. According to the ancient lore of the kitchen, of which Spoon was the current living repository, they were fed by secret underground springs, divined by the original architects. Certainly the water never stank or became stagnant.

Small steeled himself for his baptism into the religion of the goddess Hygaeia. Now that he was on the brink of the pool he was not quite so sure that his will was sufficient to the ordeal. What would Amatis have done in such a situation? Heroes swam rivers, leaped from the decks of ships into the waves, but usually they were in the grip of violent excitement. Without being pursued or threatened would they really have been able to lower themselves into an icy pool in the dark? He had never read about heroes cleaning themselves. Perhaps they never did. But Small wanted to ride a horse with the Murgans. He clenched his teeth and his fists and strode boldly down the steps. He did not need to test his will any further than that because his foot slipped on the slimy stonework and he tumbled into the cistern.

It was as if time slowed down. He watched fascinated as his outstretched hand parted the limpid surface of the pool. He observed the water travel up his arm and then came the shock as his head and torso crashed into the water. The shock was so great that he did not feel the cold at first. He was descending into a thick green twilight world that pressed upon all his senses. Seconds passed that seemed like minutes. Gilded bubbles wobbled and wavered their way up to the surface giving the impression that he was still sinking even after he focused upon the dim form of the steps. For several seconds more he was stupefied, suspended in time and space. Then it was as if a small voice within told him that he ought to get out. Suddenly he regained dominion over his physical self and lunged for the steps. Hand over hand he struggled to the surface and dragged his body, now heavy and strange, out of the pool. He drew down a great draught of air as he began to shake and tremble with shock and cold.

How long Small sat there feeling sick, cold and weak he could not tell. After a while his breathing evened out and he became once more aware of the deep silence of the place. Eventually he decided that he could trust his legs and carefully stood upright. Almost at once, a loud splash echoed around the undercrypt causing his heart to leap against his chest. Something very heavy had fallen into one of the water cisterns in the darkness beyond the glow of the lamps. He did not feel heroic at all, but try as he might he could not leave without investigating. He began to walk slowly and cautiously into the darkness.

It was easy to find the right cistern. The splash had thrown water all over the dry sandy floor and up the side of a granary silo. The surface of the pool was still agitated but there was no sign of a cause. Small strained his eyes at the faintly illuminated water. He could see nothing. Above his head a wide circular shaft ascended. Far above him he saw, not the sky, but a blue vaulted ceiling dusted with golden stars. With a shock of recognition he realised that he was at the bottom of the Great Well. Glancing back at the water he thought he could just make out a white something beneath the surface. There it was. A pale disc was rising from the depths. He bent forward to see it more clearly. It was the face of an old man. In the moment before the corpse broke surface, Small recognized the cruelly battered features of Splint the librarian.

From his seat in the gigantic inglenook which housed the kitchen furnace. Small watched as the menials gently laid Splint on the massive wooden chopping block. It was strange how life made people seem larger than they were. Looking at the corpse Small realised how pitifully tiny Splint had really been. A wave of sympathy swept over him. Poor Splint. Crippled from birth, unloved, unnoticed, so pathetically eager to please that he would make up any story he thought you might want to hear. In his mind the dividing line between the fiction in books and the fact of real life had dissolved. But what had happened to him? Had his mind finally collapsed? Had despair caused him to end his life by hurling himself down the well? Despite his eccentricity Splint had always taken his duties seriously. He loved his books like children. Would he really have just abandoned them all without telling anyone?

Small felt his eyelids beginning to droop with fatigue. The violent rubbing down with kitchen cloths that Spoon had given him, coupled with the heat of the furnace was making him drowsy. He had to sleep. The warmth in the kitchen was tempting but nothing would persuade him to spend the night with a corpse. Rising from his seat he shrugged himself into his robe and headed for the door. Spoon's men stood in groups wearing worried expressions and speaking in low voices. As he passed the makeshift bier, Small noticed that Splint's eyes had not been closed. On impulse he reached out and pulled down the lids with his fingertips. The head lolled limply to one side exposing Splint's scrawny throat. Small stared at a second mouth that had opened up in the dead man's neck. Just below the line of the jaw, close to the ear was a deep clean cut about an inch long from which a pinkish fluid was just beginning to seep.

Nine

The next morning Small rose with the sun. His sleep had been disrupted by nightmares in which it seemed that he had spent the whole night fleeing from armies of ghastly corpses through flooded catacombs. The Murgan guarding the gate was not pleased to be roused from his bedroll at such an early hour, but he had clearly received orders to let Small pass. At the Murgan camp the day had already begun. Food was cooking. People were moving about. He found Puttfark, immaculate as ever, breakfasting outside his tent. The man in white smiled at him. Small thought how strange it was that the *ulvis* should have shocked him when he first saw it. Now it seemed as much a part of the man as his robe.

"Greetings my young friend!" said Puttfark. "Sit down. Join me. Have you eaten? Here, have one of these." Small found himself holding a small lump of warm white bread which had been divided into two halves. A dark greasy object had been inserted into the cleft, along with some pungent chopped vegetables. Small ate ravenously. He was unused to such strong flavours but it appeased his hunger most satisfactorily.

"Nothing like breakfast in the open air," Puttfark said expansively. "Don't you think so?"

Small agreed. There was nothing like breakfast. Puttfark wiped his mouth on a white cloth and stood up. "Right. First we'll get you acceptable to Vulpia and then...You still want to ride a horse?"

Small nodded vigorously.

Becoming acceptable to the sinister old crone was a complicated and embarrassing process. First of all he was taken outside the camp to what seemed to him to be an exaggeratedly distant spot. His robe was taken from him and buried in the ground with just a tiny corner left visible. And after all the trouble he'd taken to get it clean! Next he was given a handful of grey slime from a pot and told to rub it all over his body and in his hair. This was then rinsed off with a bucketful of water so cold that it made him gasp and shiver. To his embarrassment numerous specimens of insect life were spotted struggling in the pool of greyish fluid where he had been standing. Wrapped in a large dry cloth he was told to sit on the ground. One of the Murgans then cut off most of his hair using a clever device with two knife blades rubbing against each other. When this was done, the old crone herself arrived carrying a small basin. The contents of the basin were transferred to every hairy part of his body and he was told to rub it in well. The substance burned like fire, but he was assured that this would pass. After a careful examination of Small's scalp, the old woman grunted in grudging satisfaction and hobbled away. To his intense delight the Murgans then presented him with a faded and worn robe of the kind which they themselves wore. He understood that this was called a *tzirt*. It felt soft and cool on his skin. Small felt reborn.

For his riding lesson, Puttfark had one of the wagon horses brought over. It was a thick-legged shaggy beast but it seemed docile enough. The horse had no saddle. Puttfark fastened a long rope halter to its bridle. He moved with an easy grace, skilled and confident; not deliberately showing off, but aware that he was impressing the young boy. He was enjoying himself. Small watched with intense interest, trying to memorize everything he saw.

"Do the horses enjoy being ridden upon?" Small asked suddenly, "How does it come about that they allow people to use them so?"

Puttfark laughed. "You have a rare talent for asking difficult questions young man. The truth is that horses in their natural state don't submit easily to servitude. They fight like any wild animal against the loss of their freedom. At first their will has to be subjected to that of their rider by means not always gentle. Horse breaking is a skilled craft. It would be a relatively simple matter to bludgeon the horse into abject submission. But then you would have made yourself a very low form of beast of burden, only fit for treadmills and carts. You would always have to carry a whip. Far better to be more subtle, rewarding the horse often with food, soft words and caresses. Then the horse will retain some spirit and perhaps serve you well at dire need.

'The art of breaking a horse to your will is first of all to teach it to depend on you for its food. Next you convince the beast that it is only free when it is out of its field and serving you. There is a wonderful irony in this since in reality it is curbed in the mouth by bronze, often blinkered, bound by leather straps, burdened by unnatural weights, and directed at every step by a will not its own. Only in its small field is it truly unencumbered and free to move at will. If the horse could not be so convinced, then it would be necessary to chase the beast around its field and break it again every time you wanted to ride. In fact we find the horse meekly submits to being bridled." Puttfark patted the horse on the neck affectionately.

Small's first riding lesson was a painful and exhausting experience. Puttfark explained how the horse could be urged forward with a kick of the heels and a click of the tongue. Sitting bareback, Small had to keep his balance whilst the horse first walked and then trotted in a wide circle at the end of the rope held by Puttfark. Trotting consisted of an endless series of collisions between the horse's backbone and the base of Small's spine. He soon learned that the key to balance and comfort was to anticipate the horse's movements and to grip the horse's flanks tightly between his knees.

Puttfark was an excellent teacher and seemed to enjoy the task. He could not have wished for a more avid and enthusiastic pupil. By the end of the session Small could keep his balance without gripping the horse's neck and, whilst in motion, had even managed to reach down and touch his own ankle, first on one side and then the other without falling off. Puttfark seemed genuinely pleased by Small's aptitude. As they strolled back to the camp Small had the strangest sensation, as if he were carrying an empty barrel between his knees.

Lubrik and Kunig were waiting for Puttfark outside his tent. They wore concerned expressions and had seemed deep in conversation. As Puttfark held open the tent for his lieutenants, Small found himself passed into the care of Banco who took him to Vulpia's tent. Clutching a small glass phial, she accompanied Small and Banco to the spot where Small's forgotten robe was buried. To his horror and shame, the corner of the robe left unburied was now a seething black mass of parasitic insects which had made their way up out of the robe and into the light and air. Vulpia subdued the vermin with a fiercely aromatic liquid from the phial. Within a very short time their inert bodies could be brushed off into the sand. Once disinterred the robe was shaken vigorously and handed back to him. Banco smiled briefly and then said, "Tomorrow." in the common speech, before turning his back and following Vulpia back to the tents.

As Small walked back towards Alligor carrying his old robe, his elated mood slowly evaporated. The events of the previous evening returned to trouble his thoughts. He was not familiar with the effects of violence, but he was certain that Splint had been viciously attacked before his body was tipped into the Great Well. Who on earth could have done such a thing? He could not imagine anyone in Alligor capable of such physical behaviour. Small hammered to be let in. As the Gate was heaved open, he caught a glimpse of the guard's dagger. As far as he knew the Murgans were the only ones here who had weapons. The guard smiled at him as he passed inside, but the smile faded as he noticed Small did not respond. Detached from the smile the man's eyes had been cold and non-committal.

Old still occupied the same windowsill overlooking the yard. Small shook him by the shoulder to wake him up.

"Greetings Old." he said.

The old man's eyes slowly focused upon him. "Small?" he said, "Is it you? You seem somewhat changed; your hair; your dress."

"Just cleaner." said Small. "The Murgans gave me the *tzirt*."

"Ah, yes." said Old, "The Murgans. They give you riding lessons and you give them the world. I remember."

"Old, I want to ask you something. Did any of the Murgans enter the library yesterday?"

"As far as I know only five entered the courtyard. Three of those went into the refectory but none entered the library itself. Why do you ask?"

"Another librarian has died. I think he was murdered. He had been beaten and there was a wound...here." Small touched his neck.

After hearing how Splint's body had been found, Old was silent for a long time before he spoke. "This is something shocking and not easy to understand. Why would anyone do this to Splint? He was so small and frail. Why so many blows when one blow would have subdued him? This wound you describe also disturbs me since it is a wound which would not have been easily inflicted whilst Splint was free to defend himself. He must have been either bound or unconscious when he was stabbed. I am no expert in violent or fatal attack but I think you are right to think that it was the cause of his death."

"Who do you think did it?" Small asked.

"That I cannot tell you." Old replied. "I am certain that it was not any of our fellow Alligorites. The wound and the attempt to dispose of the body suggest a fear of being discovered. No one who lived here would drop the body where it would both pollute their own water supply and be so easily found. In any case, the deliberate placing of the dagger makes me fear that we are dealing with an assassin, an expert in inflicting harm by stealth."

Small was depressed by the direction the inquest was taking. "So you think the Murgans did it?"

"That, my young friend, is the mysterious part. I am almost certain that no one from the Murgan camp has yet entered the library. Even if they had done so whilst I slept, it would have taken them days, if not weeks to orientate themselves. We have lived our lives in the book-city. We know it like the palm of our hand, these strangers do not. In any case they would not have had time to reach the Great Well, even if they knew of its existence. I am baffled. I do not think it was one of us. I do not think it was one of them. Yet whoever did this thing knew his way around the library, but perhaps not so well as a native would."

Small opened his mouth to speak, but then closed it again. There were so many unanswerable questions crowding into his thoughts that it was difficult to know where to begin. He screwed up his face in frustration. Old's brow was also deeply furrowed, and he stroked his beard rhythmically to aid his concentration.

Old was the first to speak. "This is all I can say. If it is not a librarian and if it is not one of the strangers, then it might possibly be a reader."

"A reader?" Small was baffled. "Are there any?"

"Very few have arrived even in my long lifetime," said Old, "but it is conceivable that one might have slipped in unobserved. The Gate is not always closed, nor is it always watched."

"But Old," said Small, "even a reader must eat and drink. If he had used the refectory wouldn't somebody have noticed him? And wouldn't he have known about the cellars?"

"Readers usually arrive with a stock of food. One even took an ass with panniers up the Great Stair. If this reader's interest took him to the Western Galleries, it would not be worth while to keep returning to our refectory. That way he would spend all his time travelling back and forth. Now, there did use to be a kitchen in the western city, and I have heard tales of terrace gardens with fruit trees and vines, but I must confess that when as a young man I went exploring, it was always hunger and thirst that drove me back."

Small was not convinced. "It is too far fetched. A reader whom no-one has seen, who doesn't eat or drink, and who has the strength to batter an old man and throw him down a well, all for no reason."

Old shrugged his shoulders helplessly. "I am as puzzled as you are. These are strange days indeed. If I did not trust implicitly in the craft of the Divine Author, I would fear that we were facing some supernatural enemy. Even so you must take extra care as you move around the city."

Old continued to ponder over the complexities of the plot until his eyelids began to droop. As Small walked away from him, his thoughts were haunted by an irrational anger. He was angry with Old for asking him to swear the oath, and angry with Splint for getting himself killed. Why had not the Murgans arrived a month ago? Then he might have learned to ride and left Alligor without a qualm. Now it felt as if he was carrying the whole book city on his shoulders. He was unaccustomed to such worry and responsibility.

His feet led him up the stairs to the Lion Cabinet. This tiny chamber was the nearest thing to a home that he had. The big cats which gave the room its name were carved rafter ends, clearly visible through the window opening. Massive and wind-silvered, they sprang out from the walls, bearing the eaves of the roof on their backs. Every evening for a thousand years they had snarled at the setting sun. That was why Small liked this room. It caught and held the last glimmer of the dying day. The Lion Cabinet contained no shelves as such, but on the right as you entered was a large press or cupboard with doors. The original purpose of the cupboard could only be guessed at, but Small found it an ideal sleeping place. In winter with the doors closed, it was as cosy as anywhere in Alligor could ever be. This was his private space. Here he kept copies of his favourite volumes. *The Mirror of Almeira,* of course, as well as *With the Horses of the Great Khan* by Zaw Pei: then *The Book of the Glory of Kings*, bound together with the wonderful *Voyage to the Land of Punt:* next to it *On the Hunting of Dragons* by Axares: Homer's *Margites* which made him laugh and Almazzar's *Nights in the Gardens of Old Babylon* with its haunting poetry. Here also were his treasures: the shells of birds' eggs; feathers of every shape, size and hue; various oddments of this and that, picked up and kept because they either sparkled or jingled, or simply because they were not books.

He was not the first to have used the room. Every square inch of the plastered walls had been scratched and scratched over again with the writing of previous tenants. Snatches of poetry; aphorisms; paeans of praise to favourite authors, usually accompanied by refutations and rival claimants; philosophical standpoints; scurrilous attacks on masters long gone and forgotten; jokes both obscure and eternal; pleas to be remembered by the Great Author; pleas just to be remembered; all overlaid and interlaced to the extent that one often ran on seamlessly into the other. Small felt comforted by the presence of so much evidence of human life. It was almost like being in a room full of people.

After a while he found himself leafing desultorily through the pages of *The Hunting of Dragons*. Because of all the unanswered questions jostling with each other in his head, he could not concentrate on any of the exciting adventures in the book and quickly reached the final chapter. Ordinarily he did not read this final part of the book because it seemed rather domestic and disappointing, but now the admonition at the head of the chapter caught his attention. It read: *Before you go seeking dragons in faraway places, make sure there are no serpents in your own palace".* Small read on. *Sooner or later a serpent will betray its presence by killing. Often the victim is killed at the moment of discovering the serpent. That is why every corpse should be carefully examined to find out what was the precise cause of death. If you fail to discover the victim of a serpent then you may expect the serpent to kill again. Often it is the weak, the old or the very young who fall prey to this subtle enemy.*

There followed examples of fatal accidents; of falling from battlements; of being kicked by horses; of drowning in fishpools; where the cause of death seemed obvious and yet when the bodies were examined, the marks of the serpent were discovered. Small felt a heightening of interest. The next section was entitled *The marks of the serpent* and was divided into three sections: *Of poisons*; *Of bruising and crushing*; and *Of punctures*. Small had no idea that snakes were so versatile. Axares listed so many different poisons, all of which left their characteristic marks on the victims' physiognomy. This one made the mouth smell of bitter almonds, another caused blistering of the throat, yet another left the tongue blackened. Some serpents even had poisonous exhalations 'a smoke like that of incense candles that killed in the time it took to take a single breath'. *Of bruising and crushing* included an interminable inventory of physical damage. Axares told the story of a young prince who had fallen down a grand staircase in full view of a dozen courtiers. His neck was broken. It seemed a simple accident, but when the serpent finder was called, he immediately noted the purple weals around the throat and the blueness of the face. These told him that the boy had been garrotted by the serpent at the head of the stair before his lifeless body had been thrown down amongst the courtiers. *Of punctures* was scarcely less comprehensive in its listing of fatal wounds. Serpents, it seemed, were extremely adept at puncturing the human body in places where it might not be noticed, and by means which would be similarly unobtrusive. Some serpents had fangs which were long and thin like needles which could go deep into vital areas and leave only a tiny pinprick on the skin. When such were inserted into various natural orifices; the ear; the roof of the mouth; the nostril; the consequences were both fatal and virtually undiscoverable. Even larger wounds could be made almost invisible if made on natural folds of the body; at the armpit, under the shoulder blade; behind the ear; under the jaw where it would be hidden by the beard.

Small read the sentence several times, letting the implications unfold in his mind. A serpent in Alligor! Was it possible? As he read on he became more and more convinced that it was not only a possibility, but a certainty. According to Axares there were many means by which blood might be prevented from betraying a concealed wound; the teeth of horn, bone, ivory or glass which the serpent snapped off inside the wound to staunch the flow; the cauterizing effects of venomous ointments smeared on the fangs. It was not always so technical, a punctured body which fell into a river, pool or cistern left no crimson pathways to lead the serpent finder to the serpent's lair. Having by this time convinced himself that there was indeed a serpent loose in Alligor, he began to read the final part of the chapter: "*The finding of snakes*". The advice of Axares to serpent finders was succinct. "*Goodness is sufficient unto itself, but evil must be nourished.* Find out where your serpent feeds and ye shall find your serpent". Even this advice was not as straightforward as it seemed, since serpents, at least according to Axares, had unusual appetites. Some would be nourished by gold or valuables, some by power, some by envy or jealousy, others by lust and yet others might feed on fear. Want of meat and drink in the ordinary sense did not seem to motivate their actions at all.

Small felt his credulity being sorely taxed. But if he had learned anything at all from his dealings with books, it was that when a great author such as Axares appeared to have written nonsense, it might not be as nonsensical as it at first appeared. Foolishness was often used to confound the wise. For all he knew, palaces might indeed be infested with supernatural serpents. On the other hand he had no doubt whatsoever that assassination and intrigue often paved the way to power for the unscrupulous and the unworthy. The advice of Axares held good for human snakes as well. A book such as *The Hunting of Dragons* placed amongst the other fairy tales in the royal nursery might well help a quick-witted royal scion save both his life and his kingdom. What was intended to save the lives of Royal heirs might also save the lives of orphan librarians.

Splint's funeral had been a melancholy affair which depressed Small for a long time. But four days of lessons on the horse gave Small a renewed sense of self-worth and achievement. He had not only acquired a new skill but the physical work of controlling the animal was beginning to tighten his muscles. He had also been given a new name. From the beginning Puttfark had found Small's name highly embarrassing and avoided using it whenever he could. For the Murgan, the degree of humility and self-effacement which the name suggested was an affront to the core concepts of Murgan philosophy - self-assertion and equality, Thus not only did he find the name insupportable but he found it disturbing even to be acquainted with someone so-named. All this he told Small.

"From now on," he said, "you will be known as *Rider.*"

The absurd upswelling of pleasure and pride which 'Small' felt on becoming 'Rider' was only slightly deflated when his horse was almost immediately taken away from him.

"We need him to pull the wagon." he was told. "The provisions are getting low."

As they watched the wagons and their escort depart, Puttfark had turned to him. "It might be a day or two before they get back. Tomorrow I think we shall take a look at your Book-City. Meet me for breakfast."

Small had nodded agreement, even smiled, but did not feel at ease. He had not forgotten the agreement he had made with Puttfark, but he secretly dreaded having to fulfil his side of the bargain, even though he could not find any definite reason why this should be so. The man in white had genuinely enjoyed teaching him to ride, of that he was sure. He had an easy-going caring manner, which if Small had known what it meant he might have described as 'fatherly'. Puttfark had the gift of making anyone he turned his attention upon feel as if they were the focus of his entire personality. Small found the effect supremely flattering, particularly when the Murgan gripped his elbow or put his arm around his shoulders when making a point. Once, when Small had complained about the buffeting he was getting from the horse, the man in white had even subjected the boy to a mock attack. Small had gasped under a rain of blows, pulled at the last moment, after which he had been wrestled off his feet. His descent to the ground had not been so gentle, but what had shocked Small most of all was not the physical contact, but that he had enjoyed the rough and tumble, had felt an immediate bonding with the man in white, and indeed with all the Murgans who shared the joke. At that moment he began to suspect what it might mean to be a man amongst men.

Small walked back to Alligor with a sinking heart. Being with the Murgans out on the plain exhilarated him almost as much as returning to the endless galleries now depressed him. The librarians seemed more and more pathetic, dirty and stupid. He was shocked by the intolerant and contemptuous feelings he now had towards them. From his niche on the Great Stair, Old looked at him with such a suspicious and accusatory manner, that he avoided his company. Small had even lost his temper with Dim. As he strolled aimlessly through galleries and corridors, he thought about his changed life. The Library seemed suddenly to be gloomy and threatening in a way that he had never before experienced. He was sure that before the Murgans arrived, the green cobweb-draped windows must have obscured just as much of the light of day; the heavy masonry and solid woodwork must have stifled the sounds of the outside world just as thoroughly; the labyrinthine architecture must have frustrated his desire for physical progress in a straight line just as it did now; but it had never depressed him so. The submarine light had always been sufficient for him to read by, and the galleries had in any case flickered with the supernatural visions kindled in his own imagination by the works of the authors. The utter silence too had never troubled him. It had enabled him to hear the sounds of imaginary worlds. It had been merely the absence of distraction, a blank wall on which he could paint more clearly the visions which the books provoked. Moving through the maze of knowledge had meant that new authors and new worlds were always coming to hand. But now he had doubts.

An author had written of ignorant people as prisoners who had been chained up from birth in a dark cave. Unable to move their heads, they were only able to see dark and uncertain shadows on the wall in front of them. One prisoner broke free and was able to see not only the bonfire which illuminated the cave, but also the interminable procession of people carrying burdens who, passing between the bonfire and the prisoners, cast their shadows on the wall. The ex-prisoner eventually found his way out into the daylight. Could Alligor be the cave, and its inhabitants the chained prisoners? What would Old say if Small told him that Alligor was a cave of ignorance whose inhabitants were obsessed with shadows and appearances?

Whether by design or accident, Small had left the Eastern Galleries and entered the old city. Recognizing the corridor in which he found himself, he moved ahead with a new-found purpose. Around the next corner was the Red Loggia. The once delicately carved and pierced crimson woodwork of the Loggia formed the grand entrance to the wooden quarter. In ages past it had been an area of inns and lodgings, now it was known as the Shambles because of its dilapidated and abandoned condition. The staircase leading down into the Wooden Courtyard had been very grand and impressive. Now it was broken-backed and subsiding into a heap of sodden red debris. The reason for the dilapidation was plain to see. The roof timbers were hidden behind a fantastic living vault of tree roots which had seeded themselves in the gutters and rain shafts of the roof. The greedy roots had pursued the fleeing moisture downwards through tiles, mortar, masonry and woodwork and forced a great fissure in the roof through which the sky could be glimpsed high overhead. Down the ages, more and more roots had forced their arthritic fingers through every crevice, gradually swelling and extending; forcing stones and timber apart until now they held the entire wooden quarter in their inexorable living grip. Thick as a man's torso they choked upper story windows and, still as thick as arms and legs, they spilled from doorways in frozen streams. Pursuing the moisture through the rotting architecture, the roots had grown out of the wooden apartments, covered the courtyard floor and unerringly headed for the well shaft at its centre. The mouth of the well was completely choked with braids and knots of jealous rootwood. Round the well were the remains of a small holding tank which the grateful thirsty had decorated with sculpture. All that still showed above the racine labyrinth were the stone figures of a man and a boy so overrun by the roots that they seemed to be wrestling with giant snakes. It reminded Small of a story he had once read.

Leaving the Red Loggia behind, Small eventually arrived at his goal. The Great Well was a good distance from the Eastern Galleries and as a consequence had been out of use for as long as anyone could remember. It was a sort of oasis in the desert of abandoned galleries. As the last source of moisture for anyone entering upon the uninhabited realms of parchment and dust, any expedition into the old city would have to begin here. Small had only visited this place once. He could remember clearing away the cobwebs which hung from the winding gear like the discarded robes of sorcerers. Now he stared at the wheels and ropes for a good few seconds before the implications of what he was seeing became clear in his mind. No cobwebs. The bucket stood on the wide parapet. When he had been here before, the wood of the bucket had been tinder-dry and shrunken. The water had all but run away through the gaps between the staves before he could wind it up out of the depths. But now its oak staves were damp and tight enough to hold an inch of water. Someone was using the well.

Small looked around nervously. This was not familiar territory for him. For the first time he felt that he might be the one who was being stalked and spied upon. He himself had often taken great delight in following the old librarians without being detected. For those who knew Alligor well there were a thousand places of concealment. He marshalled his thoughts. What would Axares have done? He began looking for signs of the serpent. They were not hard to find. Alligor was not a royal palace overflowing with food and drink. This serpent at least had to drink water. Was this where he had come regularly enough to have worn a track through the ever-laying dust on the floor? By the lip of the well the floor was dark with damp which turned the red sandstone sanguine. Whoever had been using the well had been carrying the water away with him, not towards the Eastern Galleries but into the dim gennels of the old city. The trail he had left might lead Small to the very lair of the serpent.

The parching dust raised by movement about the library caused any traveller to suffer from a dry mouth and nagging thirst. Small had the bucket almost to his lips before his own reflection in the water reminded him of Splint's untimely end in the very cistern from which this water had been raised. He quickly put the bucket down untasted. How strange, he thought, that Splint should have been thrown into what seemed to be his killer's own source of drinking water.

The path worn through the carpet of dust was easy to follow as it squirmed its way onwards and upwards through gloomy galleries, endless corridors and winding stairways. It ended at last at a substantial oak door which had been armoured with ornate wrought iron plates pinned through the wood. Small lifted the latch and pushed with his shoulder but it seemed that the door was bolted or barred from the other side. The mystery person might be standing behind the door laughing at him, or he might be far away. That was the nature of Alligor. A door could open into a tiny closed room, or a lofty gallery, or a stairway, or a corridor, and all of these might or might not connect with other levels, or other corridors, or other galleries or rooms. Small had no knowledge of this part of the Book-City. It was a dead end.

Ten

The next morning, after breakfasting with Puttfark, Small found himself leading the man in white through the Eastern Galleries. At every doorway they passed through Puttfark made a series of little turns and side-steps with his dagger half drawn. Small was mystified until he realised that the man-in-white was worried about being ambushed by someone hiding behind the door. How terrible it must be, he thought, to live in a world where it wasn't safe to walk through a door.

Small still had no idea what Puttfark might want to see or what he was going to say to him, but as usual the man in white took the lead.

"So this is your library. Where do we start?" he said.

"Anywhere you like." replied Small, "What sort of books are you interested in?"

"What sorts are there?"

"Well, there are fairy stories, poems, histories, tales of kings and their courts, of heroes and their deeds, books of science, books of law, books of religion and astrology…" Small paused for breath.

"Well let's put it this way. I'm a busy man. I don't have a lot of time to spare. Fairy stories are for children. Poetry is for time wasters. History is dead and gone. Science … any advice on how to turn lead into gold?"

Small thought for a moment. "I think they all tell how to do that."

Puttfark laughed and then waved his arm at the shelves. "Tell me. Why do all these people write books?"

"I have never really thought about it but I suppose it is so that what they knew, or felt or believed will not be lost. They write to be read."

Puttfark stroked his chin. "Let's stick with the first one, the people who write because they don't want what they know to get lost. If they know it, then it must be because they have evidence. Does that sound right to you?"

Small tilted his head in acknowledgement, though he suspected that 'feeling' was often true, whilst 'belief' sometimes involved the higher truths not susceptible to proofs and evidences. Puttfark continued with his line of thought.

"If they knew more than other men then they should have become greater than other men … I mean, if their knowledge was worth anything at all? Who could take seriously a man who claimed to have knowledge and yet was still a beggar?"

Small raised his eyebrows but said nothing

"And of those men who knew more than others, there would be some who knew yet more?"

Small found Puttfark's strange use of language rather disturbing. "You ask questions to which the answer is always yes or no. This is an overseas method of proceeding. Its use seems to be to arrive at an answer you already know. This so-called 'logic' sometimes only gives a shadow of the truth and ignores meanings."

Puttfark nodded sagely. "Even so, I prefer to stick with the truth." he said. "For example, is not the true mark of wisdom that its possessor should be happy? If he has not wealth and power enough then he must always live in fear that his neighbour might overwhelm him, shut down his livelihood, steal his wife, even have him killed."

Small shrugged and cocked his head, unable to fathom what might be the case in the world outside Alligor.

"I have just had a thought." Puttfark exclaimed, "If you think about it, out of all these wise men, these rulers of the world, one must have been the wisest of all, and he would have had wealth, riches, power immeasurable. If he had written a book then there is a very special book here, a very special book indeed. That is the book I would like to read. I would like to know the great truths about the world and how it is ruled by the wisest of the wise. How can I find it?"

Small was bemused. "I am not sure that the world is always ruled by the wise. Most of the books I have read seem to condemn the rulers of the world for their stupidity, their greed and their vice."

"But they are ruling and their critics are not!" said Puttfark triumphantly.

Small knew that there was something not quite right about this line of reasoning but because he was anxious to please he let it pass.

"So," continued Puttfark, "where do we begin?"

Small hesitated. "I ... I'm not sure. One place might be as good as another. Most of the readers came here in search of wisdom; the books are only reflections of that one great light. Wisdom usually comes as the result of reading many books on many different subjects. How else would you know if a book contained wisdom if you had not read many other books on that and other subjects? Readers usually began with one book and proceeded to many: you want to begin with many and end with one. Just as with your reasoning, you seem already certain of your conclusion."

Puttfark shrugged, "That's the way we are in Murga, methodical. We always know where we want to go and we don't stop until we get there. Perhaps I should ask you a different question. How are the books organized? What is the principle behind their arrangement? Are they arranged by language, or subject; by author or by age? That's how we would do it in Murga."

Small had never even dreamed that books could be arranged in such useless fashions. "This is a library, not a fruit seller's stall with all the apples here and all the figs there. Many books do not bear an author's name. Many authors wrote books on more than one subject. Many of the books are about more than one subject. There are almost as many languages as books and the same book can be found in many tongues."

"Then how are they arranged?" asked Puttfark bewildered.

Small had never really thought about this before. After a short pause he said, "In patterns." And as the words passed his lips it was as if he had uttered a magic spell which conjured up in his mind a momentary vision of the library as a celestial garden, infinitely diverse in its colours, types, shapes, forms and sizes. Possibilities and implications crowded in upon his consciousness.

"Patterns?" Puttfark looked at him askance. Patterns were what you found on a whore's dress.

"When the books arrived they would have been shown to someone who was interested and he would have shelved them where he thought best. Sometimes that might have been close to others of the same kind, but often he would put them with books on quite other subjects if he thought that the reader might thereby gain in wisdom. You see wisdom is to do with putting different things together so that their true nature and meanings become clearer. The way you Murgans arrange your books seems likely to divide and keep things separate which in the real world are conjoined and combined."

Putting into words what he had come to know by intuition was a strange experience for Small. It reminded him of the time when Old had explained the rules of grammar underlying the common speech. Small had been astonished to find that when he spoke he expressed himself according to rules which he had never been told about.

"So what are these patterns like?" asked Puttfark.

"Well no-one knows all of them. Some librarians use very simple ones. They put the most important books in special places. Some put them on a top shelf; others on a shelf at eye level. The central point is often used: the centre of a shelf; the central shelf; the central stack of shelves; these are good places to start when you want to know how a gallery is arranged. There are also arrangements according to number. Seventh place is very popular, particularly with Pythagoreans. Symmetries are often used. Opposite ends of shelves or stacks or even galleries may contain balanced or contrasting ideas which mirror each other in creative ways. But there are much simpler arrangements. If the librarian had a favourite working seat then the key books might simply be on a low shelf close at hand..."

Puttfark covered his eyes with the palms of his hands. "Wait! ... Wait. You are telling me that the books have all been shelved according to the individual whims and foibles of generations of weird old men who only ever arranged their own little corner of the library?"

"You could say that. But some of the librarians were very wise and knew more of the library and its books than I ever shall. Many of the galleries have infinitely subtle and meaningful arrangements"

Puttfark uncovered his eyes and strode towards a shelf. He plucked out a volume at random and opened it. He seemed deep in thought. After a while he handed it to Small. "What book is this?" he asked.

"It is a story of a king who kept a monster in a labyrinth and fed it with young men and women."

"Did you know it was here?"

"Yes."

"Do you know where there are other works concerning Kings and rulers?"

"Yes, but there are very many of them."

"No matter, we must make a start somewhere. You must find them and explain to me what they are about."

"But you said that you were not interested in history and fairy tales."

"That is true. In Murga we have no place for the past. The past is about other places. Soon there will be no other places, only Murga everywhere. Legends do not interest me. Accounts of treaties and the building of cities and monuments are not what I want to see, nor do battles and conquests interest me. A wise ruler should avoid protracted war. It is expensive, unpredictable, unpopular and it interferes with the smooth running of the state. The book I seek should be a simple theory of peaceful and uninterrupted rule; knowledge useful in all states and at all times."

The air of confident certainty with which Puttfark spoke and acted at all times, both excited and unsettled Small. "You speak as if you know the book you seek."

Puttfark looked at him. First the *ulvis* then the smile appeared. "Shall we begin?" he asked.

Small was quite unprepared for the man in white's determined and unrelenting approach to the task. The book city in which Small had grown up functioned at the somnolent pace of torpid old men whose waking and dreaming states slowly and inexorably fused together. At some stage their memories of the momentously philosophic world of books and the utterly trivial daily routine of their anonymous lives became one. In the end, the awesome significance of sunlight spilling onto an open book could render them speechless with childish wonder. Puttfark on the other hand worked single-mindedly and methodically at his task, displaying the same physical vigour in research as he had in clearing the gate, securing the city, or recruiting Small to his aid.

The activity quickly settled into a gruelling routine. Small found the books and then leafed through them quickly whilst giving Puttfark a summary of their contents. The constant to-ing and fro-ing from bookstack to reading desk was soon abandoned. Puttfark either held the book on his arms whilst Small examined it, or unrolled the manuscripts on the floor. In five hours, Small gained a more comprehensive overview of the dynastic domination of the known world than he ever would have done if left to his own devices. Alone he would have strayed into a thousand interesting digressions, Puttfark kept him relentlessly on the subject.

His eyes ached and his brain reeled. His back was stiff and painful with leaning over the books. Inside his head, empires, dominions and provinces fell to Gypsians, Hittites, Akkadians, Babylonians, Mede and Perz. The names of the powerful echoed around the galleries like a litany or an incantation: Supilamis, Cyrus, Imotep, Mursilis, Belshaz, Ozymandiaz, Sardanapal, Ammurabi, Ramsee, Tutmoz, Sardon, Assurbanipal; casting a spell of grandiloquence and awe upon the air. They looked at works of flattery, of mythification, the boasting of the successful, the slander against those whose throne they had usurped, but all were dismissed as useless by the Murgan. Accounts of every form of excess and turpitude, regal idleness and stupidity, imperial ignorance and greed were passed over as matters of little importance. Slightly more attention was granted to accounts of rule sustained by fear and cruelty, by wise council, by fair judgement, by military prowess, by feminine wiles, and even by Divine intervention, but they too were replaced upon their shelves as being too idiosyncratic and the rulers only successful by chance.

When the fading light made it impossible to read the clay seals on the manuscripts, Puttfark called a halt to the days work.

"Tomorrow I will bring a lantern from the camp." he said as he gathered vellum sheets into their boxes.

Small was horrified. "That is forbidden! No lamp is allowed inside the galleries. Flames and books are not to be brought together. Fire has only ever been kindled in the kitchens."

Puttfark merely shrugged.

As they made their way out of the galleries, the light stole from the library and bled into the dusk. By the time they reached the Great Stair they were in utter darkness. Small did not anticipate Puttfark's disorientation. He held Small's elbow, stumbling frequently and colliding with various obstacles which Small avoided by habit. The courtyard was vaulted by a starless sky. As the gate opened to let him out, Puttfark called over his shoulder, "Sleep well, Rider. We begin again at sunrise."

Through the open gate Small glimpsed the Murgan camp with its lantern-lit tents and glowing campfire. It looked cosy and inviting. He heard the faint murmur of animated conversation and a woman laughed. Both light and laughter was cut off abruptly as the guard heaved the gate shut. The rumble of the bar as it was hauled into place sounded like the closing of a sarcophagus lid. Small sighed as he turned towards the inky darkness and brooding silence of the book city. Much as he liked the Murgans, the guarded gate provoked in him a deep sense of unease. He kept meaning to ask Puttfark why the guard was there, but the man in white had a strange knack of always bending the conversation so as to draw information out of Small. There was an invisible barrier between them which made intimate inquiry impossible. Small felt that the man in white did not want to be questioned and therefore hesitated to ask.

Small crossed the courtyard and, in total darkness, began to climb the Great Staircase. In the echoes of his footsteps he listened for the tread of an imaginary assassin. Suddenly anxious, he tried to move more silently.

"Greetings Small."

The disembodied voice in the hollow dark made his heart pound. Old was still keeping watch from his niche overlooking the yard.

"Greetings Old."

There was a rustling noise as the old man shifted his position. "You have spent many hours with our Murgan 'friend'. I am interested in knowing what he thinks of our city of books." Old's voice echoed down the spiral shaft.

Small allowed the echoes to cease before he answered. "He thinks that it is filled with useless dreamings and that it is very badly arranged. He cannot find the book he seeks and is not satisfied with the ones he finds."

"Ha!" The scornful echoes danced in the stairwell. "And just what is this book he seeks?"

"It seems to be a book by a wise king on how to achieve peaceful goverment."

"Heh?" Again the echoes of Old's voice mocked Small.

"That's what he says."

The old man fell silent for a while, then said, "I know of no such book."

"Nor I," the boy answered, "but he seems convinced that it must be there."

"That is most strange. As far as I can remember, the Murgans are not interested in rule so much as making money. They are a most restless and aggressive people. Peaceful rule? It's just not their way. There is some mystery here. Just why does a high born Murgan bring his thugs and his whores hundreds of leagues into the far side of nowhere? And don't tell me that they are traders."

"They don't seem like thugs and whores to me!" said Small.

"There speaks the voice of experience!" retorted Old with as much scorn as he could muster.

"I have as much as you in such matters!"

Old snorted at the rebuff. "We are both in the dark, so to speak, with regard to their nature and their motives. One thing is certain, we know as much about thugs and whores as he does about the library. It will take a lifetime to find his book and he will soon tire."

"I do not think so," Small replied. "He is not the sort of man to give up on a task. You should have seen them clear the gate. He is a hard worker."

"Hard work will not help him here, only wisdom can unlock the library."

"Old."

"Yes?"

"I am helping him to find his book."

"Librarians do not help readers. Their only task is to care for the library. You are playing a dangerous game."

"But if he finds it he will leave."

"*If* is a small word with a long shadow, my boy, and what about his henchmen? What are they up to with Sly? Are they too searching for this same book? Perhaps you should spend sometime in the upper levels and find out."

The echoes faded. By now Small could just make out the old man silhouetted against the lesser darkness of the night sky.

"How are your riding lessons progressing?"

"Oh, Puttfark says I am a very good pupil. He has given me a new name; he calls me 'Rider'. But …"

"But?"

"He has taken away the horse I was using. It was needed to haul the wagons. They have gone for provisions. You see, he is a man of his word."

"I don't remember him promising to feed us," said Old wonderingly. "I remember Sly's suggestion, but no response."

Small did not answer. When the silence became oppressive, he took his leave of the old man.

The stillness and the pitch darkness in the Eastern Galleries did not intimidate Small. This was his domain and he knew it as no outsider could. As he passed through the Gallery of the Horses he knew where every piece of furniture was; he knew every alcove, every bookstack and every pillar. Even so he moved as cautiously and as silently as he could. In the darkness the books were invisible and mute but he could see them all in his mind's eye. He thought of them as being like sleeping friends.

The next moment he was on his hands and knees. He had stumbled over a warm yielding bundle laid across his path. As he lifted his hands from the flagstones he felt a slight stickyness. He cried out in horror and scrambled away from the bloody corpse. Terrified he squatted with his back to the wainscoting until his panic subsided to the point where the instinct for self-preservation could take over. The assassin was here and had struck within the last few minutes. If Old had not delayed him he would have been here when the fatal blow was struck. Though he had no idea whose body lay out there in the dark gallery, he was not tempted to try and find out. His only thought was to find a place of safety. Holding his breath he listened intently for any indication that the killer was still in the vicinity.

High above Alligor a gibbous moon appeared from the clouds like the face of a drowned man in a swollen midnight river. Its faint light filtered through the windows into the gallery, crept across the stone flags and up the panelling. In the instant before the dark returned to the library, Small glimpsed on the floor the crumpled heap of humanity lying in the dark pool of its extinguished life. Beyond it the secret panel which led to the upper levels appeared faintly outlined in the silver until the darkness returned.

Giving the corpse and its aureole of dark liquid a wide berth, Small moved quickly and stealthily across the gallery. Pausing only to make sure that his sudden move had not provoked any response, he felt for the tiny carved catch, opened the panel and passed inside. The faint click the panel made as it closed behind him echoed like a whipcrack around the silent gallery. But no stranger would have guessed its origin. Safely out of the gallery, Small could begin to think. Another

Alligorite had been murdered; the ragged clothing had told him that much; but who was he, and what was he doing in Small's gallery? Had he been brought here? Had he fled here? Had he come looking for Small? Did he need help or did he bring a warning? And why had he been killed? Was it to silence him? Small had an awful thought. Perhaps the wrong person had been killed. Perhaps here in Small's own domain, in the darkness, the killer had mistaken him for Small. This thought disturbed Small so much that he moved away from the entrance door and hid himself in the upper levels.

In the intestinal spaces behind the walls, the normal night time sounds of the library acquired an unearthly quality. The moans, shrieks and crazed laughter which normally punctuated the disturbed sleep of the old men, rose up through the passages sounding as if souls were in torment. These were accompanied by the booming echoes deep in the library as heavy doors closed behind aged somnambulists who shambled restlessly towards ultimate oblivion. It was a long time before sleep came.

Eleven

Small woke with a start. At first he didn't know where he was. Ordinarily the rising sun woke him, but here in the upper levels there was no daylight. His spirits sank as the events of the night before flooded back into his mind. Stiff and cold he levered himself upright and walked back towards the secret panel. Checking each spyhole as he passed it he was able to see that the Gallery of the Horses was empty: except for the crumpled form of the librarian still lying where he fell. From his high vantage point however he could see something else. Someone had stepped in the pool of blood whilst it was still liquid and left a line of footprints as he went out of the gallery and back into the library. Small caught his breath. The prints were not of bare feet. The killer had been wearing shoes. It had been an outsider. The librarians had no need for footwear on the smooth stone floors of the book-city.

Back in the Gallery of the Horses, Small approached the corpse with a feeling of dread and pity. The body was that of a very old man whose throat had been savagely cut. Copious amounts of blood had soaked the front of his robe whilst he still stood and had spread into a pool around his upper body after he had fallen. The blood was now become dark and glutinous. Small turned the body over in order to see the face. He was bewildered to discover that he had no idea who the man was. He had never seen him before. The ingrained dirt on the skin, the calloused feet and the fleas which were even now beginning to search around for a new host, confirmed that he was an Alligorite, but where had he come from? Small noticed something else. Just above the waist was another rent in the robe stained with a dark and rusty substance. Small lifted away the threadbare fabric. Between the robe and the skin was a book. Its cover was a mass of bloody finger smears through which the title could just be made out: *The Seven Lamps*. It looked like something astrological. Runnels of dried blood fanned out downwards to the leg. He tried to lift the book away but the blood had caused it to stick to the abdomen. As he prised it away from the skin, the last leaf tore in half. The small deep wound underneath was obviously an older injury. It was very similar to the one in Splint's neck.

Small was horrified and yet fascinated. If he had not read Axares he would not have examined the body with the thoroughness he usually reserved for books. The marks of the serpent seemed to indicate that this old man had been attacked twice. He had staunched

86

the flow of blood from the earlier wound by clasping the book to it; then he had staggered who knows how far to find help. Somehow the assassin had followed him through the library and caught up with him here, when he was just a few steps away from safety. It would seem that the assassin had had to forego his usual elegance in dispatching his victim; nor had he time to dispose of the body. The noise of the door opening had probably interrupted him. Small stood up, imagining as he did so the assassin making his exit. It was then that he noticed the line of tiny dark spots which ran from the dead librarian to the door. Another path to follow; but first he had to tell Old.

Old was ashen-faced as Small led him into the Gallery of the Horses. His slight frame sagged visibly as he approached the body. His chin dropped onto his chest and he sighed heavily. A slight tremor ran through his upper body. Small saw that he was crying. "Did you know him?" he asked.

Old wiped his cheek with the back of his hand leaving a paler smudge in the grime. "I knew him even though I might never have met him. He is one of us. Another poor orphan; another guardian of the books. I see myself in that pitiful bundle, but I cannot say I recognise him. In any case, naming him now would help neither him nor us."

Small lifted the robe. "See, here is the first wound. It has the same narrow opening as the one Splint received. And yet the blow was not immediately fatal. The assassin missed his aim."

"That much seems clear. But I do not think this man walked across the city with such a wound only for help and succour. He would have done better to let the flesh knit together first. I think he came to warn us." Old paused. A murmur of voices rose from the stairwell.

"It's Puttfark. I should have met him for breakfast."

Puttfark and Lubrik ducked through the archway, instinctively checking behind the doors. Old gripped Small's *tzirt* in his bony fingers and spoke in an urgent whisper, "Say nothing of your suspicions lad; listen and observe."

"What's this?" There could be no mistaking the reactions of the man in white and his lieutenant. Genuine surprise registered on both their faces, and when Puttfark turned to Lubrik with the unspoken question in his eyes, he was answered in kind. Both men were mystified.

"He has been killed." said Small, "We have found him."

Puttfark went down on one knee beside the corpse. He held the wrist between finger and thumb; then he lifted it up and let it fall back. Next he placed his hand on the chest. He turned to Lubrik and spoke quietly in his own language. "Stone cold and dead since yesterday evening."

Small had by now begun to master the Murgan dialect, but still something prevented him from revealing this. Puttfark lifted aside the corpse's robe to reveal the hidden wound. "What do you make of that?"

Lubrik's eyes narrowed. "Older wound. Two maybe three days before the other. Well placed, neat. Assassin? Should have killed him. Must have been deflected."

The blood-stained book lay beside the body. Puttfark picked it up and twisted it slightly in his hands. Each of the pages bore a slight nick on its border where some sharp edge had passed through them. He glanced at Lubrik, who nodded imperceptibly.

Puttfark stood up; his eyes searched the floor around the body. "Have you any idea who ..." he spotted the footprint, "... might have done this?" The question was addressed to Small but the man in white was now exchanging a look of utter complicity with Lubrik. Before answering Small checked that Old had also seen the exchange. The old man raised an eyebrow in acknowledgement.

"No. But it is not the first time. Two others have died. One had a wound, like that one, but here." Small touched his neck.

Puttfark nodded. "You have an assassin in your book city. He struck at this man here but the book deflected his first blow. The second cut was not as carefully placed as the first, but nevertheless was expertly struck; it both ended his life and prevented him from crying out. You must alert all your people. In the meantime, I think some of my men should come into the library. They have weapons and can patrol the galleries while we work. Lubrik, see to it." Lubrik turned and loped towards the stairway. Puttfark faced Old. "Rider here has work to do. You must arrange for the body to be removed. Find someone to help you."

Old was left alone in the gallery with a look of utter astonishment on his face. It was the first time that he had encountered the efficient way in which the Murgan organized his world. In the library such decisions were made only after long pauses for thought and consultations with everyone present.

Puttfark knew exactly where the search had been abandoned on the previous day. Without any preliminaries or conversation, Small found himself back in the gruelling routine of finding and summarising the books. As they worked their way through to the galleries which Small knew least about, the books were more and more difficult to find. The pauses whilst Small tried to work out the arrangement of the galleries grew longer, and Puttfark became more and more frustrated. It came as a relief to Small when, just before midday they were interrupted by the return of Lubrik with Kunig at his shoulder listening intently to something that he was telling him. The armed men were close behind and, bringing up the rear, was a voluminous red and yellow striped robe in which, as it approached, Sly could be seen. He was far too old and frail to manage a proud swagger successfully, but was trying his best to transform his usual shuffling gait into a noble strut. He was vanity and self-regard personified, unable to stop admiring himself; constantly re-arranging the folds and tucks of his garish garment. Puttfark, Lubrik and Kunig withdrew to a corner of the room and began to confer in earnest undertones. The armed men stood easy in a group. Sly flounced towards Small.

"Greetings Sly."

"Greetings Small. I went with the visitors to the town. What an adventure it was. We have brought back provisions. You should have seen the way the visitors bargained for the food. They disputed every coin that they had to hand over. They were so thorough, everything was checked. One merchant had mixed sand with his flour and when the visitors found out they picked him up by his ankles and shook him till their coins fell out of his clothes. Such a sight! All the townspeople treated us with such respect after that, bowing and bending and bobbing up and down. It was as if we were nobility. They even presented Puttfark with this robe … and he gave it to me!"

Here Sly preened himself once more, turning this way and that to show off the garment. Small saw that it was finely woven local cloth, but it looked thick and coarse beside his own silken *tzirt*. No Murgan would prefer it to his own apparel.

"I …," Sly paused for dramatic effect, "… am to be Quartermaster of Alligor! Through me the largesse of our noble visitors will be apportioned and bestowed throughout the Library."

"They have food for us?"

"But of course! Far be it from me to try and mitigate the generosity of our visitors, but I have repeatedly pointed out to them the weakened state and dulled sensibilities of our librarians. 'How much more expeditiously would our search proceed were we able to enlist their aid. Just a modicum of nourishment and our somnolent Alligorites would be transformed into paragons of diligent erudition'."

"You speak of a search. What are they searching for?"

Sly glanced furtively over his shoulder, before continuing in a lowered voice.

"They seek a book without a name which records the founding of their state. They have a legend that a rival king stole the book and vowed that no-one would ever read it. The book is so famous in their land that whoever is able to produce a copy of it will make his fortune."

Small was mystified, another book without a name. "How are you going about finding it?"

Sly glanced over his shoulder again and lowered his voice even more. "Many forbidden books have plain covers: they can be found all over the library."

"But Sly, it might not be shelved amongst the forbidden books and even if it is your search will take for ever."

"Precisely! But long before then, our new friends will have their minds so mazed and twisted by books which treat of occultism and savage cruelty, of lust and bestiality, of impiety and blasphemy and corruption, that they will exhaust themselves and lose their will to continue. Such is the end of all libertinism. They will give up their search."

"This is a dangerous path you are treading, Sly. Aren't you concerned that you too might be tainted by such evil? There is only one place such a search can end."

"The Cage? Come now! There is no such place. It is only a myth to frighten young librarians away from worthless distractions."

Small was taken aback. "You do not believe then in books so dark in their conceptions that they must be kept behind bars of strong iron?"

"Oh some ancient librarians might once have believed so, but I am certain that if we looked at those books today we would find them no more harmful than books which can be lifted from any top shelf in the city."

"I hope you are right in that but I think you underestimate the Murgans."

"Murgans are they?" Sly's expression changed abruptly from supercilious pride to grave cunning. "I don't care who they are, I am not the one to underestimate anybody. My search will fail, eventually, but in the meantime we will all have full stomachs. Perhaps you should ask yourself if the interests of the Library are always uppermost in your dealings with these people?"

"Mister Sly!" Puttfark strode across the gallery towards them. "I have been talking with my colleagues and we have decided that we need to store the food inside the city. We need a large, dry, airy room close to the Gate and the kitchen. There must be space for the provisions and also for accommodation, since the food will need guarding."

"Oh, I am sure no-one in Alligor would ever ..."

Puttfark interrupted Sly's protestations almost at once. "Mister Sly, somebody in your book-city is stabbing librarians. He may well be working up an appetite. My men are here to patrol the galleries, they will need a guard-room somewhere near the food store."

Sly seemed to shrink down inside his new robe whilst forcing his thin lips into an obsequious smile. His eyes narrowed as his brain squirmed in intense thought. "Of course. I will find somewhere for the food, but the accommodation in Alligor is somewhat limited you understand."

Puttfark's answer was first the *ulvis* and then a broad smile. "Nonsense, Mister Sly. The way I see it, this is a city with the population of a village. Let's go and check it out and see what we can find."

Small watched with amusement as the Murgans hustled Sly gently but firmly towards the door. The armed men smirked at each other as they moved off towards the other end of the gallery.

"I'll be back as soon as I'm able." Puttfark called out over his shoulder. "Do what you can whilst I'm away."

Small walked back to the table where he had been working before the interruption. He scooped several manuscript leaves together, and then pushed them away irritably. He was unsettled by Sly's suggestion that he was disloyal to the Library, and if the truth were to be told, he had begun to think that he might indeed have made a poor bargain with Puttfark over the horse-riding. This book search was going to be much more tedious, and take far longer, than the few hours he had spent in the saddle. But it was the discovery of the corpse which had unnerved him most of all. He could not rid his mind of the smell of blood and the thought of the jagged tear in the man's throat. Now that he was alone, the events of the night had time to sink in. He suddenly felt like retching and started up from the table as if the body was there before him. It was hopeless to try and concentrate on hunting through Puttfark's books. He had to purge his thoughts through action. There was another and more important trail to follow.

When he got back to the door of the Gallery of the Horses, the corpse had still not been taken away. He tried not to look too closely but his eyes were drawn to the body. He noticed the blood-stained book still lying where Puttfark had laid it down. His sense of duty overcame his repulsion. He walked over, picked it up, and slid it into his book pouch. Books had to be put back in their place, wherever that may be.

The bloody footprints faded after a few strides, but the spots and splashes of blood led on and on through corridors and galleries like the cryptic calligraphy of some ancient and primitive script. The tale they told of hurt and horror was plain enough. Each time the man had paused, perhaps to catch his breath, or perhaps to listen for his pursuer, the drops clustered together. Where he had struggled with a stubborn door, there were smeared hand prints and more blood as the effort tore open the wound.

Before long Small found himself in unfamiliar surroundings. He was however certain that the wounded librarian had known exactly where he was fleeing. He had deliberately chosen a twisting, tortuous, labyrinthine route that no stranger to the library could ever have followed in the dark: low vaulted tunnels with their paving worn and sunken; narrow hidden doorways; stairways so narrow and twisted back upon themselves that Small had to descend backwards using his hands. Up and down through the levels, backward and forwards across the route, and always the abandoned galleries and their endless shelves of books, mute and furred with dust and spider webs. It seemed that the librarian had tried every means he knew to shake off his pursuer, but it had all been in vain. In the dim light which filtered through the clinging plants and the cobwebs at the windows, Small could see that only one pair of feet had disturbed the millennial dust on the floor. The old man had not been followed. The assassin had known exactly where his victim was heading. He had simply taken the most direct route and lain in wait for him.

Small was relieved to find that there was little likelihood that he himself would be ambushed by the assassin, at least until the trail ended. He pressed on more quickly coming into a high shadowy hall, its tall windows closed with wooden shutters. Here and there, where a broken shutter hung by one twisted hinge, sunlight knifed through the gloom and laid a golden bar across the floor. Flying insects, luminous against the gloom, danced themselves into clouds of delirium in the light and warmth, whilst the ever-present spiders wove their destinies and span the threads by which their lives would be measured. Beyond the hall a heavy door led Small out into the open air and onto a bridge between two gigantic architectural structures. Fifty or sixty feet below him was a tiny courtyard crowded round by the roofs, terraces and balconies which encrusted the sides of the larger buildings in masonic geology. Other bridges spanned the gulf below as they leapt obliquely between the various buildings.

The door at the end of the bridge stood ajar. Small passed quickly inside. The transition from full daylight to almost total darkness left him blinded and groping his way until his eyes began to accommodate themselves to the gloom. At first he thought that he was in yet another narrow tunnel, but when he put out his hand to orient himself, it tore through the tunnel wall and released a cloud of choking dust. He stared at his hand which was now gloved with a clinging and unsubstantial gauze. Horror mounted within him as he realised that the whole gallery had been cocooned in thick spider web. Over the centuries the web's authors had spun out their plots with trails and clews until they had swagged and festooned the corners and the beams, drawn veils over the racks and shelves of books, muslinned the manuscripts and bound them each to each, eventually joining every solid surface to every other until they had made the very space and air of the room their own. Year on year the dust of neglect had settled upon the immortal webs, until the sun itself was snared in the spider weft at the windows, unable to make its way into the heart of the gallery. Even the dust on the floor had a strange texture. Small probed with his toes. It was dark with the chitinous remains of an eon of entrapped insects.

Small wrestled with his mounting panic. He hated spiders. But peering into the gloom he could not actually see any. In any case the wounded librarian had known this part of Alligor well enough to risk this gallery at night. The excitement of the chase was upon him. If he gave up here he would never pick up the trail again. On a sudden impulse he sprinted forward into the tunnel. Once in motion, fear drove him like a whirlwind to the invisible exit at the end of the gallery. By the time he reached the door he was so panic-stricken that he could not operate the latch. As he finally squeezed through into the next room he glanced back over his shoulder. The light glistened on hordes of tiny spiders which coated the webs like a dark dew. He slammed the door.

The chamber in which he found himself was not large. There was a reading desk by an unglazed window with a round-arched opening, and a sleeping shelf in an alcove. The floor was clear of dust and spattered with darkening blood stains. The bed was mattressed with loose dry grasses, green and still sweet except that is, for a patch where they had been sodden by a large amount of blood now congealed. Small realised that this was where the librarian had spent his life and where, after he had been attacked, he had taken the fatal decision to travel across the library. Small crossed to the window and peered out into a dank and narrow light well. Here and there, tiny windows pierced the stonework like ancient wounds. He leaned out to see the ground far below, but it was hidden by heaps of splintered beams, broken tiles and rubble where a bridge or balcony had collapsed. Two other doors led out of the chamber. When Small opened the first, an unyielding wall of wooden planks barred his way. The second was cracked and stained; daylight showed through in several places. The handle was smooth and shiny from constant use and the door swung easily on its hinges.

Small should have been prepared for what he found on the other side of the door. Given that the unknown librarian was living without visiting the refectory, it was to be expected that he would have to get his sustenance somehow. But the sheer luxuriance and beauty of the terrace garden took the boy's breath away. The whole was an elongated rectangle of some fifty paces in length. Vast pitched roofs angled down from all sides. Their eaves, supported on a regular arcade of pillars, formed a continuous covered walk which ran around three sides of the garden. This cloister was half hidden behind a profusion of vigorous plant life. The centre of the whole space was occupied by a large square pool or tank of water thickly fringed with succulent water plants some of which had large waxen flowers.

Small walked out of the cloister and towards the pool. Above his head there were leaden impluvia cast in the forms of leaping dolphins. Their smiling mouths gaped in anticipation of the infrequent rain. The sun felt warm on his skin. A heavy swirl in the water caught his attention. He peered into the green depths where several plump scaly beasts hung immobile except for leaf-like limbs fanning verdigris sides. Fishes! He had never seen any before. He leant forward for a better view, but with a sinuous flick of their bodies they disappeared into the submarine undergrowth. He was left staring at his own reflection in the disturbed water.

Over at the other side of the garden a flock of chattering finches descended upon a large flowering shrub. They began to devour the ruby-coloured fruit which hung in clusters from its branches. For Small, used to foraging on the roofs, this was an invitation to share in the feast. Long habit had made food a constant preoccupation, to be eaten when it was there to be had. As he skirted the pool he noticed that many of the plants bore fruits of various kinds.

The finches fled at Small's approach. The shrub was not one which he had ever seen before. Curiously it seemed to have both flowers and fruits at the same time. The flowers gave off a heady soporific perfume and dropped a thick golden pollen which covered leaves, branches and fruits as well as carpeting the ground beneath the tree. Small crammed the scented fruit into his mouth. It was impossibly sweet and had a taste unlike anything he had ever tasted before. The more he ate, the more he wanted and it seemed that he was consuming a prodigal amount. Curiously the number of fruits on the tree seemed to stay the same. The fruit seemed to last forever as he mouthed each ruby globe until it burst. The beauty of the garden seemed to envelope him. The air hummed with heat and insects. Lapis lazuli dragonflies hovered and pounced so close to him that he heard the clatter of their wings and the snap of their jaws. Suddenly he wanted nothing more than to stretch himself out in the sun, listen to the insects and inhale the enchanted atmosphere of the place. The fecund humidity of the sunlit pool mingled with the narcotic perfume of the plants and made his brain reel.

Stretching himself at full length upon the ground beneath the shrub, Small caught one of its branches with his arm. Instantly the air was filled with the golden pollen. Dusty yellow clouds swirled around him and settled upon his face and hands. He inhaled deeply. For an instant the pollen irritated his nose and mouth but then only a tingling numbness remained. Lying in the shade of the tree a feeling of lassitude stole over Small as he thought of his duties and obligations: of his duty as a librarian; of his loyalty to Old; the oath he had sworn before the Great Author; the deal he had made with Puttfark and the enormity of the task he faced in order to fulfil his part. He thought about the assassin and his victims: did he not have a duty to seek out the murderer? Why did everyone expect so much of him?

A gentle movement of the air in the garden caused the shrub to tremble. More pollen fell. He sighed and inhaled the perfumed dust from the strange shrub. He felt drowsy. The clamour of his thoughts seemed to come from a long way off, like thin high voices of distant children on a windy afternoon. The day seemed to have elongated itself. How long had he been here in the garden? It seemed like days, weeks, months, years even. It was as if his past life was receding; not just in time, but in space too. It all seemed so long ago, so far away. Did those cares and responsibilities matter any more? Were all those people who he used to know already long passed away? Did they wait and wonder for a while what became of Small before he was finally forgotten? A sweet and melancholy feeling overcame him. His eyes filled with tears as if for a loved one long dead but they seemed mingled with tears of joy because he was here in this magical garden of indescribable beauty and safety. Why should he worry? What was it that the author had said? 'Why should I strive to set the crooked straight? Why battle for the good against the evil? What good comes of it when nothing lasts and all is levelled by fast-coming death?' Why should he not be like the flowers and stay here always? He had only to bolt the door he had come in by and he would never be found.

An iridescent bird had been gorging itself upon the fruit of the shrub, seemingly for ever. Suddenly its talons relaxed their grip on the branch. The bird began to fall ever so slowly down, down, feathers ruffling slightly in the air, down towards the soft yellow earth beneath.

Twelve

Sly was not happy. Though he had forced the 'courtier's smile' onto his face, it had appeared as a twisted grimace which did little to disguise his real feelings. He was not used to being coerced either mentally or physically, and yet here he was being hustled along by the Murgans. He shrank visibly inside his new robe. It seemed that Puttfark knew exactly where he wanted his guard room to be. He had spotted a row of windows above the refectory which looked out over the courtyard and commanded a view of both the gate and the entrance to the staircase tower. Sly knew Alligor as well as anybody but even he had never had cause to visit those rooms over the refectory. Despite all his efforts to lead them astray, he soon found himself standing beside the Murgans in a gloomy corridor, ankle deep in dust, and facing a large, very solid door. The door was swathed in ancient cobwebs and to Sly's relief, firmly locked.

"What a pity!" he exclaimed. "But don't worry, I will find a small room for your men somewhere. Just give me a week or two." He turned away expecting them to follow, but the Murgans did not turn from the door. Instead they began clearing away the cobwebs and feeling with their hands around the door and its niche. The air was filled with dust. Suddenly Lubrik let out an oath. Blood welled from a wound in his palm. He pointed to a corroded metal nail sticking out of the planking. Puttfark dropped to one knee and fumbled in the dust at the foot of the door. In the dim light Sly saw the *ulvis* herald a wide grin of triumph on the Murgan's face. At some time in the distant past the nail had simply given way. The heavy key which had been hanging on it had fallen and lain unnoticed in the darkness. Once the key had been lost the whole area had been abandoned. It was not an unusual occurrence. Who knew how much of Alligor lay behind locked doors?

This room must have been sealed for centuries. Even Sly felt a quickening of his pulse as the door swung open. The opening of books has a great affinity with the desire to look behind closed doors. There is the same fathoming of the unknown, the same solving of riddles, the same giving of form to the formless. The room was large and so heavy with the accumulated silence of centuries that it held them momentarily on the threshold. Sly was puzzled. It was like no room that he had ever seen. For one thing a good portion of the floor space was covered with large glazed terracotta amphorae tall as a small man. For another, the stone walls lifted themselves seamlessly into a broad stone tunnel vault which ran the length of the room. For no apparent reason the floor sloped away from the door. Shallow channels cut into the floor ran obliquely to holes in the outer walls. Everything in the room: floor, walls, shelves, benches and a table, all were made of stone.

"Perfect!" Puttfark exclaimed, striding into centre of the room. "Once we've cleared out these jars. What's in them Mr. Sly?"

"I really have no idea at all. I have never seen anything like them before."

"Well we'd better open one and see. Lubrik, try and get a lid off."

There were forty jars. The wooden lids had been painted with molten wax and tied down with rope turned brittle with age. Using his dagger, Lubrik slashed the bindings and began to work the knife point around the hard wax sealing the jar. As the lid came off, a sweet resinous aroma filled the room. Lubrik dipped his finger ends into the opening and lifted them out glistening with a sticky-looking liquid.

"What is it?" he asked. The Murgans turned to Sly.

"It must be Meton." Sly said wonderingly.

"Meton?"

"Cedar oil." Sly too dipped his fingers in the jar, rubbed them together in the air and sniffed deeply. "The ancients used it to preserve the books from insects and such. It is an extremely costly substance, especially in this land without trees. This must have been a royal gift. No-one here had any idea this store existed. Now I see why this room is so strange. Meton can burn fiercely. This room is built to contain fire. It is quite unsuitable as a guard room."

"On the contrary Mr. Sly, it is extremely suitable. My men will move the food in right away."

Sly was horrified. "But the meton! It is a dangerous thing."

Puttfark smiled broadly and spoke reassuringly. "You just let us worry about that Mr. Sly."

Before he even realized what was happening, Sly found that the amiable Murgans had steered him towards the door and ushered him into the corridor.

"But Mr. Puttfark...!" he said, turning, but only in time to see the door slammed behind him and to hear the key turn in the lock.

Sly shuffled furiously through the library. He was angry with himself. Why had he not been more assertive? Whose library was it anyway? It began to dawn upon him that the strangers might after all be too strong for him; that lurking behind everything they said and did was the confidence born of superior physical force and the willingness to use it. Like Small before him he began to question the wisdom of

98

the deal he had struck with the strangers. He must have been muttering his thoughts aloud when a voice interrupted him.

"Sly, old friend, not disillusioned with your new acquaintances already?"

Sly became aware of Old slumped in his window seat.

"Greetings Old." His tone was sullen.

"What a fine new robe you have on. Our Murgan visitors seem to have taken quite a shine to you. What have you promised to do for them, I wonder?"

Sly was in no mood to take sarcasm from Old.

"It is more to the point what they have promised to do for us. The Murgans have brought real food for us and more is on the way. Not everybody in the library has your 'supernatural' ability to do without visiting the refectory. Perhaps you did not notice the swollen bellies and slurred speech amongst your fellows. Perhaps you even mocked their failing memories and lack of concentration as you and your small accomplice consumed your secret store. Yes! You thought you were so clever that no-one would find out. But I knew. That selfsame quickness of mind and clearness of speech betrayed you. I have heard the tales of secret gardens and forgotten kitchens. Was that where you found it? No matter now. But know this; Alligor was on its deathbed before the Murgans came. I did what I had to do. Examine your conscience Old; have you always done your duty with regard to Alligor?"

"Only gods and rogues are untroubled by their consciences. My troubled conscience seems to be all the conscience Alligor has left. I very much fear these Murgans. You should know that they only take and never give. They might seem to give, but their gifts are either of things that are useless to them, or such as will fall back into their laps at some future time."

Sly's lips crinkled with sardonic humour. "Food once given is not easily reclaimed."

"True, but perhaps the food is only given on account, against some future payment."

"They already know that we have no money here. Or do you prefer it if the librarians remain hungry and stupid?"

"In that case I would only have to wait until the Murgans leave..."

Both men were silenced by the same thought. And what then? Return to rancid oil and mildewed grains? To slow decline? Now that the Murgans had entered the Book City, Alligor was changed for ever and it could never again be as it was before.

The silence was broken by loud rumbles from Old's empty belly. Sly gave him a long knowing look before turning away. His voice rose up from the stairwell as he descended. "I must organize a meal before the Murgans lock all the food away."

Old felt helpless and defeated. Right from the start the Murgans had stopped the mouth of the Book City by guarding the gate. Now it seemed their grip was also about its throat.

Thirteen

A sandy plain, or it might have been a seashore, stretched to the horizon. There were smooth white pebbles everywhere. No, not pebbles but eggs. Eggs perfect in their curious symmetry and their satin hardness nestling in the warm soft sand. And, faraway: the sea. All was calm. Only the distant surf disturbed the stillness. A sound that seemed to swell. Louder now, and louder. And then, not the noise of the sea at all but the sound of a million eggs cracking and bursting asunder as the life within them struggled for an existence outside their brittle shells. A tide of birth swept across the plain towards him. Small peered intently at the nearest eggs, anxious to discover what form of life might emerge from these myriad calcined prisons. It was very perplexing. He could not seem to focus on them at all. They fluttered around until their wings blotted out the sand. Sometimes they seemed like shards of glass, sometimes like windblown rags. They fused and merged and parted again. It was like looking through leaves at the sky.

Small stared uncomprehendingly at the light filtering through the leaves of a tree with yellow flowers and red fruit. He was uncomfortable. Thorns were pricking into the flesh of his bare arms, legs and face. He tried to shrink like a snail but the pain continued. Something was trickling down his arm. When he looked he saw not blood but water making streaky pathways across his dusty yellow skin.

Rain. It was raining. As the rain washed away the pollen, his skin became less sensitive. Slowly he rolled over onto his side. His senses began to return. He watched the rain beating down onto the paving stone by his cheek. Slowly it bore away the carpet of pollen and revealed a surface spotted with lichen into which was carved the single word:

LOTOS

Small had awoken to a changed place. Tinted by the grey green light of the sky, the garden did not seem so benign. The plants looked alien and menacing. The transparent jade of the water had turned to jet. He stared into the inky depths. What had appeared before to be mysterious and inviting, now filled him with horror. What manner of things nameless and predatory swirled in that dark world behind his reflection? Even the metal dolphins which spewed the rainwater from the eaves in great arcs onto the pavement had changed their enigmatic smiles into *ulvis*-like sneers. It was only a passing shower but the water had soaked through his thin silk *tzirt*. He started to shiver as he stumbled back into the librarian's room.

He sat feeling sorry for himself and staring at the hissing rain until it suddenly occurred to him that the garden was completely enclosed. Where had the librarian fulfilled his duties? Where were the books? Certainly not in the gallery he had come through. No-one had been in there for years. Small walked over to the blocked doorway. The wooden boards were tightly joined together, but half way down there was a crack no wider than a hair. Small put his eye to it. It was not easy to see anything but what he could see looked like books on a shelf. He was behind a bookstack. As he adjusted his position for a clearer view his hand shifted across the boards and came into contact with a cold metal rod, curved with a ball-end worn smooth. Worn smooth meant well-used. He tugged and pushed at the rod until the bookstack moved out of its place.

Small put his shoulder gently against the boards and the whole thing swung out into the gallery beyond. He found himself in a well-ordered, well-kept gallery, noticeably free of cobwebs. It had one other door which, when he opened it, revealed another gallery as orderly as the first. He realised that this must have been the part of the library where the assassin had carried out his attack. Just at that moment, the last gust of the rain squall passed through the open windows of the gallery, through the open doors and into the garden. The disguised door slammed shut. Small whirled around. He gazed helplessly at the range of bookshelves which ran the length of the room; seamless; identical. He had no idea which bookshelf was really the door into an enchanted garden or how to open it. He might have to take a hundred books off their shelves to find it. The treacherous echoes of the slamming door ran away into the library. Small felt threatened and vulnerable. He had no idea where in Alligor he was. He looked about him as if there might be clues or directions, but could not even see the bloody calligraphy that had led him to this place. The gallery floor was spotless. The librarian had been careful. He had managed to staunch the flow of blood just long enough for him to pass through the gallery and into the hidden room. Small found the scene of the attack twenty paces into the next gallery: a large pool of dried blood, smears, handprints. The man had lain on the floor for some time.

Out of the echoes of the hidden door slamming shut came another sound: half-heard and ominous. Was it the creak of a heavy door opening? It was followed closely by the unmistakable thud as it closed again. Someone was coming. In sheer panic Small ran back into the first gallery, forgetting that it was now a cul-de-sac. Terrified he pressed himself into the corner behind the door as the footsteps approached.

The person who came into the gallery did not look like an assassin. For a start he was not wearing shoes but what appeared to be sandals improvised out of old leather book covers. He was an old man but his dress and the way he held himself did not speak of one born to the library. He was clean shaven except for large curly moustaches. He strode over to the bookshelves and rapped on the wood with his knuckles.

"Are you there?" he called in a loud voice.

Small shrank back against the wall.

"Plantman, old friend, are you unwell? It's me, Velik."

With his eyes fixed on the man's back Small sidled towards the open door. The man turned and saw him.

"Hello. Who are you?" he said.

If there had been the slightest hint of menace or cruelty in the man, Small would have taken to his heels instantly. He hesitated and the moment was gone.

"My name is 'Small' ... I mean 'Rider'..."

The man's face crinkled with amusement. "Ha! A prodigy! A boy who doesn't know his own name. No matter, I enjoy contradictions." The man's eyes narrowed, "For example, your robe doesn't match your accent."

It was given to me." Small replied.

"So was your name I think! You do not have horseman's hands." The old man had walked over to him with a hand held out in greeting. Small found his hand gripped fiercely.

"I am Velik." the man said, adding "... of that I am sure."

Small said nothing.

"Twenty years I have lived in this library and only ever met one man. Then, suddenly, two visitors in one month, and both dressed in silk..." Velik lifted his bushy eyebrows.

Small did not supply the expected explanation.

The eyebrows dropped.

"I am looking for a friend. He is a librarian. He tends the garden. Perhaps you have seen him?"

Small had decided that this was not the assassin. But if he was not a librarian either then who was he? A thought occurred to him; this must be a reader. He had a duty to be polite.

"If he is the person who lived behind the bookshelves then I very much fear that he is dead."

"Dead?"

"We found him in the Eastern Galleries. I followed the spots of blood back to here. I came out through the book shelves but the wind closed the door and I could not return. We think that there may be an assassin …."

Small could see that the man was much affected by the news.

Velik shook his head and sighed deeply before speaking in a voice thickened by emotion. "I feared as much. Listen. This is a bad place to linger now. We could be trapped if anyone came up the stairs". He glanced towards the windows, "See, the light is failing. Do you intend to return to the Eastern Galleries tonight?"

Small shrugged. "I only know the way back through the books. But even if I could open the door I wouldn't try it in the dark."

Velik laid an arm on Small's shoulder "I can offer you modest hospitality. I have lived nearby for many years. There is water, food and a solid door with a good lock on it. It'll be as safe as anywhere in the city."

Fear, hunger, thirst and simple curiosity conspired to compel Small to accept the invitation. As they climbed the steep stairs to Velik's room, Small leaned over the baluster to see how deep the stairwell was. Far down in the shadows below there was a flicker of deeper dark as someone or something ducked back into the shelter of the stairs.

Velik's room was at the top of the building. By the time they reached the door to the apartment, the stone staircase which wound around the ample stairwell had shrunk to a flight of steps so narrow that Small's shoulders brushed the walls on either side. He had to duck his head under the arch of the door.

"Welcome!" said Velik. "My home is your home."

There was something unfamiliar about Velik's apartment. It was so welcoming, so lived in, so … cozy. But these words were not in Small's everyday vocabulary. There were implications to life in a city inhabited only by orphans to whom the books were mother, father, friends and family, work, duty and religion. Velik was from that mysterious world outside Alligor where most had parents, siblings and homes; a world where books were rarely seen.

The room was large enough to contain a gallery table, a bench and a couch made from another table. Piles of books supported them because their legs had been broken off, presumably to bring them in through the narrow doorway. Indeed, books were everywhere in the room, in shelves, in heaps, piled up on every surface, but there were besides, wondrous things: things from the world outside. Best of all to Small's eyes were several brightly coloured and fantastically patterned rugs. Items so luxurious and sensual to a librarian that it was only with

104

great difficulty that Velik could persuade him to step off the one spread on the floor and take a seat in an alcove by the window. Even then he stretched out his legs so that he could wriggle his toes in the tufts of wool. The carpets were like the moss on the roof, but warm instead of cool. Evening sun streamed in through an unglazed window which opened the wall from floor to ceiling and allowed access to an extensive terrace. Fig leaves framed the opening. Out on the terrace stood unfamiliar artefacts whose purpose Small could not even guess at. A large metal pipe, recognizably part of Alligor's antediluvian plumbing, stood in a wooden frame pointing at the sky. A circular wooden stool had been converted into yet another curious mechanism. On the table close by his elbow crystal glass pebbles stood on metal rods, catching the setting sun in their tiny orbs. Those parts of the walls not obscured by books were covered in paper and parchment leaves. On them Small recognized the glyphs, arcs, triangles, circles, calculations and predictions of astrological science.

Velik meanwhile busied himself with a flask and two beakers. Presently he handed one of the beakers to Small.

"Fig wine," he said, "of my own making. A means both of preserving water and the balance of the mind."

Small drank greedily until Velik put a hand on his arm. "Careful!" he said "It is strong, ... and precious."

"I'm sorry. I never drank wine before"

"What! A novice in the mysteries of Dionysos? You must have led a sheltered life."

At that moment Small felt a most luxurious warm furriness on his bare leg. It startled him into pulling his knees up to his chest. He saw an animal had rubbed itself against him.

Velik was amused by his reaction "Let me introduce you to Sardanapalus. Sardanapalus, meet Small Rider."

Sardanapalus was a cat, a very large cat, which had insinuated itself through a very small open casement. Small had never seen a real cat before, but even if he had, he would certainly never have seen one of such prodigious proportions. Sardanapalus was a great cushion of a cat, a furry feaster, scion of a line of privileged vermin hunting cats whose race could be traced back to the time of the first Gypsian Pharaohs. Once there had been hundreds of cats in Alligor, but that was when there were readers whose crumbs and leavings attracted rodents. When the readers stopped coming, the rats and mice disappeared and the cats followed. All but a few that is, whose skill, cunning and adaptability led them either into the kitchen or up onto the roof. The kitchen cats were used as food tasters and succumbed to the poisonous mildews one by one until they were all extinguished. Sardanapalus was the last of the line of roof cats, and concentrated behind those glowing yellow eyes was the inherited genius of a thousand years of successful hunting.

Hunting was the business of his life. Where others saw only veils of foliage Sardanapalus could sense hidden movement. Where others heard only the rustle of leaves, he heard the tiny beating heart. He was a grand strategist of bird behaviour. He saw the shapes in the shadows. Stealing, stalking, pausing, pouncing, Sardanapalus came like a furry Nemesis to round off the plots of a thousand feathered biographies. Careless or merely unlucky, the birds on the roof suffered for Sardanapalus's loneliness, he fed till he was sated and then assuaged his feelings of dissatisfaction by indulging in an obsessive cruelty, toying with his victims, letting them go only for the pleasure of hooking his claws into them again and again.

Sardanapalus eyed Small warily before tip-toeing across the table. After a sort of circular dance, the cat settled himself upon a truly enormous leather bound volume which had been worn smooth by his dreaming bulk. Small could read the strange geometric script on the book's spine, *A History of Nineveh the Great*. "It's why I called him Sardanapalus," explained Velik, "even as a kitten he made that book his bed, and I have never seen a larger volume in the library."

Although the bitter-sweet aftertaste of the wine did not match its rich, heady fumes, Small found the burning glow which spread through his abdomen to be quite pleasant. Emboldened by a sudden feeling of well-being he spoke his mind.

"Velik, you did not seem surprised when I spoke of an assassin."

The old man inhaled the fumes from his beaker, sipped a little and then spoke.

"That is true my boy. This has been a dry year. My small tank became green and stinking. I was forced to use the Great Well. Many times I felt myself watched, followed, stalked like a hind. Many times I turned quickly and thought I saw ..., but was never sure. In the night I heard footsteps, the rustle of silken clothing and a hand on my door. There were screams, far away, as if someone was suffering torments. I began to think that there was an evil presence in these galleries. I wondered why the book city should be visited in this way, but having been in the world I know that depravity often needs no reason or purpose other than its own appetite for evil. But then a great gale set the clouds racing across the sky and I felt something. I could not rid myself of a feeling that it was not just a colder season coming on but that a tranquil and benign age of the world was coming to its end. Perhaps I only dreamed it. Perhaps it is a premonition of my own end."

Small understood why Splint had been thrown down the Great Well. It was Velik who drew his water there and not the assassin. Small decided not to tell Velik about this gruesome event. "I saw this wind too," he said, "Old thought it might have been a breath of evil or a demonic power loose in the world of dreams. It blocked the gate with dust."

Velik nodded and narrowed his eyes as if deep in thought. They sipped their wine and watched the troubled splendour of the sun setting. Suddenly the old man fixed a bright eye on Small and broke the silence.

"Tell me young man. You saw the garden which was tended by my old friend. Did you notice anything strange about it, anything … dangerous?"

"There were fishes in a pool and I ate some fruit. I fell asleep under a bush. I think the bush sent me to sleep. It was a very strange and frightening thing."

"I only ask because Plantman would never permit me to see his garden. He always hinted at some danger. This bush of yours, what did it look like?"

"It had red fruit and yellow flowers. The pollen was everywhere. There was a word cut into the pavement. 'LOTOS' it said."

Velik sat upright and struck the table with his hand. "So that was it!" he exclaimed. "There is a tale told by the peoples of the sea that once there was an island where the lotos grew. Those who went ashore and tasted the lotos could never be enticed back to their ships. They forgot families and friends; forgot everything and lived only for the spice and its narcotic effects. To the lotos eaters it seemed that time had stood still, that they were immortal, but it was a delusion, their lives were brief as the flowers that enslaved them. I should have known that a garden in Alligor would be of a literary nature. I wonder what other plants are growing there?"

The fig wine had an extremely relaxing effect upon Small. His day had been long and stressful: the night before broken and disturbed. As twilight fell outside he made himself more comfortable and closed his eyes, just for a moment. Within seconds he was asleep.

Velik took the beaker from Small's unresisting fingers and drank off the last dregs of the wine. Then he lifted the boy's legs onto the alcove seat and placed a rug over him. One dirty foot was left uncovered. As he tucked it under the rug Velik rubbed his thumb thoughtfully across the callused sole. Those feet had never worn the shoes he had heard on the steps outside his room. His instincts had been true. This was no assassin. He drew a long slim dagger from the front of his robe and placed it on a shelf before climbing into his own cot.

Small slept a dreamless sleep, except that he woke once deep in the night. As he looked up at the window full of stars and heard the breeze stirring the fig leaves, an indescribable feeling of longing for something lovely and lost stole over him. Tears welled up in his eyes and he gave himself over to the dangerous pleasures of melancholy. What it was he missed he could not recall. But as he drifted back into unconsciousness, the all-pervasive aroma of the lotos seemed to be wafting in through the windows and filling the room.

At sunrise he awoke with a start. His mouth was peppery and his head dull and heavy. His first thoughts were of obligations and duties neglected. He sat bolt upright startling Velik who had just come in from the terrace with his arms full of figs.

"I have to go. Puttfark will be waiting for me. You see we have an agreement

"Puttfark? That's a strange name for a librarian. In one language I know it means 'splendid pig'"

Small ignored this jibe. "Can you show me the way to the Great Well?" Velik let the figs fall onto the table. "Of course I can, but before you go could you just do one favour for me? Come. See."

Small followed him out onto the terrace which seemed to be the only clear space in a mighty quadrangle of foliage. The ancient fig writhed over every architectural surface. Whether it was one tree or a hundred was beyond knowing. Roots dipped into every nook, crevice, gutter and sink seeking the moisture which supported the greenery which had already suffocated every building in sight. Brightly coloured birds squabbled needlessly over the profligate quantities of ripe fruit which bowed the branches.

"When I was younger I clambered all among those branches. I ate the figs and caught the birds. I even planted seeds down there in the garden." He pointed down at the impenetrable foliage. "Now I cannot trust my limbs to such dangerous exercise. The birds know this and so they tempt me with their largesse. See, there."

A large crimson and black bird sat on an untidy mound of twigs and vegetable rubbish amongst the branches just below the terrace wall.

"She has three eggs in the nest. The wind must have blown her here because it is past the season. It has been so long since I have tasted an egg. I crave eggs. If you could climb down and fetch two for me … no more or she will not return next year."

Small looked over the terrace edge. It would not be a difficult climb. The fig burgeoned with horizontal branchings, but the distance to the ground was very great and made him feel giddy.

Velik saw his anxious expression. "Don't worry. I shouldn't have asked. Not everybody can climb without fear."

This last remark stung Small. It clashed with his recently coined image of himself as a potential hero. The Murgans would not have hesitated for a moment and nor would he. He swung his leg over the wall and began to climb down. It was not difficult, but because of the strange giddiness he moved slowly and carefully. So intent was he on his handholds and where he was putting his feet that when the crimson bird suddenly exploded in a clatter of wing beats and launched itself out over the gulf of the courtyard he was paralysed with shock. It was many seconds before he could open his eyes and relax his grip on the tree. He saw then that he was outside a window of the gallery on the floor below Velik's room, invisible from above and all but stifled in the glossy foliage. He peered in at a familiar scene of neglected bookstacks and cobwebbed lecterns. A flash of movement caught his eye. He caught a momentary glimpse of a figure striding through the gallery, and then he had gone. He forced his memory to disgorge what he had seen. A youngish man dressed head to foot in black who wore low-heeled boots. One hand swinging free, the other tucked inside a black silk *tzirt*. Most memorable of all was his hat. It had been like an upturned bowl from which a long black feather trailed behind, jiggling about as he walked.

In his haste to climb back onto the balcony, Small almost forgot to slip the eggs into his book bag. "The assassin! I saw him. He was in the gallery down there."

Velik seemed more concerned with preserving the eggs from Small's agitated movements. But once he had placed them safely amongst the figs on a shelf by the window, he listened as the boy described what he had seen.

"I don't suppose there could be any doubt." he mused. "He must be the one who killed my friend."

"We must get back to the Eastern Galleries and tell Puttfark. He will know what to do."

"Puttfark again? Why would I want to go with you? This is my home. I am quite safe here."

"No! You are in great danger here. Your door is locked but it would only take him a moment to climb up from below."

"If he knew that he would have been here already. The Library disorients new-comers. He has no idea that that gallery runs beneath my window. There is no direct access from that floor to this."

Velik guided Small to the Great Well. The route was typically Alligorian in its indirectness. They strode through broad galleries or ducked and crouched their way through pitch-dark gennels. They climbed stairs and descended ramps. At one moment wide architectural vistas opened up before them; the next they were confined in bowel-like tunnels. From time to time Velik would have to unlock a door, which he always locked again behind him. In Alligor such a simple act would confound any pursuer who might then have to spend days trying to find a way round to the other side of the locked door.

As they walked through gallery after deserted gallery, endless vistas of decay and disorder opened up. Rows upon rows of books, manuscripts, boxes of leaves; the endless chatter of a whole city of ghosts, lay around mute and neglected. There was not enough time in the whole world to read all those words. For the first time it began to dawn upon Small just how little life was left in the book-city. The Eastern Galleries were the last flicker of a pulse in a body already atrophied beyond hope of recovery. The library dreamed its secret deathbed dreams. Assassin or no, Old had been right, the end of Alligor was close.

They parted at the head of the stairs leading down to the Great Well. Velik grasped Small's arm above the elbow.

"Take care young man until we meet again. You must come back and see me soon. My time amongst these books has been most fruitful. I have a story to tell which must not be lost. I see decay and desolation where there should be care and order; assassins where there should be readers. But you; you have youth, vigour, innocence and promise. You will hear my story."

After he had left Velik, Small keenly regretted having made yet another promise. Everyone seemed to want to bind him to a task. He was still reviewing the onerous nature of his duties and obligations when he felt his arms pinioned from behind. He was only slightly relieved to discover that he had been seized by Pullfark's men, patrolling the approaches as ordered.

Fourteen

"How could you be so stupid as to wander off alone? My men have searched everywhere for you! You might have been killed and what then? What about our deal?"

Puttfark's angry outburst shocked Small even more than being frog-marched by the Murgan guards. They stiffened and exchanged uneasy glances at their leader's loss of control. Puttfark too was shocked. Anger was not a part of his character. He considered anger as a destructive and irrational trait. Public anger he regarded as a mark of defeat. He could not understand the strength of his feelings and told himself that without the boy he would not find the book: that the boy had made a deal: that the boy owed him. But he was alarmed by his reaction to the thought that the boy might be killed; and this for reasons he could not quite work out. There was something about Small. He genuinely liked the boy: his innocence; his untarnished mind; his willingness to learn. He was already planning an exciting future for the boy. He would teach him to control and subjugate the world to his will. Being able to introduce such an innocent to the higher pleasures of life appealed to Puttfark's manipulative character. Small would be his companion. Such desires did not unduly worry him. He had even heard of Murgans who had such feelings towards dogs or even cats. But there was more. Small was the only person Puttfark had ever met who he felt he could trust, and beyond that there were *increments*, *profits*, *potentialities* which he could not properly fathom because the Murgan language did not have words capable of expressing such things as paternal motives. He became aware that his men were staring at him with more than ordinary interest. He glared until they shuffled out of the room and back to their duties. Then he turned to Small.

"You'd better come with me. I have things to organize. The summer is ending and the tents will soon be uncomfortable. I have decided to move my people into the Library. Mr. Sly has found us a room."

Small did not quite know how to react to this news. Any change in this changeless place was exciting and interesting, but the library was for readers. Were those who had no interest in books permitted to live here? It all sounded ominously permanent.

As they passed through the galleries they came upon two Murgans manhandling a large terracotta jar almost as tall as themselves. It was an awkward shape tapering to a point at its base. Mystified Small turned to Puttfark for an explanation.

"Cedar oil." Puttfark remarked blandly, "It was in the way."

Small was none the wiser.

As they entered the stairwell, the normally sepulchral silence of the library was replaced by a tumult of noise. Voices, footsteps, doors opening and banging, bumpings and knockings, all echoing and reverberating as if a throng were passing to and fro.

Old was not in his niche as they descended the stairs. They found him on the landing below, where the Murgans were decamping into their new living quarters. A constant procession of figures carrying bundles and packages cast strange shadows upon the curving wall of the stairs. Both men and women were involved in the conveyance of the Murgan goods and chattels. Puttfark strode along the corridor and into the meton store. The room had been cleared and swept clean of the millennial rubbish which had accumulated everywhere in Alligor. There was a commotion by the entrance. Old was trying ineffectually to stop the Murgans taking possession of the room. A guard was gently restraining him from actually impeding the entrance, but from behind his arm came Old's voice, weak and hoarse with exertion.

"...by what right do you move your chattels in here? Alligor is sacred. There is no place here for thugs and whores. There is nothing here for you, nothing! Go, or the Great Author of all things will change the plot of your disgusting empire. Small! Help me! Tell them they have to leave."

Puttfark turned impassively towards Small. Small felt embarrassed by Old's behaviour, the more so since it was clearly ineffectual, but his fondness for the old man was stronger still. He did not like to see him shamed in this way. Small drew him to one side.

"Listen to me. You will make yourself ill with this excessive behaviour. I'm sure the Murgans mean no harm, but in any case there is nothing we can do about it. They are too strong. If they do not want to go, accept it, we are helpless."

"No-one is helpless who has a mind and a voice! Old whispered urgently.

"So the philosophers would have us believe. But persuasion is the only weapon of intelligence. If you would persuade someone, then don't begin by treading on their toes."

The anger left Old. He simply did not have the energy to sustain it. There were flecks of spittle in his moustache and beard, and white foam at the corners of his mouth. He looked haggard and crushed. Small put his arm around the bony shoulders.

"You have done all you can here. Go back to your window. I will come and talk with you later."

The meton store was being transformed. Coloured rugs graced the floors and walls. Veils of gauzy stuff hung at the windows. Couches and tables had been installed in the alcoves. Small was entranced. Puttfark strode over to a window, lifted one leg onto a couch which had been placed there and sat down. He parted the gauze curtain with one finger whilst he checked the yard below.

"Come over here Rider." He said

Small sat down beside him.

"We must have a serious talk"

"As you wish."

"In Murga when you make a deal it is very important that you do your part. Your life might depend on it. It's how we judge people: how they come out of deals. You promised to find a book for me. I want that book. If you find that book for me then I will know that you are the sort of man I want to ride with."

"Do you mean I could ride with you and your men?" Small was stunned. His dream might come true.

Puttfark sensed the boy's keen interest. No need to promise him anything specific. Just let him assume.

"Listen boy. This is no place for a young lad of your abilities. This whole city is a tomb, a necropolis, a graveyard. Look around you at all these old men. In five years, maybe ten, you will be the only one left alive, and then what will you do? Just find that book for me and you can ride away from this pile of rubbish; all this dead old stuff. Forget the books. Everything worth doing should be done for real."

Small was overwhelmed. He had not realised how strong a hold his dream of joining the Murgans had on him. He felt dizzy, detached, as if he was on the highest rooftop of Alligor. He was being offered the world by one who seemed to have the power to give it. In his mind's eye he saw himself, dressed in silk, turning his horse away from the Book City and into the west wind. He waved to Old at the Gate. But Old did not smile. His expression was of disappointment, sorrow, even … accusation.

Puttfark saw the elation drain from the boy's face.

"Something wrong?"

"Oh, no. At least, I will still try to find your book. I try to keep my promises. But I don't think you realize how big Alligor is, or what a terrible state most of it is in. Some galleries are little more than heaps of rubbish, some are locked. We might never find the book. It might not even exist."

"But you will still try?"

Small nodded.

"And you will ride with us?"

The boy remained silent.

"You don't want to join us?"

"Yes, but I have other obligations. I ... have sworn an oath."

"An oath? Who to?"

"It is a secret oath sworn before the Divine Author of All Things."

"The Divine Author? Wasn't that who the old man was shouting about? Can't we just go and ask him if he'll let you off?"

"You don't understand. He is not a mortal scribe, but the Author of this whole world."

Puttfark looked at him in such blank incomprehension that Small tried to explain. "We learn that in the very beginning there was the Divine Mind in which there was the potential for everything that came to be, even the Great Author himself. The Universe began when He spoke the word which was His own name. Thus it is said that in the beginning was the Word. He spoke more words and as the word was uttered, that thing came to be. As he spoke of the relations of things so did the Great Plot unfold. This was how He created our universe, just as a poet might make a verse. In this kind of divine shape forming, one word might bring into being more than one reality. So do the poets speak of the metaphor and the cosmic word. These are mysteries of God."

"So he's your God and everything you do is controlled by him?"

"Not everything. Just as the authors tell us that no matter how carefully they plot their books, the characters take on a life of their own and shape the story from within; so are we mortals able to choose our courses through the world. But should we make a moral choice which offends the natural order of things, then our lives will take a tragic course, until we have purged ourselves of our transgressions. The ordering of nature is given to the Divine Author alone, and it is He who controls all our endings."

"Ha! In Murga we plot our own lives from beginning to end."

"I would not be so sure. Perhaps one day you will wake in the dark hours of the night and hear the scratching of the Great Author's pen."

Puttfark was not in the mood for superstitious rubbish, nor did he like being lectured. He needed to be in control. "So this divine author is your god. What did you promise him?" Puttfark noticed the startled look in the boy's eyes.

"Nothing ... I mean ... I swore to somebody else. To take care of the Library."

The *ulvis* heralded Puttfark's broad smile. "I see," he said. But what he saw was that the boy was still holding something back: something important. His attention shifted to the door. Small turned to look. One of the young women from the camp had entered the room. In her arms she carried two fat stone flagons. Puttfark called to her, "Imperia, is that wine you have there?"

She turned towards them. As she drew near, Puttfark spoke to her in his own language. "The dust in this shit-heap gives me a throat like a desert latrine." He gave her a conspiratorial wink and pointed at two places on the table. Small understood the insulting reference to Alligor, but did not protest because he was too bedazzled by the smile which the woman turned on him. It had that same exciting effect as at the camp, but at close quarters there was something unsettling about it. The eyes seemed too watchful; too interested. He was fascinated.

The flagon was quickly broached and the wine decanted into small tumblers of cloudy green glass. Puttfark beamed across the table. "This is real Murgan wine: black as Sa'than's toenails and twice as strong!"

Small picked up his tumbler which indeed resembled nothing so much as a pot of ink. He tilted it slightly against the light. There was no redness in the smear it left on the glass. He watched as Puttfark took a good swallow of the wine before he tasted his own. It was very sweet, with subtle unfamiliar flavours like low voices on the edge of sleep. A heady perfume arose from the disturbed wine, which for some reason made him think of the lotos pollen. The wine burned into his insides in a most pleasant manner.

Puttfark held his glass under his nose. "I once knew a man who said that the fumes from good Murgan wine made him think of old wealth, strong fortresses and high-born women. To me it smells of winning, always winning. It's like drinking the blood of enemies. It makes my heart swell with courage. So. Tell me, where did you disappear to?"

Small had not had a chance to tell his news. "I followed the spots of blood till I found where the librarian came from. I met a reader and saw the assassin."

"'You saw him?"

"He was dressed all in black silk. He wore low-heeled boots and a hat."

"A hat?"

"Like a little upturned bowl with a long black feather on it."

Small noticed Puttfark's features tauten almost imperceptibly. "He is a Murgan, isn't he?" he asked.

Puttfark did not respond. He was considering options.

Small pressed on,"… do you know who he is, why he is here?"

Puttfark was silent for a few moments before he spoke. "This is not good news. You and your librarians are in great danger. In fact your whole library might be threatened. The man you saw is almost certainly an assassin. He is well known … in certain circles. His name is Rottko."

"A Murgan!"

"Perhaps not by birth, but certainly by instinct."

"I don't understand. What is he doing here? Why don't you just talk to him and get him to leave?"

"In Murga nobody does anything unless they are paid to do it. He has been paid to come here and do a job …"

"So you too are here because you have been paid to come: paid to do a job?"

Puttfark shrugged.

"But you said you were traders."

"We trade our services for payment. Just as you trade your lives for food and lodgings, we are paid to bring things to market. Life is all trade."

Small took a sip of the black wine. "Is Rottko looking for a book?"

"I would think so."

"Is it the same book?"

Puttfark nodded assent. "In Murga the book has been known about for a long time," he said, "but everybody thought that it didn't exist anymore. Lost, destroyed something like that. But then rumours started. A Library City in the East which had every book in the world."

"But what exactly is this book?"

"It is as I said. A book by a wise ruler on how to govern. It is the book on which our state was founded. That is all I know."

"So Lubrik and Kunig are searching for the same book?"

A nod of the head.

"But why is it so important? Who wants it? What are they going to do with it?"

"Powerful people in my country see it as Murgan property. The legend says it was stolen. We always reclaim our own. All agree that it should be returned to Murga, if only to prevent it falling into foreign hands. Some want Alligor to be brought under Murgan control, but garrisons are expensive. Others argue that it is more important that the book does not fall into the hands of an enemy than that it be found. Meanwhile certain wealthy individuals thought it might be a worthwhile investment to pay someone to look for it. I was paid to put together an expedition to find a 'valuable commodity' for my

116

employer. Rottko has been paid to do much the same. Unfortunately his methods are more direct. Besides being an assassin, he is also an expert at extracting information by inflicting pain. I don't know how long he has been in Alligor but you can be sure that his time has not been wasted. Who knows how many old librarians he has finished off? Who knows what they might have told him?"

Small thought of the cries which Velik had heard. "They could not have told him much or he would have left by now." he said.

"If he suspects that the book is here but that it can't be found, he might well have been ordered to make sure it never will be found."

"How could he do that?"

"All he needs is flint and tinder…"

Small was thunderstruck.

Puttfark's face turned dark and impassive. He spoke slowly and deliberately to Small. "So you see, young man, it is very, very important that you find the book for me. If you fail to find it, Rottko will torch your library and you will break your oath. Find it and I think even your divine author will admit that you have done your part of the deal. With the book on its way back to Murga, no-one will give a God about your library anymore."

Small was too numbed by the implications of what he had heard to protest. As he drained the glass of black wine to the dregs he noticed that the Murgan captain had only taken the one mouthful of his own. Puttfark continued speaking.

"Mr. Sly has promised that in return for food the librarians will all help in the search. A meal is being served in the Refectory. I suggest that you go eat. You have a busy time ahead. I will come later. I have to talk to my men. They need to know who they are up against."

Puttfark watched him leave. The boy was still holding something from him. A secret oath. No matter, there would be a way of bringing it to market. Every deal was possible. It was just a question of finding the offer that couldn't be refused.

Old was not in his window seat. Small assumed he would be in the Refectory. The courtyard was all activity and bustle. At the foot of the stairs, food in baskets, in jars and in sacks, was being unloaded from one of the wagons ready to be carried up to the Murgan quarters. Through the Great Gate he could see the horses being fed the hay and other feedstuffs heaped upon the second wagon. A group of Murgan guards now heavily and openly armed, stood watching by the Refectory door as the last few bundles of goods and chattels from the camp were carried in through the Gate.

As he looked on, two burly guards escorted Tentpole and Dim to the Refectory door. Tentpole looked anxious and resentful, but Dim wore his usual broad smile and open expression. At the door they were held up whilst one of the Murgans patted them in a most intimate and embarrassing fashion all over their upper bodies, not even leaving out their armpits and thighs. Apparently satisfied, he granted permission for them to enter by jerking a large square thumb over his shoulder.

Small could not divine what this curious ritual might portend. When he too was given the same treatment, he asked the Murgans what they were doing. They merely smirked at each other. The blond giant passed him into the Refectory with a sideways jerk of his head. "Don't worry. Just checking." he said.

The Refectory was more crowded inside than he had ever seen it. Nearly every librarian he had ever known, and not a few he had never seen before, were all assembled for the first proper meal to be served in Alligor in living memory. His heart sank as he surveyed what was almost certainly the last muster of Alligor's finest. The ingrained dirt, the rags, the blank, disinterested expressions of the merely old, the slack-jawed imbecility of the irretrievably senile, the uncontrolled drooling of those who had begun the final descent into terminal drowsiness, all served to prove Puttfark right. These were all the troops that Alligor could field in its final battle. Small would soon be the only one left. Sly, his eyes glittering with desperate intelligence, seemed a prisoner of his new clothes. He was flanked on one side by the urbane and inscrutable Kunig, and on the other by Lubrik: tense, alert, eyes flickering to and fro like flies trapped behind a window.

Spoon and his helpers, having finally come into their own as the servants of appetite, stood glistening, flushed and full of hubris in the savoury smog issuing from the kitchen door. Across the room the book menials huddled together at their table, suspicious, cynical, trying to work out their position in this new state of affairs. Nearby, Dim, sitting bolt upright, head and shoulders above the rest, eyes bright, whimsical smile firmly in place, a monument of health and strength in this temple of decrepitude.

"Thmall! Thmall!" he waved and beckoned excitedly. Behind him, a nervous Tentpole leaped to his feet, "Please Small come and sit next to him before he has the table over."

As Small squeezed in next to Tentpole, Dim put a massive brotherly arm around his shoulders and hugged him forcefully. "Thmall! The thtrangerth! The thtrangerth they've got mummieth with them!"

"What?"

"Mummieth! Ladies!"

"Oh. Yes. Ladies." Small had forgotten that the others had only just discovered the Murgan women.

"It might be your mummy, Thmall, come back to get you. It might be mine. She said she would come back."

Dim was trembling with excitement. Small's spirits sank. He would have to disappoint poor Dim again. "Not all ladies are mummies, and your mother would be an old lady by now."

"No. She's young and pretty, like these."

"Wait a minute Dim. You speak as if you knew your mother. How could you remember her? You must have been a baby."

"No. Not a baby. I walked here with her. She was young and pretty. She said she would come back for me."

Small's heart sank further. "Dim, listen to me. None of these ladies are your mother. They are too young. They come from too far away. They have never been here before. You mustn't think such things."

Dim lifted his arm away from Small's shoulder. For a moment his forehead wrinkled in thought, a perplexed expression passed across his open face. But then his countenance was as untroubled as before. "You never thaw my mummy. You don't know her."

Small opened his mouth to speak, but then thought better of it.

The general hubbub was interrupted by a sudden commotion at the door.

"Get your hands off me! Let me go! You Murgan thugs!" Old floated into the room between two grinning guards who held him up by the armpits his feet dangling in the air. No sooner had he been lowered to the ground than he attempted to force his way back out by burrowing between the two big men. He was gently repulsed and firmly guided back into the refectory. It looked as if he was going to make an appeal to the other librarians, but at that moment Puttfark swept in through the door, accompanied by at least ten heavily armed men. They walked in step, just as the military manuals advised. Their faces were stony and impassive. As one they turned to face the diners and slapped their sword hilts. As intended, the diners were both impressed and intimidated into silence. Puttfark bounded lightly up onto a bench behind them and began to speak.

"Greetings, men of Alligor! For those of you who do not yet know it, I am Puttfark. I and my colleagues have come here on a business enterprise on behalf of an employer in Murga. We seek to recover an item of stolen property, a book, which has a value peculiar to the Murgan nation. On your behalf, Mr Sly ..." he turned to Sly who gave a sickly 'courtier's smile'. "... has offered your services in the search.

119

In return we will feed you with good food at our expense. Mr. Sly assures us that an improvement in diet will quickly transform you all from your present lethargic state into diligent researchers. I trust that this will be so; I hope that this will be so, since the amount of food will be strictly limited. Only those of you who are able to help us will be fed. The others will have to continue as they did before we came. Unfortunately we have agreed with Mr. Spoon ..." a nod here towards the kitchen, "... and his staff that they provide their skills and facilities exclusively to us. So communal meals will only be served to those in our employ. Anybody who does not work for us cannot expect to be fed here."

"Villainy! You are going to starve them to death! We will never do your work for you! Begone and take your slimy business with you." Old was almost incoherent with rage.

"Ah. Mr. Old I believe." Puttfark smiled. The *ulvis* stayed on his lips for so long that he seemed to be savouring it. "I insisted that you be brought here so that you could hear all I have to say. You have resented our presence in Alligor since the moment we arrived. You have repeatedly abused me, my men and our womenfolk. You see us as a threat to your Library but I want you to know that we are not your worst enemies. There is a far greater threat to your city of books. A violent assassin, a cruel torturer is at large in Alligor. If you doubt me ask your young friend. This man has already killed several times and will certainly kill again if he gets the chance. He is searching for the same thing as we are and will stop at nothing to find it, or, if that is not possible, to destroy it. If you want to save your people and your books you must make sure that we find the book first and quickly. Whilst your men search, my men will give you protection. As you can see, they are experienced professionals, but few in numbers. Protection will be limited to those involved in the search and to those galleries in which they are working. I think you will admit Mr. Old that we share a common interest. You want us to leave as soon as possible. The moment we have the book we will go. In the meantime we have a common interest in looking after both the library and its inhabitants. Think long and hard on these things Mr. Old."

The man in white turned to address the room once more. "We have a fine meal prepared for you. This meal you may eat without obligation. The next must be earned. Enjoy! Enjoy!"

A ragged cheer was instantly drowned in a great rattle of bronze cauldron lids as Spoon led his phalanx of food bearing minions out of the kitchen and into the refectory. In a greasy parody of the entry of the Murgan guard, the food servers made a fair attempt at keeping in step with each other before scattering anarchically amongst the tables. There could be no doubting the quality of the food. Spoon had excelled himself. Wonderful bread, warm soft and aromatic, sat next to dishes of beans pulses and cereals. Green leaves straight from the plants enfolded morsels of spicy rice laced with nuts and olives. A skin full of sweet honey beer was taken from table to table.

The Murgans sat apart from the rest. Puttfark was in excellent spirits and sipped black wine with his food. Small ate ravenously tearing at the bread and stuffing it into his mouth, alternating it with handfuls of beans and rice. He satisfied his hunger quite quickly: years of barely enough to eat had caused his stomach to shrink. Looking round he noticed Old, still standing with arms crossed and a defiant expression on his face. Small felt sorry for him. He got up and walked over to where he stood.

"Old, you must eat." he said.

"Never! It would choke me. I would rather die."

"Old, you cannot die. It would break your oath."

The old man turned to him with a crestfallen demeanour.

"Look around you, Old. How many librarians can you see who are capable of looking after the library in any way at all? Only you, me and Sly even know what is going on here. We have to keep our strength up and our wits about us."

"Is it true about the assassin?"

"Yes I saw him. Velik also knows about him."

Old lifted his eyebrows. "Velik?"

"A reader. Puttfark is our only hope. We must find his book, whatever it is, as quickly as possible and then they will all leave us in peace. Otherwise we will be picked off one by one and Alligor burned to the ground by this Murgan madman."

"Listen lad. From now on there will be no more peace in Alligor. Once our librarians have had their bellies stretched by all this food do you really think that they could ever go back to starvation rations of rancid oil and mildewed grain? Have you seen the galleries after Sly and his new friends have been through them? All the books scattered about and nothing put back in its place. It is the end."

"It would only be the end if it was all burned down. It won't help anything if you are dying of starvation. You are just tired and overwrought. Come. Eat. Tomorrow we will talk about what to do."

Small had to coax Old to his first mouthful, but after that the old librarian ate as voraciously as his shaking hands would allow. The Alligorites became more and more animated and rowdy as their bellies were filled. Another skin of beer was brought round. There could be no denying it; there was more merriment and goodwill here than he had ever seen in the Book city.

As Small took in the festive scene, he noticed one of the Murgan guards lean over Puttfark and speak to him behind his hand. Puttfark looked around the Refectory and then nodded his permission. The guard beckoned to his squad at the door. They stepped back and the women filed in.

The women had taken great care over their appearances. Their clothes, their hair, even their faces had been transformed into works of art. They looked like goddesses. The room was hushed into stunned appreciation as they took their seats. The hubbub resumed only when the kitchen menials brought them their food. Small noticed that several of the women had carried the strangest devices with them into the room. There was one that looked like an animal skin stretched over a wooden hoop, another was a box overlaid with threads or strings, a third consisted of dried plant stems bound together. These they laid on the floor next to them whilst they ate.

When the Murgans had all finished eating, their tables were cleared and pushed back against the wall. The women picked up their strange devices and lined up with the open space in front of them. The skin-covered hoop was lifted into the air and one of the young women began to hit it vigorously with a short bulbous double ended stick.

"BOOM-ba-da! BOOM-ba-da!" it went. Small's heart felt as if it was trying to catch up with the insistent rhythm.

Dim was baffled. "What is it? What are they doing?"

"It's a drum! I think it's a drum!" Small shouted back

The Murgan men nodded their heads and tapped their feet in time with the drumming. Suddenly the zither and pipes joined their hypnotic and repetitive melody to the compelling beat.

"It's music, Dim, music! The authors write of it."

Small felt the hairs rise on the nape of his neck as the two young women from the camp stepped forth into the clear space, moving rhythmically and sinuously together but not touching. They rolled their hips and raised their shoulders, their arms and legs intertwining in a thrilling and graceful candle-flame of a dance. The music took hold of Small. His heart beat like the drum and he felt that he wanted, had to do something, he did not know what, jump, run, shout, break something. It was all most exciting. He was not aware of standing up, or of having left his place at the table. He was only aware of the urge to be as close as possible to the source of this extraordinary experience. He wanted his senses to be filled with music, rhythm and movement. The music got faster. More women joined the dance. He found himself standing beside the Murgan guards.

The music and the movement induced a state of high excitement in the room. Small watched the surprised expressions of the librarians turn to smiles. Their hands tapped the tables in time with the beat, their feet twitched on the floor. He wondered that mere sounds could have such an effect on people, but he could hardly keep still himself and had an almost uncontrollable urge to hurl himself into the dance.

The spell was suddenly broken by that most feared of all phenomena for a librarian, the smell of burning. He caught the sweet acrid reek in his nostrils and turned instinctively towards its source. The Murgan guards were wreathed in a bluish haze. It seemed to be coming from a small pear-shaped clay lamp which they were passing from hand to hand. It had no visible flame and at first he thought that they were trying to light it. But as he looked on in amazement one of the Murgans lifted the lamp to his mouth and inhaled deeply from its spout before passing it on. Small could hardly believe his eyes. From the man's mouth issued a plume of blue smoke which assembled itself into a cloud and floated up into the vaults. The man was immediately bent double by a spasm of coughing, but then he threw back his head and gave a loud high-pitched hoot of what seemed to be joy. Small was baffled.

The lamp made its way along the line of Murgan guards to where he was standing. By this time most of the Murgans wore broad smiles and were gyrating to the music. His neighbour took a mouthful of the smoke and then turned to Small.

"Here," he said, "If you want to hear the music of the gods try some of this. Just suck out some of the smoke and hold it in your chest."

Small took the strange object in his hand and looked at it carefully. It fitted snugly into the palm of his hand. There was a hole in the centre where something combustible was glowing redly. It felt warm and comforting. With the drumbeats pounding in his ears, he raised the thing to his lips.

It never got there. A strong hand gripped his forearm. Puttfark extricated the device from Small's palm and handed it back to the guard.

"That is not for him." He said.

Small was not disappointed but only curious. "What is it?" he asked.

"A drug. It makes people feel happy for a while. They enjoy singing and dancing and … things."

Small was intrigued. "So why not for me?"

"It has other effects: more subtle. It makes people not care. If they are poor and without hope, this drug makes them happy and content to be so. It is a politicians dream."

"But you let your men use it."

"I don't think I could stop them. Their existence is both banal and dangerous. I need bodyguards who do not think but who only react; bodies not brains. So in their case the drug is useful."

"But how?"

"The drug affects the judgement and dulls the sensibilities. I do not want them to think about the extreme acts they are sometimes called upon to commit or to dwell on them afterwards. Working outside Murga it is easy for bored soldiers to weaken and go native. Even for them to be affected by what you call 'morality'. It is like a disease. The drug is a medicine to prevent my men getting sick from it. As for you, young man, I need you to find my book, and for that I need your brain, your mind, nice and sharp and active. Take my advice, forget the pipe and stick to wine and beer. Those things carry within them their own punishments for over indulgence. Their effects on the mind are not subtle nor do they linger."

"What is the name of this drug?"

"It has a thousand names but the one everyone remembers is the one that gave the assassins their title. One day I might tell you the story."

Puttfark strolled back to his place, pausing only to exchange a few words with the blond giant. Instinctively Small knew that he would never be offered the drug again. The thought did not trouble him at all. It was a mark of high privilege, and anyway, who needed drugs when there was music and dancing?

By this time all the Murgans were responding to the music. Even the men rocked their hips and rolled their shoulders to the rhythm. As the guards danced they swung the purses at their belts and ogled the women in a most comical manner. Small laughed out loud and wished that the music would go on for ever. It seemed to energise him. He was enchanted by the women too. Their dance seemed to be an invitation, but he was not sure if he should approach them. It must have been an hour later when Puttfark made the gesture of drawing his thumb across his neck. The music ended abruptly. The vaults rang, the women hooted and the men made strange high pitched shrieks by inserting their fingers in their mouths. Small decided on the spot that he would simply have to learn how to do that.

The man in white addressed the room. "It will be safer if you sleep here tonight. My men will put down straw for you all to sleep on. Dream the dream. We start work at first light."

The music played in Small's head long after the instruments were still. The images of the banquet danced in his mind's eye. Even in his sleep, the girl with the sinuous arms and the calculating eyes enticed him into the sunset, but however fast he galloped his horse, he could never catch up with her.

Fifteen

For those who had the stomach for it, breakfast was the remains of the banquet. There were not many takers, nor was there much time. At first light the Murgan guards burst into the refectory and began, none too gently, to rouse the sleeping librarians and chivvy them towards the door. Along with his appetite, Small had lost the euphoria of the previous evening. He felt irritable and vulnerable. He was uneasy about being told where and when to sleep, and faintly suspected that the overnight guard on the refectory door was more to keep everybody in than to keep anyone out. When he was jostled by one of the Murgans he reacted angrily and was more shocked by the blank, disoriented look in the man's eyes, than by the glossy blade that suddenly appeared in his hand. The authors had not written about heroes on drugs. He was not sure what to think about it.

Alligor's finest tottered into the blinding light of the courtyard. The fresh air was invigorating after the foetid stable-like atmosphere of the refectory, but they were not allowed to enjoy it for long. Soon the guards had everyone on the move towards their new workplace.

Like all things the Murgans set themselves to do, the search through the galleries was determined, organised, and methodical. It seemed part of their character to be undeterred by seemingly endless or superhuman undertakings. Tasks the very thought of which overwhelmed the common mind, seemed to provoke them to feats of dogged persistence. If there was an advantage to be gained from counting the grains of sand on a beach, the Murgans would set about doing it. It was as if they feared to leave stones unturned for others to look under. There was something compulsive about their behaviour, like the gnawing of trapped rats.

The first days of the search saw the old men stumbling back and forth with scarcely the strength to carry the books. Dazed and confused by the unaccustomed activity they bumped into each other and frequently forgot what they were supposed to be doing. But gradually the work settled into a productive pattern. In five days they had gone through fifteen galleries. With a shock of realisation Small worked out that in six months they could cover half the city.

There could be no doubt that most of the ancient librarians were being transformed by the whole experience. The food the Murgans provided, though never again so varied or plentiful as on that first evening, was adequate and supplied regularly. It strengthened bodies for the walk to and from the galleries and the endless carrying of books. It was the first regular exercise that most had ever done. They ate with appetite and slept untroubled sleep. The sudden and intense social activity connected with work in the galleries was like a physician's tonic to men long accustomed to solitary and sedentary lives. Lethargic shuffling bundles of raggy robes soon had a spring in their step and a brightness and intelligence in their faces. They became animated and their characters began to emerge. In short it constituted a revival little short of the miraculous. They worked with a will and were innocently grateful, just as the Murgans had planned. For a few of course it had all come too late: too far gone to respond, they wandered off and continued to waste away.

It might have been possible to admire the Murgans for their industry, perseverance and even their altruism, were it not that their single-minded pursuit of their goal was just that: single minded. From the start Puttfark thought that replacing the books in their places on the shelves was a superfluous waste of time. When Small protested that the books must be replaced, two of the most infirm and confused librarians had been reluctantly assigned to the task. After that all pretence of leaving the galleries as they found them was completely abandoned.

Because every seventh day was dedicated to the official Murgan deity, work in the galleries ended for the week as twilight fell on the eve of Sa'than's day. The ancient librarians were marched off by the guards to the refectory. Small's own importance as a linguist was acknowledged by the privilege of being able to make his own way to and from the galleries. As the tramp of feet and the murmurings of the old men faded away, he heard activity in the next room. Curious he went to see and found Old frantically gathering manuscript rolls, tablets and books into his arms from the table. When he saw Small he let them all slump back onto the tabletop.

"Small, it's hopeless, just hopeless. How can we possibly know where they all came from? What if the One were to come now? He would never be able to find the manuscript. Not any more. All order and arrangement is lost. It is as if the Library is stricken by the old man's disease of bewilderment and misplaced memory."

Small put a hand on the old man's shoulder. "I have been thinking about the Library." he said. "When it was first thought of it was in order to preserve important but dangerous truths. Only one book was really important. The rest were only accumulated to distract the casual reader. I do not believe that even King Holman himself realised what the Library would become; how it would grow into the Book-city. It is like the oyster. A tiny grain of sand sticks in the animal's bowels and round it grows a pearl of great price. The manuscript is only a grain of sand. When I think of all the great and wonderful literature in this place, I cannot believe that it is all just a dark cloak for a fugitive. I think that all these books are worth saving. I think that the Library is more important than any one manuscript, whatever it may be. If the price of preserving the Library is to lose the manuscript forever, then so be it."

Old shook himself free of Small's hand. "What are you saying? Without the manuscript the Library would be just a meaningless heap of words. And anyway, how do you know that this mysterious book they are looking for is not the manuscript itself?"

"I have also thought about that. But how would we know? We don't know where it is or what it is. It might be on this desk. It could be anywhere: it might be nowhere. Can we really be so sure that in all the centuries it has never yet been found and taken?"

Old opened his mouth to speak but then thought better of it and lapsed into silence. Some minutes later he spoke again. "You must find it. You must find the manuscript before they do. Nothing is more important."

Small was dumbfounded. "How can I do that?" he said.

"I don't know. But you are young, you have intelligence, you know the Library. You must find the manuscript and read it, only then will we know what to do and what is important. The paths through the book-maze are still there, but the Murgans are obliterating them. If they cannot find what they are looking for they will destroy everything. They might do it even so. It is their way."

"You ask too much of me. It is impossible."

"The Murgans don't think so. You admire them so much; perhaps you should take a leaf out of their book and be as positive as they are. You must at least try. There are paths and ways through these books that connect the thoughts of those long dead each to each. I always imagined Alligor as a spider's web. The spider does not set out to create a beautiful pattern. Every structuring thread is laid according to a blind instinct to connect, to catch and to hold. Neither do the flies perceive the fatal and invisible design. But when the light catches the threads, the whole is at once visible; all the shining threads lead the eye to a central point. Light has this mysterious quality of ordering chaos. The scratches on a scoured metal plate seem completely random yet when a candle is held close they all form circles around the reflected flame."

"What are you trying to say?"

"The light of understanding, if it is bright enough, can not only reveal hidden patterns, it can even impose order where there is only chaos. In short, nothing can withstand the full power of the human intellect consistently applied. In past times young librarians were much more rigorously exercised. They were hard pressed by able minds. But out of the softness of many hearts, you Small were allowed free rein and much leisure. Your mind has never been properly tried. Now we shall see if you can awake your mind and put it to work. You say that all the books are equal. Not so. Otherwise there could be no meaningful arrangement. Real composition is about unequal things and one thing being more important than all the rest. Here is your mission. Find the book."

Silence descended. Old resumed his helpless shuffling of the chaos of pages and volumes on the table. Small mumbled his leave-taking and headed for the Eastern Galleries. He had no intention of spending another night imprisoned in the refectory. He thought of going up onto the roof but then changed his mind. He would go to the Lion Cabinet. The chances of a single assassin being able to stumble upon a single boy in the labyrinthine architectural hive of the Book City were not good, but even so he took elaborate precautions against being followed. He doubled back, took intricate detours, hid and waited. No-one was following him.

The carved lions still snarled at the afternoon sun streaming in through the windows. It was as if the original builder had sought to guard his books against the seductive light of the decadent day. *Hic sunt leonis*, he seemed to have wanted to say, and yet here, at least in this tiny room, there had been nothing at all; an empty cupboard in an empty room filled only with the all conquering sunlight.

Small bolted the door and flopped into his bed. He drew his knees up to his chest. He felt tired. Not the overpowering fatigue which is the reward of those who labour long and well, but the paralysing lassitude which overtakes those whose tasks seem hopeless and endless. A chill wind of evening blustered at the window opening. The summer was ending. The setting sun shone out bright and hard from under grey and rainless clouds. There was only one cure for the way he felt. Small pulled his threadbare bedding around his legs and picked up one of his books.

Nights in the Gardens of Old Babylon was the perfect evening book. It was a book of Autumnal reflection, of looking back on a full life, the poetry of a golden age. Almazzar's Babylon was the capital of an old civilization slipping into that comfortable decadence which would eventually atrophy its heart. Almazzar had captured the essence of the city that never sleeps, the big ripe fruit, the beacon of nations, the heart of all darkness. Day and night its streets and alleys heaved with a greedy and atavistic multitude. But up where Almazzar sat on the pinnacle of the great stepped pyramid which symbolised the world mountain, the incessant noise of the city was faint and faraway, like the black murmur of diseased blood in the head of a man with fever. Small loved to imagine the antediluvian city made from unfired clay, notorious as the great Harlot of the Nations.

The hearth fires that feed her hungry children
Cloak the city in a blue veil that is her only robe.
A thousand lamps sparkle like sequins, mirroring the stars which
spangle the heavens.
Babylon the Great takes her ease in the cool of evening
Her face is in the sun a beacon to the nations, her veiled body is a
shadow on the plain.

The poem was divided into seven cantos and described a ritual ascent of the great central ziggurat which dominated the city. Each step of the mountainous edifice was a wide terrace planted as a garden of paradise. The rare and beautiful trees, shrubs and herbs spilled over the terrace edges and hung down in swags and festoons. As the pilgrim gained each successive level, he divested himself of the layers of his material life; badges of rank and fine clothes, weapons, servants and slaves on one level; memories and habits on another; on the fourth level law and justice ceased to operate; all duty and religious ritual ceased on the fifth, "here", he wrote cryptically, "we deliver our children into the hands of time"; on the sixth level the pilgrim took leave of lovers and companions of sensual pleasure, the temple prostitutes and venal neophytes with whom he had shared the revels of the ascent. Then came the descent into the dark heart of the ziggurat, the fearful narcotic death and grateful spiritual rebirth of the 'purified' soul. This ritual was too secret to be revealed in any book, but its power was evident in the faces of the initiates as they ascended from their erstwhile tomb and into the light of a new dawn.

Almazzar's image of that holy ziggurat rising above the filth, squalor and degradation of the streets had always intrigued and fascinated Small, but it was Babylon, the greatest market in the world, which really caught his imagination. Here was a wealth of description: foods of every sort; rare fruits and exotic meats; quenching drinks from the melted snows of winter and fiery draughts stilled into volatile flammability; perfumes, philtres and potions enough to provoke or suppress any passion; slaves for every purpose; slaves of every age, sex and race; blond with lapis eyes like the sea gods and dark like ebony idols oiled with unguents; giants and dwarves; cripples and athletes; infants and grandfathers; miracles of craftsmanship in both metals and woods, precious or common, tortured, beaten, twisted and carved into an infinity of fantastical shapes; fruit and leather, coral and silver, everything from apes to ivory, from armour to ordure, all was for sale. Like the ruined twin towers of Moloch, built to reach Heaven and destroyed by who knows what mighty force, Babylon was the very image of vanities and appetites which could never be sated. Small wished he could have seen the great harlot of the nations for himself. Even though the luxury and barbarous excess was rooted in poverty and putridity so profound that its inhabitants had deified the filth itself by inventing Beelzebub, as Lord of the fat black flies which polluted every clean thing and plagued everything which lived in it: even though Almazzar had described it as an evil and iniquitous place: from the first time Small read the book he had ached to be in that teeming throng just for one day.

It was obvious that the poet had been torn between a horrified fascination with the life in the streets where every form of vice and human iniquity was practised with varying degrees of blatancy, and a deep and abiding respect for the vibrant intellectual and spiritual speculation which it provoked in him. Not for nothing was Babylon known as the nursery of religions. Almazzar was perhaps the first to realise that no great books could be written in Paradise. What was it, he asked, about the nature of literature and art which made them vital in times of injustice and tyranny, and moribund in times of justice and contentment? Like many before him Almazzar compared the pursuits of the soul with those of the body. Was not the soul of the artist like a lover pursuing his beloved? And was great love not a passion, and were not the passions the symptoms of struggle and discord between reason and appetite?

In Babylon writing and religion were almost one. They had not invented the art but they knew it for the divine gift that it was. The Mesopotamian gods did not bring magic swords or eternal life. They came bearing clay tablets written with right words. These divine laws, proverbs and aphorisms were gratefully received, but the Babylonians were a nation of merchants. Their wealth was based on written records, treaties, accounts, laws, contracts, receipts and payments. The written law which guaranteed religion also sanctified the business contract. In their gratitude the Babylonians gave their best writing back to their gods. They did not know rhyme and metre, but their

131

hymns and chants were made vivid by means of repetitions, parallels, similes, metaphors, choruses and refrains. They made Poetry a proper sacrifice to the gods. It became the language of the gods and the guarantee of divine inspiration. Old even thought that their religion was an antediluvian prophecy of the coming of the Divine Author.

On the seventh level of the ziggurat Almazzar had renounced his favourite courtesan with a final song. Now that Small had been in the company of women and felt the power of their music, he began to realise how deeply felt this parting had been and why he had been moved to write his lyric:

Dance to the beat of her drum
That virgin never entered or possessed
Dance to the beat of her drum
That harlot who sold herself in the market place
Dance to the beat of her drum
That queen who ruled the markets of the world
Dance to the beat of her drum
In whose name argosies crossed the oceans
Dance to the beat of her drum
At the sound of her name a thousand sons left home to seek her out
Dance to the beat of her drum
A speaker of many tongues
A mother of many religions whose prodigal offspring squandered
their inheritance and denied their birth
Dance to the beat of her drum
For all men must take her, leave her and go on
And her name is Babylon.
Dance to the beat of her drum

Women, music and poetry: now that he had experienced all three, Small realised that they engendered a similar excitement and seemed tangled up in each other's existence. These mysterious affinities gave him a sense of baffled wonder that was not unpleasant.

From the summit of the ziggurat where the seven stony idols caught the sunlight Almazzar looked down upon that city of appetite with all its brawling and posturing, animal coupling, gluttonous feasting, frenzied acquisition. He wondered at the equally fierce promptings of the appetites of the soul which it engendered. Where the man in the street caught at the faithless harlot who sold everything and gave nothing, the artist chased a goddess ever virgin in the careless hunt perpetual, who allowed no liberties, never surrendered her virtue and yet rewarded her suitors handsomely.

Babylon was no more. This much Small knew. Almazzar had seen in the city of cities a blown flower. He had seen the worm in the heart of the rose. All worldly beauty was a peak or a high point followed by inevitable decline and decay. Only the beauty of ideas was eternal and even that had to be guarded with unceasing vigilance. Babylon had blossomed in the sun and fallen so quickly that the ships of distant nations, loaded low with luxuries, still called to trade for years afterwards. They found only desolation; a city of dried clay dissolving back into mud; a resting place for shepherds; their campfires aromatic with the cedar beams of fallen palaces.

By the time the light failed, Small still felt restless and excited. There was more to life, more to poetry than even he had suspected. It was like the dancing girl in his dream; ever beckoning but always out of reach. He was in the mood for a quest; for an adventure. He made up his mind to rescue Velik from the assassin. He lay awake for some time listening to the wind moaning around the eaves of the Book City and fell asleep thinking about the Great Gale and all the changes it had seemed to herald.

The morning came hard, bright and cold. The wind from the night before still buffeted its way across the rooftops and ruffled the open book on Small's bed. Awakened by the lifting of the pages, he closed the book and put it back in its place. His empty stomach prompted him to action. He would find Velik. He swung himself out of bed, closed the cupboard doors and set off. The trail of bloodstains had darkened into invisibility. But Small was able to find his way partly by following the footmarks in the dust and partly from memory. The whole journey seemed shorter this time but the dark gallery which the spiders had made their own still filled him with horror. He screwed his courage to the task by telling himself that there was no risk, but that danger was, in any case, a defining element of the adventure he was embarked upon. He hurled himself down the dark tunnel before the timorous and rational side of his being had time to point out the contradictions in all this.

The librarian's room was as he had left it, except that a cloud of fat black flies rose from the blood-caked bedding as he entered. Behind its door the garden lay silent and serene in his mind's eye. It was still dangerously attractive and he felt strongly the pull of it as he turned away. For a long time he crouched with his eye to the crack in the hinged bookshelves. Only when he felt satisfied that there was nobody in the gallery beyond did he pull the lever and push his way through the secret doorway. Opening the catch from the other side was not as simple. Small had to strip two entire shelves of their books before he discovered both components of the opening mechanism. He smiled inwardly when he realised that the catches were operated by pushing two books back onto them. The first was a boxed manuscript of *The Use of Ornament* by Niksur and the second *The Secrets of the Grammar* a scroll cut into leaves and bound in ivory plates. Carefully he replaced all the books, resisting the temptation to read Niksur's fascinating treatise only because it was written in 'gergo', an infuriating allusive script more like a word game than a language.

Bars of blinding sunlight slanted into the galleries as he passed through them to get to the stairs. Ordinarily this would have been a comfort, but here in the assassin's domain it was a complication. The brighter the sunlight, the blacker the shadow. In the library every gallery, every shelf, every book, every manuscript and every one of its leaves had its shadow. The simple presence or absence of light and its infinite gradations created forms not only in the eye but also in the mind. There were stories about the things which lurked in the shadows of Alligor: ghosts, incubi, djinni. Even after a lifetime in the gloomy book-rookery, Small still found some dark corners immanent with unspeakable menace. The library at night was a world of the memory passable only to those who knew her well. It also became a world of the imagination. Any glimpse of movement in the shadows was heart-stopping. But as the authors never tired of saying, 'without shadow nothing could be as clearly seen'. That is why shadows are said to be the very essence of the maker's art, indeed they are the art itself.

Then Small remembered *The Mirror of Almeira*. When Amatis had been hunted and tempted to hide himself he had thought deeply about the nature of sunlight and shadow. There are shadows which are a sanctuary and a place of security; a hiding place from real daylight fears: there are also shadows which are themselves a threat; shadows which conceal nameless terrors; but there are also shadows whose fearful contents are only in the mind. You can be safe in the shadows but then you must always hide from the light. Just as Old had said, every form of refuge has its price and the strongest fortress has the smallest windows The light is a tempter. Precious things can be placed in the shadows for safe keeping. The thief will not be tempted to steal what he cannot see. The rich man will not covet what is kept hidden from his sight. The poor man will not feel the want of what he is kept in the dark about. The tyrant will not censor what he cannot detect. Amatis realised that the way you use the shadows, determines whether you are the hunter or the prey.

There is an instinct which every animal seems to possess that it can feel when it is being watched or hunted. Even the tiniest of animaliculae expresses its anxiety in its behaviour when it feels itself present in the awareness of another. Small heard nothing. No doors slammed or creaked. Nor did he see anything move in the shadows or freeze in the light, but as he made his way towards Velik's room his footsteps became softer his hearing more acutely tuned. Somewhere deep in his being he felt the infinitesimal pressure of an active intelligence bent upon him.

The cat was sleeping. Even in sleep his muscles tensed for dream pounces, his claws flexed and retracted and his teeth gleamed through a lip curled to bite. Without any natural enemies the cats of Alligor had developed all their predatory instincts to the highest degree. The slightest of vibrations was enough to bring Sardanapalus from the edge of sleep. The slightest of movements, though forty paces distant in the shadows at the end of the gallery, and he was completely awake and alert, his eyes widening into dark transparent mirrors.

Rottko had known that Velik's visitor would return. He did not know yet where the old man hid himself, but he had worked out where the best place was to intercept anyone moving around in this part of the ancient rats' nest. His instincts were as sharp as any cat's. He felt Small's presence in the gallery as if it was a change in the wind. It was like a pressure on his senses. He smiled to himself and moved silently to his chosen place of ambush.

Sardanapalus had seen black birds before. He had even seen them inside the galleries. Crows and ravens squabbled with rivals and nested in neglected bookcases. None of their offspring ever lived to fly further than where Sardanapalus was waiting for them. Now he did not stop to sharpen his claws on any volumes of ornithology. He saw only plumpness in motion and the tantalizing tail feather behind a distant shelf. The ancient compulsion to stalk, to catch, to bite, to rend and tear overmastered him and corrupted all his other instincts.

Small felt the menace becoming more and more tangible with every step he took. Soon he was only moving forward one bookstack at a time; every sense straining; his whole will marshalled against the desire to flee back where he came from. By the time he reached the last gallery before the stair he was almost paralysed with the sense of threat.

Rottko heard the stealthy movements in the shadows and allowed his mouth to straighten into a brief smile of triumph. His hand went to his belly and found the comforting firmness of his dagger hilt. He tested the edge of the weapon with his thumb but only out of habit: it was always sharp. He froze as he caught his first glimpse of his victim. A young boy! He would have to be careful. Boys could be slippery as eels. Running through the eventualities in his mind he adjusted his plan of attack.

Sardanapalus saw the tail feather stop jiggling. It was a moment he knew well. Apprehension of danger held the prey immobile, hoping it had not been seen, but poised for flight if it had. The cat balanced itself: rump swaying, tail switching gently, eyes fixed wide with the intoxication of total absorption. He measured the gap and savoured the moment. The slightest quiver of a muscle by his prey would trigger his attack.

Small was dry-mouthed with fear. Twenty paces had never seemed so far. Stealth was no longer relevant. Retreat might be as dangerous as advance. He steeled himself for a dash to the stair.

Rottko could see the boy: knew what he was thinking: prepared himself for the disabling lunge.

On the shelf in front of Small's face was a large book of leaves bound between wooden boards. A parchment label had been tucked under the bindings: *The Shield of Manly Virtue*. His fingers closed around the edges of the book. He scarcely knew why but he felt reassured by its familiar weight. He lifted it from the shelf, clasped it to his body and then ran for the door.

Rottko moved like a striking snake.

Sardanapalus pounced.

Small saw the shine on the blade as it stabbed at his thigh. He thrust the book at it and let go when he felt the impact. There was no second strike. Half-blinded, Rottko stumbled around in uncomprehending agony his eyelids stapled to his eye sockets by eight sharp claws. The largest cat west of the mountains sat firmly on his head like a furry cap with a puzzled expression. The more Rottko tried to shake it off the tighter the cat held on with its claws. The assassin tried to stab at his tormentor but the point of his dagger was embedded in the wooden book cover. He flailed desperately with his strangely leaden arm.

Sardanapalus adjusted to his unexpected situation very quickly. From being rigid with shock he was now tensed for flight. As Rottko reeled close to a bookstack the cat leaped away, raking the assassin's face from scalp to chin as he did so.

"God ... God ... Goddinhell!" Rottko fled too, clutching his streaming eyes, colliding with the stacks and sending books and rolls to the floor in clouds of dust.

Sardanapalus scampered away to find a safe place where he could lick his dignity back into shape in private and muse over the strange taste on his claws. Small pounded on Velik's door and almost fainted with relief when it was opened to him.

"You came back!" The old man's face lit up with pleasure. Small pushed him aside and threw the bolt.

"You seem a little agitated."

"He tried to stab me!" Small began to tremble as his body drained off the excitement that had propelled him up the stairs.

Eventually Velik managed to sit the boy down with a cup of fig wine. "This will stop you trembling."

Small drank the wine in one gulp. "I came to rescue you!"

"And instead you have led the assassin to my door and I have rescued you."

"You don't understand. Puttfark says that if the assassin cannot find the book he is looking for he may well burn down the whole library."

"The whole library? Is it possible? This is a big place. Can you not just find the book and give it to them? Which book is it?"

"That's just it. Nobody knows. I wish I could just ride away from this stupid place and never come back."

"This stupid place," Velik looked horrified. "Do you know where you are young man? Do you know what this place is? No? I will tell you where you are. You are inside the mind of the world. Everything is here: the wisdom, the foolishness, the memories, the hopes, the fears, the beliefs. If you are unwise enough to search for such things, you will even find those unspeakably evil impulses which lurk in the dark corners of the human consciousness. Nothing is so esoteric or mysterious that it cannot be found. Go down a corridor, climb up a stair and there you will find it.

"Dig deep enough here and you will uncover the roots of the world, and if you find the roots you will know the tree and its fruit. The rustling leaves of this tree are made of parchment or paper or leather. On them you will read the mountains and the seas, the rivers and the clouds, the herbs of the earth, the birds of the sky, beasts of field and wood. You will read all the things made by human hands: cities and roads and ships; clever machines and even more wonderful inventions such as words and symbols. And beyond: the topmost leaves try to catch the stars and reach out for the infinite mysteries of the universe.

Reflected on them you will see gods and angels and things unknowable. And we? Like little finches we hop from twig to twig and try to grasp the whole from a sampling of tiny parts, not realizing that trying to understand the world is like trying to read a thought in the mind of God."

"Puttfark says that Alligor is a mausoleum, a necropolis." said Small.

"In a sense he is right," Velik said, "This is a city of ghosts and each book is a sarcophagus. But when we raise the lid all those dead selves live again. Each time we open a book we achieve a victory over Death. The author speaks again from beyond the grave and we ourselves are able to live many lives in one. Thus Alligor can also be seen as a symbol of life itself. It has but one way in and one way out. We enter as children knowing nothing. We leave as children but knowing just how little we know. Thus it is said that a wise man discovers his ignorance. Only a fool regards himself as wise."

Small thought this last remark was rather pessimistic. Was Velik just another old man trying to put him in his place? "Tell me Velik," he asked, "Have you ever ridden a horse?"

Velik put one fist into his waistband and thumped the other onto the table. He fastened his gaze onto Small. "Ridden a horse? I have ridden hundreds of horses. I have ridden camels, mules, donkeys, even once upon a time on an elephant. I have sailed the great ocean in fishing boats, dhows, galleys, triremes and quinqueremes. I have seen the banks of crimson oars splinter in the shock of battle. I have been becalmed in seas of glass, driven before storms on waves as high as mountains, attacked by pirates, rammed, shipwrecked and washed up on desert shores."

Small was impressed. Here was a man with knowledge of the real world. "This sounds to me like a full and exciting life," he said, "and yet you choose to live here in the great library like a hermit. What brought you here? Why do you stay?"

Velik's expression softened as a faraway look appeared in his eyes. "That, my young friend, is a tale that no one has ever heard," he said, "And yet the instant that I set eyes upon you I realized that if the tale were ever to be told, then it must be told now and to you. Seeing you made me realise that my story was nearly at its end. The lamp must be handed on to another lest it flickers and dies." He adopted an orator's stance and started his tale.

"When I was a young man such as you are, I found myself possessed of an insatiable desire to know the truth about everything. Being young and in the springtime of life, the stories that held my attention often concerned members of the female sex. I read of the noble Scheherazade who risked her life and saved the citizens by her quick-wittedness and story-telling prowess. I also read of the evil Princess Liboce who ruled her country without a husband from her palace by the river and had her lovers thrown into the swirling waters when she grew tired of them. Often I heard wonderful love songs and poems describing women who were veritable goddesses: beautiful, clever, loyal, strong and wise. Naturally I wanted to meet such a one. "Where are these wonderful women to be found?" I asked. "Why, they are all around you!" I was told. Now I had already investigated the female population of my home town very thoroughly. No such women had I ever seen. Nor was this surprising since it was the local custom to keep young maidens incarcerated in the family dwelling, uneducated in anything but sewing and preparing food. Once married, their domestic duties filled their time. In my country a woman who had read a book was something monstrous and unnatural.

'I was however convinced that these women must exist somewhere or else how could images of them have lodged so firmly in the minds of men? And so I began to look for clues in books and writings. I sought out wise men and engaged them in discussion. I befriended rich men so that I might devour their libraries. I became a collector of books. It was through my collecting that one day I heard tell of a man who bought and sold ancient manuscripts in a distant city.

'The city was called Kubala. It was very ancient and beautiful. It stood on a hill and its white buildings flashed in the sun. Even the streets were made of stones which had been fitted perfectly each to each by skilful masons. I found the bookseller's shop and introduced myself. The bookseller had gained much wisdom from all the books which had passed through his hands. He was glad that he could talk to a fellow lover of books. After several days during which we talked of many, many things. I told him of my quest for the woman in the works of the poets and philosophers. He listened politely to me although I felt that he found my tale amusing. When I had finished talking he asked me why it was that I sought this woman. I answered that in the first place I wanted to know if such a woman existed and if so what she was like. The bookseller said that to seek such a woman only out of curiosity might not be sufficient reason. I protested saying that more than being merely curious; I wanted to hold a position in the court of such a one. Upon hearing this, the bookseller chastised me for my pride and materialism. If my quest was pursued only from prurience and ambition then I would not get far. On hearing this I was deeply offended and told him that my quest was of such deep and abiding interest to me that he did me great injustice to belittle my motives thus. In fact so strong was my desire to seek out the woman highly blessed that I would rather say that I did it for love of the woman, since no other word seemed fit. This impressed the bookseller because he said that if that was truly the case, then I was worthy of the task I had embarked upon. My efforts would surely be rewarded. After all this I was convinced that the bookseller knew more about the woman than he was willing to say.

'Now each morning when I made my way from my lodgings to the bookseller's shop, I liked to vary my route. Kubala was a beautiful place cris-crossed by winding alleys which led to exquisite squares and courtyards in which fountains played and vines hung down from roof gardens. Many lesser alleys led off each little square and many a time a flight of steps and a glimpse of sculpture beckoned me to explore the city. Who could resist? Every square was different from all the others. Sometimes there were open-fronted workshops: a lamp-maker, a bell-foundry, makers of astrolabes and musical instruments. Sometimes there were taverns or shops among the houses. Some of the houses had elaborate balconies, others carved shutters. All the houses had overhanging eaves supported on rafter ends carved and painted with great fantasy. Some had been shaped into the forms of dragons, others naked men. In wet weather the rainwater from the roofs spewed out through the mouths of animals made of lead or wood.

'Those old time builders believed that when you built a house or a palace, you stole a piece of the green earth and of the blue sky which would have otherwise have been there for the enjoyment of passers-by, be they men or gods. That was why they sought so skilfully to ornament their buildings for the delight of all who saw them, so that the passer-by should smile on the building and not be tempted to utter a curse on the house or its inhabitants. For indeed who could tell what effect all those heaped up curses might have? Thus had Kubala become a beautiful city. So you see when I walked through the city I did not look down at my sandals, but usually I looked up at the buildings. That is how I came to see her. I had seen the palace before. It had a balcony with shutters intricately pierced and patterned. On this day the street was busy, but I noticed that one of the shutters was open. Through it I glimpsed a lady with beautiful eyes who smiled at me from behind her veil. Modestly she showed the palm of her upraised hand in greeting and invitation. The window closed. I stood in the street staring at the house. My heart beat faster. I looked around me. No-one else had seen her. I was not even sure of what I had seen.

'From that day forward I always passed by her house, but it was a long time before she showed herself again. The next time she beckoned to me with her hand. When I moved closer she whispered a few words to me which were difficult to understand because of the thick veil she was wearing. Yet I was certain that she wanted me to return the next day. You can imagine the state I was in. I could not eat or sleep. I seemed to be possessed by a kind of madness. I was certain that this lady was the object of my quest. My Imagination swooped and soared in anticipation. The next day I found the door to her palace ajar and an aged servant conducted me to the inner courtyard where the lady was waiting for me. This time her veil was sheer and transparent and through it I could see the face of a woman no longer youthful but not yet ravaged by age. It was a face of calm repose and yet beautiful enough to lay a glamour on any man who beheld it. As she worked at a tapestry, we talked for hours: of myths, their origin and meaning, and of all the other mysteries which grip the human mind. We spoke of the elusive nature of wisdom itself, like a maiden who makes her lover pursue her, running further into the wood each time he approaches. Finally she hinted at the existence of one greater than herself who she followed.

'The following day I returned, hoping to resume our conversation. Imagine my surprise when I found the house shuttered and empty. The neighbours told me that the lady and her household had left at first light for parts unknown. Despite her having lived next door for several months, they did not know any more of her than that her name was Sophia and that she came from the East. I was devastated. Even with such a short acquaintance I had thought myself as her confidante. Now I realised how little I really knew of her.

'My friend the bookseller listened to my tale of woe with great interest and sympathy. When I had finished he confessed that in his youth he had once had a very similar experience, also in a distant place. It might even have been the same person, in which case it was clear that she was no ordinary woman at all since she seemed not to have aged in forty years. In his opinion the lady was one of the immortals, perhaps even a goddess in disguise, but certainly a being who had lived many lifetimes. This would account both for her great wisdom and also her nomadic and hermit-like way of life. I determined on the spot that I should not rest until I had found the divine lady. Both the bookseller and myself agreed that the best way to do this would be to first learn her true identity, since that would tell us about her family, her haunts and habits.

'To this end I travelled both far and wide earning my living as a storyteller and sage. I visited every land known to ..."

Small interrupted him, "Did you visit Murga?"

Velik's countenance became clouded. "Why would you want to know about such a place?" he asked.

"Did you?" said Small.

"Yes, but I curse the day I ever heard that name."

"Will you tell me truly what it was like?" said Small earnestly.

Velik rubbed his chin and looked at the floor. Then he began to speak again. "I had heard of a rich and powerful country whose symbol was a woman. The traders and mercenaries of this country seemed to be everywhere I went, and yet their homeland was far west of the mountains and across the gulf of oceans. From time to time I met people grown wealthy on "business" as they call it, who could not praise this country, which I soon learned was called Murga, highly enough. For these it was the key to the riches of the world and the natural home of "freedom". Everyone else I asked seemed reluctant to talk about Murga in case something bad happened to them. But what or how I never could find out."

"That is just as Old told me!" said Small.

"It was all most intriguing and so I determined to visit Murga myself. If this was indeed a goddess who struck out at her enemies from far away, then I needed to know about her. I crossed the mountains and took ship for the main port of Murga which was called New Adam. Never have I kept company with such a set of evil and contentious people as were on that ship. Only through luck did I survive that floating hell where the strong preyed upon the weak. Each morning pools of blood on the deck bore witness to violent transactions in which gold or food changed hands. I noticed that the wealthiest passengers had employed bodyguards to ensure a safe passage for themselves and their goods. I earned a little money from storytelling, but most of the time I tried to melt into the crowds on the lower deck. You can imagine the relief I felt when after weeks at sea, land was finally sighted.

'From faraway the Murgan port of New Adam looked like a giant's crown, but as we drew closer, the tall buildings looked more like broken fangs in the maw of a dragon. To enter the harbour the ship had to sail between the legs of a colossal statue of a naked whore carved from stone. In one hand the figure carried a scourge of bronze and in the other a full purse. Words were carved upon the base of the statue which read:

Come all who will. Come all ye dissatisfied, poor and worthless. Come all ye thieves and vagabonds, beggars and tramps. Come all ye bankrupts and debtors. Come all ye who have no good name. Come all ye of violent passion. Come all ye parent haters and neglecters of children. Come all ye loose women and unnatural men. Come all ye followers of strange and cruel religions. Come all ye traitors of men and betrayers of women. Come all ye that the world scourges, so that only ye love wealth and power; I will forge out of you a scourge for the whole world.

'The statue must have been hollow because I could see faces of people peering out of the eye sockets far above me. I asked a sailor what was the meaning of this figure. He told me that this was the symbol of Murga and it stood for freedom to do anything you wanted to. So revered was this statue that it was the ambition of every Murgan, once in their lives, to climb up and see the world through this woman's eyes.

'My relief on leaving the ship was short lived. Before I even left the waterfront I was robbed of what little money and food I had managed to earn on the voyage. As the gang of young cut-throats walked away, I shouted "Stop thief!" expecting honest citizens to aid me. Most ignored me completely. More than a few laughed openly.

'The long straight streets were filled with a mongrel throng who seemed to have assembled there from every corner of the earth. The first thing I noticed was that although clean, well-fed, and respectably dressed, every single person carried a half-concealed weapon. Both sexes, from the smallest infant to the oldest crone, never let their hands stray far from the hilts of their knives.

'Their buildings were tall and impressive in their bulk, but at street level they were forbidding and fortress-like. These buildings had neither art nor culture in their making, but were made up only of straight lines. Nor was there any art or fantasy employed in the openings for windows. Like the hatch grilles on slave ships, each rectangular aperture was identical to every other."

"How bizarre," said Small musingly.

"So I too thought at first." continued Velik, "But on such high buildings, no-one would see any ornament unless it was gross and gigantic. In any case no Murgan would have dared take his eyes off his neighbour to look upwards even for an instant."

"Do the Murgans not hate living in such hideous surroundings?" said Small.

"As with their stone whore it seems that they see the values of their society reflected in their architecture. All Murgans are supposed equal; therefore all have the same openings. The rich simply have more of them."

Small could not be sure if Velik was being ironic. "But if their makers of beautiful things are not employed on buildings, then what do they do?" he asked.

"That's just it! They do not have any true poets or artists as we would recognize them. It was something which perplexed me greatly whilst I was there. All over the known world I have held people in thrall with my storytelling, often I have felt the divine wind of inspiration carry my words to the audience, and yet in Murga the people seemed unable to pay attention for more than the time it takes a summer cloud to pass in front of the sun. It was not until I sampled their entertainment for myself that I understood why. Their dramatic artists concern themselves with only three things: lust, violence and sensation. In Murga any poet or dramatist is doomed to failure if he does not provide his audience with a regular and frequent succession of incidents of these sorts. Consequently, the entertainers vie with each other to provide ever more explicit and sensational happenings to excite the jaded appetites of their audiences. Murder and mutilation are so commonplace as to be unremarkable other than in the novelty of their commission. Nor do they stop short of portraying those sacred intimate moments between men and women which should be enacted only within the sanctuary of privacy. Indeed there is no act so foul or so perverse that they will not show it. They will go to any lengths to outdo each other and make their name. The Murgans still talk with admiration of one entrepreneur who pulled down the theatre on top of his audience for a final earthquake scene. Scores were injured, several died, but the man's reputation and his fortune were made."

Small's credulity was being sorely taxed, "This I cannot believe." he said. "This is surely some trick of your storyteller's art."

Velik hung his head. "If it is then I learned it in Murga. It is with great shame that I tell you that I sold my storyteller's soul there. I had to escape and storytelling was my only trade. I gave the Murgans what they wanted. I quickly became rich and well known. I was able to afford bodyguards, I was invited to the ugly houses of the high-born. I began to understand just how rich, how powerful and how dangerous these people really are. I know what you are thinking. How can a nation with so little culture and learning be a threat to all the ancient and noble peoples of the earth? But it is precisely their disregard for everything that all other nations hold dear or have ever valued in their past that gives them their terrible strength. I still cannot understand exactly how they destroy their rivals. But wherever I travelled their ways and customs were replacing all others.

'Once I dined with one of the wealthiest of them all. At one point I questioned his morality. It was not a word he had ever known. When I explained it to him he dismissed it as merely another set of chains such as slaves wear. "That is our strength," he declared, "In the battle for the world, we Murgans are free. All our opponents are trying to fight in chains. Some of them are chained to the land, some are chained to their past, some are chained to their families, some to their priests, some to each other, some to their god. Some tie themselves up in your morality. Only the Murgans have no chains at all."

Small had never heard such a depressing tale. His soul protested at such unremitting criticism. "Surely the Murgans must have some bond which holds them together." he said at last.

"Yes their common aim and purpose is in their appetites. Other nations might be driven by honour and glory, or by love of country or of family. But Murga is driven by appetite alone. Just as hyenas fight each other but hunt in packs, their appetites prompt the Murgans to unite. In Murga every appetite can be serviced instantly, at a price of course. They all dream of being rich enough to be able to satisfy instantly any desire that goads their senses, be it for food or drink or power or lust. That is the freedom that Murga offers her creatures. They are unstoppable. They will corrupt the world."

"This is a dark and compelling tale you spin, old man." said Small.

"Would that it were only a tale," answered Velik.

It was Small who broke the silence. "So the lady of Murga was only a whore of stone?" he said.

"Alas, even that would have been shameful enough," said the old man. "But whilst I lived amongst the Murgans I became aware that a far more sinister being held the females of Murga in her thrall. The Murgan women were loud in their cursing of the gods of the East as ignorant savages who would bind all women up in chains. All the mighty gods of thunder and storm and sea-wave, of light and starry darkness, they put aside like bankrupt husbands and abused them as wife-beaters and rapists. But in their unguarded moments I heard the women of Murga offer whispered supplication to a secret sovereign power. The name that escaped their lips was *Lilith*."

The old man paused for dramatic effect. Small was impressed but unenlightened. "Lilith? Who is that?" he asked.

"In Murga," Velik continued, "all knowledge is available at a price. I discovered that Lilith is thought to be one of the immortals. She was created at the beginning of the world as a perfect mortal being. Her beauty was unsurpassable, her mind as sharp as a scimitar. However such was her power that all men were captivated by her person. They became entangled in her golden-red tresses and quickly became her slaves. Thus she despised them all. This unhappy state of affairs had not been foreseen by the Great Maker and so he decided to remove her from mortal society. Despite being relieved of the burden of mortality, Lilith was not happy with the transformation. She was immortal but not a goddess. She had enjoyed wielding her power over mortal men. Also it had been foretold that she would be killed by one of her children. Since she was one of the original parents of the human race, all children were in a sense hers. This tormented her with doubt. She could no longer wield her power in the world itself, but because she existed on the borderline between the realm of the gods and the realm of mortals she found that she could intervene at that point where mortal life begins. The lady Lilith became the punisher of love, the preventer of life, the stifler of hope."

"I ...I don't understand," said Small.

"I say it plain. She is the slayer of innocent unborn babes; the patroness of untimely birth. She sees every new life as her potential assassin and conspires to prevent it."

Small was horrified. "This is some Murgan horror story you have been tricked into believing. I fear you have become like Splint and confuse your stories with your memories."

Velik said nothing for some time. Then he sat back in his seat and said, "You are an innocent. We will speak no more of that accursed place. But know this, I have not told you a fiftieth part of what I saw and heard in Murga: some things I will never tell; some things I wish I could forget."

There was something in Velik's manner of telling the tale that gave Small a chilling cognition that the tale was true. As the old man continued with his tale, his gift for storytelling shone through and his face became animated once more. Painted war galleys cut through sparkling turquoise waves until the bronze ramming prow splintered their crimson planks. Blood splashed onto polished decks or clouded the crystal sea with purpure. The shards of damascened blades flashed like fish as they sank to the ocean floor. But Small could not lose himself in the poetry. The fear that the Murgans had seduced him, had tricked him, had manipulated him, floated up through his mind like the corpse in the cistern. It hung there accusingly amongst the galley slaves still chained to their benches in the sunken wreckage at the bottom of Velik's memory. It lurked at his heels as Velik led him across the great sand sea in a caravan of camels to the windowless walls of the city on the barren plains. As the still youthful Velik entered the Great Gate of Alligor, the shadow of doubt slipped in with him.

"So you see, it was almost as if my footsteps had been directed to this place. Many times my life was spared when all around me perished. First on the ship when the pirates were slaughtering all my fellow passengers, I was knocked into the sea. In the sea I could not swim and yet a broken spar floated under my hand. Then the winds, notoriously fickle in their moods, chose to blow me to the beach. Finally to be plucked from the arid sands of the limitless Zahar and brought here, here of all places!"

"You speak of confusing stories with memories. I hardly believe it myself. Sometimes I feel as if I have always been here and my life in the world was just a dream. But then, I reach for my little pouch. And then I know for certain that my life had an Author." From the front of his robe Velik pulled a little pouch made of animal skin. It had drawstrings at its mouth. He tipped its contents onto the table. A jumble of unfamiliar objects rattled against the wood.

"What are they?" Small asked.

"This one is a sea shell which I found on the beach. I kept it for its beauty and to remind me of the charity of the sea. These four coins are from Murga, see the name and the device of an eye contained in a triangle. These represent the world I left behind. This one here is one of the living grains that the camel driver gave me and which eventually were to sustain my life and spirit. This last is a forged link from a chain used to fasten slaves to their benches. I must have picked it up on the ship. I keep it as a symbol of my moral duty."

By accident or design Velik had arranged the objects in a circle with the chain link at the centre. Now he scooped them all back into the pouch. "Ah!" he said, "Here comes Sardanapalus to remind us that it is time to eat."

Velik busied himself with dishes and beakers. He laid out strips of dried fish and fowl next to hard cakes and figs. The golden wine transformed this frugal fare into food fit for gods. The meal was short but satisfying. The wine seemed to make everything glow with a kindly light.

"So you never did find your divine lady?" Small asked.

"Do you really think that after I had already gone through so much that I could give up so easily?"

"You found her?"

"But of course I did!"

"Where did you find her?"

"Why, I found her right here in Alligor."

There was something mischievous in Velik's expression. Small was incredulous. "In Alligor?" he said, "But there have been no women here for at least a hundred years. The Murgans are the first anyone has seen."

Velik threw his head back in silent laughter. "Ha! Perhaps no-one saw her because they were not looking for her. Perhaps they did not look in the right place, or perhaps they saw her but did not recognize her for what she was."

Small was mystified. "You mean she was in disguise." He asked after a short pause.

"Oh this lady can appear in so many disguises that without her veil she usually passes unrecognized by anyone."

Small pondered on this revelation. He reminded himself that Velik was a self-confessed teller of tales; a professional inventor of falsehoods. There was only one way to be certain. "Velik," he asked, "I would very much like to meet this lady. Would that be possible?"

Velik waved his hand expansively. "I don't see any reason why not. She comes most mornings and evenings. Let us look at the weather outside." He moved to the window. "Yes, fine and clear. I expect her this evening."

Small was still convinced that there was a catch to this tale. "I am very curious to hear how you found her. Will you tell me the story?"

Velik slapped his knee noisily. "I said that I would and I shall."

"I have already told you of how I was plucked from the seashore by a caravan of camels. The captain of that caravan was a learned man. He was a lover of knowledge and carried a small collection of books about with him on his travels. Often in the cool of the morning he would face the new-born sun and chant a favourite poem. It was, he said, an offering to the Great Maker. He once told me that he was convinced that when the first men had witnessed the rising of the sun it must have been the beginning of all philosophy and all wisdom. During those long desert nights whilst the stars wheeled over our heads, we talked of wisdom, of books and of their meanings. So it was that we came to talk of the Book City. He told me that once he had picked up an old man who he found sitting by the roadside. This man told him that he had spent half his lifetime searching for wisdom in the Great Library of Alligor. He told the caravan captain all the world's wisdom was in that place and that the Library contained every book that there ever was. Every mystery, no matter how large, no matter how small, had been written about in its books. The more I heard about it the more I came to believe that if I wanted to pursue my quest, I must visit this library. I left the caravan some twenty leagues north of here and walked the rest of the way.

'I imagined that Alligor would be a bustling city with ample opportunities for a storyteller to earn a living. Alas I found it silent, deserted, abandoned and decayed, but with its treasures still there for all who cared about them. The caravan captain had given me a sack of grain as a parting gift; otherwise I should have starved to death in those first months. I planted some of the seed but mostly I lived by consuming my meagre store and a little foraging: wild fruits, birds' eggs, anything I could find. Eventually I settled here. There was water from the roof, figs, earth in which to plant my seeds and most important of all, this terrace open to the sky.

'Why did I not leave? The books had me in their grip almost from the first day. From time to time I was hungry, thirsty, cold, even lonely, but everywhere I looked I seemed to catch glimpses of my Lady Highly Blessed. Here she was mentioned, there described, in another place she was there but in disguise, in yet another she was being sought. Always and everywhere she was veiled, mysterious, yet always promising greater and yet greater revelations.

The days turned into weeks; the weeks into months; the months into so many years that it frightened me to count them. I had thought that I was learning more and more about my elusive lady, but then one day I realised that all I really knew about were her many disguises. She was Astarte, Ashteroth, Ishtar, Isis, Shiva, Athene. She was Kypris Queen, Typhon and Tiamat.

'It was about that time that something curious happened. My lust for books had lured me deeper and deeper into the Library: into subterranean rooms and galleries with thick walls and primeval furniture. Suddenly I came upon a room filled with manuscripts some of which were so old that they crumbled in my fingers. They were written in an ancient form which at first I had the greatest difficulty understanding. Luckily I had encountered similar tongues on my travels. Soon the ancient script was giving up its secrets to my eager eyes. And do you know? In all those books in that gallery there was not one single word written about my divine lady. Of course I checked over and over again, but not in that gallery, nor the next, nor the one after that could I find the slightest hint of her existence. Here was a conundrum that might have baffled a casual reader, but in thirty years I had come to understand the library: how it had been built and how it had grown to be what it was.

'I remembered that once, whilst on my travels out in the world, I had seen a wondrous thing. I came upon a high wall of rock caused by the earth shearing, tearing and thrusting upward. And embedded in that mighty cliff were the bones of beasts from earlier creations. Fierce dragons and gigantic unknown monsters lay crushed between the layers of the rocks: each successive creation laid above the one before to make a ladder of time in the stone. I saw that the whole cliff was a history book with each layer of remains as a chapter, each following the one before. Remembering this made me realise that the Book City also had a history and that it too was a history book for those who knew how to read it. The very earliest parts of the library were filled up with books collected in the very earliest years of the library's existence. Only when there was no space left were more galleries constructed. It was these very earliest galleries which I had stumbled upon, and in these were the very earliest books of all; some already ancient when the library was built. And in these books my lady did not appear. Suddenly I knew that there had been a time before men knew of this extraordinary lady. Then I knew what I was searching for."

Velik paused for rhetorical effect. Small asked the requisite question. "What was it you were searching for?"

"Why the accounts of her coming of course. And I did not have far to look. Her coming was noted in every land. It was recorded by every civilization which had writing. In fact the telling and re-telling of her story was considered of such importance that it became a religious duty. Accounts of her every movement were written on the orders of kings and emperors and the very wisest men of all struggled to describe what they had seen."

"And what had they seen?" asked Small, rather bewildered by the grandiose turn the tale had taken.

"The coming of my lady was the occasion of a battle in the heavens between the very gods themselves; a battle in which the world itself and everything in it was nearly destroyed. And everywhere the story was the same. The mighty warrior god ever crimson with rage who had held the supreme position in the heavens: he who was everywhere revered and worshipped by the strong and the powerful as heaven's bright star was challenged in his own domain by a newcomer. This newcomer appeared from nowhere, her bright shining hair flying out behind her as she crossed the heavens. A goddess of terrible beauty she was, brighter than the moon goddess, and even the sun god could not extinguish her brightness. As all the peoples of the world looked on, the mighty god of war was toppled from his throne by a goddess who at one time was a bull with horns and at another a flaming serpent. As they grappled together locked in a passionate embrace both fell from the heights of heaven. They came so close to earth that the terrifying steeds of the warrior god were clearly seen by mortal eyes for the first time. 'Terror' and 'Rout' men called them because of the great showers of stones which fell to earth in their passing. The goddess came so close that her horned crown could be seen atop her unbound hair. That was how men know her for a virgin for everywhere it is the custom for married women to bind up their hair. As she passed by, the goddess gathered up the oceans to her like a skirt and held them high as the mountains. The warrior god erupted and boiled with fire. He discharged thunderbolts and cast showers of black stones upon the earth with great force but even so he was overthrown and banished to a far corner of the heavens from whence he has never returned. So did Venus Ishtar usurp the throne of Marduk Ares. She sits in splendour and magnificence as Queen of Heaven whilst he glares malevolently from afar.

'Here on our insignificant world the mountains had shifted on their foundations, the seas had changed their levels and rushed over the land, whole nations and their cities had been utterly destroyed; even the very poles had changed places. The passage of the sun across the heavens was interrupted; the seasons were disordered so that no-one knew the times of planting and gathering. Plagues of foul pests swept across the lands. That …" Velik paused for breath and effect. "was the story of the coming of my lady."

Small was not sure how to interpret what Velik had said. "That is indeed a powerful story. But I have read these stories before. They are stories of the gods of peoples ignorant of the Great Author and those kinds of stories are intended to be understood in a different and more mysterious way than the stories you tell of your travels. Even I know this."

"That is quite right, young man." answered Velik, "But you know that in all made-up stories there may be a kernel of truth, like the stone in a plum, which remains in the mouth after the sweet soft pulp has been swallowed. Spit out that stone into fertile ground and a whole new tree might sprout from it."

Small thought about this. After a while he gave up. "I just don't understand what you are trying to say. You first spoke of the lady with the veil as a real person of ordinary size, who lived in an ordinary house, and was known to her neighbours. Now you tell me of a mighty goddess, a queen of heaven, big enough to shake the world. Can they both be the same person?"

With one of his characteristic theatrical gestures Velik sat forward in his seat and placed his elbow on the table. "If you remember," he said, "I started my quest by trying to find the original of the lady described in the works of the poets. The lady Sophia was but another type or image of that enigmatic original. No woman could read the works of the poets without being inspired with a will to such power and wisdom. The poetic idea of the all powerful female who could vanquish the warrior god and bind up the whole world in her hair, revealed to educated women a new idea of their potential which was not to be found in everyday life. Thus did the goddess of wisdom and beauty stamp her image on her acolytes like a seal on wax. Of course such women do not fit easily into the world as it is ordered by men, so to avoid the obvious perils of becoming a cynosure they tend to live in a manner both secretive and nomadic."

"So you are saying that ladies such as Sophia model themselves upon the images of the poets which are themselves a shadowing forth of a collision between worlds? Are the destructive motions of great lumps of rock in the heavens such a good model for women to copy?"

Velik laughed and twirled his moustache. "You have an innocent way of getting to the heart of things!" he said. "The natural world has ever been our model. Do not men do the same? What mighty warrior does not model himself on the fierce lion and wish they had its strength and courage. Yet proverbially it is the lioness who defends her cubs to the death, and is it not a simple matter for a woman with a bow to slay any lion? Look, you won't understand I know, but the love that a man feels for a woman is only as strong as the story that he tells himself about her. She may only be a mere woman, uneducated even, but let her give herself the right airs and graces and not reveal too much of who she really is and the man will convince himself she is a goddess. Men like to believe that love is a great power, a divine thing, so that their great foolishness over women is explained. Like many other things the feelings of men and women are shaped by stories they hear and stories they tell themselves."

Velik glanced at the window opening. "The light is fading." he said, "It is nearly time for you to meet our lady in person."

In preparation for her appearance he began to carry various pieces of arcane apparatus out on to the terrace. Getting down onto his haunches he squinted up into the piece of water pipe and made adjustments. Then the crystal pebbles on their metal rods were carefully aligned in conjunction with it. Finally satisfied with his arrangements he grunted and said, "What do you think of that?"

Small let himself be adjusted like the water pipe and put his eye close to the nearest glass pebble as Velik directed.

"What do you see?"

"I see the horned moon!"

"Just so! But that is not the moon, those horns are the crown of the goddess Venus Ishtar."

"But it appears so large."

"The glass pebbles cause the light to swell. They make small images larger. Here! If I turn the apparatus towards the Moon herself look what you can see." Velik swung the pipe around and re-aligned the pebbles. Small squatted down once again and held his eye to the pebble.

"Her face is like a stained map that I once saw, but it is scarred and pocked with circles. This is indeed a wonder. Where did you get this magical device?"

"When I was searching for the stories of the coming, I found a book with an ornamented cover. It had many precious jewels worked into the metal of its binding, jewels such as thieves and naughty people would prise out and steal, but two of the jewels were plainly worthless, mere glass pebbles. Only when I read the book did I find that these were the most precious jewels of all, made from purest meteoric glass and ground to perfection by secret arts. Such is the nature of true ornament, that it can lift you above the everyday and into the heavens."

Small was impressed but also perturbed by Velik's revelations. He took his eye away from the apparatus and addressed his host. "So these religions that guide and direct the conduct of so many mortals are only the work of silver tongued liars?"

"Do not be so hard on them. Those early scribes and poets did not have the words with which to describe the catastrophic events which they had witnessed. Any man can only describe the unknown in terms of the known. The planets were generally believed to be gods, only when they came closer did their true nature become apparent. The scribes had no clue of celestial mechanics. Their main task was to make sure that what had happened was recorded and remembered. What had happened once could happen again. There would always be wise men who could penetrate beyond the veil of the myths. But if the stories were forgotten who then could foresee the danger if once again a dangerous hairy star appeared in the heavens? We cannot fathom the vastness, the mystery, the horror, the magnificence of the creating

153

power behind our universe. But by using images and metaphors we can perhaps show something of it, by fragmentary and reflected gleams and glimpses, like gold and jewels in a cave might catch the sunlight and indicate the riches within. For the very greatest ideas we use the very greatest images we have. The greater the image the greater is that which it conveys."

"But Velik, the priests and the people make sacrifices to images of these gods. They live their lives in the belief that these gods are supernatural beings with will and intelligence. They have no inkling of their true nature."

Velik shrugged his shoulders resignedly as he answered. "There was always a danger of the story becoming more important than the truth, of the gods becoming more important than the natural facts they represented. That was the risk in making gods out of natural phenomena. The priests' power depended upon the people believing in the gods as real beings and thus they would always suppress the astrological truth at its foundation, but belief in the gods was also an extremely useful and valuable civilizing power. In a very real sense the gods are much more important than the heavenly bodies. Thus it might be said that the poets and authors - those 'silver-tongued liars' - were a great moral force. Perhaps your 'Great Author' might be an idea close to the truth about the relationship between the Creation and its Creator, between Nature and Divinity. Indeed the more I think about it, the more interesting it seems."

"And do you think that another such star could appear?"

"But of course, unlike our lady Venus, they come and go all the time. Some return over and over again and their returns have been calculated."

"I would very much like to see such a hairy star sweeping across the heavens, provided it didn't come too close!"

"And so you might." Velik replied. "According to the wise men who have studied such things there will be a very large travelling star in the sky next year. Look to the heavens when the sun rises in Aries and if the authors are right then a mighty comet will hang in the sky."

"By Euhemerus!" exclaimed Small, "That will be a sight to see!"

Small spent several hours on the terrace observing the heavens whilst Velik explained the nature of the celestial bodies and their motion. By the time he laid down to sleep he had been told the names of all seven planets, what they looked like and why their movements were so various. He knew about the fixed stars and their constellations and the celestial highway of the zodiac. Amongst the procession of people, animals and mythical beasts which travelled along it, he had seen a ram, a bull, a lion, the Queen of Heaven, two fishes, a centaur archer and a scarab. There was also a sign of ill-omen. He was pleased to find that he already knew all their stories. He fell asleep in a state of pleasant bewilderment; his brain a blizzard of decans, asterisms, signs, sigils, degrees and arcs. Midway through the night he was half awakened by the book in his book bag digging into his side. He resolved to shelve it but by the time the birds greeted the sun he had forgotten all about it again.

After the frugal breakfast was over, Small pleaded with Velik to return with him to the Eastern Galleries.

"The assassin knows where you are now. Before long he will discover how to get in."

"That may be so," Velik replied, "but I think I have a better chance with one Murgan in an area that I know well than with twenty in a place I know not at all."

"But Puttfark's men are not bad!"

Velik merely gave him an old-fashioned, sideways look and said nothing.

Small's face lit up. "I have it! You can live in Plantman's room. You will be quite safe there behind the secret door. I know how to open it now. There are plants and fish and birds for you to eat. I will be able to come to see you without being ambushed."

Velik's eyebrows lifted in anticipation and a broad grin ruffled his moustaches. "You know, I think that might indeed be interesting. I have always wanted to see that garden."

Small helped the old man to pack some essential items into a bundle and they walked as cautiously and as silently as they could to the Plantman's domain.

After Velik had been shown how to open the secret door he paused for a few moments by the blood-stained cot, then with a deep sigh he followed Small out into the garden. Before long Velik was behaving like an excited child.

"The Lotos!" he exclaimed, "It really does exist. See what a strange plant it is - no, not one plant but two - look carefully and you will see how the plant with the flowers entwines the other. It is a parasite like ivy or the golden bough. This other bush with the red fruit is the host."

Small kept his distance. Velik moved on.

"Now! Here are the flowers of literature indeed. The marigold that always turns her face towards the chariot of Apollo as it crosses the sky; the scarlet anemone which sprang up where the blood of Adonis fell; the myrtle sacred to Venus; the bush of Laura; the earthly remains of Hyacinth, Narcissus and Crocus, lovers all. And here! The scarlet

155

rose, noble flower of Venus, Queen of blooms, just coming to bud. Beware her sharp thorns that inflict the wounds of love. Now here is a noble shrub, but one I do not recognize at all."

Small scrubbed away the lichen and moss from the pavement with his foot. The word 'ALMUG' eventually appeared. He gasped.

"I know of this plant. It is one of the trees which the Queen Hatshepsut brought from the South to Solomon in his kingdom of Punt. It is the rarest and most precious tree in the whole world. Perhaps some of the other plants from Solomon's garden are here. Small scrubbed away at the pavement and discovered first OLIBANUM then SPIKENARD, ALOES and CASSIA. Velik kept up his excited commentary all the while; the gum of one plant was used for royal incense, the flowers of another perfumed the beds of maidens; yet another gave spice oil from its bark. And always there was a story to go with each plant.

The sheltered northern corner of the terrace garden was bathed in warm autumn sunlight. In the embrace of the cloister stood a tall bushy plant. It bore myriads of long narrow serrated leaves like pale green spiders or grasping hands. A sickly familiar smell hung in the air.

"Ah. The assassin's plant," said Velik.

"Puttfark spoke of it too," said Small, "The Murgans burn its leaves in a pipe. It makes them happy. Do you know its story?"

Velik adopted a suitable stance with one fist in his waist and the other hand held out away from his body and began to tell the story.

"Once there was an evil and unscrupulous warlord whose ambition and cruelty knew no bounds. He lived in a high and desolate region and was only kept there by the courage and cleverness of neighbouring rulers. As time passed his frustration turned to hatred of his rivals but he could do nothing. One day he heard of a travelling merchant who was selling a plant to cure all ills. He caused the man to be brought before him and questioned him. 'It was a plant' the man said, 'that made people think that they were in paradise even though they might be in the darkest dungeon'. This gave the wicked warlord an idea. After he had thrown the merchant into a dungeon he gathered a band of his most trustworthy men around him, went to a village where his face was not known and gave drugged beer to the young peasant men. After they had fallen asleep he kidnapped them and carried them off to a high and beautiful valley in the mountains which looked down on the clouds. When the gullible peasant boys awoke they found themselves dressed in fine new clothes, being served the very best of food and drink by beautiful houris who attended to their every wish. The warlord explained to them that they had died and were now living in

156

paradise. They were immortal and could enjoy the fruits of this place for ever, except that from time to time they would have to go back into the mortal realm in order to perform certain tasks for him after which they could return.

'Perhaps because all the food they ate contained quantities of the merchant's drug they really did believe that they were in paradise, or maybe the drug just made them forget the warnings of their parents and elders and then trade their honour for this new pleasant existence. Who can say? Whatever was the case, from time to time, the warlord put these gullible young oafs to sleep once again and took them down to the plain. Each time they awoke they were instructed to kill one or other of the rulers who were thwarting the warlord's ambitions. They were given copious quantities of food laced with the resin of the plant to dull their judgement and then led to the place of ambush. The warlord told them that they should not fear death since if they were to be killed they would merely wake up as before in 'paradise'." At this point Velik rubbed at the paving with one of his makeshift sandals. "See, the plant is called ASHIZ, those under its influence are the *Ashizim* or as we would say 'assassins'."

"Wondrous!" Small said, "How stupid those young men must have been."

"Perhaps, but the drug made from this plant is very subtle and insidious. It corrupts the ability to reason and its effects linger on. I have heard of rulers who planted fields of it close to troublesome cities before they raised their taxes. The citizens danced and smiled as they were reduced to penury."

Small thought about this and also about what Puttfark had said on the subject.

"Velik I must go. Will you stay here and keep the doors locked? If anything happens follow my footprints and the blood spots and you will get to the Eastern galleries."

He left the old man thumbing through Plantman's small private collection of botanical books. "Ah!" he heard him say, "the milk of paradise…"

Sixteen

The great search seemed to have been interrupted. The old men sat or squatted around talking earnestly amongst themselves. Sly hovered by the window. As Small walked up to him he saw that the old man was even more agitated than usual.

"How was I to know?" he said, half to himself and half to the boy, and continued gnawing at the insides of his cheeks and twitching at his robe with nervous fingers.

"Know what?" said Small.

"That it was real. That it existed. That the stories were true."

"What ...?"

"The Cage."

"You found the Cage?"

"I didn't know. One book led to another. It was as if a path had been laid. I had to follow it. I couldn't help myself and then suddenly there it was.."

"But what was in it?" Small was alarmed but fascinated.

"Books of course. Many books. It is locked but the Murgans are fetching tools to break it open."

Sly seemed distracted, about to scuttle away. Small gripped him by the shoulders and tried to look him in the eye. "Sly, what have you done? The Great Author alone knows what evil things might be in there."

"Don't accuse me, Small. You know these people. They never give up. They would have found it eventually. You might even have led them to it yourself."

It was Small's turn to look away.

When the Murgans returned they were carrying a variety of brutal looking metal implements. As they swept through the gallery, Small followed, pulling Sly along with him.

Like so many other nooks and crannies in the bowels of Alligor, the entrance to the Cage room was difficult to find and even easier to miss. It would have been impossible to stumble on it by chance. In some remote past time the weight of the colossal door had fatigued the metal of its hinges and settled immovably onto the floor. Since then it had been impossible to close it. The massive cobwebbed locks and bars were useless. The door remained eternally ajar. The chamber was cramped, pentagonal and unlit. The cage itself stood in the centre. Vertical metal bars as thick as a man's arm had been socketed into the floor and the vault. They enclosed a tall rectangular cabinet with a built-in lectern. On one of the horizontal straps which bound the bars to each other there was an archaic inscription in an all but forgotten language. Small could not make it out but Sly clutched his arm. "I have seen that inscription before somewhere. If only I could remember."

The Murgans lit a lantern. Small gasped in horror. "It is forbidden!"

Puttfark held out a calming hand. "Don't worry. We will be very careful."

The guards began to work on the cage door, levering and prising with their iron tools. The lantern cast their weird shadows onto the walls. It was as if demons stood at the shoulders of the onlookers. Lubrik stood against the wall smirking and joking with Puttfark. Small heard snatches of what they were saying. " ... If not the book then something of real value ..." With his nose pressed against the bars, Small could just make out the bindings of the volumes in the cabinet. Strangely, instead of words these books had painted pictures on their spines: an apple, a flower, an ear of corn, a wheel. It was the first time he had ever seen it in Alligor, but he knew that this had often been used in the past for secrecy. Illiterate servants could be asked to fetch books without ever knowing their contents. Only the keeper would know the contents of important books. As an added security measure each volume in the cabinet had a strong chain attached which hung in a loop from a metal ring in the ceiling.

In the end it took an hour of incessant pounding with iron hammers and wedges to distort the lock sufficiently for the cage door to be levered open. When the Murgan guards finally stood back and wiped the sweat from their faces with the backs of their arms, Lubrik stepped into the cage. One book lay on the lectern. He picked it up and opened it. Looking over his shoulder with a knowing and lascivious leer on his face he lifted the book away from the lectern to show the others. There was a brief glimpse of a curious coloured illustration; a sort of mouth surrounded by swirling moustaches; before the chain which bound it to the lectern tightened to its limit. Instantly the floor fell away and Lubrik vanished into the dark void beneath. His final shriek rang in Small's mind long after the echoes had died away into an ominous silence. The book swung to and fro in the air until the counterweighted floor rose back into place. As it did so the chain shortened and the book slid back onto the lectern.

Nobody moved.

"A pleasure to enter ... "Sly mumbled in his ear.

"What ...?" Small was in a state of shock.

"It's what the inscription says. 'A pleasure to enter: a pain to leave.' It's a version of the old proverb. 'Where pleasure leads you only pain can release you.'"

Puttfark began to issue orders. Shelves were torn from bookstacks and laid into the Cage. The floor was opened once more and the lantern held above it. Puttfark shouted Lubrik's name into the shaft and then listened until the echoes died away. A coin was dropped into the void. It made not a sound. The shaft seemed bottomless.

The blond giant shook his head in disbelief. "It must go all the way to hell," he said in an awed voice.

Lubrik was written off. The books in the cabinet were prised from their chains and handed out into the light of the corridor. Small had a superstitious dread of the contents of the fatal Cage and refused to handle them. Puttfark opened them one by one whilst Small and Sly took turns at translating their titles and contents. The boy began whispering some of the titles, *A Thousand Curses of the Name of God by Zalaman*, *The Uses of Pain*, *Sacrifices to Moloch*, *The Usurpation of the Will*, but after a while he refused even to say the words, only shaking his head to indicate that it was not the book they were looking for. Finally it appeared that the Murgan Constitution was not in the Cage.

Puttfark had grunted with pleasure as he heard each title. It was as if he had discovered a great treasure. Small looked at him puzzled.

"There are those in Murga who will pay handsomely for such interesting things" he explained.

Small was shocked, "These are forbidden books. They belong to Alligor. You must not take them."

Puttfark turned towards him, an expression of mild surprise on his face. The *ulvis* appeared followed by a wide reassuring smile. "Perhaps that will not be necessary. If they are interesting we will have copies made."

Somehow Small knew that when the Murgans left Alligor the books would leave with them.

The opening of the cage hardly interrupted the search. The Murgans were truly relentless in the execution of any task which they set themselves. As the days passed, more and yet more galleries were laid waste. Small found it increasingly depressing to walk back and forth each morning and evening through the rooms strewn with discarded books and unrolled manuscripts. The unaccustomed gaps on the shelves were like the pauses in a conversation when the person being talked about passes by. Small saw them as mute accusations.

Somewhere in the chaotic tangle of masonry and literature, Old heaped jumbled armfuls of texts back onto shelves in a futile attempt to restore some appearance of order to the library. Small dreaded meeting him.

If the aged librarians had qualms about their role in the sack of Alligor they did not show it. On the contrary they seemed to become ever more sprightly. There were even small scuffles over the carrying of books which Small put down to their enthusiasm for the task. Several librarians had sufficiently recovered command of obscure languages mastered in their youth so as to be able to help vet the hundreds of volumes examined each day. When dusk brought all work to an end, many of the old men carried full book bags at their waists. Small took this as a sign of reviving interest in the library until he noticed that the book bags were always empty in the morning. A little more thought caused him to wonder what pleasure they could possibly elicit from all this literature during the hours of darkness.

As work ended he found himself walking back to the refectory beside Tentpole whose knee problem seemed to have been miraculously cured by his improved diet and regular employment. "Your book bag is full tonight Tentpole," he said, "What are you reading in the dark?"

Tentpole looked distinctly uncomfortable. In his naivety he clutched defensively at the bag as he answered. "Oh, nothing much," he said, "just light reading for leisure hours."

"And the authors?" Small asked, not sure what was going on but certain that 'light reading for leisure hours' was a concept wholly alien to Alligor and its keepers.

Tentpole grinned guiltily but did not answer.

"Here let me see."

Tentpole made a half-hearted attempt to fend off Small's prying fingers but then realised how determined the boy was and gave up. Small examined the books. As he lifted each from the bag he saw that they were all elaborately and richly bound. Wafer thin gold plate and chased silver was embossed with jewels, turquoises and tigerseye, or studded with lapis, jade and amber. Dismissing this ostentation as the whim of some profligate monarch, Small read the titles: *Goat Racing*, *The Usefulness of Sewers*, *The Diseases of Camels*. What possible interest could Tentpole have in such subjects?

"It is always a good thing to broaden one's mind by reading in new and strange subjects," Small said, "but these …?"

Tentpole smiled nervously before speaking. "Yes, yes they are aren't they? Must go, must go ..." He held out his hands for the return of the books.

Small could only hand them over even though he still felt that something was not right. Tentpole scuttled off into the gloom trying to catch up with the other librarians. Did all the old men have such eccentric reading habits?

Something was going on in the courtyard outside the refectory. The Murgans were dashing around in a most anarchic manner kicking up the dust with their feet until it hung in the air like pink smoke. They were tossing a kind of round shaped bag to each other. Small noticed how skilfully they were able to pluck the bag out of the air and hold it in their hands. Then the bag was thrown short and it fell to the ground. Unbelievably it sprang up again straight into the hands of the blond giant. Small was amazed. The giant spotted Small and hurled the bag over the heads and reaching hands of the others. The bag fell towards Small who held out his hands to catch it as he had seen the Murgans do. He mis-timed his grab hopelessly; the bag hit him square in the face and rebounded across the yard. Only his pride was hurt since the bag was filled with nothing heavier than air. Amidst guffaws and jeers he shouted excitedly. "What is it? What is it?"

There were exclamations of disbelief. "He's never seen a ball before!"

"Of course I've seen a ball. But never one filled with air. What are you doing? What do you call this?" he asked the blond man.

"This is just having fun."

Small found the concept unfamiliar. "What does that word mean in your language?"

"You must know what 'fun' is." The man answered.

"In our common speech it signifies a trick, a ploy, a cruel hoax. You seem to have given it another meaning."

"Its what ever makes you smile or laugh and forget your troubles. It's anything that throws a coloured veil over grey reality. You know, playing games, music, dancing, drinking and eating, the company of women. In Murga these are the goals of life."

Small could feel the undoubted attractions of 'fun'. But nevertheless considered their description as 'goals of life' more than a little extravagant. How could tossing a ball about, swigging wine and guffawing loudly be compared to honour, duty, loyalty, wisdom and all the other lofty ideals of the authors? Of course in a society that pretended to equality, the 'goals of life' had to be achievable by even the most ignorant peasant: hence 'fun'. He pursued the bouncing ball with intense delight as it rebounded from the library wall and into his fumbling hands. He threw it back into the melee just as the distant rattle of spoon on cauldron heralded the meal. As he walked into the refectory he pondered the difference between the 'fun' of the Murgans and the more common words such as 'enjoyment' and 'happiness'. 'Fun' was somehow 'innocent', but in the same way that savage tribes were 'innocent'. It had no moral depth to it. Because of this it could be just a childish game with a ball, but it might also be cannibalism and torture. The Murgans seemed to have cut the bonds between duty and pleasure and made them opposites.

Small was surprised to find the refectory almost empty. He had expected to see all the librarians sitting reading the books they had taken from the galleries. The lamps were lit, the meal would soon be ready and yet only a handful of diners were at the tables. What, he mused, could be more important than food? His thoughts were interrupted by a great bellow. Inflated like the Murgans' ball with equal measures of food and self-importance, Spoon bounced through the kitchen arch followed by his foot soldiers of food, for all the world as if he were lifting a siege. On seeing the empty tables he stopped dead in his tracks. Behind him his kitchen troops collided and rebounded off each other with much cursing and dropping of lids. Steam rose to the vault. Grease dripped on to the stone floor. Spoon's great round head, shiny and red as a ripe boil, remained immobile. In the silence, beads of perspiration gathered on his forehead, coalesced and ran into the puffy folds around his eyes which slid from left to right and back again in their fleshy slits.

"Ur," he growled. "Where are they?"

No answer was forthcoming. Small sat swallowing saliva in anticipation of the food. Spoon strode ponderously over to his table. With a loud clatter he dropped the heavy ladle which served him as both marshal's baton and knout onto the table. Leaning heavily on his immense and sweaty knuckles he stood over Small. The table top bent under the weight. The cook's laboured and fetid breath rasped through its constricted passageways.

"They have finished their work in the galleries but they are not here," Small said. "I don't know where they are. Perhaps they prefer their food cold."

Spoon's features contorted horribly as deep beneath the fleshy surface of his face the muscle and tendon strained and tautened in displeasure. He drew himself up to his full height, "Feed them," he hissed, spitting the words disdainfully over his shoulder with a half turn of his head. His minions obeyed.

Small ate quickly, noting that each mealtime he seemed to have to eat more and more before he was full. When he had finished he went in search of the librarians. He was sure that they had entered the Great Stair before him, but they had not reached the courtyard. The only inhabited place which led off the stairwell was the corridor which led to the Murgan apartments. Outside the apartment two Murgans were struggling to manhandle yet another of the large terracotta oil jars towards the stairs. He stepped into an alcove whilst they passed. In the darkness a hand was laid on his shoulder. He jumped violently.

"Greetings Small," whispered Old.

"Greetings," Small replied, trying to search out the old man's face in the gloom.

"I have not seen you for some time young man. What have you been doing?"

Small was still in a state of pleasurable agitation from the game in the yard. He began to tumble out a disjointed account of the experience.

"A ball? What kind of a ball?" Old spoke with the distracted and irritable tone of one interrupted in a reverie. His face, barely visible in the failing light, appeared out of the alcove.

"It was a bag of air. They call it 'fun'." Small was also irritated that the old man had not been listening.

"They trick you into neglecting your duties with a bag full of nothing and you come and tell me about it as if it were a great event." Old folded his arms tightly across his chest and half turned away.

Small touched the old man on the elbow. "No, you don't understand. They threw it at me but it didn't hurt. When it dropped on the ground it sprang up again into their hands. It made me laugh. They call it 'fun' but it means something different in Murga. It's something that makes you happy and makes you forget all your cares."

Old shook his head in disbelief.

"They make you happy to forget the library, the books, your colleagues, your duties. It's just another Murgan trick. Whilst you have 'fun' they take over the library and steal all the books."

"But in Murga everybody wants to have 'fun' all the time. It lets them escape from grey reality."

"If I lived in Murga I too might want to escape from my 'grey reality', but isn't all of life real?"

Small was used to having his enthusiasms quashed out of hand. The Murgans never did that. They seemed always to be so positive about everything; except the Library. He decided to change the subject.

"What are you doing here?" he asked.

Old leaned back into the shadows,

"I at least have not forgotten my duties as a librarian. When I see librarians taking full book bags from the galleries and returning with them empty, I want to know where the books are going. And you?"

"The same. I swear by the Great Author. Tentpole had the most curious bagfull of books I ever saw. He was not in the refectory, neither were the others. I wanted to know where they were."

Old leaned forward again into the half-light and nodded towards the Murgan apartments,

"They are here," he said.

Small peered around the old man's shoulder into the gloom of the corridor. Sure enough, shadowy figures lurked in alcoves and doorways. From time to time they bobbed out and peered anxiously at the Murgans' door.

"What are they doing?" he asked.

Old shrugged. "They go in one at a time with their books," he said, "then they come out again without them."

"But what is going on?"

"I do not know," Old answered. "Another Murgan trick, perhaps."

Small was baffled. Reading books was completely out of character for the Murgans.

"Perhaps you ought to take a stroll through the upper levels." Old suggested warily.

"There are upper levels here too?"

"Of course."

"But that would be spying on them. They are my friends." It was a half-hearted protest.

Old ignored him. "You would have to be very quiet and very careful. If they discovered the upper levels existed we would lose an important advantage."

There was the noise of a door opening. Small and Old ducked back into the shadows as one of the aged librarians emerged from the Murgan apartments and scurried past them. His empty bookbag slapped against his thigh. Back up the corridor the door opened again and another librarian went in.

"Show me the way up." Small whispered to Old.

This district of Alligor had been built long before the Eastern Galleries. There was no wooden panelling here and no carved faces to twist. As the librarians all moved one dark recess closer to the Murgan quarters, Old led him into an archway which had just been vacated. A door led into a cupboard with barely enough room for them both to stand in it. Old bolted the door behind them. His voice sounded loud and close in the pitch blackness,

"There are book shelves in front of us," he said, "The entrance to the upper levels is behind the books."

Small heard him operate the hidden catch and sensed the book shelves swinging back. The disembodied voice spoke again,

"I will hold the door open till you return."

Like a blind man, Small stepped forward into the unmistakable icy atmosphere of passed time and decay. For a second or two he was completely disorientated by the chill of silence and neglect which washed over him. He had heard of demons who lurked in the darkest corners of the Library waiting to feed on the souls of those who were disheartened and disappointed with their barren and futile lives. Now as his courage drained away in the mind-numbing stillness he was enveloped for the first time by the demon Despair. It whispered of endless constricted lives, of wasted, wasted time, of dead time, of unfulfilled existence, of unfinished books, of unused notes, of voices suppressed by the all-stifling masonry of the Book City. In a darkness so thick and palpable as to be almost visible, he had a premonition of disillusionment. Did he really want to see behind the Murgan veil? Old coughed nervously in the darkness.

Small started forward, using his hands to feel his way up the narrow stone stairs. He explored the upper levels in the same way. The heavy fireproof vaults were of dressed stone. Each spyhole was plugged with a suitably massive inverted cone of the same material. Each plug had a metal handle by means of which it could be lifted out. The view through the spyhole was restricted by the small diameter of the opening in its lower end, but because of the conical recess he could see more of the room below by simply moving his head. The Murgan apartment was lit by a flickering yellow light. He could not see its source but he knew where it was from the shadows it cast on the wall. He could feel warm air on his face.

Small adjusted his viewpoint until the angular figure of Tentpolu came into sight. He was laying full length on a couch. Small tilted his head further over and saw that a Murgan woman was sitting at the old man's shoulder. She was stroking his wrinkled cheeks, scalp and forehead in a slow rhythmic manner. From time to time she bent over the old man; pushing her ample breasts against his arm. With an expression of imbecile contentment on his face, Tentpole stared blatantly at the woman's bare throat.

Small was no cynic when it came to human motives, but his heart sank at the scene before him. Even allowing for his total ignorance of women and their ways, he knew that spring and winter didn't come together like this. The authors had a word for what was going on down below and it wasn't 'charity'.

The woman bent over Tentpole again and murmured in his ear. He immediately plunged his hands into the bag at his waist and pulled out the books. These he handed over to her. She examined their bindings front and back, but did not open them. Small heard her murmuring approval as she handed them to an unseen figure who had approached her from behind. Tentpole wriggled back into a comfortable position, but it seemed that his sojourn in paradise was at an end. The Murgan woman stood up and walked out of Small's field of view. The beatific expression faded from Tentpole's face and he raised himself painfully from the couch and walked towards the door. Small wanted to know what was happening to the books. He carefully replaced the plug in the spyhole and felt his way in the dark to another one. Now he could see that an open fire was burning brightly in the corner of the room. A fireplace had been cleverly constructed from loose bricks and stone. Its slanting flue directed the smoke through an adjacent window and into the night air. Beside the fire sat Vulpia. With one of her mottled and bony hands she held *The Usefulness of Sewers* down on her knee; in the other she held her stiletto. She used the blade to prise out the semi-precious stones from their mounts and then to strip off the wafer-thin silver foil from the binding. The body of the book and its wooden boards she tossed into the fire.

Small was stunned by the sacrilegious nature of the act. A loud male voice in the room below forced him back to into reality.

"Was it poetry or history?" it cried.

A female voice replied, "What's it to you? Are you turning into a librarian?"

"Ha, ha, ha! Don't you know that poetry burns brighter than history or philosophy? Less ink!"

At first Small was too stunned to move. He could scarcely believe what he had just seen. Then, his hands shaking with anger, he replaced the heavy plug in the spyhole and crawled quickly back to the stair. Beyond caution he hurled himself down the steps falling headlong down the last of them. Still blind with fury he scrambled to his feet and in the pitch darkness ran straight into the arms of Old. Small tried none too gently to push past him. Old struggled to hold the boy.

"Wait, wait! Hold, hold! Not until you have calmed down. Now tell me, what did you see?"

"They are whores. You were right." Small's voice trembled with emotion. "They prostitute themselves in return for richly bound books. They strip off the gems and metals and then they burn the books on a fire to keep themselves warm at their work. The men make the poets ridiculous. They say that they burn brighter. The Murgans must leave. I shall tell them to go. I am going to strike every librarian in the corridor with my hand."

"No. You will do no such thing." Old hissed as he clung tenaciously to Small's arms. "You will calm down first, whilst we decide what to do. That was the advice you yourself gave to me, remember?"

Small stopped trying to push past the old man. He realised that he had only the vaguest notion of what he was going to do and say.

"If you are not in control of your emotions you might alert the Murgans to the upper levels. The librarians are as timid as sheep, you need only reprove them. If you are violent you will only drive them into the arms of the Murgans. Remember these Murgans use violence the way other nations use ploughs. If they succeed in provoking you to violence and opposition then they will have you in their power, since they have the strength, the numbers and the weapons. If the librarians ask for their protection then you will find yourself alone and an outsider."

Small had by this time suppressed the first hot rush of anger. "You speak sense, but even so I must stop this destruction of books. I have to confront the Murgans and it must be done now. I will take care not to reveal our secret."

Old was faint with the effort of restraining Small. He knew that he had done all he could to prevent the boy from acting without thinking. His aching arms dropped to his sides. Instantly Small passed by him and out into the corridor.

Small pulled the few remaining librarians out of their niches and alcoves and, after admonishing them severely for neglecting their duty with regard to the books, sent them to the refectory. He did not need to knock on the Murgans' door. The sound of his raised voice had caused the guards to open up. Light and warmth spilled into the corridor.

"I want to speak with Mr. Puttfark," he said to them.

Puttfark wore a genial expression and held up his hands beside his shoulders as if surrendering himself. Small did not wait to be asked the nature of his business but began to speak right away.

"Your purses are filled by pillaging the munificence of cultures civilized beyond your understanding. Your apartment is made warm and luxurious by the burning of literature not your own ..."

Puttfark flinched as if he had been struck. "Wait!" he said. "Either your language is too grand for us or you are speaking in riddles. Come, speak plain. What has upset you?"

"Your women are burning our books; books which they ask from the librarians in return for their favours."

The smile faded from Puttfark's face. His features tautened.

"This I cannot believe. I am sure that you have been misinformed. But I promise you that if such things are happening then I will stop them right now. Wait here while I find out."

The door closed behind him and Small stood in the darkness listening to the murmur of voices coming from the room. The door re-opened. Puttfark and the light emerged.

"The women were simply rewarding the old men for helping in the search. They thought the librarians should have some fun in their lives as a kind of goal to work towards. The old men brought the books in sheer gratitude. They chose pretty books because they had read that women prefer such things. You have to understand that my guards and my women are just simple folk. They do not know the worth of literature but only the value of the materials from which the books are made. They were wrong to break them and I have told them so. The fire was intended for rotten or broken wood. My men collect it on their patrols. There was never any intention to burn books. I have given orders that no more books are to be burnt, but to speak plain, the books themselves were not innocent."

"What? What do you mean?" said Small, completely taken by surprise by this last remark.

Puttfark put an avuncular arm around Small's shoulders and began to walk him slowly away from the Murgan apartment. "In Murga, men and women are all equal. No man would dream of abusing women just for being women. Our authors are the same. They would never ever write anything which even suggested that women were weaker or less intelligent than men. But in the past, and outside our state, in lands less free, many ignorant authors have written of women as inferior beings unequal in their capacities. Such wrong-headedness has no place in Murga. We do not suffer such books to exist. In Murga even one term of abuse is enough to condemn a book. Our women cast such books into the fire in the same way that they would cast off an abusive husband. The books which were burned were of that type. Of course

169

no guilt attached itself to the jewels and silver of the bindings so they were saved."

Small was at a loss how to respond to all this. Strange lands had strange customs but he was sure that the woman had not even opened the book before it was destroyed. Did she know it already? Perhaps its title had two meanings. Was it a cruel allegory? There was no way now of finding out.

"Tell me," said Puttfark suddenly, "why do you keep books in the Cage?"

"Some books are evil and pervert the minds of those who read them."

"Then why not burn them?"

"We would never do such a thing. Books are like people. There are good and bad and there are truly evil books. But all are precious to the Great Author. As with murderers and thieves, we keep them locked up where they can do no harm and yet may still serve an admonitory purpose."

Years spent reading about the art of rhetoric made Small fully aware that Puttfark was trying to put him onto the defensive by mounting a shrewd counter attack. Unfortunately the man in white had chosen an inappropriate analogy. The one skill that Alligor taught above all others was the remembering and connecting of seemingly random facts. Small did not give Puttfark time to pursue his line of attack.

"Anyway, you speak of respecting women as equals and yet one of those books you took from the Cage was about torturing women - not just ridiculing them - but actually tearing them to pieces. I saw it - and yet you said that it was interesting and that Murgans would pay well for such a book."

It seemed a long time before Puttfark answered.

"One day the whole world will be Murgan. Our aim is to create a better life for everyone. There will be one world, one language, one religion, one people. But such a dream cannot come about by merely talking or asking people nicely to change their ways. Only overwhelming power can make this new world, and overwhelming power needs to be supported by overwhelming wealth. If anything is to be bought and sold in this world, then it is best that Murgans do it. We cannot have those who disagree with us, and live in error and inequality, becoming wealthy, because you see, wealth is power. It is therefore the birthright of every Murgan to be able to make money from each and every commodity that he can."

"But such a book is evil. Surely you would not expose it in the market place?"

"We are in a battle for the world. Knowledge can be a weapon in that battle, if we have it and our enemies do not. Evil itself is also a weapon. It's like a severe and undetectable poison. We prefer to have it in our hands in case it should fall into the hands of others. When the end is a better world, the end justifies the means."

Small had been so certain of his case against the Murgans but now he was not so sure of his position. Puttfark always managed to achieve that effect. Perhaps the women were so unsophisticated. Perhaps the book really was insulting to them. The Murgans committed the most blatantly evil deeds but they always seemed so sure of their rightness and in the end their actions seemed almost noble; an essential part of making a better world. Perhaps he would have felt better if burning the books had not been so immediately conducive to the Murgans' own comfort. He had so little knowledge of the outside world. How could he judge?

When they reached the end of the corridor, Puttfark held him by the shoulders and looked him in the face. "Trust me," he said, "There will be no more book burning whilst I am here in Alligor. How about a ride tomorrow? Meet me for breakfast?"

Small found that he had been manoeuvred to the staircase. He nodded in the darkness. The man in white turned away. Small listened to the receding footsteps and heard the door close. From out of the darkness came the voice of Old.

"I heard all. Do not feel bad. You did well. This man is like a scorpion. He insinuates himself into the smallest crevice. He is impossible to catch hold of. He twists this way and that and if you are not careful he fills you with poison."

"But what he said about the authors abusing women, might the Murgans be right?"

"Pay no attention. The authors abuse everybody and everything. Such chastisement is part of their task. Would you rather they were a crowd of flatterers? As far as I am aware, the follies, vices and evil habits of men have been the subject of almost every story ever written and yet I have never heard a single complaint that men are abused."

"But women are not men."

"There may be authors who criticise women too fiercely, just as there are authors who praise them too highly. For myself I know nothing about women at all so I cannot judge. If they are indeed inferior then they might need protecting. If they are fully equal and would stand with men in the market place then they must expect to be spattered with everybody else when the market carts go by. In any case the women we have here are Murgans. They would not even trouble themselves to throw books on to a fire unless they could make some material gain from it. Nor incidentally do they stroke the greasy pates of old men out of the goodness of their hearts."

In the silence they heard distant laughter from the Murgan quarters.

"Small. You know what your task is. You must find the book they are seeking and get rid of these people. It is the only way."

Seventeen

As Small crossed the courtyard in the grey light of dawn he noticed Sly slumped against the refectory wall. He looked the very picture of dejection.

"Good morning Sly," he called, "Are you ill?"

"Good morning small one. No, I am not ill. A little sick at heart, perhaps, but it will pass."

Small had never seen him in such a defeated mood. All the crackle of intelligence seemed to have been dowted in him. Only a sullen glow remained. He walked over to him.

"Tell me old friend. What is wrong?"

"Wrong? I am wrong. All my life I have been reading about the great courts of emperors and kings. I familiarised myself with their etiquette, with their ritual, with their behaviour. I learned a thousand grades of address. I could offer my condolences to a Grand Vizier on the death of his mother's sister. I could commiserate with a King on a sleepless night, and all without the slightest breach of etiquette. I knew how to huzzah a victorious general without appearing to be a peasant. All the duties of a courtier I learned. One day, I thought, one day a great and noble personage might come to Alligor: perhaps to consult a rare volume; perhaps to donate a collection of books; perhaps even from idle curiosity; and then, Sly, the perfect courtier would be on hand to welcome, to guide, to instruct, to negotiate the salvation of our Book-City, our venerable edifice of literature. And so I waited. I waited a lifetime and no-one came. Then one day the Murgans arrived. At first I thought they might be nobles. Then I believed that they were an advance party: that the nobles would follow after. I smiled. I courted them. I negotiated with them. It is only now that I realise that I have been mocked and ridiculed by a band of freebooting riff-raff who despise the very idea of nobility. They talk only of freedom and equality and have no respect for any traditions but their own. And now I have shown them the Cage and loosed all its devilments onto the world."

Small could see that Sly was suffering in the grip of the demon Despair and that he had a duty to cheer him. "The authors say that we should always see our mistakes and disappointments as a process of learning about the world. To be truthful with you, all the books that I have read about Courts and courtiers have told of intrigue and conspiracy, falls from favour, of princes deposed and of high and mighty men always afraid of the assassin's blade."

173

"Then I have truly wasted my time."

"Do not think so. No time is ever wasted on imagining things to be better than they are. Perhaps you have only mistaken your vocation. If you find yourself to be a poor courtier, perhaps you might make a better author. You complain that the high and mighty people never came here. But all the great and good of the world are already here. They are hanging around in the library on every shelf just waiting to discuss all kinds of things with you whenever you want. Could you not write a book about a perfect courtier in a perfect court? Then the library would always be ready for the Monarch to come, even if it is a thousand years from now."

"But I would need parchment, ink, pens ..."

"Many books have blank leaves. Many books are unreadable from mildew or vermin. Their pages could be scraped clean and used again. There are blocks of ink everywhere. They need only to be dissolved in water ..."

Sly's shoulders had slowly lifted by imperceptible stages. His eyes had narrowed. He had found the plot once more. "You won't tell anybody?"

Small laughed aloud. "Trust me." he said and was turning to leave when Sly caught at his sleeve. "Look over there." he murmured conspiratorially. A group of the Murgan women were entering the refectory. "Why are all these unmarried women travelling without their families? They should be chaperoned. They will have no reputation when they come to marry."

"Why not ask them?" Small replied.

The new day was clear and bright. The sun had not quite lifted clear of the level horizon as Puttfark and Small rode away from the picket and out of the shadow of Alligor. The horses were skittish because the wind was hard and fierce. It lifted the pink dust just off the ground so that it swirled and smoked in threads and skeins across the plain. Soon they found that they were riding across a turbulent cinnamon ocean of dusty light. It was a magical experience. Puttfark turned towards him in triumph.

"Freedom!" he shouted, "Doesn't it make you want to ride to the end of the world?"

"To the end of the world!" Small shouted as loudly as he could and kicked his horse into a gallop.

They pulled the horses up after about half a league. Small was breathless and exhilarated. Puttfark leaned over in the saddle and gripped him by the arm.

"This is living!" he said, "A fine horse and a bag of silver: what more could any man want?"

Small noticed the instinctive touching of the weapon hidden in his waistband, but it was now such a familiar part of the Murgan body language that he thought no more of it. Puttfark inhaled deeply and threw out his arm at the landscape.

"This world is bigger than you can possibly imagine. There are lands to discover, deals to be made. The world is at our feet. Murga is unstoppable. They speak of Kings, of priests, of generals: let them believe what they will; the world is ours because we know how to use it. Ruling is their business, our business is *business*. With every commodity we trade we sell more freedom, more independence. With every deal we get stronger and our opponents get weaker. Forget your falling-down library and your rotting books. Don't be Small, be Rider! Join the winning side. You are young. You are quick. I can show you how to get everything you could ever want; horses, riches, palaces, women, adventure. Why, you could even meet some of your precious authors: if you had the time."

Puttfark saw the shadow of doubt pass across Small's face. "Listen," he said, "we have our faults. We are only men; no more, no less. We can't be perfect. We don't even try to be because the deals we have to make are too difficult, but we do try the best we can … and we never give up. That's why we always win. Your authors write of heroes, but there can only be heroes in books. Perhaps in a perfect world we could all be better people. This world takes heroes and crushes them flat. Ordinary people love to see heroes fall. It makes them feel better about being so weak. They think, well, maybe I am not so bad after all. Join us. Be Rider. You won't ever be a hero but you will be a winner."

The man in white glanced back over his shoulder. Two swaddled horse riders were approaching across the ocean of swirling dust. Puttfark turned his horse and cantered over to meet them. After exchanging a few words with them, he turned, waved and shouted to Small.

"Business!" The wind flung the distant word across the plain to where he was waiting. Puttfark galloped back to Alligor. The two riders came on.

As the newcomers cantered their mounts towards him, Small knew that the two riders were young women long before they unwound their burnooses and showed their faces. The wind pressed the sparkling patterned material of their dresses against their bodies and made it billow behind them like shimmering wings. From time to time the

175

wind lifted the hem of their skirts. Slim brown knees appeared above soft white boots. Their bare faces and forearms glowed in the sunrise as they gripped the reins with tight fists inside supple leather gloves. All this Small saw. His pulse quickened.

The two girls smiled but did not speak. They tilted their heads at him alluringly. It was the same expression as at the camp. Small tried to decide how to greet them.

"Greetings," he said rather lamely.

Their smiles broadened. He blushed suspecting that they were mocking him.

"Puttfark has asked us to keep you company. He has some, ah, business to take care of," one of them said.

"He seems to be a very busy man," Small replied politely and then, "I don't know your names yet."

"I am Violanta," said the girl with the dark impenetrable eyes.

"I am Imperia," said the other. "And who are you?"

"Puttfark calls me Rider"

"Rider, eh? And I thought you were Small. We shall have to find out if you have earned your name."

The blatant innuendo was lost on Small. "How do you like Alligor?" was all the response he could muster.

Imperia tossed her head and looked around her. "It's boring: so flat, so empty, so poor. We like towns and cities with lots of people. We like music and dancing. We like business!"

"My friend Mr. Sly wonders why you women are all unchaperoned."

"Why are you not chaperoned Mr. Small Rider?" replied Violanta with a provocative tilt of her head. "From where I am sitting you seem in much greater danger of losing your innocence than we are."

Small's thoughts were in confusion. His reason was being seduced. Alligor and all its authors had not prepared him for the sensual insurrection he was now experiencing. He floundered on. "But I am a man. Men don't need chaperones."

"No more do we. In Murga men and women are equal. They are not treated like chattels. We do not have to be bridled and tethered like horses. We can roam wherever we like. Perhaps you would rather we were all locked up at home and forced into marriages with old men like the women on this side of the mountains?"

"No, no I am glad that you are free," Small answered, "but is it not dangerous for you?"

Violanta laughed but Imperia's face clouded slightly and she pressed her hand to her belly. It was plumper than her friend's and

176

seemed at odds with her slim athletic frame. Small floundered on, "What I mean is won't men take advantage of you?"

"They could try!" they said almost in unison, instinctively touching their weapons. The outlines of their daggers were clearly visible beneath the flimsy material pressed against their bodies by the wind. Violanta pushed her dark ringlets away from her face. "We take care of our own business," she said, "We do our own deals."

"What exactly is your business?" asked Small, fascinated and awed by these exotic creatures.

The two girls exchanged the briefest of complicit glances.

"Show business." said Imperia.

"But what do you show?" asked Small.

"That depends on how much our clients pay. Our business is entertainment. We have entertained at all the finest courts. We sing; we dance; we are also actresses …"

Small was shocked. In the common speech the word 'actress' was synonymous with the word 'whore'. But then again, the true meaning of so many words in the language of Babel was unclear to him, and these girls did seem so friendly, and so attractive.

"You don't have any money here do you?" said Imperia.

"No," Small replied, "We don't ever buy things. We never have."

"But you have to have things like food and clothes. How do you get them?"

"In the past those things were given freely by the people who valued the Library and what it contained, but something seems to have changed in the world outside. Perhaps they have forgotten about us."

Violanta assumed a mocking smile. "I think everybody west of here is too busy making money to read books."

Imperia giggled, "And everybody to the East is too busy worrying about not making enough."

Small was unsettled by all this pragmatism. "So you are not at all interested in books?" he asked.

Imperia looked skywards and thought for a while. "I like pretty books," she said, "Golden or silver books with lovely jewels on them. Knowing that they belonged to somebody rich and successful makes me interested in them. Perhaps you could find some and bring them to me. I would be very … grateful … and I know that you would enjoy my gratitude … very much. Much more than all those old men."

Before he could respond the young woman had kicked her horse into motion. The other followed and they were quickly lost in clouds of pink dust. Small lifted his reins to follow but then held back for reasons which he could not have articulated. Although he was hardly aware of it, his peaceful childish state was now fully embroiled in that adolescent civil war between instinct and reason. With these Murgan women he seemed always to say the wrong thing and to misunderstand everything. He felt like a buffoon. He was so ignorant of the outside world. And he had no money. These women always seemed to be interested in money. Perhaps only libraries staffed by male orphans could exist without money. He thought of all the stories he had read which involved courtship and marriage. There were some which involved poor people, but either the poor boy found a great treasure, or discovered that he was really a prince, or was rewarded by the ruler for some brave act. Perhaps after all it was the way it all worked in the real world. Women liked rich men. He would have to get some money if he wanted to be taken seriously.

He tethered his horse to the picket line in the shadow of Alligor. Above the banks and drifts of pinkish dust the Book City was an endless red wall which hid the sunrise and blocked his path. Never had he felt so frustrated with his life. Old wanted him to find the book the Murgans were looking for, but that was an impossible task. The Murgans were right; the only way to find it was by sheer dogged persistence. It could take a year or more. He made his own decision as he passed through the gateway. If Old was right and the Gropius manuscript was the one really important book in Alligor, then that was the book he had to find. After he had found it he would give it to Old for safekeeping. Then he could leave with the Murgans whether they found their book or not. He would have done his duty. The secret of the Library would be safe. The other librarians would have to find some way of rearranging the books and carrying on. Perhaps they could strip some of the precious materials from the books and trade them for food. He knew that the Murgans were not heroes. He knew that they were not noble or virtuous. He even knew that they were violent by profession, but his appetite for adventure had been awakened. He longed for the companionship of these men so confident in their own powers and abilities. He wanted to test his manhood against the world and plant his feet in the footsteps of other men. Above all he was fascinated by these strange and liberated women. If it was a choice between Alligor and the world, he would choose the world.

Small strode through the library with a new found sense of purpose. The search for the book had moved away from the Eastern Galleries. The old men could now muster a score of languages between them. Small was no longer as essential to the search as he had been at first, but his absence would be noted. Since Puttfark was busy, Kunig would be in charge. The Murgans were persistent and methodical but their search would take far too long. There had to be a better way. Small had his own search to think about. In the meantime he needed to be undisturbed. The Lion Cabinet would be the right place. The tramp of shod feet alerted him to an approaching patrol. He cut away into less frequented galleries and began the meandering ascent to his private room.

It was with some surprise that he suddenly came upon the blond giant and one of his fellow guards. They were manhandling yet another of the giant glazed jars of cedar oil through an archway. Small could see by the way the jar glistened in the dim light that it was leaking its contents. The men cursed as they struggled to grip the slippery amphora. As he watched, the inevitable came to pass. Both men lost their grip at once and the jar descended abruptly onto the stone floor. Instantly the aromatic oil forced its way out through a wide crack which split the container from base to neck. The two men leaped back to avoid the oily tide and the broken vessel shattered into fragments at their feet. The echoes clattered away into oblivion. The two Murgans stared open-mouthed at the spreading pool of oil. Where there should only have been pottery shards, there was a glutinous crouching figure of a dead man.

"Goddinhell!" said the blond giant in an awed voice.

Small stood with the two men staring at the oily corpse. The dead man looked as if he had been carved from yellow wood. He had a cruel face with a healed scar which curled his lip. From his ear hung a heavy golden earring thickening at the bottom with a swelling bead of the meton. His tattooed torso was naked to the waist but his legs were wrapped in voluminous trews, now dark and sodden and hanging down over his open sandals. One hand gripped an antique bronze stabbing sword; the other held a serrated dagger.

"Who the God is he?" the blond one asked, looking at Small for an answer.

"I do not know. No librarian would have tattoos and earrings, and readers may not carry arms."

"He's a thief." The second Murgan was looking at the other side of the corpse's head. Small walked around the pool of oil to look.

"See the ancient law-mark" The man pointed to where half the dead man's ear had been cut off. "They always did that to thieves."

The blond giant spoke again. "Here is a mystery. An armed thief dead in a jar of oil."

Small bent down to pick up the broken mouth of the jar. A royal cartouche had been impressed into the soft wax with which the lid had been sealed. It was still legible. Small was amazed to recognize the mark of King Abab.

"This corpse has been in the jar for half a millennium," he said, "The oil must have preserved him. What bizarre plot put this man here?"

"He is not the only one," said the blond man's companion.

"What do you mean?"

"I have carried five of these jars across the library. They all had something in them that bumped and scraped against the sides."

"You mean that all these jars contained corpses?"

"Seems so; and there are forty of them."

Small was dumbfounded. "It would indeed be a cunning author who could account for such a strange occurrence."

He left the men to muse over their accident.

Alone in the Lion Cabinet, Small began to apply himself to the seemingly impossible task of finding the manuscript. Old had spoken of paths through the Library; of Paths of Light and of Paths of Darkness. The dead librarian Knowall had written about *The Shining Path*. What sort of path could lead a reader to just one book in a whole city of literature? Those who had placed the book in the Library had intended it to be found by someone who was a stranger to Alligor. With such a massive and shifting collection, the paths which led to it must be simple and quick. Otherwise the One might spend a lifetime among the books whilst the Evil of Knowledge swept through the world unopposed. There could be no written clues since no-one knew what language the One would speak. Written clues might even be followed by another reader, perhaps out of mere curiosity and the whole plot be revealed out of its proper time. That left numbers, patterns and images. Let the One come from wherever, he would understand that two and two made four, and that the roof hereabouts was supported on the backs of lions. Small was pleased that with a small amount of thought he had been able to make so much progress. Already his task seemed less daunting.

Two hours later he still had not been able to think of a single way in which either numbers or images could lead him through the Library. There just did not seem to be anything in the book city that was organised or systematic enough to link all the various suburbs and precincts of learning. The fabric of Alligor was the work of long ages and short epochs. It had been funded by the pride of extinct dynasties, shaped by the forgotten philosophies and redundant religions of dead schools and lost academies. So various was it in all its parts, that styles of building, styles of painting, styles of carving, even the types of joints in the furniture, all changed from gallery to gallery. What kind of plot could possibly run through such an extended cultural labyrinth?

He had read that some cities were held in bond by the sheer weight of their heavy stones pressing down on their foundations; others were bound together by cunning masonry and skilful connection of wooden supporting members. There were even cities in which the fabric was prevented from disintegrating by means of strong iron chains attached to its constituent parts. Alligor was different. Its inhabitants were held in thrall by ideas. Instead of the physical agents such as cement or bitumen or chain, the organizing principle in Alligor was that of ideas and the connections and associations between them. Its commerce was in the bringing together of things artificially separated. Alligor was a mind pregnant with ideas. Alligor was a book with many stories. Alligor was a story of all the world, told by all the world.

Small knew nothing about the world but he did know about stories. He knew that they had to have a beginning, a middle and an end. He also knew that they had to have a plot and that the plot ran through the story like a thread, turning this way and that, doubling back on itself, sometimes visible, sometimes invisible as the author tied his knot. Just like a thread the plot had to have two ends and the meaning of the story was revealed in its untying. If he was to understand the plot of the Book City, Small realised that he must begin at the beginning. Alligor had only one entrance. Every reader must enter by that gate. If there was a path through the labyrinth then that must be where it began.

Small stood at the head of the Great Stair and faced the door. For the newly arrived reader the Eastern Galleries were the very first suite of rooms he entered. They were the vestibule through which the Temple of learning was approached. In all the years he had lived and worked amongst the books Small had never before remarked this obvious fact. He paced the length of the first gallery trying to see this place as something more than a mere storehouse. Was it a riddle, an opening chapter, a sign post, a formula? The books sat inscrutably on their shelves.

What were all these books? Pythagoras had said that everything was number. Could the books be tokens or calculi? Were they arranged in numbers triangular or square? He began by counting the bookcases. Next he found the numbers of shelves. He started to count the individual books, but forgot his totals and gave up. In desperation he even counted the windows and calculated the number of flagstones on the floor. None of this provided a single indication. After an hour of futile addition and subtraction he stood facing the door which led out of the gallery still without any idea of how to proceed. Staring stupidly at the door he noticed something odd. There should have been ten of the large double-sided bookcases in the room, but there were only nine. Four pairs were equally spaced and then here by the exit was a single bookcase facing an empty space. He could not say why, but the asymmetry of the arrangement was irritating. The more he thought about it, the more it perturbed him. This was the very first gallery. Why had the tenth bookcase never been built? He tried to return to the problem in hand but the missing bookcase kept intruding into his thoughts. It would have been the last bookcase in the room. It would have been important in any arrangement. First, last and central positions were often important in the patterns of the library. He walked over to the single unpaired bookcase. The central shelf was larger than the others. It contained nine books of leaves. Nine books, nine bookcases? Each book sat in its own individual wooden compartment. It was a permanent arrangement.

He was acutely aware of the silence as he lifted out the first book. He wiped the dust away from the label. *Travels to the End of the World*, next to it *Odyssey*, then *Journey to the Underworld; Up-country March* by Xenophon, *Alexander's Celestial Journey; To the Outer Sea* by Hanno; *The Making of Maps* by Scylax. If it was a signpost then where was it pointing? Once through the door it was possible to turn either left or right. Small reasoned that it would be unduly perverse to have a signpost on the right side of the exit to indicate a left turn and so turned right. The gallery he next entered had its full complement of bookcases. On the central shelf of the last bookcase on the right were eight books. Once again each had its own partitioned compartment. They were treatises on number, arithmetic and calculation. Through the doorway another corridor led right and left. He turned right.

In the next gallery there were seven books on their partitioned shelf, but the shelf was two levels below the centre of the bookcase. Small heaved open the massive wooden door. To the left a corridor curved away into utter darkness; to the right a stairwell spiralled up into the light and down into the gloom. He scampered down the stairs past the first landing and then on to the second. The gallery door stood ajar. Everywhere was dust, dilapidation and cobwebs. Six books here, this time on the left and on the top shelf. Through the doorway a stair

182

ascended to a high landing with a stone balustrade. There were two doorways. He passed through the one on the left.

By this time Small was exhilarated. There could be no doubt about it. He had found a path. Five books led to four, four to three, three to two; finally he stood in a gallery in such an ancient and ruinous state that he almost despaired of being able to complete his quest. Some of the bookcases had disintegrated entirely; others leaned drunkenly against each other having spilled their contents onto the floor. It was difficult even to reach the end of the gallery let alone find the last bookcase. He clambered over the heaps of decaying wood and rotting vellum, all the while whispering apologies to the Great Author for the damage he was inflicting upon the books beneath his feet. The last bookcase had been pushed over until it rested at an angle against the wall. Small crawled into the cave which had formed beneath it. There could be no mistaking the volume which had occupied its central shelf. It was even larger than the bed of Sardanapalus. He tugged and manoeuvred it out into the light. It was a massive treatise on hunting called *The Hunt Royal*. Small turned the massive leaves. The book described the hunting of a variety of beasts from lions and unicorns to, implausibly, a white whale. He was baffled. Was this the manuscript around which the library had grown? How could such a book counter the evil of knowledge? As he turned the beautifully illustrated leaves dedicated to Diana and to Orion a scrap of parchment fluttered to the ground. He placed the book carefully on a pile of rubbish and picked up the fragment. Words had been written on it. He read: *Penman here on the Shining Path yr.1414. A Royal Hunt indeed! But alas the beast escaped my hounds.*

This was not the manuscript itself but only a marker on the path. Small did not know what to think. The last person to get this far was three hundred and sixty-three years ago. At that time the book city must have been fully staffed and well visited. Even so Penman had lost the trail. What hope was there for an apprentice librarian in these modern times when the only thing that bound the library together was cobweb and the only thriving things the poisonous spiders that spun them? For the rest of the day Small hunted hopelessly through adjacent galleries until his throat was raw with the dust and dirt; his hands and face filthy with the grime of ages. The onset of twilight alarmed him. He did not know where he was and needed the light to find his way back. The thrill of the chase had made him incautious, he had completely forgotten about the assassin. He was also hungry and thirsty. Finding his way back was no simple matter. The signposts were all pointing one way. In his excitement he had not memorized the route he had taken. Before long he was hopelessly lost. Furious with himself he ran on through the darkening library. Sooner or later he must find a familiar landmark.

When he first heard the noise it was a low burbling murmur which mingled confusingly with its own echoes. As he advanced cautiously towards its source it became a voice, and then, as it acquired definition and characteristics, it became recognizable. It was Dim. But who was he talking to? Small strained his hearing to catch another voice, but in vain.

Dim was talking to himself. "They call me Dim. Do you want to play? I won't hurt you. I pull the book thledge. You can ride on it. I'm hungry. Nobody wants to play with me. My mummy was very pretty. I have to be a good boy. She promithed ..."

Small was too irritated and too thirsty to try and make sense of what Dim was saying and so interrupted his soliloquy. "Dim? Are you alone?" he said quietly.

"Yeth," came Dim's reply, and then, "Its you Small! You've come to see me."

"Not on purpose, I'm lost. What are you doing here?"

In the gloom Dim's bulky form seemed to sag and shrink. "The mummies don't like me." he said, "They think I want to hurt them. The men hit me and laugh at me. They say if I come back they will hit me again."

Small was just not in the mood for sorting out what had happened. There had clearly been a misunderstanding. Dim was not used to the physicality and the horseplay of the Murgans. That was all it was. "Can you show me the way back to the Eastern Galleries," he said. "I will take you to the Refectory. No-one will hurt you. The Murgans are my friends. I will explain everything."

Dim gave a heavy sigh. "I will show you the way but I won't go back. They will hurt me. They have knives."

Small was exasperated. Dim could be so stubborn. "Show me the way then and I will find out what has been happening."

Quite how Dim found his way about the Library was a mystery to everybody. It was a part of the strange way in which he had been touched by the Divine Being that he had never ever been lost in Alligor. Even in the dark he always knew what was around every corner. Soon they were back in familiar corridors. Small took his leave, but felt a restraining hand on his elbow. Dim's voice boomed in his ear.

"Small? Have I been a good boy?"

"Of course you have."

The hand released its grip. Small broke away and started to jog down the corridor. The voice spoke again. "I'm very hungry," it said.

A wonderful aroma of food issued from the kitchen and caused Small's mouth to water as he crossed the Great Courtyard. Two Murgans were posted at the entrance to the Refectory. When he tried to pass between them they threw him back unceremoniously.

"No work: no food. Those are our orders."

Small was unutterably shocked. "But I worked yesterday!" he said.

"You worked yesterday: you ate yesterday. Work tomorrow and you can eat tomorrow."

"But I went riding with Puttfark. He is my friend."

The guards smirked at each other. "Then talk to him tomorrow when he gets back from his business trip. Meanwhile we have our orders. If we don't follow them then we won't eat either."

Small was too shocked and demoralised to argue. Stupid guards, stupid booksearch, stupid Library. He turned away and stamped his way back into the stairwell. He tried to analyse his anger. Before the Murgans had arrived he had often gone without food. Now his hunger seemed to be his master. His stomach was protesting loudly and felt as if it was consuming itself. He had to eat something. What was happening to him? Even though it was almost dark, he decided on impulse to go to the roof. Up there he would be able to forage something or other; fruit perhaps, or flower seeds.

He entered the upper levels. This time the tiny door and the passage beyond it were a serious struggle. He had a momentary panic when he realised that if he did get stuck then there could be no rescue. No-one would even know where he was. A few more Murgan meals and the roof of Alligor would be closed to him for ever.

The fierce wind of the morning had scoured all the clouds from the sky. The western horizon still glowed with a narrow ribbon of deepest crimson shading into green-blue. Before this ghastly daylight finally disappeared, Small was able to find some windfalls. Squatting in the dark he ate figs soft and rank with the odours of fermentation and rot. They were by turns sickly sweet and tainted with the familiar tangs of mildew. For the first time he felt a faint disgust at the pocked and blemished bird leavings he was eating. Philosophically he stifled a yearning for the bland wholesomeness of a Murgan breakfast. After all a full stomach was a full stomach once the palette had been swilled clean with rain water.

The wind seemed always to blow from the same quarter nowadays. The morning's gale had subsided but the gilded weathercock still faced west. Small felt too sated and lazy to climb up onto its back and so he laid full length on the warm stones of the roof and clasped his hands behind his head. Above him the stars wrote their silent poetry as the heavens rose and fell. He tried to remember all that Velik had told him about the movements of the planets and the patterns of the constellations. Venus Ishtar hung on the horizon like a jewel of light, unspeakably beautiful and terrible, like a promise and a threat at once. The red eye of Mars Ares stared balefully at her from the zenith. Between them both Small marked the blazing jewels on the sword scabbard of the giant hunter Orion where he hung askew in the Eastern sky. He tried to make out the other constellations, but without Velik's pointing finger and the accompanying stories, they did not look like the things they were supposed to represent. Was that a Bear or a plough?

The food made him drowsy and relaxed. Staring up into the heavens he felt strangely disembodied. Beneath him the books slept on their shelves like seeds in the ground. Puttfark would have said like corpses in a catacomb. He wondered how many people had lain here just as he was doing with the whole wisdom of the world below and the greatest mystery of all above. He thought of the very first librarians. But then he suddenly realised that this whole roof landscape had been built later. The original readers and librarians would not have been here above the library at all, they would have been down at ground level in the courtyard. In its first days the library had been an immense hollow square of architecture surrounding a vast open space. Would there really have been room for a thousand tents in the Great Courtyard? What a sight that must have been. What discussions there must have been after the light had left the library and the readers returned to their camps. And then, when the last voice had fallen silent, all eyes would have turned from the dark buildings of the library to the bright architecture of the cosmos. Contemplating the vast, ineffable, ungraspable immensity of it all would have stilled any tongue. What did they think when they looked up at the zodiac forever passing across the sky like a serpent which hid its tail in its mouth? Did those ancient readers recognise the same endless cycle of people, their attributes and the beasts which accompanied them as they processed across the heavens on their shining path?

His reverie was interrupted with a jolt. A *shining path*. A path defined in pattern, story, order, arrangement and sequence. He thought of Alligor itself. Of the ancient ceilings dusted with golden stars. Of the original building which snaked around the central square and ended where it had begun just like the shining path of the zodiac. Perhaps the shining path was not a path through the library, but a

186

library that was itself a path; and Alligor not just a library with a serpent, but a serpent library which concealed its end in its beginning.

The further implications of this momentous revelation suddenly dawned on Small. When the manuscript was first hidden, only the original quadrangle had been built. Over the millennia, architects had filled the Great Courtyard with their additions, but as Velik had discovered, the first books stayed where they had been put. If the manuscript was anywhere it had to be in that original part of the building. Small realised that at a stroke he had just eliminated nine tenths of Alligor from his quest. He was exhilarated.

Small passed an uncomfortable night, partly from restless anticipation of the next day's activity and partly from the chill damp air. If eating the Murgans' food had made him more susceptible to hunger, then sleeping in the humid warmth of the Refectory must have lowered his tolerance to the cold. Stiff and irritable he rose with the sun. White mist tilted eerily in the still air above the pools and flashes of rain water. The cold West wind had brought autumn early to Alligor. Plants which had travelled here from the South now bore scorched and darkening leaves. Their fruits had fallen before they ripened. Shrivelled and shrunken they lay about on the ground, scorned even by insects. The more temperate vegetation had already begun to take on the richer tints of decay and decomposition, as if nature was a widow masking her lost youth with finery. The birds and insects too felt the changing season and squabbled over the fast ripening food with a new urgency. Some of the birds which queued to drink and bathe already felt the pull of the sun as it retreated before the cold and were gathered into chattering flocks for the long flight south. As he filled his book bag with as much edible matter as he could forage, Small mused over the way Nature's fecundity always expressed itself in death and decay, and how all her bounty, what men feed upon and call riches, originates in the ending of life. What was the profligacy of autumn if not a great symbol of the vanity of all material things?

As the rising sun showed between the roofs, Small set off through the long shadows to the dark archway which led back to the world of problems and responsibilities. Before he ducked through the doorway, he turned for a final look at the private kingdom of his childhood. He had quite simply outgrown his rooftop paradise. It was not just the physical restriction of its secret entrance, but also that he could no longer find enjoyment in the solitary pleasures it afforded him. The golden weathercock creaked loudly as it turned to face a freshening

187

breeze from the East. As Small plunged into the darkness of the upper levels he wondered why he had never before noticed what a mischievous expression the cock wore on that other side of its face.

If all things had their seasons then it was also late autumn for the library itself. Alligor had grown fecund in its decay and pregnant with significance. It had the same profligate and promiscuous character as Nature herself. Almost in parody of the trees from which they had been fashioned, the bookshelves cracked and split and delivered their contents onto the ground. 'Here are my riches' they seemed to say; 'choose, take, devour, digest: or let them lie, as you will'. The ideas in books seeded themselves in the mind. There they were nurtured, grew, blossomed and formed the seeds of other books and each book was the seed of a new library. Small had always known that Alligor was a repository of memories, but the notion that the memories themselves had a history and were arranged accordingly was quite novel to him. Having grasped the notion of sporadic building and collection over several millennia, he now felt as if he was walking through the pages of a history book. The outer perimeter was so obviously older than the rest; he wondered why he had never realised how significant that was. It was the only part firmly fixed in time: the rest was a chaos of ages. Thus Alligor itself was a chronicle set in stone for those who knew how to read it. He had often read about buildings with stories carved or painted on their walls, but now he saw that the walls themselves told their own history.

Humans are creatures of habit. Left to their own devices they draw the patterns of their lives and, even though they derive no pleasure from it, they go over the familiar lines of their designs again and again. Eventually they forget that other patterns are possible. Before long the fear of change becomes so strong that they develop an almost religious aversion to difference. They invent laws and taboos to forbid the making and taking of other paths. So had it been with Alligor. Certain doors in constant use were familiar to all; others remained stubbornly sealed, not by bolts and bars, not by fallen debris, but by force of habit. Small knew that he must enter the perimeter of the Book City but was at a loss as to how and where this was to be effected. The Eastern Galleries were the obvious place to start, but he could not recall any doorways other than the ones he always used.

When he stood on the landing at the top of the great stair he could only gape incredulously at a huge entrance sealed by double doors three times the height of a man. It was as if they had appeared by magic. True, they were hidden in deep shadow, but he could not believe that he had never noticed them before. He knew that they had always been there, but because they were never used they had gradually become invisible until their final elision from the librarians' mental map. And yet they were so big and so grand.

Two leaping dolphins fashioned in bronze served as door handles. He paused with his hands on the backs of the fishes. This was the latch to unlock the whole library: these the doors through which all the great philosophers had passed. He pushed and the doors swung silently apart to reveal a vast and gloomy architectural space, its true extent lost in shadow. The ceiling was a double vault carried on a central colonnade of pillars. Each supporting pillar rose to a capital in the form of a ram's head. Curling horns bore the lintels from which the starry vaults sprang. Originally the right-hand wall had been pierced by ample window openings but now only a single casement admitted the light. All of the other window openings had been blinded, filled with the masonry of later and less skilful operatives only concerned with guarding their own acquisitions. The detritus on the floor lay deep and undisturbed. Each time he set down his foot, a puff of dust arose which spread and hung in the still air. The gallery was so wide and high that even the spiders had been unable to reduce its ample proportions. Great swathes of their filthy web rounded every angle and joined every eminence each to each like the webs between the toes on a duck's feet. The bookshelves were masked in ancient filament. The work of millennia of spiders sagged with fistfuls of accumulated dust and insect debris. Great swags festooned the ram's heads and the window bars. Feathered skeletons of birds hung in the cloud-like firmament of cobweb above the window, just as if they had been stopped in mid-flight.

Everywhere was debris and decay. The gallery seemed to have been abandoned without ceremony or forethought. Books lay open on the lecterns where their last readers had abandoned them. One bookstack had been emptied and its contents still stood on the floor nearby. All and everything was masked, veiled, transformed or hidden by the all-pervading web which covered everything with its subtle insubstantiality. Everything was connected and everything obscured. All the different volumes had congealed into uselessness because their arrangement was no longer visible. All were still easy to extract but impossible to find because they were now veiled by the iniquitous web. Only the spiders profited from their appropriation of the library. They held their fat bodies motionless on the invisible filaments anticipating the faint vibrations of their next meal.

The gallery had one remaining window. Small stood on tiptoe so that he could look down into the courtyard. Far below him he saw the woman Imperia. She was vomiting against a wall. He saw her kick dust over the mess before she walked away. Small wondered if the Murgans might have brought illness into Alligor. He drove the thought from his mind. Where the daylight spilled into the gallery through this one half-blinded opening, it lit the opposite wall above the shelves. Small could just make out ancient painted pictures. He yanked at a swathe of obscuring web then quickly jumped back to avoid the cascade of dust which descended to the floor. When the dust cleared he saw a tree on which was hung the fleece of a golden ram. It sparkled with fragments of crystal which had been embedded in the plaster. Coiled around the tree was a mighty serpent. The only other image which could be seen in the gallery was of young men planting saplings in a bare landscape. Everywhere else the spiders had drawn a veil over the precious archives and the rooms which contained them. Small's heart sank at the prospect of having to clean every book and manuscript, every carved wainscot, every painted wall in four miles of perimeter galleries. He walked the length of the gallery. Another double door barred his way. He tore at the swathes of dirty web which hung across it like curtains. The gauzy stuff clung to his fist and wound around his forearm. One sharp tug and it all fell down revealing a large human figure carved in the stone tympanum at the head of the door. A king in full armour sat on his throne. He had been painted all in crimson. One hand held a sheathed sword stark upright, the other rested on a grounded shield. On the shield was the head of a ram in gold. He was the very emblem of power and dominion but, further than this, Small could only guess at his identity because the ancient carver had not cut a name on his creation.

More leaping dolphins opened the doors. For upwards of an hour Small made his way through endless suites of lesser rooms, smaller galleries, claustrophobic archives, abandoned reading rooms, lobbies and stairwells. Each had a painted starry vault; each had its own painted and carved motif. Here was a painted Medusa's head, there a great whale fish. On the ceiling over a large marble reading table a warrior held a bloody knife and a lion's head. One formerly splendid rotunda had seven sisters on the facets of its vault. For each larger room there seemed to be three smaller chambers, each with its own esoteric figure. Small could make nothing of it all and he began to wonder if these images were all random like the painted devices on the book covers in the Cage. Were they only there so that readers could identify individual rooms? Then he came upon another giant set of doors with dolphin handles. The gallery beyond these doors was even larger than that of the ram king. It had a single barrel vault supported on a broad entablature. A stone frieze of horned ox skulls ran all around the room. All the visible imagery was to do with bulls and cattle. Maidens leaped acrobatically over the horns of bulls. A strong man cleaned out a bull's byre. Another wrestled with a bull. Dark-skinned worshippers carried a golden bull calf. A bull ran into the sea bearing a maiden on its back. Small was excited. He knew of a pattern which began with a ram and a bull. If the library had been constructed on this same pattern then up ahead, probably just before the wall turned the angle from north to east, there would be another grand gallery.

The face of a dusty queen looked down on him as he tore open the doors and sprinted onwards, vaulting over collapsed shelves, toppled lecterns and heaps of abandoned literature in a frenzy of anticipation. Over his head hung a giant hunter armed with a club. The gallery seemed familiar. There were footprints in the dust. They were his own. *The Hunt Royal* was perched on its shelf just as he had left it. He ran on. A hare, a dog, and a ship flashed overhead as he passed through room after room. Finally he stood before the dolphin doors. Only then did he allow himself to doubt his theory. What if the walls were covered with elephants? He need not have worried. The first thing he saw was a sunlit patch of wall on which two identical male figures were hauling a chariot in which sat a divinely beautiful woman and a naked child. He did not know the story but he knew the twins were the third sign of the zodiac after the ram and the bull. He shouted out loud, whooped and leaped and fell about until clouds of dust rose high enough to choke him. With convulsing lungs and streaming eyes he fled to the other end of the room. Over the door a figure with a sceptre of snakes peered at him from beneath a winged helmet. He was too excited and triumphant to look back over his shoulder at the long succession of doors he had left open and the arrow-straight trail of fresh footprints in the dust, else he would have seen a long line of running script which told the story of his recent passing in plain language. Outside the gallery of the twins the library immediately turned east. Golden bars of bright sunlight leaned against the south facing windows. He swept the dust triumphantly from a sunlit table and sat in the warm light to eat and reflect.

His positive mood was soon tempered. He had discovered the grand design by which the original building had been laid out. Alligor was built in the image of the zodiac. The major galleries had been assigned to the major constellations of the shining path: but what of all the other rooms? And how did it all relate to the books? Was the entire decorative scheme merely a clever artistic device so that readers would always know where they were? And where in this great architectural cosmos was the manuscript? It seemed unfair that he had come so far from his starting point and yet still had no clearer idea of where or what he was looking for. He decided he needed food for thought.

Small emptied his bookbag onto the table. Along with a cascade of wizened fruits in every stage of damage and decomposition, came the book which Plantman had carried across the library. It landed with a thud. Its outer leaves were spotted with juice and pulp. Cursing himself for not shelving it when he had the chance, he tried to wipe off the worst of the mess with his sleeve. The juices were sticky. Several leaves turned over until the book lay open at an illustrated page. He found himself staring at a picture of the Crimson King, identical in every detail with the carving he had seen over the door. But here the author had written names: MARDUK ARES MARS. RULER OF THE HOUSE OF THE RAM. With this sudden shock of recognition Small turned more pages. He found the Queen of Bulls, the horned goddess VENUS ISHTAR, divinely beautiful without her dusty coat and cobweb veils. The helmeted man with the serpent sceptre was THOTH HERMES RULER OF THE HOUSE OF THE TWINS. There were other images which he remembered from the ceilings of the lesser rooms. The Persian with the Lion, the Sea Monster and the Hare were all minor asterisms which surrounded the zodiacal signs. The book named and explained them all. Their stories were recounted, all their associations and influences listed, along with which colours were theirs and which stones and, of course, which books had been accumulated in their various domains. Even the dolphin door handles were explained as the symbols of the stars rising out of the sea curving overhead and plunging back. Hardly believing in his good fortune Small realised that what he was holding in his hand was a complete guide to the iconography of old Alligor. When Plantman had fled across the library he had not clasped just any volume to his wound. Knowing how important it was that *The Seven Lamps* did not fall into the wrong hands he risked his life to put it beyond their reach. Perhaps somewhere in this iconographical encyclopaedia was a clue to the whereabouts of the library's greatest secret. Small began to read at the beginning.

Know that these are the words of Kalil, a dutiful servant of Alligor, who thought long and pondered deeply on the nature of the library and all it contains. Here I set down my humble opinions for lovers of mysteries. There is no wealth but life and life is not just the mere fact but it is life in the fullest sense both physical and spiritual. We live in a material cosmos but it is also a spiritual cosmos. We inhabit a universe of meaning which language has created for us. The moment we start to describe anything in words it is transformed, metamorphosed, and forever connected to disparate concepts. This is because all language is metaphor and as a consequence all material things have a symbolic existence. All visible things are emblems to us. Thus it is that when we describe the unknowable, ungraspable heavens, the heavens become a book, indeed a whole library of books written in celestial hieroglyphs. We need only describe the sun as the chief body in the sky to attach to it all the attributes of a mortal king. The heavens become his court, and he himself the quick racer in his solar chariot. Likewise the zodiac becomes a ring of great power by which all others are ruled. Words are not the real things they describe but symbols which bring those realities to mind. But words change the meaning of everything to which they are attached.

There are those who account themselves learned because they can name a thousand different things, be they pebbles or stars. You too may have a command of such facts, but facts are as useless as pebbles on a beach, or stars in the sky, until they are marshalled into meaning, connected each to each and woven into dreams and stories. Do you have pebbles? Are they hard and round? Then hurl them from slings; make roads from them; use them to count your flocks. Do you have stars? Do they shine? Then use them to steer your fishing boats from one stinking dock to another. Or you can make each pebble a magic talisman and each star a divine jewel and they become moral signposts to a better life. You can even weave your dreams from them. Here in the library we find that imagination can be far stronger than knowledge, that myth can be more potent than history and that meaning is a richer notion than truth. To understand Alligor you must understand that it too is a symbol which conceals more than it reveals.

The book itself was comprehensive in its description of Old Alligor. Small learned that each of the four sides of the original building represented one of the four seasons and contained major galleries dedicated to the zodiacal signs associated with them. The Ram, the Bull and the Twins were the spring signs presided over by their planetary rulers Mars, Venus and Mercury. The four corners of the building were dedicated to the major winds. Here where spring and summer met, the West wind was represented as a lightly clad youth bearing flowers. Where winter met autumn, an old man in thick clothes carrying a conch shell was the howling North Wind. Small also learned that the Eastern Galleries were in fact on the western side of the book city, but were so-called because the windows of the western side of the quadrangle had all faced East, just as those of the summer side had faced South.

Small leafed through the book several times. He could not find any mention of either secret rooms or hidden manuscripts. No book of special importance was even hinted at. The last chapter contained a curious final summary:

Learned men speak of looking at the stars and gaining wisdom thereby. But the empty spaces are as important as the brilliant points of light, because the darkness between the stars is an essential part of their arrangement. It was out of the dark spaces that the starry images and their outlines were conjured by the mind.

There was a good deal more in this mystical vein before the book ended abruptly where the last page had torn away. Small deeply regretted not having had the courage to peel away that final paragraph from Plantman's wound. He knew that this was an important book, but he still felt that he was missing something. He recognised the strange language which the authors used when their texts had two meanings. Kalil was trying to tell his readers something.

Out of habit more than anything else, he opened the book into two equal halves. Carefully judging the thickness of paper in each hand, he eventually arrived at the exact centre of the volume. There was an illustration of a young maiden holding a stalk of corn. The sign of the Virgin and the end of summer. Was the Virgin the central sign of the zodiac? He was not yet so familiar with the shining path that he could remember all the signs and their places. He went through the book counting the signs before her and the signs after. There were five before her. There were also five after. He counted them over again. He had not made a mistake. One sign of the twelve was missing. Spring had her three houses, and so did summer, but autumn had only two. The centaur archer and the lady with the scales both stared at the place where the ill-omened Scorpion should have been but was not. The hairs rose on the back of his neck. *The empty spaces were as important as the brilliant points of light.* Was this Kalil's way of drawing attention to one particular gallery? What better place could there be in which to put an ill-omened and deadly book than the house of the Scorpion? It was quite possible that the gallery itself had been omitted by the Architect, but Small had come too far to be thwarted now. The hunt was up. The beast would not escape this time.

As an autumn sign the Scorpion's place would be on the Eastern perimeter of the Book City. If he ran fast enough, he could be there well before dark. After putting the remaining fruits back in his pouch, he tucked *The Seven Lamps* back under his arm, swung his legs over the edge of the table and ran to the dolphin doors. As the leaves swung open he shouted in frustration. A solid wall of masonry blocked his path. This was why these galleries had fallen into disuse. They led nowhere. He could not get through; he must go round. How long or labyrinthine the detour might be was beyond knowing. But at least his movements would not be random. Now he knew the layout of the book-city he could use the sun to navigate his way around the obstacle.

Eighteen

Rottko scurried through the maze of galleries like a spider; moving from dark place to dark place; listening for any movement; pausing often to let the muffled echoes of his footsteps die away. His face, disfigured by the cat's claws, was a terrifying mask. From each puffed eyelid, a pattern of livid and puckering lines zigged up into his hairline. Dried blood in broken tracks marked his cheeks and temples. Sardanapalus had signed his name across his forehead in that most ancient of cursive scripts. Rottko's streaming eyes and half closed lids blurred his vision and caused the library to swim before him. It felt as if his eye sockets had been filled with burning grit. Other men might have fallen down and wept, but the hatred of the world which had made an assassin of him, was more powerful than any physical pain. He bore a grudge against the whole earth just for having been born into it and would not rest until he had stabbed it in the heart. The pain in his eyes transformed him from a mere murderer into a dark supernatural force.

He had only the vaguest idea of where he was. Reasoning was futile. It could not help him to find the boy. In the savage state he was in, more primeval and intuitive senses were operating. Each locked door, each blind alley, each fruitless detour served only to hone his predatory instinct. He would find the boy. He just knew. He paused to listen. The silence in this city of books had strange qualities. It was such an unnatural place. There always seemed to be sounds just beyond the reach of the senses: conversations in far off rooms; the murmur of a crowd; the echoes of shouts; the distant rumble of who knows what ancient machinery; even faint and ethereal music. He had not liked this place from the moment he set foot in it. Some places; some jobs; they just had a bad feeling. This was one of them. He looked about him at yet another room full of rubbish and dust. Or was there something? He blinked to clear his streaming eyes. Something not right? The leather binding of a large book on a collapsed bookshelf gleamed in the half light. Gleamed. No dust. No cobwebs. It had been handled recently. Rottko looked up from the book. At the end of the room a succession of doors opened into gallery after gallery. Just before his eyes filmed over he saw the line of footprints leading into the far distance. His lips drew away from his teeth. It was not a smile.

By the standards of Alligor it had not been much of a detour. Small had spent just over an hour trying to circumvent the bricked-up door. It had been a frustrating and interminable time of locked doors, blocked doors, switches from higher floors to lower floors, of dead ends and wrong routes. Finally he found himself in a room decorated with lions and ruled by the Sun King. Back on the shining path once more, he began to jog through the summer galleries. Once upon a time these rooms must have been the warmest and brightest in the whole library. Where traces of the windows still remained he could see that they had been especially large and fine, their heads filled with carved stonework pierced by star and moon shapes into which fragments of coloured glass had been inserted. Now there was more shadow than light in these galleries. Everywhere was dilapidation and decay.

Just before he turned the corner from summer to autumn, Small turned to look back the way he had come. For the first time he felt a twinge of apprehension. The line of footprints told the story of his passing as plain as the day. His return journey would be especially hazardous. The light would be failing. He might be ambushed at any point. But he had come too far and it was now too late to do anything other than press on. He ran faster, dreading having to spend any more time than he had to in these dark and alien galleries. There were no more detours. He passed through five small rooms and then came up against the familiar dolphin doors. He grasped the handles and pushed his way in.

Although there was very little light in the room, he saw right away that it had been looked after until relatively recently. The books and rolls were tidily installed on their shelves, and the tables were clear. A thin film of fine dust covered everything, but there were only a few cobwebs in high and inaccessible corners. Over the door a female figure held a set of scales in perfect balance. This was Venus Ishtar, ruler of the House of Scales. From what he could see of the decorations they looked more beautiful and harmonious than any he had seen in the whole of Alligor but he did not have the time to examine them closely. He pressed on through room after room after room until he came to another set of dolphin doors which opened onto a very large and spacious gallery. Centaurs disported themselves all over the vault. Many carried bows. Hunting dogs of all kinds ran with them through a landscape without fences or walls. Small hurriedly consulted *The Seven Lamps*. No doubt at all, this was the house of the centaur archer Sagittar. Over the door sat Jupiter, a gilded bolt of lightning clasped in his hand, his eagle by his side, enthroned as the ruler. Small was perplexed. Where was the gallery of Scorpio?

He retraced his steps, checking every gallery against Kalil's description until he came to a door which led off the main route. It opened into a gallery without any other illumination than the dim light which spilled in through the entrance. He would have passed it by, but there was a quality about the darkness which gave him the impression of a very large space. When he looked at Kalil's book there did not seem to be any corresponding entry. He left *The Seven Lamps* on a table and with a sense of mounting excitement he groped his way into the darkness. The door kept closing itself. He noticed it was on rising hinges. It took some time before his eyes became accustomed to the gloom. The room was a domed polygon. There were no windows. Since the shelves ran all around the walls it looked as if the gallery had been built without any source of natural light. Apart from the shadowy rows of books and the central table, only two features were discernible. One was a sort of hook shape in gold leaf high up on the vault which reflected the light from the doorway; the other was some kind of metalwork structure which had been fixed to the centre of the ceiling.

The day was coming to an end. Small realised that soon there would not be enough light left to read by. For a while he wandered aimlessly from shelf to shelf picking out books at random and carrying them out into the light, hoping he might pick the right one by chance. Many of the authors were well-known to him. The most magnetic and emotional orators, the greatest seers, the most subtle and secretive diplomats, all were represented here. Works by bitter and dogmatic critics sat with those of ambitious and violent generals. Arcane works by the most occult and painstaking researchers rubbed shoulders with manuals of butchery and treatises on ironmongery. Here and there amongst the patterned bindings were plainer, unmarked texts pertaining to the diseases of the secret parts of the body or else to the violent passions connected with them. None of the books Small opened seemed remarkable enough to build a library around. If he were to check every book in the gallery he might be here for a week: perhaps more. And how would he know the book? Small stopped his random searching. There must be a significant arrangement somewhere: a signpost perhaps, a marker of some kind. This was a room filled with the writings of subtle thinkers. Perhaps the subtlety of the arrangement would be too great for him

The metalwork hanging from the ceiling intrigued him. He decided to take a closer look by piling up some of the library's heavy furniture onto the table underneath it. More by touch than by sight he was able to identify it as an ornate corona of six lamps joined by a flat circular band and fixed by long rods to the vault. Letters had been raised up on the flat band by hammering them out from the inside. He traced them with his fingers. It was an exceptionally archaic script but luckily the words were simple and similar in many tongues: *Strike no flame in the library lest all wisdom be consumed.* This was indeed a strange thing. Fire was not permitted anywhere in the Library where books were kept. He had never seen a lamp in any other such room and yet here was a whole tree of lamps in a room without light. Why a lamp here? Why the warning? Why a room without light anyway? He shifted his attention to the surrounding vault and the golden hook. From up here he could see that a gigantic scorpion writhed across the shadowy ceiling. This was the place! His eyes followed the black tapering body and its segmented tail until it ended in the deadly golden hook at the end of the monster's tail. It was indeed a prodigious weapon. Plated in gold-leaf and dripping with gore it looked capable of stabbing clean through a man's body and coming out the other side. The painted sting was on the curve of the vault, about fourteen feet above the floor. Small moved around to the other side of the corona in order to see it better.

He noticed that the painter had done a curious thing. The scorpion's sting was surrounded by a rectangle indicated by a fine painted line. Small angled his head and screwed up his eyes trying to make out what the painter had done. It was not a painted line at all. It was the gap around a small door. With the light getting fainter every minute, Small dragged at the large and very heavy table. He could only move it an inch at a time and his feet kept slipping on the smooth stone floor. When it was in position he climbed up onto the table, but even then he could not reach the little door. Climbing down again he raised a smaller table on top of the first, and then a stool on top of that. His eyes were still not level with the door but by raising his arms he could just touch the bottom of it with his hands. His fingers felt a slight blemish on the painted surface where a handle might once have been; otherwise there was nothing. In sheer frustration he struck the door with his fist. Instantly it fell open enveloping him in a cascade of dust and debris. When he opened his eyes he saw that beyond the door a smooth and empty tunnel of masonry led up to the open air. Faint evening light filtered down through it onto the metal candelabrum. He could see that the cups of the lamp were filled with dark tallow. The wicks were intact. These lamps had never been lit. The door in the vault squeaked faintly as it swung slightly on its hinges.

He climbed down again and looked around. There was now enough light to see that the ceiling was a vaulted dome, plastered and painted with the gigantic and fearsome scorpion which snaked from the skylight across the vault and down the other side to where its claws embraced the doorway which led out of the place. Somewhere in this room was the most important and dangerous book in Alligor. Small strode back and forth. He looked carefully at the King in black armour over the door. His face was sensual and cruel. His sword was drawn and threatening. On the walls were dark and disturbing images of torture and flaying, cruelty and sensuality. He recognized the hedonistic King Sardanapalus reclining on his vast yellow bed whilst his wives and concubines were slaughtered before his eyes. Elsewhere a muscular hero chained to a rock had his eyes pecked by eagles. With the daylight beginning to fade and the shadows creeping out of their hiding places, this was not a place in which to contemplate staying the night. He had to solve this final riddle quickly.

The failing light illuminated the corona of lamps. It was a work of fine craft. Six cups filled with tallow sat on the circular band which was linked by rods to a large central ring. Curious, Small moved around the gallery so that he could look up the shaft into the daylight. He found himself looking through the large central ring of the corona into a steep and narrow shaft which passed through the vault and out of the building. He stared at the lamp. A lamp which must not be lit? It made no sense. No librarian would ever light that lamp. Only the very worst sort of reader might do such a thing. Then there was the shaft, narrow and dark as a chimney. What use was that? Unless … unless it *was* a chimney and not meant to let light in but to let smoke out. What if the dark tallow in the cups was not intended to light the room at all? What if they were in fact incense candles? In the growing darkness of these unfamiliar galleries it was natural for Small to suspect everything of having a sinister and serpentine design. He remembered Axares; the hunting of serpents; and their poisonous exhalation: *a smoke like the fumes of incense candles that killed in the time it took to take a single breath*. He was certain that the lamps were a fatal trap for the wrong sort of reader. The self closing door was to contain the fumes. The chimney was to flush out the poison after it had done its work. Like the book on the lectern in the Cage, this was a trap intended for those who needed everything in plain view, who wanted the world unveiled, those who murdered to dissect, those who would tear apart a great wonder in order to sell the materials from which it was made. With a rush of understanding Small realised that the gallery of Scorpio was a room designed to be dark. It contained a secret which could be found in the dark. He closed his eyes and waited for his thoughts to calm.

His five senses were now reduced to four. Hearing? As little use here in this silent room as anywhere else in the Library. He listened until the silence overwhelmed his senses and he began to hear those ethereal and distant noises always just out of earshot. He shook his head to banish them. Smell? Mildew, dust, decay and an overpowering impression of age beyond remembering. Taste? Just the bitter dryness of the eternal dust. Only Touch remained, but it was touch assisted by intelligence. Hadn't he read the inscription on the lamp through his fingertips? Still with his eyes closed he began to move around the room running his fingers along the shelves of manuscripts and books of leaves. As he turned the angle between each side of the room some part of his mind began to count: ... *four, five, six* .... He stopped and opened his eyes. Turning slowly he began to count the sides of the room starting from the door. This room had thirteen sides, but only twelve contained book shelves. The thirteenth was the door. Twelve sides? Twelve houses of the zodiac? The Scorpion lived in the eighth house. Starting from the left of the door Small counted out the sides of the room. The shelves of the eighth side were stuffed with hundreds of volumes. He closed his eyes and ran his hands all over the books and shelves but found nothing. He counted the shelves. There were nine. He stamped his foot with frustration. The light was almost gone. He ran back to the door and counted out the sides again but from the other side of the door. This time there were twelve shelves on the eighth side. He quickly touched the shelves until he came to the eighth from the floor. It was just above eye level. Unlike all the others, this shelf had a vertical partition on the left hand side; a partition just wide enough to insert a single slim book of leaves. He stood on tiptoe and thrust his hand between the partition and the corner. Unwilling to accept the inevitable he felt into every corner of the space. It was empty. He stood gripping the edge of the shelf in utter despair. Was this really the place? Had the manuscript been found, taken away, destroyed? Had it ever been here? His finger scratched irritably at a rough spot on the shelf. It began to trace the curving shape to and fro, to and fro. All of Small's attention suddenly concentrated into that fingertip. Not just a rough spot: not just a shape, but a letter crudely scratched or carved into the wood: a letter from an ancient language, a language originally stabbed into the soft clay from the banks of the great rivers, a letter G in its regal form. The mark of the man who would be king: Gropius.

The ancient stories were true. He had been here. It was typical of the man that he would leave his mark to taunt anyone who came after him. But what had he done with the manuscript? Had he laid his own dark clues through the library? Small thought not. The shining path was structural, architectural, it could not be re-arranged. If Gropius had moved books around, the librarians would soon have put them back in their proper places. Whatever he did, he had to do quickly before he was recognised. This room was the symbolical resting place of the manuscript, shelved anywhere else and it might be lost forever. It must be here somewhere. He sat down in the gloom and began to think.

Small did not know much about the astrological sign of the Scorpion, Kalil had not written about it, but he had read about the creature itself. Its sting was sudden and out of all proportion to its small size. It was a creature of darkness. It hid in the shadows. He looked around him. This was a whole room of darkness and shadows. Gropius must have hidden the manuscript expecting man of dark intellect. A man not afraid of using violence. A seeker who had little respect for books or libraries. A man too impatient to be distracted by the subtleties of the librarians. Small knew a man like that. How would Puttfark approach the gallery of the Scorpion? In his mind's eye the man-in-white entered the room, instinctively doing his little side-step to check behind the door; and then Small knew where the manuscript would be. Until now no librarian had ever feared the assassin behind the door. In an ordinary world no reader would dream of it. But in a world turned upside down ….

He pushed the entrance door right back against the bookshelves. Part of the bottom shelf behind the door was in the deepest darkest shadow in the room. He let the door swing away from the shelves and groped around for some time. An extra shelf had been put in at the bottom of the stack leaving just enough room for a single volume to be pushed in horizontally. He felt around until his fingers closed on the object which lay there. It appeared to be a slim leather book of cut leaves bound with straps. He swept off the thick dust with his sleeve and tilted it towards the last glimmer of light. Tooled into the leather was a single word GROPIUS.

He had his book.

Small carried his prize out of the darkening gallery and into the twilit outer chamber. He held the book up at arms' length before him with mixed feelings of triumph, awe, and dread. He swung around so that the failing light would fall on the book's cover. Now that the hunt was over he felt unsure, uncertain, even fearful of what he had done. This unremarkable leather bound volume in his hands was the seed from which Alligor had grown. He thought of how strong men had freed the stones from the living rock; how stone carvers had dressed the rough stones; how masons had raised them into the architecture needed to hold the books. How whole forests had been felled so that armies of joiners could roof the walls and vaults and carpenters could furnish the galleries. Plumbers, plasterers, painters and glaziers had all worked their arts and then passed on. For thousands of years books had been carried to this place. Millions of books had been assembled. Hundreds upon hundreds of librarians had devoted their lives to the service of the book-city and its contents. All over the world poets had rhymed, historians recorded, geographers mapped, astrologers charted, storytellers spun their yarns and tied their plots; all wholly unaware that they were helping to weave the great veil, the impenetrable cloak that was Alligor. And all this effort was to keep this one little book safely concealed.

He stared at the book in his hands trying to grasp its enormous significance.

"This is it," he murmured softly, and then in a loud voice which sent treacherous echoes dancing through the Library, "This is it and I have found it."

By now the library was beginning to lose its shape in the twilight. Roofs, supports and floors began to blend. Architecture, furniture and books melted together. Books became walls; walls lost their solidity in the darkness. The light was draining out through the few openings left in the masonry. In this chamber of shadows and shapes in shadows, Small sensed movement. He turned. The shadow spoke.

"Give it to me," said a voice like a studded boot on a stone. The ghastly face of the assassin emerged from the darkness. "Give it to me. It belongs to Murga. It is mine."

Small clasped the volume to his chest paralysed with shock. "This is not the book you seek," he said "This book belongs to Alligor."

"You lie," rasped the assassin, "I can see the name on the cover. That book belongs to Murga. Just lay it on the table and back away."

Rottko's face was not just disfigured by claw marks; it was also contorted with hatred. Rottko was not a forgiving man. Someone would have to pay very heavily for the assassin's pain and humiliation. Small sensed rather than saw the blade appear in Rottko's hand as the assassin began the slow choreography of professional violence. Whilst Small had been standing rigid with shock, Rottko had moved with a slow side-stepping motion until he had the boy penned in between two tables.

The assassin moistened his lips before he spoke again. "Just lay the book on the table and back away," he said.

Rottko shuffled closer. Small noticed his puffy eyelids and streaming eyes. The assassin pulled out a cloth from his pocket to try and clear his vision. Small moved towards the table holding the book out in front of him, but then his heart began to pump panic into his limbs. He acted instinctively and unexpectedly: ducked and rolled under the massive piece of furniture and leaped to his feet on the other side. Rottko swung his arm in a swift arc across the table, but only sliced the darkening air. Before the assassin could recover his balance, Small was off and running through the dark library. Still holding the book, he sprinted as fast as he could out of the autumn galleries and back towards the part of the Library he knew. Fear gave him strength and speed he did not know he had. He ran on until he felt sure that his pursuer was not at his heels and then he ran some more, only slowing to a fast walk as he approached the outskirts of the Eastern city. The blood was pounding in his head and his breath came in gasps. It reminded him of the Murgan music. Slowly he became aware of a counter-rhythm in the darkness behind him; fast, insistent, growing louder, closer, shod feet running; breath panting; still in pursuit: Rottko. With a cry of alarm Small sprang into a run. Panic now had him in her grip and he sprinted blindly on through the galleries. He had no thought of where he was heading, only that it was away from that terrible sound.

He turned a corner and there in the distance was movement, life, safety. A Murgan patrol making its way out of the Library. He could hear their voices.

"Help me!" he called out, "Help me!"

The men turned towards him, surprise and alarm on their faces. Weapons appeared in their hands. They craned their heads to see more clearly. Then Small heard the awful breathless voice of the assassin from behind him.

"Catch him, he has the book!"

Small skidded to a halt. Suddenly everything was clear. The Murgans were all together in this. Puttfark must have joined forces with the assassin right from the moment they knew he was here. The patrols had probably been supplying him with food. Axaris had written 'Find out where your serpent feeds.' If only .... The guards began slowly and deliberately to advance upon him. Rottko stumbled out of the gloom, breathing harshly and clutching his side. Small looked around desperately for an escape. There was a low arched doorway between the bookshelves on his left. Neither the guards nor Rottko could see it. The door might be locked, it might be jammed, it might be a cupboard or a dead end, but there was nowhere else to go. Six full-grown men were advancing upon him with drawn weapons. He had not the slightest doubt that they were going to kill him. He was numb with terror. He moved as if he was underwater. The Murgans were gradually shepherding him into the space between the book cases.

"Just throw the book to me," said Rottko, cutting arabesques in the air with the point of his stiletto, "and you won't get hurt." Every muscle and fold of his damaged face belied what he was saying.

The first guard had moved to where he could see into the bay between the bookcases.

"There's a door!" he shouted.

The Murgans rushed towards Small who turned and hurled himself at the door. It opened a fraction and then jammed. Extreme terror and the primeval instinct for survival propelled him through the impossibly narrow opening. So extreme was the power of the reflex that he neither feared injury nor felt the pain as he scraped his head and chest through. For an instant the strap of his bookbag snagged the latch. Grasping hands reached out blindly for him, but then he was away. A thrown dagger rebounded harmlessly from the wall and clattered along the dark pavement at his feet.

The Murgans crowded at the door trying desperately to force their bodies through the gap. They had neither the youthful physique nor the extreme motivation to get past the door. Rottko was seething with rage.

"One of you go tell Puttfark. The rest of you smash down that door." he said as he put his knife away. The boy was lucky, very lucky to have escaped him twice. Rottko was not superstitious but he respected the science of luck. Successful assassins never underestimated the goddess Fortuna. She could be a formidable ally or a deadly opponent. She only held sway over those who submitted to her rule, but he had seen skilful assassins meet their end because they thought that their strength and cleverness were enough. You might take advantage of her favours but she was a capricious whore who quickly grew tired of her paramours. The boy's luck might hold for a while but sooner or later it would leave him. Until then he, Rottko, would leave nothing to chance.

Nineteen

Small hid for some time in a dark corner of a room which had several escape routes. This time there was no pursuit. Despite being very shaken by what had happened, Small felt that to do nothing would be to play into the hands of the Murgans. They were methodical and thorough. By the morning they would have had time to plan ahead and organize themselves. Guards would be doubled and alert and the Murgans would probably have convinced the other librarians that he was a dangerous renegade. The other librarians would feel glad that the Murgans were guarding them even closer than before. If he was to act at all he had to act quickly. He had to find Old and tell him what he knew. Old was the senior librarian. He would take responsibility for the manuscript. Small decided to visit him in his window niche overlooking the courtyard.

It was now almost night, but here in the Eastern Galleries the darkness was Small's friend. He knew every inch of this part of the city by heart. He did not need light to move around. Unless the Murgans were prepared to sit silently in the dark all night waiting for him, he had the advantage. Somehow he knew that patience was not their style. Their every impulse was to act, not to wait and see. His pulse quickened as he moved noiselessly on bare feet through the darkness. The only sound was the swish of his silk tzirt which he silenced by holding his arms tightly to his sides. Then there was only the subliminal whisper of his breathing. Ordinarily the creaking, groaning and thudding of doors would have betrayed his passing through the library, but the Murgans had insisted that all the doors be wedged or jammed open. It was a Murgan foible that their 'government' of Alligor should be as open as possible. Their excuse was that if anyone was attacked they would be able to hear their cries for help. But the truth was that they simply didn't trust any situation which they could not oversee, any conversation which they could not overhear. Their own quarters were of course always locked and guarded.

Small felt reasonably safe walking in such a familiar place since the Murgans could not move around without giving themselves away. They needed lanterns in the dark and the tramp of their heavy shoes echoed through the galleries. The musky perfume they used betrayed their presence wherever they went. Even so he paused and listened at every doorway. When he reached the stairway he extended his hand into the window niche which Old had made his own. The old man was not there. He felt the chill night breeze on his hand. One of the glass panes had been recently broken. He was beginning to be anxious about his old friend when he heard voices down in the courtyard. By climbing into the niche he was able to see the lamplight spilling out from the refectory door. A distinctive red and yellow robe flared into view. It seemed that Sly had also negotiated the privilege of sleeping outside the refectory. The garish robe headed for the great staircase.

Sly's discontented mutterings grew louder as he ascended the stair. When Small could hear the soft scuffing of the librarian's feet on the stone steps he spoke.

"Greetings, Sly," he said.

"Eeaagh!" Sly was so startled that he lost his footing as he jumped back.

"It's only me," Small said.

"Small? What do you mean by scaring me half to death?"

"Sorry Sly, I was looking for Old. Do you know where he is?"

"He is where you will be if you don't run off and hide somewhere where the Murgans won't find you."

"What?"

"They grabbed him and dragged him away. They said that you and he were thieves and murderers, that you had found their book and were planning to run off with it and sell it; that you were killing everyone who tried to stop you."

"That is a complete lie! The Murgans are in league with the assassin. They have been feeding him whilst he tortured and killed every librarian he could find."

"But you have got their book?"

In the darkness Small clasped his book bag tightly to his body. "No. Not their book. Another book."

"As you say, but they are so certain that you have the book they are seeking that they have called off their search. Tomorrow is a holiday for the librarians. There will be music and dancing in the refectory, but of course that is just to keep us all out of the way whilst they hunt you down. I hope you realise that you are in grave danger of losing your life. These people use violence as casually as we use these stairs. I would not like to be in your position."

Small kept silent whilst he thought about how vulnerable he was. His skin crept with apprehension.

"This other book you have found," Sly spoke in that more familiar wily tone which he adopted when he thought there was something of value being kept from him, "What is written in it?"

"I don't know," Small replied, "At the moment I found it, the assassin found me. I had to flee for my life. Then it was too dark. Anyway it is perhaps a dangerous book and not intended for the casual reader."

"A book too dangerous to be read? Then why was it not in the Cage?"

Small felt that he had already revealed too much about the book.

"You said that the Murgans took Old. Where did they take him?" he said.

"That I cannot tell you. Perhaps he is in their quarters, but they have set up other little dens for themselves in the Library. All of them have heavy doors and strong locks. He could be anywhere."

Small's heart sank. Of course Sly was right, but the least he could do was to find out where Old was being held. He began to take his leave, but Sly had not finished.

"He is sure to be guarded and if you try to find him the Murgans will catch you too. Best hide somewhere close to your secret food store until they go."

Small felt as if he were being accused of disloyalty. It made him very uncomfortable. "I have no secret food store. I only gathered what I found as I roamed around."

"You should have shared it with the others, then we might have defended Alligor more effectively."

"There was never enough to share. I gave some to Old."

Sly muttered something under his breath as he continued on up the stairs.

The Murgan quarters were close by. He could check if Old was there and avoid being caught by using the upper levels. When he reached the landing the corridor was silent. He moved as quickly and as quietly as he could towards the door which led into the cupboard. In the pitch dark the minutes passed. It took him a long time to find the catch which caused the bookcase to swing open. Finally he felt his way up the narrow stair and moved cautiously across the vault. From time to time the low murmur of conversation rose from the room below. Small chose the spyhole furthest away from the voices and then, very slowly and very carefully, lifted out the stone plug.

The room was lit with lamps and there was a fire in the makeshift hearth. He could not see what fuel it was burning. He could not see who was talking, but it seemed that there were only three people in the room; at least there were only three voices. One of them belonged to Puttfark.

"You are a businesswoman. You know the nature of the business. You've done this stuff before and you know the risks. You named your price and the deal went down. If the money was not enough then you shouldn't have signed the contract. There were plenty of others only too willing to take your place. I did you a favour and now not only do I get these extra medical expenses, but I have to put up with your complaining as well."

A young woman stifled a scream of rage. "Expenses! Expenses! Cast your mind back three or four months. Where was the bodyguard who should have been outside the door when that fat caliph was raping me? Busy helping you with one of your private deals I expect."

Puttfark snorted contemptuously. "We had to travel fast to get here. The horses had to be fed and all the forage was in the town. Your fat caliph was asking too many questions. You only had to keep him occupied whilst we bought the supplies. Anyway, you told me you could take care of yourself."

"You told me that you would look after me!"

"You're still alive aren't you? You'll live to spend your fee. Anyway I expect you've done this before."

The young woman's voice was flat and level with suppressed anger. "Oh yes, I've done it before, but those were unavoidable accidents, I accepted the risk. This was preventable. You could have prevented it, but you messed it up, just as you've messed up this whole operation. The great Puttfark! Beaten by a worn out old man and a stupid boy!"

A cackle of humourless laughter interrupted the argument. Puttfark did not like it. "What are you laughing at Old Bag!" he shouted, "You were supposed to make sure this didn't happen."

The laughter stopped. "I'm paid to keep them healthy. Getting rid of mistakes is extra. You know the deal."

Small recognized the voice of the old crone Vulpia: the vermin killer, the book-burner, and now? He still had not the slightest idea of what they were arguing about. He decided to move to another spyhole.

From his new vantage Small could see that the young woman was Imperia. Her voice had been so distorted by emotion that he had not recognized it. She was laying on a couch, her arms crossed over her breast, her hands gripping her shoulders. Her face was white and drawn. She looked ill. Puttfark stood by the window, legs apart, arms folded. Vulpia sat by the fire tending a small cauldron. She held her hands over the boiling liquid.

"If you don't want me to do this say now before I mix the potion. These herbs are not cheap."

Puttfark shrugged and nodded assent. The old crone turned to Imperia. "Do you still want to go through with it?" she asked.

Imperia looked away. "Do I have a choice?" she muttered.

"Not really, and not if you want to keep working."

The young woman gave the slightest of nods. The crone dropped a handful of dried vegetation into the cauldron and spoke without taking her eyes away from her work, "Anyway, the medicine you have already swallowed will probably be enough to do the trick. This is really only to make sure."

Small was mystified. Something was about to happen but he had no idea what it might be. The old witch added more ingredients to the cauldron. Several minutes passed in an uneasy silence. Then the infused liquor was decanted into a small cloudy glass tumbler and given to Imperia to drink. She stared at the glass for some time before drinking its contents. She continued to stare into the empty glass until Vulpia prised it from her fingers.

"How do you feel?" Vulpia asked her.

"Goddinawful."

"Good. That shows that it's working." The old woman then turned stiffly to Puttfark. "You don't have to be here. We can manage without you."

"I want to make sure I get what I'm paying for," he replied. "I want to see it happen. I've been taken like that before."

The old woman spat into the fire. "Don't worry," she said dryly, "you'll get your money's worth."

Small watched with growing unease as Vulpia's drugs tightened their grip on the young woman. Her face sallowed to a corpse-like hue. Beads of sweat formed on her forehead and cheeks. Dark, wet patches discoloured her bodice. Her mouth sagged open. Suddenly her body convulsed.

"Lilith be praised, its starting," Vulpia said, and she began to unfasten Imperia's bodice. The young woman's head jerked from side to side. Her nose was streaming and saliva began to drool from the corner of her mouth.

Small was shocked. What terrible disease was this? He had never seen anything like it. The convulsions continued, each one now accompanied by awful screams which increased in volume and duration with every fresh spasm. By turns Imperia's face turned dark with exertion and then relaxed into plague-like pallor. After some time Vulpia moved around to the front of the couch and sat with her back to where Small was. He could no longer see what was happening to the young woman except that she had drawn up her knees and her dress

210

seemed to have ridden up her thighs. The screams increased in intensity until they were almost unbearable, then, abruptly, they stopped. Imperia began to sob quietly.

"Is this what you wanted to see?" said the old woman and held something up for Puttfark's inspection. Small only caught the briefest glimpse of what Vulpia held in her hands before she moved out of his field of vision. What he saw reminded him of the contents of a half-devoured bird he had once found, only much larger, the size of the Murgans' ball.

Imperia lay still on the couch naked up to her waist. It was then that Small knew the illustration in the book on the Lectern in the Cage for what it was. He knew he should not look. He knew that it was wrong for him to be here. He knew he should flee from this chamber of horrors; but he also knew that he had to know for certain what the old woman had shown Puttfark. Numb with apprehension he moved back to the first spyhole. Vulpia was cleaning her hands with a cloth. Small could not see where she had put the thing. Then Puttfark strode into view. He kicked at a leather bucket with the toe of his boot.

"Ha! It looks just like that fat oaf of a caliph." he said.

The kick had disturbed the contents of the bucket. Its contents swirled and rearranged themselves. A tiny white human foot appeared above the rim of the bucket and then sank slowly back into the gore.

Small cried out with all the energy of his heart and lungs an involuntary wail of horror, pity and outrage.

Rottko stiffened into instant alertness. He was not sure what the sound had been. He had never heard a cry quite like it, but the scuffling noises above the ceiling were plain enough. He strode across the room, homing in on the source of the noises. Suddenly his eyes were filled with dust and sand. He cursed and rubbed his lids until they cleared. It was then that he noticed the tiny hole in the vault. The dust and debris which Small had dislodged whilst scrambling across the vault were still trickling out of it. His mind closed like a rat-trap on the situation.

"Guards! GUARDS!" he shouted.

Small's headlong scramble through the pitch dark ended when he collided with a vertical surface which should not have been there. Almost stunned by the blow to his head he slowly realised that in his rush to confront the Murgans and do (he still didn't know what), he had missed the head of the tiny stairway. He blundered around in the total darkness unable to find his way back. Trying yet another direction he found that this section of the upper levels was vast and labyrinthine. After stumbling on for several minutes he knew that he was completely lost. He slumped to the floor in utter despair. Besides revulsion at what he had seen and his own impotent attempts to do something, he felt disillusioned, gullible, betrayed and sullied. That he could ever have dreamed of a life of adventure with the Murgans; that he had ever thought that they were heroes because they were clean and comely; now that he had seen his heroes for who they really were, he writhed with embarrassment and loathing. There could be no doubt. He had seen what he had seen. There could be no explaining it away, no appealing to a greater good or a greater freedom. What he had seen was unmitigated evil. And for it to be done here of all places; here in the library, where unwanted orphans were so valued, so necessary, so vital to the very survival of the book-city; here where even Splint and Dim had found a home; where even *their* services were valued.

Old had been right. Velik had spoken the truth. Once again the Evil of Knowledge had risen in the World. Murga was the Enemy and he, Small had almost led them to the Manuscript. Whatever this mysterious book was: talisman, amulet, antidote, counter-spell; he only knew that he must keep it out of their hands at all costs and keep it safe for the One. But where was the One? Who was the One? Did he even exist? If he came how would anyone know? And if the test of the One was that he could find the Manuscript, what would he do now that it was not in its proper place? Small wished that he could talk to Old. Surely he would know what to do.

The silence was broken by the faint tramp of shod feet and the shouts of command and response as the Murgan guards arrived from the Refectory and began to throw a cordon around the whole area beneath him. He knew from Puttfark's reaction that he had given away the secret of the upper levels: yet another stupid mistake he had made. Now Puttfark would not sleep until he had opened a way into the space above his quarters. Small had to get as far away as possible if he did not want to be caught. He navigated in the darkness by always moving away from the sounds of the guards.

When the martial noises faded he became aware of another sound. At first he thought it was one of those strange ever-distant sounds which hung around the library like ghosts, but as he approached, he recognised it. It was Dim. Small felt a sudden rush of shame. He should have brought some food to his friend. Poor Dim must be near to starvation by now.

After an age of blindly feeling his way through the darkness, Small stood above the room where Dim was babbling to some imaginary friend. Though he scrabbled around on his hands and knees he could not find any way down into the room. Finally he climbed down a cavity in the wall and found himself behind the wainscoting but there was no door. He shouted Dim's name at the top of his voice.

"Is that you, Thmall? Where are you?"

"I'm behind the panelling. I can't get out."

"Then you have to go round."

"I can't go round. You have to help me."

"What shall I do?"

"You have to break a panel. Kick it or hit it with a stool."

"Oh I can't do that, Thmall. All the librarians have told me that if I break things I am a bad boy. I mustn't be a bad boy."

"Dim you won't be a bad boy, I promise. We can fix it afterwards. If I don't get out of here I might die. You would really be a bad boy if you let me die. Please Dim, break the panel."

Dim was silent for some time. "You won't tell anybody?" he said.

"I won't tell anybody."

There was a crashing blow and the wainscoting heaved violently against Small's shoulder. The second blow splintered the panel. Dim's massive hands tore the shards of wood out of their housings. Small found himself lifted bodily through the panelling and into the room. He felt Dim's arm round his shoulders, and his massive hand smoothing his hair.

"You won't die now will you?" said a worried voice next to his ear.

"No, I won't die now." Small replied.

Dim sighed with relief.

"Here." said Small, fumbling in his book bag, "I have some food for you."

Dim put the wrinkled and damaged figs into his mouth and swallowed them without even chewing. Small felt the big hand trustingly held out for more. "I'm sorry that's all there is," he said ruefully.

There was a long silence before Dim spoke again. "I'm thtill very hungry," he said.

In the darkness Small blushed with shame. How could he have been so blind, so selfish, so stupid as to trust the Murgans? And now what was he to do? He could hide the book, but what use would that be? The Murgans knew it was in Alligor; they even knew what it looked like. They wouldn't give up looking for it, even if they had to torture every librarian to death, and eventually they would catch him too. He couldn't hide for ever and then all they had to do was threaten to hurt Old or even threaten to burn the Library and he would have to tell them where the Book was. Which ever way he approached the problem his reason steered him towards the unthinkable. He had to go away from Alligor and then, even more unthinkable, he had to take the Book with him. This he just had to do, but how? The Gate was guarded and the whole of the Eastern Gallery area was patrolled by the Murgans. He had read Mungara's treatise and he knew that they would already be locking doors and sealing corridors. By morning he would have to pass perhaps a dozen checkpoints to reach the stairwell. He had to act now or he would be unable to act at all. The desperate situation forced an idea into his mind that was so rash, so dangerous that it exhilarated him.

"Dim," he said, "can you find your way to the Great Well?"

"Yeth," came the answer out of the darkness.

"Can you do it now in the dark?"

"Yeth."

"Then take me there now."

"Are you thirthty?"

"No, but I am hungry. Would you like some food?"

Small felt his hand being gripped. The way Dim found his way around in the dark was truly uncanny. Night had fallen and the Library was in utter darkness. With no moon, or even starlight, there was nothing to see: nor did Dim need to touch walls or furniture. The only things he touched were doors, their handles and latches. Small had often asked the big man-child how he did it, but all he could say was, 'I know where to go'. From time to time Dim cleared his throat with a slight cough which gave a sort of sound picture of the space they were in, but this was too seldom and too random to be of any use.

As they walked through the darkened Library, Dim whispered constantly as if in conversation with some unseen person.

"Who are you talking to?" Small asked.

"The people."

"Which people?"

"My friends."

"But there is nobody here."

Dim said nothing. Small tried another approach. "Who are these people? Do I know them?"

"I don't know their names."

"What are they saying?"

"They are saying numbers."

Dim had not progressed far in the mathematical arts. He could only conceive of 'one' and 'more'. Small thought about this before asking which numbers the people were saying.

"One," said Dim and then added, "Lots of ones."

Dim began his whispered conversation once more.

"Stop it Dim, you are frightening me."

"No, you mustn't be frightened. They like you. They are your friends. They want to help you but they can't."

"Why can't they help me?"

"I don't know. I think they are dead."

"Enough! Tell them to go away."

Small and Dim walked on in silence. After a while Small spoke, "Have they gone away?"

"No. But they won't talk to me."

Another silence. Dim stopped abruptly.

"What? What is it?" asked Small.

"We're here."

"Where?"

"The Great Well."

Small leaned forward and reached out his hand. He felt the parapet of the well. "Dim, how did you know that? It's too dark to see, you didn't touch it, you didn't even cough."

"Oh, I've been here before."

Small shook his head in disbelief. Then he felt for the windlass and the rope. His hands followed the rope to the bucket. He checked the knot.

"Dim, I want you to do something very difficult for me. If you can do this you will be a very good boy and I will bring you something to eat. I want you to let the bucket down into the well by winding the windlass."

"That'th easy."

"Dim, listen, I am going to stand in the bucket so it will be very heavy, but even if your arms get tired you mustn't let go. If you let go I will fall down the well. Do you understand?"

"Yeth."

"Now when I shout 'Stop' you stop winding, but you mustn't go away. You must keep holding on to the handle and when I shout again you have to wind the bucket up again. Can you do that for me?"

"Oh yeth! It'th like pulling the book-sled. 'Thtop' and I thtop. 'Go' and I go again."

"Take hold of the handle Dim. Are you holding the handle?"

"Yeth."

Small climbed carefully over the lip of the well and reached out until he could feel the rope wound tightly around the heavy wooden spindle. He gripped the spindle with both hands and swung himself out

215

over the void. As he wound his legs around the rope which hung from the spindle he tugged the bucket off the parapet. It jerked and bounced on the end of the rope. Still holding tightly to the spindle he placed his feet into the bucket and, very cautiously he relaxed his arm muscles until his full weight was bearing down on it.

"Ready Dim? Start unwinding. Go!"

The windlass had four straight handles. Dim began to lower the bucket into the well hand over hand by grasping each handle in turn and letting it pull away from him. As Small descended inch by inch into the pitch dark, he twined his arms around the rope to take some of the weight off the bucket handle. He knew when he was fully inside the well because the sound took on that quality peculiar to narrow shafts and tunnels. It took a very long time before he heard the change in the air which told him that he was out of the well shaft and dangling below the huge vault of the undercroft. By the faint far-off glimmer of a single cresset lamp he could see that he was suspended over the centre of the cistern, but the dark water below him sent back no reflections. He began to pull on the rope and thrust his feet in the bucket away from him. Slowly he began to swing like a pendulum from side to side. The further he descended the wider was the arc until he was swinging over the lip of the cistern on both sides. When the bucket had descended to within a foot above the lip he was able to jump lightly onto the paving. He held on to the rope until he had placed the bucket securely on the lip of the cistern, then he shouted up to Dim, "STOP!"

Far above him the faint creaking of the windlass stopped. He mouthed a silent prayer to the Divine Author that Dim would remember to wait for his return and then walked between the huge troll-like grain silos towards the light. He was intrigued by a faint blue glow in the shadows below one of them. He went closer but recoiled in horror when he realised that the faint phosphorescence emanated from tainted grain which had spilled out of a silo. The Divine Author alone knew what infernal fungal poison had infected the ancient store.

He opened the kitchen door slowly until he could see through the gap that there were no Murgans in Spoon's domain. The door to the refectory was still closed which meant that the meal had not yet been served. Hoping that he would not be noticed, Small slipped through the door into the overwhelming heat, light and bustle of the dinner preparations. All the kitchen menials were busy lifting, carrying, stirring, pouring, ladling, running to and fro. A huge tureen of steaming savoury stew stood on a table. He snatched up a bowl and was about to take some when an enormous hot damp weight fell on his shoulder. It was the hand of Spoon. Small turned his head and found himself staring into the head cook's broad and sweaty features. The folds of flesh shuddered into speech.

"Not from that one my little rebel," the flesh said, "That's special. For the Murgans. Most particular about their food you see. Always want theirs' kept separate. Only the best for them. Prepared special."

From deep inside Spoon's constricted chest there came a ruttling, rumbling sound. His jowls heaved, his fleshy chaps smacked and his tongue writhed. Finally he ejected a great gobbet of phlegm onto his ladle. With a beatific smile on his moist countenance he plunged the ladle into the Murgans' pot and stirred it cheerily and vigorously. Then, half turning he bellowed, "Who's the King of the Kitchen?"

All work stopped momentarily as the menials shouted their response.

"Spoon! You are! King of Alligor."

With acclamations still ringing in his ears he bent down until his mouth was close to Small's ear. "Oldest rule in the world," he said, "Always treat the people who cook your food with the necessary respect. Ur!"

Tyranny can exist in many subtle forms. Likewise the revolt which it inevitably inspires can express itself in a variety of ways. Every worm turns, even when it knows that it will be immediately crushed beneath the boot heel but, other worms take note, recognizing the tyranny for what it is, is the first stage in its overthrow. One small act of defiance can be the catalyst for an oppressed people to begin to assert their independence. So Spoon's pathetic rebellion inspired Small to strike back at the Murgans for all the evil they had brought to Alligor. He had intended to try and slip out through the refectory. Now he had another and a better plan, but he had to be quick. Snatching up a wooden bowl he ran to the cellar door and descended into the inky dark undercroft to where the heap of tainted grains still lay faintly fluorescing on the pavement. He scooped them up with his bowl and ran back up the steps into the kitchen. Whilst no-one was looking he tipped the lot into the Murgan pot and stirred it briskly. He scoured the bowl with clean sand from the big pot by the sink and then rinsed it thoroughly with water from a pitcher. He stuffed his mouth with as much food from the librarians' pot as he could, filled the bowl for Dim and then packed his book bag and the front of his robe with bread. By this time the menials were lining up in front of the door which opened into the refectory. They marched on the spot with remarkable esprit de corps whilst chanting in low voices a blasphemous hymn to appetite.

"What do you think of my troops?" bellowed Spoon from across the kitchen, and then, "Better disappear before I open the door."

As Small slipped back into the undercroft, he heard Spoon order the advance.

"Feed them!"

Small hurried back to the cistern beneath the Great Well thinking about what he had done. The blue grains were supposed to be dangerous, but just how dangerous were they? Would they bring on sickness and diarrhoea? Or hallucinations? Or worse? For an instant he regretted what he had done. In his memory the ball bounced in a game of Murgan 'fun'. He thought of running back to the kitchen, but it was only a momentary impulse. Other images quickly supplanted the first. The Murgans had callously tortured and murdered without compunction wherever it served their interests. They would do the same to him if they caught him. Now the Book-City would strike back. All the Murgans would eat from the pot and the poison would disable them long enough for him to slip out of Alligor. It was his only chance. It might be the world's only chance. After all he had sworn an oath to stop anyone following the Dark Path: by any means necessary.

The bucket was where he left it. The rope still hung over the water. He stepped into the bucket, took a turn of the rope around his free arm and shouted in a voice which echoed to the ends of the catacombs, "Go! Dim. Go!"

Far above his head the windlass creaked into motion.

Sitting in the dark with Dim eating noisily by his side Small felt relief, elation and a quiet pride. He had conquered his fear, taken great risks and succeeded in what he had set out to do. More than this he no longer felt powerless and impotent.

"Wath I a good boy?" boomed a voice close to his ear.

"You were a very good boy, Dim."

Now all that remained was to think hard about what he must do next. The Murgans usually ate in two sittings. How long would it be before the poisoned grains took effect? Too quickly and the second sitting might be warned: too slowly and it would be morning. He needed to be where he could see the guard on the Great Gate. The moment the man doubled over and ran for the privies, he could make his escape. On one of the horses picketed outside the walls, he could be miles away before dawn.

The enterprise would be highly dangerous, but it was not only the element of risk which caused him to linger over his meal. Alligor was his life, his world. Everything he had ever known had been contained within its walls. Now that it was imminent, he found the idea of cutting all these ties and heading out over the plain deeply disturbing. He only knew of the world outside through books. Sitting here in the dark with his helpless friend, his first instinct was to burrow deeper into the Library and hide for as long as he could. But no matter how long he lingered, his reason would not be silenced. He had to go.

Dim began to whisper to his friends once more. There were times when even Small felt as if Alligor were a living thing. Was it a companion, a mentor, a protector? A great and ancient master had written that like all truly great architectural achievements the value of Alligor had nothing to do with the number or preciousness of its stones. Its glory was in its age. It had been weathered by the passage of seasons, times and ages; it had watched the decline and birth of dynasties; it had survived the changing of the face of the earth and of the limits of the sea, and it stood as a symbol sibylline and wise beyond words. And who is to say that the walls of the buildings in which we live might not soak up something of the joy, the aspirations, yearnings, dreams, pain and despair of the lives which they enfold? Had not the poet spoken of the deep sense of voicefulness, of stern watching, of mysterious sympathy which we feel in ancient walls? Small thought that he heard a hubbub of voices in the darkness: intimate yet distant, impossible to place or fix in space, as if a throng were gathering for a ceremony.

Alligor spoke. Or rather, the moon came out, and, down long corridors, rooms glowed in whitest silver light. Walls and floors were tigered with slant stripes. The beautiful ancient masonry appeared skeletal, magical, looking like the phosphorescent bones of a colossal whale on the midnight floor of a deep ocean. Ripples of darkness pulsed through the Library as cloud stragglers passed across the face of the moon. It was as if Alligor was showing him the way. He stood up.

"I have to go, Dim," he said.

"Can I go with you?"

"No, it will be dangerous and difficult."

"Will you bring me food?"

"No, I will be gone for a long time. If you are hungry you must ask another librarian. Sly sleeps in the galleries. He will feed you."

Small set off towards the Great Stairwell, passing through pools of bright moonlight and darkest shadow. Preparing to leave was a poignant experience for him. He felt the need for a memento, a keepsake and so he made a detour to the Lion Cabinet. Once there, he looked over his meagre store of possessions. He was about to enter a bookless world, what else should he take with him but a book? And what better book than *The Mirror of Almeira*? Amatis its hero had survived on his wits when every man's hand was against him. It was an uplifting tale illuminated and illustrated in gorgeous colour. He stuffed the book into his bag. He noticed his ancient ragged robe lay where he had thrown it on the bed. In a sudden fit of self-loathing he tore off his Murgan *tzirt* and pulled on his own threadbare garment. With a final glance around the moonlit room, he turned his back on the only place he had ever thought of as his own.

From Old's window niche he could see into the Courtyard. Lamplight spilled out of the refectory door. A faint hubbub punctuated by shouts and laughter rose up from the feasting Murgans. Clouds of blue smoke billowed out of the refectory door. The guards were smoking their assassins' drug, numbing their sensibilities against unconscionable acts. In the shadows by the Gate there stood, not one, but two Murgan guards. They looked heavily armed and alert. Had they already eaten or were they waiting their turn? Perhaps the blue grains were not poisonous at all.

Somewhere in the galleries a door slammed. The moon came out. He shrank back from the sill feeling very vulnerable. What would Mungara have advised in his military manual? 'Plan your escape routes' most likely. Nothing was happening in the yard. He decided to try all the doors which led off the stairway. Although he had expected as much, he felt sudden alarm when he discovered that they had all been locked, bolted or sealed. The Stairwell had been made into a giant trap. He raced to the head of the stairs and began to move through the galleries. Here too all the doors had been sealed apart from the single route through the main galleries. Turn a key or shoot a bolt on any of the remaining doors and anyone in the galleries would be trapped with only one way out: through the Courtyard. He heard a muffled thud as another distant door was closed. Someone was out there. They were still sealing off the escape routes. He was trapped.

Even with all the doors locked there were still many dark corners and recesses where he could hide, but the Murgans were thorough. They would be sure to check every hiding place. Hiding in the galleries was too risky. There was only one safe place; the upper levels. At least the Murgans hadn't found the secret panel in the Gallery of the Horses yet. Clouds passed desultorily before the moon causing the galleries to slip in and out of utter darkness. When he reached the Gallery of the Horses it was perfectly dark. He stood immobile listening for movement and waiting for the moon to reappear.

In the first flicker as the silver light returned his heart stopped. Puttfark was standing two or three paces in front of him! Small turned and ran for his life. Puttfark leaped after him. There was only an arm's length between them. Puttfark was fit and fast. Halfway into the next gallery and Small could feel Puttfark's hand twitching at the back of his robe trying to catch hold. He yelled in terror and tried to pull his shoulder away as he ran. A dread feeling of failure began to drain his will and strength. Then, unbelievably, up ahead in a shaft of moonlight he saw Dim, standing with a quizzical smile on his face, unable to understand this latest game.

"DIM!" he shouted as he ran past him, "Grab him! Hold him! Don't let him GO!"

Puttfark gasped as he was stopped dead in his tracks by the massive arms around his chest. His legs flew up in the air still running. Small sprinted out of the gallery, slammed the massive door, shot the bolt, and kept running. Then he realised what he had done. He ran back to the bolted door shouting despairingly at the top of his voice, "Dim! Let him go! Let him go! STOP!" He fell to his knees in front of the keyhole. Dim was sitting on the floor with his legs straight out in front of him, for all the world like a big child. He still wore that puzzled smile. His hands clutched his chest. In the bright moonlight Small could see the inky runnels of blood welling out from between his fingers and darkening the front of his robe. He had to help him, but where was Puttfark?

Distant shouts rang out. They seemed to be coming from outside the building. Small ran to the window. A hundred paces further along the wall, Puttfark had broken a window and was leaning out shouting to the Guards in the Courtyard.

"He's here! We've got him! Get up here and unlock this door, but don't let him slip past you."

The guards disappeared from view as they headed for the Great Stair. Small unbolted the door, ran past Dim and shot the bolts on the next one. When he got back Dim was sitting in a wide pool of blood which was beginning to run away across the uneven floor.

"Dim! What were you doing here? What has he done?"

"I was looking for Thly but all the doors were clothed. I held the man like you thaid and then he hurt me with hith knife. Wath I a bad boy?"

Small put his arm round the broad shoulders. The wound looked very bad.

"No, Dim you are a good boy, a very good boy."

221

"My mummy thaid I had to be a good boy. She thaid if I was a good boy she would come back for me. When she comes will you tell her that I am a good boy?"

"Yes of course I will," said Small. His eyes were filling with tears. He felt the big shoulders beginning to tremble. Dim grunted and took one hand away from his wound. He stared at the palm wet and black in the moonlight. The sound of blood spattering onto the floor skittered around the walls like a trapped bird. Then he relaxed, his eyes went up and he fell back dead into Small's arms.

More shouts. Heavy blows rattled the locked door on its hinges. Angry, terrified and distraught, Small laid Dim gently on the floor and then ran for the Great Stair.

The Gate was now unguarded. If he could only slip past the two guards coming up the stairs he could escape. But how could he hide? The treacherous moonlight knifed into every room. He prayed for clouds and kept running. The guards were stamping around in the first gallery at the head of the stair. They carried long shiny swords which flashed hideous shards of moonlight all over the vault. They were very thorough. They thrust their sharp blades into every dark nook and cranny. They stood on the tables and looked over the tops of the bookstacks. They even looked behind the door as they left. Small was forced to retreat through gallery after gallery until he could hear Puttfark pounding on the door behind him. In desperation he ran to a window. Beneath him was a sheer drop of forty feet of smoothed stone. Above him, sailing in a wind-scoured sky full of stars, the moon flooded the earth with her pitiless brilliance. Then, out from behind the eaves of Alligor came a large wedge of silver edged sable cloud, reaching towards the bright disk of the moon like the hand of a jealous god. It would be his only chance.

The sudden darkness took the Murgan guards by surprise. They were at opposite sides of the gallery with their backs to each other thrusting their swords under the furniture. They froze, trying to orientate themselves and straining their ears for movement. Small had started moving as soon as the dark descended. He did not need eyes here. He passed between the Murgans with the slightest whisper of bare feet on stone. He heard them stiffen in their silken shirts, but they were blind. He was fifty paces away before the light returned. He heard shouts: a bolt was withdrawn and then the clatter of hard shoes behind him as he hurled himself down the winding stairway.

The courtyard in front of the Gate was bathed in bright moonlight on three sides. Deep shadow cloaked the other wall. Laughter and light spilled from the Refectory doorway. Inside, the Murgans were relaxing after eating their meal. The blue grains did not seem to have had any effect. Now, faint shouts came from behind him as Puttfark and the guards reached the head of the stairway. Small would have to risk crossing the courtyard. He sprinted for the shadow at the foot of the wall and crossed to the corner by the Gate without being seen. The serpent handle on the bar of the Gate gleamed in the moonlight. He would have to draw the bar and open the Gate in full view of the open refectory door. From where he was crouching he could see the Murgans passing their filthy drug from hand to hand. They seemed very animated. The shouts of Puttfark and his guards were getting louder as they ran down the stairway. It had to be now.

Small took a deep breath and ran for the gate. He caught the snake handle on the run so that the sheer impetus of his forward movement yanked the bar into motion. He heaved with all his strength and the heavy bronze bar rumbled slowly into the wall. As soon as it had cleared one half of the Gate, he reached for the thick metal ring that served as a door pull and, bracing his feet in the dust, he heaved the door open a foot or two. It was enough. At the very moment when Puttfark burst into the yard, Small slipped out of the Great Gate of Alligor and ran as fast as his legs would move him across the empty moonlit landscape.

The Murgan horses picketed outside the Gate snickered and checked in alarm as he crossed in front of them. His feet pounded the dust and his pack slapped against his back. No time to loose the horses. An outburst of shouting and uproar behind the Gate told him that the hunt was up. Small had only covered about three hundred paces but already his legs were aching and his shoulder hurt from the weight of his pack. He felt his knees begin to weaken. Behind him the Great Gates were swinging open: the Murgans swarming out and heading for their horses. They could not fail to see him in the bright moonlight. By now he was taking short painful breaths and his stride was faltering. About twenty paces ahead of him the ground rose slightly into a low mound covered with scrub. Beyond it there might be some cover. An ominous pounding of hooves sounded behind him. His breath came in sobs. The slight incline almost made him stumble as he reached the crest of the mound.

Suddenly the ground at his feet seemed to erupt. A great pale horse complete with rider staggered to its feet right in front of him. He stopped dead. Horse and rider turned in a tight circle which brought them back facing him. The excited animal rolled its eyes and arched its neck. The rider, face turbaned and body muffled in dark clothing managed to control the dancing horse. For a moment the rider seemed to hesitate. Then, with the thunder of hooves loud in his ears, Small reached out for the gloved hand which was extended towards him from above. Almost before he had scrambled up onto the horse's rump he felt the rider's waist tense. With a great kick the horse leaped into rapid motion across the moonlit plain.

Small wrapped his arms around the rider and gripped the horse with his knees, terrified that he might fall off. Even so he bounced uncontrolledly on the horse's rump. He risked a glance over his shoulder but his pursuers were just dim shapes in the dust cloud kicked up by the horse.

"Go faster, go faster!" Small screamed the words in the language of Babel before he properly understood what this meant. Despite the buffeting and panic of this headlong gallop across the plain, some part of his brain had registered the powerful horse, the silken clothes, the heady perfume, and told him that the slim strong torso that he was desperately trying to hold on to belonged to a Murgan.

The horse galloped on. Despite its double burden, Small saw that the other horses were being left behind. The clouds of dust lifted by its hooves made it difficult for their pursuers to see where they were going. On the rising broken ground the other horses had to slow down or risk laming themselves. Small wondered when the poisoned food would take effect. He'd seen them eating it. Surely it must work soon. What would it do to them?

Small saw that up ahead the ground was broken by a series of gullies. These clefts in the earth were choked with low bushes and stunted trees rearing out of impenetrable moon shadows. After a swift backward glance the rider urged the horse into the densest, darkest thicket of all. Wheezing and snorting, the horse slowed to a canter and then a walk. Small still clung tightly to the rider until an expertly delivered straight elbow to his abdomen shunted him backwards over the horse's rump. Winded by the blow and stunned by the fall onto the hard ground, he sprawled helplessly on his back. The rider dismounted and with skilful bridle tugging and knee work forced the horse to lie down on its side. Small was still trying to take a breath when he found himself being tugged and pulled over to the horse. Attempting to rise he almost impaled himself on a long double edged dagger which was being held against a soft part of his neck. The blade caught the moonlight. No words were necessary. He lay still and kept quiet.

The Murgans were just outside the entrance to the gully. They were making a lot of noise but so far they had not emerged from the dust cloud. There was a lot of shouting and their horses seemed to be getting more and more nervous. Cries of alarm gave way to unearthly screams. Angry voices shouted orders. Small realised that the tainted food was beginning to take effect. Even after all that had happened he still felt an extra wave of shock sweep through him. He had never before harmed anyone at all and yet from what he knew of the poison it could even be fatal. The rider half rose and peered into the moonlit haze trying to puzzle out what was happening. Horses reared and turned, or galloped off in random directions. Daggers and swords flashed in the moonlight. It seemed as if the Murgans were battling with invisible demons. They screamed and babbled as if possessed. One by one they toppled off their horses to lay twitching and screaming on the broken ground. Only the man in white was unaffected. He shouted at his men until he alone was left in the saddle. Amidst the settling dust Puttfark caught as many loose bridles as he could and led the animals back to Alligor.

Small tried to get up. The rider stiffened. Small sensed uncertainty. "It's all right," he said," they will be out of action for many hours. Perhaps longer ..." He tried to sound reassuring.

After a short pause for reflection, the rider stood up and began to unwind the black turban from around head, face and neck. Small watched astonished as the rider shook out long dark hair which fell in tresses around a slim white neck. The rider spoke for the first time as the last coil of the head dress fell away.

"Magic ... or poison?" she said.

His rescuer was a young woman.

Momentarily the question attached itself in his mind to the extraordinary figure of the girl rider, then, pulling his thoughts into order he answered. "Poison ... but not necessarily fatal. I didn't want to hurt them ... I just had to escape." Small could not gauge her reaction to his words. Her expression did not give anything away.

"You can stand up now." she said and began to lift the horse back onto its feet.

Small had to hurl himself sideways to avoid being trampled by the animal. The girl seemed not to notice.

"I'm impressed," she said as she turned towards him. In the bright moonlight Small saw the *ulvis* curl her top lip before she smiled. What had seemed slightly sinister on Puttfark was strangely interesting on her face. High-born Murgan or not, he realised that she was little more than a girl. Her confidant manner and athletic bearing suggested a maturity beyond her years. "Those men ...," she lifted her head towards the faint whimpering noises coming from the gully entrance, "they are professionals. Expensive killers. The best. Somebody paid a lot of money to get them here."

"They said they were traders." Small was not yet thinking clearly. He felt strangely disembodied, intoxicated. He could not take his eyes off the girl.

"Yes, they would, wouldn't they?" she said.

Small felt stupid and gullible. Why had he not listened to Old?

The girl's expression became impassive again as she tethered the horse to a bush. "I followed them here. They travelled fast. They took risks. They avoided towns when they could. They came for something of great value."

Small did not speak as the girl came back towards him. He saw the girl's arm flexing as she gripped the dagger inside her robe. She looked him squarely in the eye as she spoke. "So. What's in the bag?"

Small had not even decided in which direction he was going to run, before the girl anticipated him, "You can run off if you like but there's nowhere to hide for about ten leagues in any direction. Even without his men, the white leaderman will ride you down in a day or two. You have no food, no water and no horse. I am your only hope of getting away. I'll be generous. I'll settle for half of what's in the bag."

Small thought fast. There were two books in the bag. She could not possibly know that either of them was important in any way. He needed her help. It was a risk he had to take. Slowly he unlaced the sack and tipped out the contents onto the ground. He picked up *The Mirror of Almeira* and gave it into her hand. She rustled through the vellum leaves. The gilding flashed in the moonlight. Suddenly she snapped the small volume shut and thrust it close up to his face. "What the God is this?" she said menacingly, "Are you trying to trick me? Back off!"

As Small took a step backwards she bent down and picked up the other volume. "Books!" she hissed, "I risk my life for Goddin' books! Tell me boy, what sort of city is that?"

"It's Alligor. It's a library," Small answered, "It's full of books." He was frightened. The girl was becoming extremely threatening. Her eyes were wild, her stance aggressive. As he slowly backed away from her, she was beginning to stalk him, her dagger half-exposed. Then she paused.

"Wait. Stop." she said, "You risked your life to get these things away. I want to know what these words say." She ran to the horse and fumbled in the saddle bag. Clearly impatient and cursing violently she squatted down, struck a spark to tinder and transferred the flame to a tiny ceramic lamp which she placed carefully on a large stone. "Come here and read this for me."

Small took *The Mirror of Almeira* from her outstretched hand and opened it at a random page.

"Read," she said, "and no tricks. Don't stop until I tell you."

Small tilted the precious book towards the flame. Moonlit purple and grey turned to red and gold in the lamplight. The colours of the illumination glowed. He began to read. "*Amatis was not only a mighty warrior but he was also well formed in body and face. His movements were so graceful and he was so comely that even married women in the street would turn their heads to catch a second look. There were of course many handsome brutes in the Khan's army, but Amatis was different. He didn't spit, scratch himself in public or kick children. He was charming, polite and gracious. He could recite poetry and discuss difficult things with wise men. But what made him even more different was that he did not pursue women. This made him totally irresistible to all female creatures who despise any male whom they can easily seduce. Wherever the Khan's army was billeted, the local beauties would straight away begin their own campaign to ensnare the handsome Amatis by ambush, entrapment and subterfuge. But no matter how long the siege, Amatis never fell. He was ever faithful to his beloved Poeisia. Through all his hardships; even though he knew that he might be discovered by the Khan and executed at any moment; even though he knew that his life might be ended at any time by a chance arrow in a skirmish; he was never unfaithful to his beloved. From the moment he set eyes upon the beautiful and fascinating Poeisia his soul was hers and hers alone. Many men saw her beauty and desired her madly but only to Amatis did she open the door to her soul. It was a great, great love between them. And each would have lain down their life for the other. Amatis had promised to return and make her his wife. She had promised to wait for him. It was the great love which they shared that gave them their faith and fortitude. The Great Khan himself, with all his wealth and power could neither catch hold of the one nor break the will of the other. Such is the power of true love.*"

"Stop!" Her face was so close to Small's own that he could smell her skin. Her expressionless mask had slipped to reveal the bright expression of the girl she might have been. "Is there more written in this book about '*love*'?" Her voice was strange and quiet.

"Oh yes," said Small, "It's a love story. It's supposed to be the greatest of all time."

"Ha! It can't be true." she said, but there was doubt in her voice, "*Love* cannot be so powerful, can it?" Again, the light in her eyes. It was like a beacon seen across a midnight ocean.

Small was confused. "I ... I'm not sure. Many authors speak of it as if it is a divine and noble thing. I do not think it is a thing that could be invented, but I know so little of the world ..."

"Have you yourself ever known this '*love*'?" she whispered.

All small knew was that most of his mental energy was being occupied in examining the exquisite curvature of the girl's lips, the flare of her nostrils, the dark hairs of her eyebrows and that extraordinary moonbrushed hair. "I ...I ...I don't think that, ... I mean. I never saw a woman before the Murgans arrived. I'm not an expert."

The light went out. The girl stepped back. There was a slight snick as the dagger went into its sheath. "This is the deal," she said flatly, "I'll get you out of here but only if you read to me about this '*love*'. It is something I need to know about. I need to know if there is any such thing. Is it a deal?"

As they rode across the moonlit plain, Small had many hours to think over what had happened. The books were back in his pack, but one thing was certain, he had just escaped death by several hairsbreadths. Had the girl not been there, Puttfark's killers would have ridden him into the ground; had the girl not asked him to read *The Mirror of Almeira* she would have stabbed him without a qualm. The girl herself remained an enigma. She was a high-born Murgan, so why did she help him? Why did she not just kill him and take the bag? Why did she have this desire to know about 'love'? From the way that the authors wrote about it he had always thought that love was something that everybody knew about. Could it really be something that only existed in books?

The moon had long since set and the dark sky was being washed by a cold pale dawn when Small noticed that they were approaching a small oasis. It seemed to be the only vegetation in a sea of pink dust which stretched to every horizon. As the horse plodded in amongst the trees, Small slipped exhausted from its back and collapsed onto a grassy bank shadowed by foliage. He fell asleep instantly. When he stirred some time later it was to find that he was securely bound by his wrists to one of the trees. He was vaguely aware of loud snoring coming from where the horse was tethered. As he drifted back into unconsciousness he thought how curious it was that he had never read in any book that horses snored.

Twenty

When Small awoke he had no idea where he was. The events of the night only returned to him gradually. His wrists were no longer bound but the rope was still loosely wound about the tree. When he tried to get up he found that every muscle in his body was telling him a painful story about the journey on horseback. It seemed to be a work of many chapters, with appendices. He hobbled painfully towards the horse which snorted and flattened its ears threateningly. He decided to keep well away from the giant beast.

The oasis had formed around a small pool of water overgrown with dense vegetation on three sides. The water was brown and murky but not stagnant. Falling on his knees Small drank greedily from cupped hands until he noticed that he was being observed. The girl, naked except for a thin leather belt around her waist, stood facing him in the water at the opposite edge of the pool.

"You're drinking my bath water," she said, without any shadow of modesty or embarrassment. "If you've finished you'd better keep a look-out, out there." She waved her hand at the western horizon. In utter confusion, Small stumbled off into the bushes. Unable to resist a backward glance, he saw her reach for her clothes. In the cleft between her buttocks the long slim dagger hung in its sheath from the belt.

Small did not believe for a moment that Puttfark would simply give up. He knew that somewhere out on that red plain the man in white was already organizing the pursuit. Even so, when he saw the distant dust cloud it gave him an unpleasant jolt of fear.

The girl received the news calmly and continued grooming the horse. "It's not Puttfark," she said, "Wrong direction. He won't be on our trail until tomorrow at least."

Small was relieved. "That is good to know," he said.

"We can't be sure," the girl replied from beneath the horse's belly, "Only horsemen travelling fast raise dust like that. It won't be traders. Are your book readers so keen that they gallop to your library in bands?" Small smiled at the idea, but the girl remained impassive. "I think we should keep out of their way," she said, "They can't know that we are here and if they are in such a hurry they won't hang around for long."

They hid in the dry bed of a river which had cut itself a deep gully some half a league from the oasis. They did not hide their tracks but made a long dogleg from the oasis to the gully so that they could see if they were being tracked. It was at least an hour before the horsemen came in sight. About twenty in number, they swept into the oasis cavalry fashion with drawn swords, but they were like no cavalry that Small could possibly have imagined even in his wildest dreams. They wore extravagant and gaudy dresses like women's. Their long hair was piled up into the most outrageous ornamental forms and tied with bright ribbons. Ornate jewels dangled from their earlobes. On their feet were strange pointed and heeled constructions. Even from a distance Small could see that they had crimsoned their mouths and kohled their eyes. Small listened to their strange raucous voices and watched their exaggerated movements with utter bafflement.

"Sa'than but you've just had a lucky escape," the girl said.

"Who are they? What are they?" Small asked her.

"They're Warholl from Murga. Paid troublemakers with very nasty habits."

"Warholl?"

"They make war on all that is holy."

Small thought about this. The word Holl in the common language meant terror.

"But why do they dress up like women and behave so strangely?"

"They're other. You know, they don't chase after women, they prefer boys. They'd be delighted to meet you. But I should warn you. They don't ask permission and they usually torture their lover boys to death. Don't let their appearance fool you, they are experts in violence."

"Why are they here? Where are they going?" Small asked.

The girl shrugged. "Difficult to say. But somebody is paying a lot of money to give this area a bad reputation. Whatever your friend in white is doing in that library he doesn't want anybody stumbling in on him. The Warholl will soon frighten everybody away."

The ladies from hell settled down for a short siesta. Small and the girl had no choice but to do the same.

Small gazed about him at the plain. Looking first in one direction, then in another he could not see anything to disturb its utter monotony. To every horizon there was nothing that was of the slightest interest to him. Eventually his gaze settled upon the girl. She had begun grooming her horse with rhythmic movements which sent shimmering waves of highlight pulsing through her loose long hair. It was some time before Small could bring himself to speak. He rubbed the spot on his throat where she had held the dagger.

"What should I call you?" he said at last.

She did not answer immediately, seeming to be engrossed in her work. Then she said, "I am called Domina."

Small was impressed. "Does that mean you are from a noble family?"

The Girl cast him a scathing glance over the horse's rump. "We don't have nobility in Murga, only people who are rich and powerful."

"Are you rich and powerful?" he asked.

"If I returned to Murga I might be," she replied enigmatically.

Small thought about this whilst he watched the girl continue her task. "Then your family is rich and powerful?"

The girl grunted something monosyllabic which Small assumed was assent.

"Do they not worry that you are alone and so far from home?" he continued.

Domina frowned at him. "Why would they do that? I am old enough to do business for myself."

Small sighed. He had the by now familiar feeling that the girl thought him naive and ignorant. Had he made another blunder? All that he had ever read had convinced him that parents had a deep and abiding interest in their offspring. Was this just another literary convention, like romantic love? It was all very unsettling. Perhaps the girl was being deliberately perverse. "But your parents must love you very much. Do they know where you are?" he said.

On hearing the word '*love*' Domina fixed him with a fierce stare. "What have parents got to do with '*love*'?" she demanded. The question was not rhetorical.

Small was bewildered. Had he made a mistake? He knew nothing of parents or love except from books, but he felt that the word '*love*' held some kind of strange significance for her. It suddenly dawned on him that he had never heard the Murgan word for '*love*'. Nor had he heard the girl use anything but the common speech term for it. Perhaps it was a language problem. "What is the word for '*love*' in your language?" he asked her.

"We don't have one," she replied, "It is not a concept that any Murgan would understand."

"But *you* understand it, don't you?" he said.

"I have heard of it," she mumbled, and began tugging at a stubborn tangle in the horse's tail.

Small felt that she was holding something back. "Where did you hear of it?" he asked cautiously.

Pausing in her work, she brushed away a strand of her hair that had stuck to her sweat-dampened cheek. She looked at him for some time whilst she decided whether or not to answer his question. Finally she spoke. "I had a servant, a woman. She had been forced to come to

Murga to work off a debt. She came from the mountains to the east of here. She talked constantly of this '*love*'. She said that in her country when a man had '*love*' for a woman, he would devote his entire being to her welfare. He would do everything he could for her happiness, and even lay down his life in her service if it was necessary. He would always stay faithful even when she became old and ugly. All this he would do and never ask for money."

Small nodded his agreement. "That is just as the authors say."

Domina continued. "She spoke of a man who had '*love*' for her back in her own country. One day he would come for her. She was so convinced of this that I ordered my bodyguards to kill him on sight if he ever turned up. Good servants are hard to find and I didn't want to lose her. Even so, one day she disappeared. A man had been seen. After she had gone, I thought about all she had said to me. I thought it would be rather fine if someone had '*love*' for me. Quite apart from anything else I could save money on wages for my bodyguards. They had turned out to be useless anyway."

Small felt that Domina was slightly missing the point. "I am no expert," he said, "but I am sure that love is a sort of mutual thing. The woman also devotes herself to the man."

Domina flashed him a glance of lip-curling scorn. "Don't be ridiculous! Why ever would I want to do that?"

Small bit his lip and fell silent. It was all quite perplexing. Why did the authors write such things if they were not true? What would cause anyone to devote their lives to another like that anyway? He had to admit that, examined rationally, the whole thing seemed somewhat implausible. "Is that why you came here, to find love?" he asked her.

"I am here on business." she answered tersely.

"You mean that you are looking for bodyguards who will work for love not money? Why are you Murgans so obsessed with protection? Is Murga really such a violent place?"

Domina began to groom the horse again. "In Murga protection is the key to wealth. There is always someone who will take what you have by force if it is not well protected. To do business; to make money; you must be able to pay for protection. It is not cheap. When I was just nine years old, I earned the money for our family's first proper bodyguards."

She spoke of this achievement with obvious pride. Small felt that he should be impressed. "At nine!" he said, "How did you do it?"

"I was very fortunate. I had a very wealthy old uncle who had a taste for young girls. My parents made a good business deal with him. I lived with him for five years. I earned a lot of money."

She made a strange shaking gesture with her hand which left Small baffled. "I still don't understand. What exactly did you do for the old man?"

"You know. Entertainment. A bit of dancing, a bit of stroking, a bit of rubbing," she answered blandly.

Small felt as if a large book had fallen on his head from a high shelf. "The authors have a name for that sort of thing." he said, "Pr ..."

"Business?"

Small decided it might be safer to keep the word to himself. "But Winter and Spring like that, it cannot be a good thing," he said, "the authors would call it immoral. You were not even betrothed. Were your parents so desperate for money? Are there no laws in Murga to protect children from such evils?"

Domina laughed. "You foreigners!" she said, "You all keep your children in chains. You regard children as incompetents and extensions of their parents will and character. In your countries, children have no separate legal rights, but Murga is the home of freedom. We Murgans do not see children as slaves or chattels. They have the same freedoms and rights as adults. I went to my uncle of my own free will. It was just business."

Small's mind was in turmoil. The way she described it seemed almost logical. Freedom for children seemed a noble thing, but something in him felt uneasy about the whole thing. Surely freedom must be balanced by care and discipline otherwise it would be mere license. More freedom must be a good thing, for who would want to be a prisoner or a slave? Yet in Murga freedom seemed to lead to evil consequences. Even the bonds of love and duties of parenthood were seen as fetters on the general liberty; a liberty that meant mothers were free to kill their unborn babies; children free to prostitute themselves. It was all so confusing. Small felt completely unbalanced and helpless. Murga was so successful, an expanding global empire, its every citizen an efficient killer, born and bred to 'business'. Not only were all Murgans totally convinced that their way of living was better than any other, but they also seemed able to convince everyone they met that the Murgan way of life was better than their's. The arguments were so simple as to seem unanswerable. How could anybody argue against more freedom?

There was something else which bothered him. He distrusted Murga and all it stood for. This girl before him, still vigorously grooming her horse, was a Murgan. And yet despite his fear of her dangerous temper and her sharp dagger, he was not now planning his escape. For some reason he found that just watching her, just being with her, was strangely pleasant. The musky perfumed smell of her hair and skin had a strange narcotic effect upon him. It seemed to have been in his nostrils ever since the escape from Alligor. Even more than this, and despite her obvious ability to look after herself in every way, he sensed vulnerability. He felt intuitively that she wanted someone to take care of her. Since the only other living beings in this crimson landscape were the Warholl, Small unconsciously appointed himself as her carer, temporarily, and only until a hero came along.

After a long pause he said, "You are spending a lot of time grooming your horse."

"It keeps him from getting restless," she replied, "We are upwind of the other horses but he might sense their presence and call to them if he is not distracted."

"What is your horse's name?"

"He is Lucifer."

"Is that not a strange choice of name? To call such a beautiful, obedient beast after a king of demons who tried to depose God?"

Domina paused to clean her combs and looked at Small, her head tilted slightly and her eyes narrowed. "You know nothing," she said, "Lucifer is the bright morning star. The god of this world, the giver of freedom, the breaker of chains, the spiller of wine and blood."

Small fell silent once more. Murga was like the world behind a mirror in which everything the authors said was reversed.

The sun had climbed high into the heavens before a sudden bustle at the oasis and a distant drumming of hooves signalled the departure of the Warholl. Scrambling up the bank, Small was just in time to see their parti-coloured forms vanish into the clouds of pink dust kicked up by their horses. Domina vaulted onto Lucifer's back from where she watched intently as they disappeared. "They are in a big hurry to get somewhere ... Lucky for you," the *ulvis* heralded a wide smile, "Come on, let's get moving."

Small moved to mount the horse but she had already walked Lucifer on. Over her shoulder she called, "I walk. You ride. A lady and a beggar on horseback would be conspicuous."

"To whom?" Small shouted, waving his arms at the empty landscape. But she did not reply and he had to run to catch up.

It was late afternoon before they saw the first signs of human habitation. Low walls built of unriven field stones bounded areas of cultivated land. Drifts of red dust made it impossible to guess if there were any crops planted. Soon after Small became aware of a wailing

234

sound which came from behind a low, mud-brick dwelling off to the right of the road. The farm was poor enough but had signs of being well kept. The walls had been recently patched with fresh mud and no garbage was to be seen in front of the door. A large apple tree stood in the farmyard, its ripe fruit weighing down the tips of the branches. Suspended from one of the larger boughs of the tree hung the body of a young man. It swayed gently at the end of a crude rope. His hands were bound behind him and he was naked save for a piece of torn patterned silk tied around his waist. His face was swollen and dark. His open eyes bulged and yet he seemed to wear a bizarre smile because a piece of orange fruit peel had been inserted into his mouth between teeth and lips. Rouge and Kohl had been crudely smeared on his mouth and eyes.

Small, numb with horror watched as Domina walked Lucifer over to the tree. She stood up in the saddle, spun the body round and began to saw at the rope with her knife. It seemed a long time before the body fell to the ground. The thin wailing from the farmhouse became a wild shriek. Domina dismounted and strode towards the noise. Small felt as if he were sleepwalking as he stumbled after her. "What has happened here?" he asked.

"Warholl," she said simply.

The old woman had been tied to an ancient ox-collar which her tormentors had wedged into a door frame. As soon as she was untied she ran to the body and cradled the dead youth in her arms. She took out the orange peel, tore away the fragment of silk and wrapped her shawl around the corpse. She was unable to remove the rope. The blood knot had been well tied, it had bitten deep into the flesh and it was tight and hard. The old woman's cries were so piteous that Small was moved to help her. He turned to Domina fully expecting her to cut the knot, but the girl was staring intently at the scene as if trying to work out what was happening.

"Domina, please cut the knot." he said, as the old woman continued to claw ineffectually at the rope. The girl did not move. "He's her son. Please cut the knot." Still Domina stared but did not move. Small walked towards her, his hand outstretched. "Give me the knife," he pleaded, "I'll do it."

The knife flashed into sight so quickly that for an instant Small feared for his life.

"Never try to take my knife," she spat, "I'll kill you first," then she bent down and cut the knot.

The old woman continued to rock the body to and fro. All the while she was wailing and keening. Now she was forming words. "He was a good boy. Full of courage. He knew right from wrong. He stood up to them. Who will avenge him? What kind of a world spawns such devils as those who did this?"

Small remembered what Old had said. "Fear a world in which the evil of knowledge is abroad." But this was beyond mere cold calculation. This was the evil of total unreason. This was evil bordering on madness. The old woman subsided into a low moaning.

Domina turned to face him. "Why is she doing that?" she asked. "I don't understand. He is worth nothing now and yet she is still upset."

"He's her son," said Small, "She loved him very much. Your parents would do the same if it was you who died."

"No they wouldn't. When my brother was killed they cursed a lot because they lost money in a deal he was handling. But they didn't wail and embrace him. This old woman is very unhappy. Is she in pain? Did '*love*' do this to her? Is this because of '*love*'?"

Small was trying to analyse his own feelings. He did not know either of these people and yet he was on the verge of tears. The more the old woman wailed and tore her hair, the sadder he became. What had the philosopher said? 'We laugh with those who laugh and grieve with those who grieve'. Why should that be so?

Domina reached out and brushed his cheek with her thumb. She examined it carefully as she climbed on Lucifer. "You are crying!" she said in an astonished tone. "This is completely ridiculous. Murgans would never behave like this. Come on. We have to get going or you will be next to taste the orange."

"We can't just leave her'" Small protested.

"There is nothing you can do. The crops are buried in dust. The farm labourer is dead. She is too old to go anywhere and Puttfark is on his way." she turned Lucifer about and shouted over her shoulder, "Old woman, those devils will return. They will ask you about us. Tell them nothing."

Back on the road Domina walked the horse at a gruelling pace. Small soon understood that this was not going to be a stroll through the countryside. No matter how fast he walked, he continually found himself being left behind; forced to break into a jog to catch up. The plain seemed to go on for ever. There were no trees and very little plant life of any kind. From time to time they passed heaps of rubble which had once been buildings. Only the stones remained. The roof timbers and doors had long ago been used as fuel. The Ancients had been right. Trees should be held sacred. They provided shade, shelter and fuel; their roots bound the land together. The people who lived on the plain around Alligor had squandered their inheritance; slashed and burned their woods and forests with no thought for the future. As they stripped their landscape of its groves and arbors they had been too greedy and foolish to replant. The day came when they shivered in their cots and were forced to eat their food raw. Without the trees to re-make it, the very soil of their fields turned to dust at their feet. He wondered if those last inhabitants as they stared into the embers of their house timbers had learned anything from their folly, before they were forced to walk down this same road, never to return. Were they even now hacking and burning some other landscape to dust?

He jogged until he was level with the horse.

"You must tell me your name." As usual Domina spoke without looking at him. "It will seem odd if I don't know my servant's name."

"In Alligor I am known as Small."

The horse stopped. Domina turned her head slowly in order to stare at him.

"Come again?"

"Small. I was left at the gate. I ..."

"Small?" The girl's lip curled in utter disgust.

He blushed. "The man in white called me 'Rider'."

"Ha! He really took you for a ride, didn't he? 'Walker' would be more like. 'Dustkicker' perhaps?"

Small was beginning to find the *ulvis* not quite so endearing as before. The girl's scorn cut him like a whip, but when she lifted her face to the sky and laughed, his fascination with this strange creature revived. He stared at her with frank interest. When Domina saw the way he was looking at her, she suppressed her mirth with a shake of her hair and kicked the horse into motion.

"Let me explain to you the ways of the world," she said. "In this backward part of the globe, a young woman without protection attracts attention from men. This attention is usually unwelcome, but it can develop from being merely annoying to being dangerous and even fatal. It's best if such attention does not arise in the first place. If it looks like the woman has a man to protect her, this can act as a deterrent. Unfortunately you are as skinny as a dog, and the way you carry yourself is all wrong for a bodyguard. But, I have seen young men with your build who were fast and deadly with a blade. Perhaps you can give that impression. The right name might help, something like *Slot*, or *Cutter - Shiv* perhaps? Got any ideas?

Small had his own idea of how he wanted to appear. "How about Amatis?" he suggested.

"That's really funny. So funny it might get you your throat cut."

237

"But if Amatis were to meet a young woman travelling with somebody called *Slot* or *Cutter*, he would straight away set about rescuing her."

"You might have a point there. There's always some young thug out to make his name. Best avoid any hint of a reputation." She fell silent and the horse plodded on.

"I've got it," she said suddenly, "*Sharp*! That's your new name. 'Sharp'. See? It has two meanings, like a knife with two edges, sharp thinking and good with a blade. Perfect!"

'Sharp' contemplated his new persona with interest. Was there a veiled compliment in there somewhere? He wondered.

By now the wine-coloured dregs of the day were gathering in the west and evening was upon them. 'Sharp' side-stepped a large patch of animal droppings which lay in the road.

"That's the third," said Domina. "Animals mean people. There must be a village ahead. I think we will try to find somewhere to stay the night. The horse needs fodder, and I need to wash some … things. Can you remember how Puttfark's men looked and moved?"

'Sharp' nodded uncertainly.

"Show me."

'Sharp' straightened up, squared his shoulders and adopted the rolling gait of the professional thug. As an afterthought he curled his lip into an *ulvis*-like sneer. Domina's eyes widened at the transformation. "You look …," she paused as she searched for suitable words, "…like a complete idiot!"

Small was visibly deflated.

"But it will have to do. Just remember to keep silent."

It was dark by the time they reached the clustered buildings which had once been a village. Many looked as if they had been abandoned for years. One or two still had roofs. Skeletal cattle in crude pens huffed and groaned as they passed by. At the heart of the village was a cross-roads. There they found several bony horses and a camel tethered outside what looked like an inn. A murmur of voices and a glimmer of light came from inside.

Domina dismounted. "Tie up the horse whilst I see if this place is safe. We wouldn't want to walk in on a Warholl dinner party, would we? Come when I call and try not to look soft."

The inn fell silent as Domina closed the door behind her. The room was filled with men whose gimlet eyes glittered in the fire light. The place looked and smelled like a rat's nest. Behind a rough trestle, a stout bearded man had frozen in the act of dipping a pitcher into a large earthenware jar. As she strode over to him, her hand curled around the handle of her weapon.

"Are you the innkeep?"

"Yez I am." His dialect made his speech as thick and cloudy as the brew in the jar.

"I need food and lodging for the night for myself, a manservant and a horse." Domina felt the eyes of all the men in the room boring into her back. With her thumb she flicked over the thong which kept her dagger in its sheath. She already knew which three she would kill first, if she had to.

The innkeeper placed the pitcher carefully on its uneven base in the centre of the trestle. "Well, lady, the room is no problem, and the stable is empty, but to tell truth what with the dust storm and they Murgans buying everything up, we're struggling to feed us selves."

"I can pay." Domina held out two pieces of Murgan silver on her palm.

"Oho! More o' that evil eye money. I got plenty o' that. Trouble is, there ent nothing left to spend it on. Funny thing, how of a sudden like, this whole countryside is swarming with …" he spat ostentatiously into a heap of foetid straw. "… Murgans. Happen you passed 'em on the road?"

"I try to keep out of their way." She did not like the way he was looking at her, nor the angry mutterings from the corners of the room.

"Strange that, 'cos I could've swore you was one of they too." As he spoke he tugged at her silken sleeve with a calloused thumb.

With a jolt she realised that she was going to have to fight her way out. She needed the door open and a distraction. Time for that idiot to earn his keep. She half turned away from the trestle. "Sharp!" she called out. All eyes swivelled to the door. All bodies tensed. The latch lifted slowly and 'Sharp' came in. With his upper body held rigid he turned himself sideways as if his shoulders were too broad to fit through the door opening. His arms hung away from his sides in what he hoped was a muscular and thuggish manner. But with his threadbare robe that hardly covered his bony knees and with a totally lunatic expression on his face he looked utterly and completely absurd.

For a moment the room held a stunned silence. Then as one they all exploded into helpless laughter. Amidst the general uproar voices cried out "It's a clown", "It's a buffoon" and "Give him food, let him play for his supper."

Domina was taken completely by surprise. She had planned for all possible scenarios of violence and mayhem, but confronted by a room

239

full of men rendered helpless by mirth, she completely omitted to kill any of them.

The innkeeper was a transformed man. Tears of laughter streamed down his face. "Gods of the Amelakites! I've never seen anything so funny in my life. God knows we have little enough to laugh about these days. If your man can amuse us for an hour or two I can find you something to eat."

Domina forced a smile for the innkeeper whilst bundling the bewildered Small into a corner. "You heard?" she whispered. "You have to earn our supper. Can you do it? Can you amuse them?"

It was perhaps lucky for Small that he had only seen the room filled with laughing genial peasants. "What do they want me to do?"

Domina shrugged her shoulders. "Tell them a story: something to make them smile."

Small had never spoken to an audience. He tried to remember several books on rhetoric that he had read. But the vague recollections of balanced or contrasting phrases, of ornamental arrangement, of suitable or unsuitable metaphors, and of florid Asiatic oratory, were no help. He remembered how Velik had let himself be swept along by the tale: changing his voice to suit the subject and miming the action with his hands and body. The room fell silent as he stepped out in front of the trestle.

"I tell of a man," he shouted loudly, and then in a more intimate voice, "a man like some of you. A gardener by trade, which is, as you know, a kind of farmer of plants. And of his love for the beautiful daughter of a mighty monarch." Small paused and turned towards the landlord "There is also an innkeeper in this story," he said.

The audience turned in their seats, murmured knowingly, winked at each other and smiled in anticipation. Small thrust his fist into his waist as he had seen Velik do and began.

"There once was a mighty Khan who ruled over many lands. His beloved queen died after giving birth to only one daughter. This princess Poeisia was the apple of his eye and he applied his great wisdom and fatherly care to her upbringing so that her life would be happy and fulfilled. When she came of marriageable age he invited many suitors to court and the royal palace was made gay with dancing, feasting and merrymaking. As a great ruler he had a duty to make marriage alliances but as a loving father he did not wish to compel her to sacrifice her happiness for reasons of state. He hoped that she would choose willingly. Much as Poeisia enjoyed the festivities and the attention of the young princes she could not commit herself to any one suitor. She knew her duty as a princess, but did not find any man amongst the strangers with whom she would like to spend her life.

'To escape the bustle of the court she would often walk in the queen's garden. The garden was a miracle of the gardener's art, perfumed by rare blooms, shaded by resinous pines and overhung by a cornucopia of luscious fruits and succulent nuts. Fountains played and water splashed freely. A winding path led down to a tiny overgrown harbour where a royal pleasure barge could sail in through a gateway from the ocean. In this paradise on earth Poeisia had passed her childhood years in guileless pleasure, but like all earthly paradises, this garden had its guilty secret.

'Although no-one was allowed into the garden but she and the gardener, the gardener had a son to bring up in the craft, and so the gardener's son became her secret playmate. His name was Amatis. Even though it was forbidden, Poeisia often shared her thoughts with the gardener's son. They talked of this and that, of her joys and sorrows, and even of things which she could not tell her father. He often brought her flowers and would even show her poems he had written. As is the way in such things, the two young people became more than friends and Poeisia suddenly knew that Amatis was the man she wanted to be with always. This was a serious problem. Amatis risked his life every time he spoke to her. For a peasant to seduce a princess was punishable by death. It was an impossible state of affairs which threatened to have a bad end.

'Poeisia foolishly decided to tell her loving father that her heart was won by a nameless commoner. The Great Khan listened to his beloved daughter. He was greatly surprised, disappointed and angry but he did not show it. He reasoned with her, reminded her of her duty to her father, her mother, her people and her country. He pointed out to her that such romantic liaisons did not last and that the young man would probably desert her. The Khan could remain calm because there was a standard procedure in such cases. He would find out who the young man was and have him kidnapped and killed. The medicine was strong but the cure complete.

'Poeisia knew her father loved her and was convinced that he would eventually agree to the marriage, but Amatis was shocked at what she had done. He decided to go away to visit his uncle until the Khan was won over. In the dark perfumed garden the lovers embraced and exchanged their vows, the one to return, the other to wait. Then Amatis took his leave. He escaped the waiting assassin only because he knew the garden so well and his ambusher knew it not at all. He escaped in a small boat from the harbour and went into hiding. Instead of collecting his fee, the failed assassin fled for his life, and the Khan offered a reward of a thousand gold pieces for the arrest of 'Amatis the palace gardener, enemy of the state'. When this failed, the Khan decreed that a militia army be conscripted from the common folk to flush out the errant gardener. Poeisia knew nothing of all this.

Amatis was a stranger in his uncle's village so that when the local people heard of the reward, many were suspicious of him and asked, 'Who is he? Had he been a gardener?'. Things became very dangerous for him when the militia arrived at the village. What was the best place for him to hide?"

Small's story telling was interrupted here whilst the audience offered suggestions. It seemed that wells and cattle byres were the most popular bolt holes here on the plain. Small waited whilst the villagers used up their limited store of ideas.

"Amatis was much cleverer than that. He devised a bold and cunning plan. The best place to hide an ear of corn was in a corn field. The best place for a young man to hide was in a field of young men. He grew a beard, changed his name to Sitama, became a zealous recruit and joined the militia. In the months that followed, Sitama quickly rose through the ranks because of his energy, his persistence and his determination. No-one was more thorough than Sitama the soldier in searching for Amatis the gardener. But somehow the wily gardener always slipped through the net.

Years passed and the two reputations grew. Whatever disturbed the civil order was blamed on Amatis: the elusive enemy of the state, the mischief maker, the thief of time, the enemy of reason, the almost supernatural cause of all misfortunes. Sitama: the hawk, the tireless hunter, the sudden descender, the loyal dog of war, the Khan's right arm, was sent to quell the disturbance. The reputation of Sitama the soldier came to the ears of the Khan who ordered him made a captain. This meant a splendid new suit of armour, a purple cloak and a summons to the royal palace. He knew that this would be dangerous but he would risk it for the chance to see Poeisia. The Khan had never seen his face. If people expected to see a gardener they would see a gardener, if they expected a great soldier hero, that is what they would see. Anyway he knew that it was the very last thing anyone would expect Amatis to do."

After a hesitant start, Small had warmed to his task. He found the right level for his voice and before long something strange happened to his audience. The hard weather-worn faces, pinched by hardship beyond endurance, eyes dulled from watching too many things wither and die, foreheads knotted by adversity, lips twisted into asymmetry by unanswered prayers and murmured curses, slowly relaxed as the magic spell of the story and the teller caught them in its snare. Eyebrows lifted, eyes widened, mouths opened slightly, and grown men became children again with the wonder engendered in their unlocked imaginations. Soon they were unaware of anything but the stream of words. Small felt the power of the tale. It was a poor enough rendition but these poor illiterate farmers seemed to be hearing much more than he was telling them. It was as if they were willing the story into existence. It was just as Velik had described it. His words were being carried on the divine wind. From time to time the farmers laughed or made exclamations, but never so loud as to interrupt the story.

Without pausing in his tale he glanced over at Domina to see if she had noticed the effect he was having. He was amazed to find that she too had the rapt expression of the wondering child. Only one face in the room remained unmoved. In the corner behind the door a dark, bearded man with regular features, no farmer he, twitched at his travelling cloak and fondled his beaker. He lubricated the cynical half-smile on his lips often with his tongue. He seemed relaxed but his eyes missed nothing. From time to time he darted surreptitious lingering glances at Domina.

"Sitama put on his splendid new uniform and set off for the capital city. He left his old armour and cloak in the tavern where he was billeted. No sooner had he left than the innkeeper entered the room to lay fresh rushes on the floor. The innkeeper admired the armour and uniform which hung from a peg on the wall and wondered what he might look like if he were to put it on. This he duly did. For some time he strutted around the room in the uniform and armour. He drew the sword and flourished it in the air. He made martial gestures as he had seen the soldiers do. He was so pleased with himself in his new guise that he decided to go downstairs into the main room and see if he would be recognized. He pulled the helmet low over his eyes and tied the leather cheek pieces well forward.'

'Recognizing the armour and the uniform, several drunken soldiers saluted him as he came down the stairs. He was even more amazed to find himself the object of admiring glances from the women in the room, who were however, it has to be said, not of the best character. This last however made him giddy with vanity and almost before he knew it he was out in the street. Soldiers saluted him, even wealthy citizens stepped aside for him to pass, and everywhere the flashing eyes of even the most respectable womenfolk spurred him on. The innkeeper felt like a king among men. He squared his shoulders, thrust out his chest like a cockerel, and strutted up and down in the busy market place. He was so pleased with himself that he did not notice the surly and unfriendly looks which the local men cast upon soldiers. Eventually the fear of being recognized overcame his vanity and he headed back to the inn.

It was then that he spotted several of his regular drinking partners down a narrow alley. He decided to play a trick on them before revealing who he was. "You there! Stand up and account for yourselves," he shouted in a loud aggressive voice. The men started like rabbits, coins fell to the ground, but their shocked and guilty expressions quickly darkened into anger as they realised that they were five against one. Clubs and knives appeared in their hands. The innkeeper was alarmed. "Wait! Stop!" he said, struggling to untie the helmet, "I am your friend." Which of course they took for a sign of cowardice and rushed upon him. The innkeeper was terrified and took to his heels. But in the streets he could not take off his helmet for fear of being recognized. He ran as fast as he could around the corner. There he stopped abruptly. A squad of heavily armed soldiers was marching straight towards him. The soldiers mistook the innkeeper's flailing arms and strangled cries for the signal to attack and immediately charged after the hapless man. Around the corner they ran into the five armed ruffians and a melee developed which spilled out into the market place.

'The market traders only saw two things: their market stalls overturned by brawling men, and the hated out-of-town soldiers beating the heads of locals, so of course they all joined in. The soldiers found themselves outnumbered and reinforcements were sent for. As is always the case in such circumstances, by evening a sleepy and prosperous province had become a bonfire of revolt raging out of control. The soldiers knew of only one name which could be attached to such a serious disturbance - Amatis. An urgent dispatch was sent to the Khan begging him to send Sitama back as soon as possible.

'After Amatis had fled the king's assassin, the Great Khan had lost no opportunity for persuading his daughter that the gardener was a worthless adventurer. For her part Poeisia argued that she loved him even so, and thus the debate centred on what was the nature of love and the role of parents. The Khan was well aware of the potent nature of the affliction but saw it as his duty to warn his daughter against too willing submission to her inclinations. "You speak of love as if it were something light and harmless like a bottle of perfume or a perfect fruit, but love can be like a terrible army," he argued, " that lays waste your lands. The god of love is its charming general who stands at the gates of your city and says 'Open up and all will be well.' If you do so he will enter with his army and take over the government. If you don't then he will try and force his way in. Either way you will be left stumbling amongst the ruins of your own fair city. Love can be like a handsome stranger on a camel in a caravan who pulls you up behind him and carries you off to distant lands. Everything seems a great adventure until you awake one morning to find yourself sold into slavery. You speak of your feelings as if that was all there was to it, but are you certain that those feelings are really love? Might what you feel be really lust and no more than the pleasurable feeling you have when you feed on a roast carcass at a banquet?"

'Poeisia found it difficult to counter her father's arguments. She replied that the pleasure she felt was more like the pleasure of being in the temple on a feast day, as if senses and spirit were lifted together. But her father insisted that the pleasure she felt in the temple was in large part due to the knowledge that the rites of the temple were performed for the good of the whole nation, and that such selflessness was in no way to be compared with the sort of selfish begetting which she desired. Poeisia thought her father was exaggerating. "But how could the begetting of a single child make any difference to the well-being of the whole nation?" she asked. The Khan was adamant. "A King or queen would no more think of marrying for lust or even love than they would of giving up their throne or selling their people into slavery. Too many lives hang upon their choice. Their position is god-given and so their duties are divinely ordained. Poeisia was intransigent. "Then I wish I had been born an ordinary peasant and could have my child born of passionate love."

'The Khan was not impressed. "Do you really think that it would make any difference? That you would not then have similar responsibilities? A man, a woman, they are like kingdoms, indeed they have within them thousands upon thousands of citizens yet unborn. Whole kingdoms of the future. When we make our alliances we must be very careful. We observe that children learn by imitating their parents in all they do. If the parent is unruly, a drunkard, a weak fop, promiscuous or violent then there will be an effect upon their children. How often do we see criminality or promiscuity running in families? We observe that children are chained to their parent's weaknesses and that they pass on these chains to their children in their turn. Chains of this sort are almost impossible to break. Give up your responsibilities and embrace passionate love and you set an example for your children, which they will pass on to their children, and they theirs', until you have a whole village of irresponsible and passionate offspring, Within

245

a couple of generations that village of descendants will become a town, and that town a city. Think about it and you will realise that the fate of nations will depend upon your fit of passion just as surely as if you had been a monarch."

'Such was the nature of the discussions which Poeisia and her father were wont to have. However no matter what arguments the Khan used, Poeisia remained stubbornly faithful to Amatis. The Khan then decided to try to distract her by introducing her to other desirable young men, and who could be more desirable and attractive than a dashing military hero? The reports of both men and women with regard to Sitama had convinced the Khan that his Militia captain was eminently suitable to the task in hand. Sitama was summoned to the royal palace. Of course no-one recognized the gardener's son when he arrived dressed in his magnificent armour and cloak. With his newly-grown beard and fine clothes not even his own mother would have known him. Indeed when he was ushered into the royal presence even Poeisia saw only a handsome stranger before her. However, as they talked together she found herself strangely attracted to him. She felt as if she had known him all her life and was shocked to discover herself falling under the spell of his charm. Was love such a temporary and fickle thing that she should fall for another man so soon after declaring her undying faith to Amatis?

'The Khan was overjoyed when he saw how successful his plan had been. He made sure that the young soldier had every opportunity to be with the princess. For her part Poeisia seemed anxious to spend as much time as possible talking to the young soldier. Sitama had soon made two conquests, since the Khan himself enjoyed the company of his brave young captain and found himself wishing that he had a son just like him. "How can you dream of marrying a peasant," he said to his daughter one day, "when there are fine soldierly types like Sitama here?"

'The courtly conversations were rudely interrupted when a messenger arrived with news of the dangerous revolt which, although no-one knew it, had been started by the innkeeper's foolishness. When the Khan asked the messenger who might be behind the uprising, the man knew only one name capable of inspiring such mayhem. "Amatis!" he cried. Of course the handsome militia captain looked up when he heard his real name. Poeisia instantly recognized her lover for who he was and knew that he had fulfilled his promise to return. The Khan was too busy to notice. He had to act quickly and decisively. A daughter in love with a peasant was one thing but a revolt was much more serious. It was far more important that Sitama should quell the revolt and kill that accursed gardener than that he should lie around flirting all day. Sitama was told to choose a horse from the royal stables and return to his post immediately. Once again the lovers were parted without even being able to exchange a few words of farewell. Back with his troops, Sitama was able to restore order to the province very quickly, but of course Amatis managed to slip away yet again. The Khan congratulated himself on the success of his strategy and resolved to make Sitama a noble. The innkeeper had eventually crept back into his inn and taken off his disguise. Afterwards he told all who would listen that he for his part did not envy the soldiers or their lifestyle and that it was far too dangerous for his liking. Of course Poeisia and her lover were to be re-united many years later, but that is another story: in fact that is several other stories. But hearken to the moral of this tale. Never judge a thing by its appearance, since nobility is not always a matter of birth alone. Neither fine clothes nor rags say much about the man inside."

There was a short appreciative silence before the shouts and banging of beakers on the tables began. It had been a plain enough tale but the reward for its telling was such as Small had never had before. To be a travelling storyteller might indeed be a very fine thing. The audience were smiling and bright-eyed. They milled around him, wanting to be close to the source of their enchantment for as long as possible. They touched his robe in thanks. They fumbled in their clothes with rough and crabby fingers for small coins, hoarded and precious in this poor land, and pressed them into his hands. He was given a drink, then another. A meal appeared, cold, homely enough but not stinted. There was no doubt that it was as good as the innkeeper had. Small and Domina ate hungrily and without pause whilst the peasants stood round smiling. This was still a world where fair work deserved fair wages: where skill and artistry were rare and precious, things to be bought at any price. As they ate, Small several times caught Domina sneaking sideways glances at him. He tried to see but he could not tell what lurked in those dark and lovely irises.

Domina was perturbed. She was well aware that she had let her attention drift several times during the telling of the tale. She had got away with it but knew that she might well have been knifed or bludgeoned whilst her guard was down. It had been a stupid lapse. The innocent air of this child-man had a strange lulling effect on her. She was constantly being surprised by her reactions in his presence. She had been anxious that he tell the tale well and pleased to hear him praised, and it was not just because his skill would fill her belly. There was more to this boy than met the eye and she was not sure she liked it.

By ones and twos the crowd drifted into the dark night until the room was nearly empty. Whilst Domina went with the innkeeper to see to the horse, Small followed the woman to a small chamber with two low wooden cots. He lay down in his clothes and went to sleep almost at once. When Domina came into the room he did not even stir. She looked at him in disbelief. This boy wouldn't last two minutes on his own. She suppressed a very un-Murgan thought and climbed into her rickety cot. Through the window the cold stars wheeled the world into the small hours.

There was banging and knocking, and shouts. Small groped his way out of unconsciousness.

"For the love of God stop that snoring!"

Small had no idea where he was or who was shouting. The snoring was very loud. Faint recollections stumbled around in his head. "It's the horse," he mumbled. "It's in the stable. Why are you knocking us awake?"

Scornful laughter from several voices. "Have you got a horse in there with you? Then shut it up. Keep it quiet."

The snoring was still loud. It was in the room. It was Domina. He rose wearily and crossed over to where she slept. It was difficult to make her out in the dark. He bent over her. The musky perfume of her sleepy warmth washed over him. He had a strong desire to bend closer, to bury his face in her hair, but even as he moved the snoring had stopped and a dagger blade was pressed into his stomach.

"What the God are you doing?" she said.

"You were snoring. You woke the whole inn."

"I don't snore. Try to get into bed with me again and I'll kill you."

Small began to protest his innocence but gave up. When he was close to this girl he was no longer really sure *what* was in his mind.

A pale sun brought a cold dawn. Small had slept in his clothes and now sat with his feet in the ashes of the fire downstairs to get warm. He scratched at his vermin bites. Domina, after washing and dressing herself in their room, went into the backyard with the innkeeper's woman. Their manner was so mysterious and conspiratorial that Small could not help being curious. He got up and walked into the yard. Domina was crouched over a tub of water rinsing and pounding what looked like lengths of cloth. The cloths were stained with blood.

Small was shocked. "Have you been wounded?" he asked. "You should have told me."

She looked at him with the now familiar expression of scorn and disbelief.

"Don't you know anything? All women bleed. It's normal. Usually men are intelligent enough not to poke their noses into it."

Small was dumbfounded. He had made another foolish error. But if it was so normal then why did the authors never mention it?"

Once on the road with the sun warm on his back, Small pondered over the mysterious issue of blood. He wished that he had read more books on physic. His thoughts were interrupted by the pounding of hooves in the road behind them. He turned and saw that it was the man from the inn. The one who had not been caught by the tale.

Domina stared fixedly at the road ahead. "Leave this to me," she said. "Whatever happens don't try to interfere or you might get hurt." She dismounted and pretended to adjust her stirrup.

The rider almost ran Small down as he pulled his horse to a standstill and dismounted next to Domina. Small found that the stranger's horse was a barrier preventing him from seeing what was happening. He had to run round in front of the horses.

The stranger was tall, well built and not ugly. His chin was smooth but he had a thin moustache above a long sensual mouth. He smiled a thin-lipped smile before he spoke to Domina.

"Having trouble?"

"Not yet," she replied rather coldly.

"Travelling can be full of unforeseen circumstances, especially for one so young," he said, "… and desirable," he added, and waited for a reaction.

Domina ignored him.

He continued. "I saw you in the inn last night and I thought to myself, a beautiful young thing like that, travelling without any real protection, could get herself into all kinds of trouble. What she needs is a real man: to look after her."

Domina turned to face the man. Small noticed that her hand was on her dagger inside the front of her clothes. "I have no money to spare for bodyguards. Sharp here is all the protection I need."

The man turned to Small with a sneer. "YAA!" he shouted. Small jumped back in alarm. The man laughed in derision. "Where I come from a sickly child like that would have been strangled at birth. He couldn't even protect you from an angry goose."

Domina had not flinched when the man shouted, nor had she taken her eyes off the man's face for an instant. "That is my business," she said, "and I cannot pay you."

The man had moved very close to Domina. He put his hand on Lucifer's saddle close to her shoulder. He grinned lasciviously as he bent his face down towards hers. "Oh I wasn't thinking about payment in money. There is nothing to buy in this land of beggars. I was thinking of quite another, more pleasant form of reward. Payment in kind so to speak. A body for a body?"

The stranger pressed his hips against the girl, pinning her against the flank of the horse. Small had seen enough. He hurled himself at the man intending to pull him away from Domina. The stranger did not attempt to wrestle with Small but suddenly butted him hard with his forehead on the bridge of the nose. As Small fell back concussed and blinded with pain, he felt a vicious kick in the abdomen which drove all the breath from his lungs. He fell to the ground with blood spurting from his nose and with his breathing paralysed.

Domina remained impassive. The man was no longer smiling as he curled his other arm around her waist. "You see how much safer you would be if you made a deal with me?" he said quietly.

She did not try to push him away but angled her head back so that she could still stare unflinchingly into his face. "Perhaps," she said, "but when would this payment in kind fall due?"

"Oh, let me see. Right now, I think. Payment in advance. It would be … safer." The man smiled faintly at his own wit.

Domina shrugged. "I suppose we could do business. But not here on the public road. I wouldn't want us to be seen."

It was the man's turn to shrug. "Choose your spot."

Small was still fighting to make his lungs work and choking on the blood from his nose. He tried to shout but only faint gasping and crouping noises came out. He watched helplessly as Domina strolled with the stranger to a patch of scrub. All the way the man's hands roamed over the young girl's body. When they reached the cover Domina turned towards the man and their bodies came together. They stood motionless for several seconds. The man sank to his knees. Domina stooped over him as he went down. Then she straightened and began to walk back towards the horses. The stranger remained kneeling; his chin down on his chest. It looked like he was praying.

Small was still not thinking clearly. It was not until Domina came closer and he saw her hand held carefully away from her side so that the blood running down her forearm, over her knuckles and dripping from the point of the dagger did not mark her silken clothes. He

250

watched as she pulled some cloth item from the man's saddlebag. He watched her scrub the sticky blood from her arm where it had run down from her hand. He watched as she cleaned the reeking hand which had pushed the blade into the man's body. He watched as she carefully polished the blade which she had twisted and turned inside him seeking as many vital severances and ruptures as would end his life. It was only then that he realised that she had killed the man.

Domina stuffed the bloody rag back into the man's saddlebag and lifted his water skin off the horse's withers. She pushed the horse off the road and slapped its rump. It cantered away over the plain. Spurting water onto her hands she walked over to where Small was still writhing on the ground.

"Get up," she said. "Next time listen to me."

Small clutched his aching body with both arms as he stumbled along after the horse. His eyes were half closed and he felt sick from the salty taste of blood in his mouth. For the first time since his escape he longed to be back in Alligor. It now seemed like a haven of sanity and security to him. Adventures in books had always seemed so fine. How many times had he read about fighting and killing and thought it grand stuff. But when it actually happened in real life it was not exciting at all. It was disgusting and frightening. What were the authors up to? Was everything they wrote about so false?

He looked at Domina. All those future histories he had been composing in his head since he met her were just castles in the air. She had looked like a young girl, but now he realised that she was an animal of an entirely different kind to him. She was a monstrous shape-changer. She was angel and she-devil. She was a Murgan and a killer without conscience. He was deeply afraid and not just because of what she seemed capable of doing but of what he felt she had already done to him. He was helplessly in emotional bondage to her. He had wanted to look after her but she was always looking after him. He could not do anything for her. He was worse than useless.

He stopped walking. Tears of pain and humiliation welled up in his eyes. His nose felt bulbous and ugly, big as a skinful of water. His insides hurt. He watched the horse walk on into the distance, then he shuffled to the side of the road and sat down slowly and awkwardly.

Lucifer plodded on, raising puffs of pink dust at every step. Domina was deep in thought. She had no idea why they were being pursued, but by this time their pursuers were almost certainly on their trail. It might take them a day or two to find out which direction they had taken, but then they would be moving fast. Avoiding the Warholl had been doubly lucky. Puttfark would first try every other route than the one they had come down. Helping the old crone at the farm had been a mistake though. The Warholl would know right away that someone had passed by, even before they started breaking her arms and legs to get her to tell them who. The innkeeper might delay them for an hour or two by sending them down the wrong road, but they would get the truth out of him when they returned. Would he have the sense to run away and hide before they came back? Once Puttfark knew that they were heading east for the mountains he could easily overtake them. She could have taken the dead man's horse but if he had travelled this road before, it might have been recognized. Horse thieves were usually butchered on the spot. Keeping to the road was risky, but leaving the road would slow them down. They had to move faster.

It was then that she looked back and noticed that the boy wasn't following. Behind the horse the dust whirled away across the plain. An empty road stretched into the pink distance. It was obvious what she had to do. The boy was a liability: a hopeless imbecile. He had nothing of value for her. If she abandoned him she could be out of any danger in a couple of hours of hard riding. He might even be safer on his own. He could walk parallel to the road and duck behind a bush when anyone came by. The deal had been to help the boy escape. She had done that. Now the boy was nothing to do with her, nothing at all. It had been a bad mistake to get involved in a deal without profit. She must cut her losses and get out.

Small was sitting hunched over his knees at the side of the road. He heard the horse approaching and looked up. Domina held out her hand to him.

"Get on the horse," she said.

Twenty-one

Puttfark rode his horse in a mood of cold fury. He had never before had a mission go so catastrophically wrong. Five men dead on the spot, seven more gibbering madmen with hands and feet going black with gangrene. Rottko, that smirking scorpion, on his way back to tell the paymaster all about it. And, to cap it all, having to work with these Warholl. Sa'than! The way they had pulled the old woman to pieces. They were worse than wild animals. They had got the information, but it just wasn't his style. No finesse. And all this because of a naïve boy, a foolish innocent. He still could not work out how the boy had arranged his getaway. He must have made a better deal; but who with? Thinking about the boy made him especially furious. The boy had betrayed him. The deal had been struck, not in so many words, but struck none the less. The manuscript was his. The boy was his. By the terms of the bargain he owned the boy's future. He would have been the empty beaker into which could be poured all the pleasures of the world, in measures which he, Puttfark of Murga, would decide. Why should anyone not want that? How could the stupid book be worth more to him?

When the Warholl moved through a landscape it was in a miasma of perfume and death. Puttfark was not a man to be troubled by either death or violence, that was his trade, but there was something about these openers of fatal orifices, these body piercers, which made him tense and uneasy. He did not share the strange appetites which animated their lust for butchery and he felt excluded from the unnatural bonds which bound them together. With their ribbons, tassels and bright brocades they seemed all flounces and frills, but when they lifted their *tzirts* there was black leather, metal studs and small sharp weapons buckled all over their bodies. Working with the Warholl was like riding a tiger; it was prudent to make sure the beast was kept well fed.

It had not been easy to get the Warholl to help him. They had no orders from the paymaster to take part in a manhunt. They had only been paid to terrorise the district and seal off the library. In the first white heat of anger at being bested and betrayed, Puttfark had dangled the young boy as bait before Okni, their captain. He was already beginning to regret this rash act. He needed their help to find the boy, but now he had to work out how he would be able to pluck the boy and the book away from these simpering sadists and get both back to Murga. The one thing he had to avoid at all costs was catching up with the fugitives on the open road. If that happened he would not be able to prevent the Warholl having their way with the boy. If they so much as suspected the value of the book they would take that too, even if they had to kill to do it. He was in a very dangerous position and he would have to play this particular game very skilfully if he was to recover his losses. Best let Small get as far as the nearest town, since only he, Puttfark, could pick him out in a crowd. The Warholl would have to trust him to go in alone and find the boy. Once he had him it would be a simple matter to slip past these twisted queens and away.

At first sight the village on the cross-roads seemed deserted. The starving animals were the only indication of human activity. Without any orders being given Okni's gaily dressed cavalry spurred forward to surround the place just in case anybody tried to sneak away. Okni was reaching for the latch on the tavern door when Puttfark stepped into his path.

"Let me handle this."

Okni pouted disapproval. "You might spoil your nice white clothes."

"I'm in charge of this manhunt."

"If you say so, pretty boy."

Puttfark flushed with rage. "Don't call me that! I'll go in first. You just watch my back."

"I never take my eyes off it for a moment."

Several of the Warholl sniggered at the innuendo. Puttfark flashed a fierce stare at them. They smirked back at him without flinching, without fear. He was in their power and they knew it.

Two or three peasants and the tavern keeper froze in apprehension as Puttfark walked in.

"We are looking for a young lad. Simple in his manners, dressed in a raggy robe, barefoot, carrying a bag, probably with a horse." Puttfark waited for a reply. No-one moved. No-one spoke.

Behind his back Okni sidled into the room and struck a pose. "Come on now darlings," he lisped, "talk to the lovely man. Don't be petulant"

A tall stoop-shouldered farmer boy standing against the wall sniggered nervously. Okni half-turned to him. The hum of his sabre as it flashed an arc across the room was only interrupted by the slightest of snicks as it passed under the boy's chin. Seconds seem to pass, then the head lolled over at an improbable angle and blood began to spatter onto the floor. It was already a corpse which crumpled into an untidy heap against the wall.

"Now, answer the nice man's question." Okni said quietly.

Naively all the peasants looked at the gray-faced tavern keeper, who shrugged hopelessly.

"There was a young lad came here, a stranger, but he went. He took the road south to Metafia."

Puttfark knew right away that the tavern keeper was lying about where the boy had gone. It was brave of him, but stupid. It would cost him his life if the Warholl found out. But a wild goose chase was just what Puttfark wanted. It would give the boy time to make the nearest town.

"Was the boy alone?" he asked.

The tavern keeper struggled with his conscience, but his resources of courage were draining away with the blood of the man on the floor. "There was a young girl. That's all."

"A girl? Local?" Puttfark asked him.

"No. I've never seen her before."

Puttfark found this unexpected new element in the game puzzling. Could it be part of an elaborate false trail? Something to keep them guessing. Something to buy time? He turned to go, then paused, "Tell me. On the road east, how far to the nearest town?"

"Twenty leagues at least. The other side of the mountains."

Puttfark saw the guilt and uncertainty in the man's eyes. Now he knew where the boy had gone. Okni had also seen enough to begin to have suspicions about the man-in white. Puttfark was far too subtle and dark in his methods ever to betray a simple motive, but Okni had seen what he had seen.

"You believe him?" he asked as Puttfark remounted his horse.

"Not really. But the boy might have lied to him or doubled back, we have to make sure. If he is heading east we can always catch up with him later."

As he rode on, Puttfark allowed himself a moment of quiet self-congratulation. The situation was still difficult, but now they were all playing his game. In his mind he reviewed strategies, options, trajectories, timetables and intersections. He could not find any obvious errors. It seemed the fickle goddess was back on his side.

Twenty-two

Domina cantered the horse for an hour or so and then they dismounted and walked.

"Lucifer hates carrying two. It is very painful for him," she explained. "We will have to keep giving him a rest or he will be exhausted."

Small also felt the need of a respite from the jarring motion of the horse. After they had walked for some time he asked her where they were going.

"The innkeeper's wife told me that there is another inn up ahead. It's where the land begins to rise out of the plain. Beyond that, the road leads up to the high pass. It is the only way through the mountains."

"Will we stay the night at the inn?"

"No. We are travelling much too slowly. We can't risk being overtaken."

Small looked over his shoulder at the road they had travelled. It was arrow-straight and empty all the way to the horizon.

"But we don't even know that they are following us," he said.

"They are Murgans. I don't know why they are here or what they are looking for, but you have somehow messed up their business and poisoned their countrymen. Believe me, they will hunt you down and, they will never give up. It is the Murgan way."

Small thought about this depressing news for several minutes before he spoke.

"Domina, you are a Murgan, why are you helping me?"

"I told you. It's just private business. We have a deal."

They walked on in silence. Up ahead the horizon was now continuously serrated with mountains. The massive accumulations of rock were clearly visible amongst the swirling clouds and vapours which veiled them. Small had never seen anything so awesome.

The moment the landscape began to rise out of the plain, it became more verdant and more fertile. It was as if they had risen above all that was low, arid, poor and oppressed and entered into a higher region where nature was free to grow and express itself. At first there were patches of scrub and thorn, but then isolated trees appeared. Imperceptibly the bare autumn countryside carpeted itself in meadow grasses until everywhere seemed green and growing. Water splashed and gossiped in the valley bottoms. Soon they were riding through dense patches of woodland which clung to the steep hillsides. The sheer redundancy and variety of the landscape lifted Small's morale.

When they reached the inn it was a solid structure of warm grey local stone which nestled amongst the rolling foothills. Fat cattle and sheep chewed contentedly in their paddocks. Alerted by the cockerels, plump hens fled squawking at their approach. They dismounted and entered a walled and gated courtyard on the south side. A woman's head popped out from a doorway.

"I will be with you presently," she called out. "Take a seat and drink water from the fountain."

They sat on a bench made from a great tree which had been worn smooth by countless travellers. The woman duly arrived. She was matronly but still young. Her hair was tied up and decently covered. Her arms were bare to the elbow. She rubbed her hands clean on her apron as she approached. Small was fascinated to see that she had with her a small child who hid behind his mother's voluminous skirts and stole shy glances at the newcomers.

"Greetings," the woman said, unsure as to which of them she should speak. "What can I do for you?"

Domina was busy taking off her riding gloves, "We will need food and drink." she said. She did not look at the woman as she spoke because she was checking and memorising every possibility for ambush or escape which the inn provided. "There is also a horse to be seen to."

"I'll call my husband," the woman replied. "He will do the ostlerie and turn the horse into the paddock. There is still grass enough."

The innkeeper was a not unhandsome man with a genial face and a kindly demeanour. Small noticed how he put a gentle arm around his wife's shoulders as he greeted them. He saw the woman smile unselfconsciously as she placed her hand on his. He also saw how they pressed their bodies slightly together. The child's head appeared between them at knee level. Small smiled in sympathy and pleasure. It was just as the authors described the loving family. He glanced at Domina to see if she had noticed, but she had her back to them all and was unwinding her turban.

They ate indoors. The room contained a bright cheerful fire which served for both heating and cooking. After they had eaten their fill, the innkeeper came and sat down with them. He lifted a narrow-necked jug from a shelf and poured wine into beakers for them all. When she had cleared the table, his wife joined them. Travellers were rare so late in the year and their conversation could be a rich source of entertainment. It was clear from the way the innkeeper's wife glanced

257

from the shy skinny good-looking youth in rags to the haughty young beauty in silk, that she was highly intrigued by these particular birds of passage. The innkeeper did most of the talking, but from time to time his wife whispered conspiratorially in his ear. Small chatted with the friendly innkeeper not realising how skilful the man was at drawing information out of his guests. Small tried always to turn the conversation away from where they had come from and to ask questions about where they were going.

The innkeeper laughed. "So," he said. "You don't want to tell us where you are coming from and you don't know anybody or anything on the other side of the mountains. I think you are running away and don't want to be found."

Small could not hide his dismay. Domina shook her head and looked up at the ceiling.

"Don't worry," the innkeeper said tapping the side of his nose, "You can trust me to hold my tongue. I've seen it all before."

The conversation was interrupted by a loud halloo from outside. Another traveller had arrived. Whilst the innkeeper went to investigate, his wife tended the fire. Domina walked over to the window then returned to her seat.

"Nothing to worry about," she whispered, "It's just a local."

The traveller entered the room a few minutes later and stood before the fire warming his hands. He greeted Small over his shoulder in a familiar manner as if he knew him already.

"I heard you tell the story at the tavern at the cross-roads," the man said. "It was excellent. The best I've heard. Mind you, I've not heard many proper stories. May I sit down with you?"

The innkeeper's wife brought the man a beaker and he poured wine into it. He waited until she left and then began to speak in a low voice.

"I enjoyed your story, and even though you kept me awake with your snoring ... er, horse, I will tell you something. After you left, strangers came. They were dressed like women but they were armed. They were savage as animals. They killed a youth just for laughing at them. They asked about you and where you had gone. The innkeeper sent them off in the wrong direction but it won't be long before they find out that he lied. I did not want to be there when they returned so I got away as fast as I could. I think that you too should move fast and hide well."

True to his words, the man left as soon as he had eaten. They listened as he urged his horse into a fast canter up the road.

258

The innkeeper returned to his wine. "That was a frightened man if I ever saw one," he said. "I have a strong feeling that big trouble is following you up this road."

Small said nothing.

The innkeeper took another mouthful of wine. "I know that man. He is an honest fellow. So it would seem that your pursuers are a bad lot. I might be able to help you. You say you want to take the high pass over the mountains. It is very late in the year and we have had a strange hard wind that has disturbed the seasons. The first snows will come early this year and then the snow will close the pass. If it snows before you reach the top, turn back straight away. My advice is not even to try the pass. I have a friend who lives north of here: very secluded. He needs help with his animals. You can hide there."

Domina interrupted him, "They will find us wherever we go. We have to cross the mountains now."

The innkeeper shrugged. "It will be cold up there. We have some warm clothing, not a lot, but better than none. Without it you will certainly freeze to death."

"I will buy all you have, and food," she replied and stood up. "I must saddle the horse."

Small's eyes followed her to the door.

"That is a fine-looking young woman," the innkeeper said. "My wife says that you are in love with her."

Small blushed ingenuously.

"Ha! I thought so. No need to be ashamed. It can happen to anybody. It even happened to me."

"You love your wife?"

"Of course I do, and she loves me."

Small was delighted to discover that love really did exist in the world. He would tell Domina. "And your little boy," he added, "you love him too?"

"What strange questions you ask! Which father doesn't love his children?"

Small felt vindicated. The authors had not lied after all.

The innkeeper adopted a more intimate tone. "This young woman you are travelling with," he said, "She is a strange one. A fine horse, fine clothes and the air of a noble. She seems to bear herself like a man. The way she treats you, neither as a servant nor as a companion, it's … interesting. My wife says she holds her feelings so deep down inside that they can hardly get out. My wife thinks she might have feelings for you but hides them by treating you badly."

The innkeeper seemed to be waiting for a reply. Small was dumbstruck. He did not know what to think. Just then, Domina appeared at the doorway and the innkeeper left to fetch the clothing.

"The innkeeper loves his wife," Small said.

"What …?" Domina was incredulous.

"The innkeeper loves his wife, and he loves his child. Didn't you see?"

"At any moment a bunch of heavily armed deviants will arrive and tear you apart for fun and you talk to me about love? Are you mad?"

"But you said you wanted to know about it. That was the deal."

"The deal was also that I helped you escape. It won't be much of a deal if we are both dead."

Whilst they had been talking, the innkeeper's child had entered the room. He was gripping a young hen tightly to his chest. The hen was protesting loudly. The child was trying to show his pet to Domina. He shouted the bird's name over and over in a shrill voice. Suddenly Domina shouted "Goddinhell!" grabbed the bird, wrung its neck and placing her boot in the centre of the child's chest propelled him violently across the room. She tossed the dead chicken after him. The child struck the wall and sat abruptly. Then he began to wail and screech at the top of his voice.

Small was shocked. "What did you do that for?" he asked, having difficulty being heard above the wails.

"I hate children. They are like little pigs, noisy and dirty."

"But they don't know any better. He's only a child. He wanted to show you his pet."

"Children must learn not to annoy people. In Murga he would have been protected or armed. His bodyguard would have kept him quiet, he would have drawn his weapon or someone would have done what I did. We are all on our own in this world. The sooner children learn to take care of themselves the better - and that goes for you too. No Murgan child would have allowed themselves to get beaten up on the road as you did, and that's because they learn young."

"That's not fair. I was trying to protect you. If you had not been alone on the road the man would not have followed us."

"In Murga a woman does not need chaperones. She is free to go wherever. The man followed us, I dealt with him. Such things happen in the real world. You can only live in your kind and gentle dream world of books because I am protecting you."

260

Before Small could answer, the innkeeper returned. He dropped two bundles of clothing on the floor and swept the wailing child up into his arms. The child pointed at Domina and redoubled its cries.

"I killed his chicken. I did not know it was a pet. I'll pay for it," she said.

The innkeeper looked at the feathered bundle on the floor and then at Domina. His face clouded, but then he shrugged, "I will find him another. He will soon forget. See what of this you can wear."

The child was handed to its mother who cuddled and caressed him until the unhappiness subsided. Small saw Domina observing this process with more than ordinary attention. They took all the clothing which fitted them. Small was amazed to find a novel garment which consisted of two tubes of woollen material which covered his legs. They were called 'trews'. He discarded his ragged librarian's robe in favour of a longer belted coat with a hood attached. It was patched and torn but respectable. The innkeeper insisted he also take some woolly pieces of sheepskin to tie on his feet. When they had finished, Domina gave a handful of silver to the innkeeper and went to tie the bundles onto the horse. The innkeeper held Small back by the elbow.

"Good luck," he murmured in his ear, "but be careful. There is a dark shadow on that girl."

Small looked over his shoulder as the horse turned the first bend. Husband and wife waved to him. The child buried his face in his mother's bosom.

Twenty-three

Small had never experienced anything so overwhelming as the mountains. The higher he climbed the more exhilarated he became. He could understand why holy men and poets climbed up to the high places for inspiration. There was something godlike in being able to rise above the plain and to comprehend at one glance the whole pattern of the Maker laid at your feet like a rich carpet. The arduousness of the climb towards the high pass meant that they had to pause frequently to rest. Drawing the clear cold air into their lungs they would invariably turn and look back the way they had come. Small fancied he could see Alligor on the far horizon and when the sun set he looked for its gnomonic shadow across the plain. For her part, Domina searched for the inevitable dust cloud that would reveal their pursuers. Early each evening they would find some rocky wall to guard their backs and, whilst the horse pulled and champed at the lush greenery skirting the forest, they would build a roaring campfire from fallen pine branches. With winter so close they huddled together to keep warm in the chilly mountain night and before long the girl's head would be resting on his shoulder. Small would read from *The Mirror of Almeira*.

"To love,' said Poeisia to her father, 'and to be loved in return is to know that there is a God.' 'To be old,' replied the Great Khan, 'is to know that God can be cruel as well as benevolent. This great love you speak of can cause violent pain, pain too great to bear. Drive this adventurer from your heart, my daughter, lest it takes your whole life to convince you that he will never return.' But Poeisia would not listen, 'Better a life spent in forlorn hope of something great than in the certainty of something mean. I promised Amatis that I would wait; he promised that he would return. Only death can release us from our oaths."*

"Pah!"

"What?" Small was startled by Domina's snort of derision.

"That is completely ridiculous." she said, "No Murgan would ever make a deal like that."

"But do not Murgans get married as other peoples do?" asked Small.

"Of course we do: lots and lots of times; every few years in fact."

"But I thought marriage was something you were only supposed to do once."

Domina gave him the by now familiar twist of the mouth expression to let him know that he was a complete idiot. "Marriage is business." she said, "No Murgan in their right mind would ever marry for any other reason. If a woman marries a poor man she halves her fortune; if she marries a rich man she may double it. The value of a marriage in terms of assets, connections, business opportunities and security is all worked out to the last copper coin before the deal is struck."

"So you would never marry a young man without wealth or prospects?"

"What stupid questions you ask. Where would be the point? Marriage is business. Who would be so foolish as to strike a deal with a beggar? Where would the profit come from?"

As usual Small struggled to defend his cherished authors against the girl's sledgehammer logic. "But what if a woman met a very attractive young man but who had no money?"

"She would hire him of course."

Small was momentarily silenced. Never had he heard anything so depressing and so logical. "So it never happens?" he asked.

Domina thought for a moment. "Only very rarely" she replied, "and only amongst the very poor. A woman will sometimes marry if she needs a labourer or a bodyguard and can't afford to pay wages. The man will take a share in any future business. Otherwise why would anybody want to do such a thing?"

"For love?" Small said quietly.

A shadow of doubt settled on Domina's face. Her frown made Small think of a crumpled page in a fascinating book. He always wanted to smooth it out with his hand.

"Ha! That word again." she hissed, "I don't believe in it."

"Perhaps if you don't believe in it then you will never find it." Small suggested.

"What do you mean?"

"Amatis speaks of a leap of faith. He knew that for a gardener to declare his love for a princess was an action punishable by death. He was not sure that she loved him, or even that love existed, but he believed that it was so. More than this he thought that if Poeisia did not love him then his own life was not worth anything anyway. So he summoned up his courage and opened his heart to her. He called it a leap of faith."

Domina gave another snort of derision. "We Murgans only deal in facts. Faith and belief is for fools."

"I don't know but it seems to me that if two people believe in their love for each other then they form an unbreakable bond, a knot of unshakeable belief. Perhaps even Murgans have to accept that as a fact. There can be no way of disproving it."

"Or of proving it?" Domina sat back with a smile of triumph on her lips.

"But if you believe that you are happy, you just are. It is something beyond proving." His voice tailed off into silence. Domina had lifted her dark intent gaze and was looking intently into his face as if she was searching for something she had missed before. Small found this strangely exciting. Wild impulses stirred inside him but his courage failed under this fierce scrutiny. He turned away embarrassed. The silence hung in the air like a struck gong.

"Read me some more." Domina said.

Small would quite happily have climbed every mountain in the world just for the sake of these magical evening moments. Even after the light had gone and he could no longer see the words, he frequently continued the story from memory or improvised shamelessly until Domina's loud snores ended his readings.

On the third day they looked back into the late afternoon light and saw a dark column of smoke pointing like the finger of Sath'an at a particular spot on the landscape.

"The inn." said Small in a flat voice.

Whilst he grieved at the fate which he had brought upon the kindly innkeeper and his family, Domina was silent, working out the practical consequences. She quickly calculated that Puttfark would overtake them sooner rather than later, but said nothing. That night they rode till it was too dark to see their path and lit no fire. They awoke cold and stiff-limbed to find themselves enveloped in mist. Everything in the forest was dank and dripping with moisture. They prepared the horse in silence and began to climb onwards and upwards through the clinging atmosphere. By midday they were back in bright sunlight again, having climbed above the clouds into a realm where only the highest peaks could be seen rising like islands in an enchanted waveless sea. The afternoon wore on. Above the cloud ocean, titanic accumulations of blinding white vapour billowed up silently into a high infinity of deep azure sky. Little by little the sunlight was shut out. Small wondered that something so bright and splendid should cast such a large shadow. He watched awestruck as it spread across the vaporous seascape like a dark stain. Beneath the spread wings of the gathering storm, new veils of cloud obscured the plain. A chill breeze became increasingly boisterous and the first flakes of the snows that would eventually close the pass, whirled in the air.

At this height the forest had thinned until the stunted trees seemed huddled together and flinching in the bitter cold. The wind lashed at them for their temerity. Any patch of ground still in shadow held the white hoar frost of the previous night. They came to a narrow escarpment which ran out of the forest and across the face of a great peak. Broken ground fell away on both sides. The wind drove snowflakes in flurries up the bare mountainside and into the sunlight far, far above. Domina tugged at his sleeve as she paused in the shelter of a large pinnacle of rock. She had to shout against the roaring of the wind. Her voice sounded thin and child-like. "I have to put on more clothes or I'll freeze. I think you should do the same."

Small nodded agreement and began to unpack his bundle. The horse backed nervously to the end of its tether as they clawed at the panniers.

"It's just as the inn-keeper said," he shouted, "Winter is come early. I fear we must turn back."

"That's not possible," Domina shouted back, "Puttfark and his gang are too close behind us."

"How do you know?"

"It's not difficult to work out. They are all mounted. From the time they set out from the inn they would have been making two or three miles to every one of ours. Even without the snow they would have caught up with us before we topped the pass." She began to wind the burnoose around her head.

Small found that he had lost the heat generated by the exertion of the climb. The cold had begun to grip him. His teeth chattered and his forehead ached. "But the inn-keeper!" the wind snatched at his words, "He said that we should turn back at the first sign of snow. The first snow always blocks the pass and once blocked only spring sunshine can open it!"

Domina's answer was muffled by the burnoose about her face but her eyes told Small all he needed to know. It was their only chance. They had to make it to the summit before the snow closed the pass.

"But if we can make it so can Puttfark! You said so!"

"Think about it." She gripped his arm. "We knew there might be snow. The inn-keeper told us so. He gave us all the clothing he had to spare. Puttfark and his men are in silk *tzirts*, travelling fast and light. The moment they come out of the trees they will freeze!"

"Like us?"

"Possibly, but at least we have a chance. If we turn back we will have no chance at all. I prefer a chance of freezing to death to a certainty of dying at the hands of the Warholl!"

Small did not answer, but continued to struggle into the unfamiliar clothing. Where self-preservation was concerned he could trust any Murgan. The way Domina marshalled the facts, the decisions seemed to make themselves. Without her aid his mission would have ended where it began. Not for the first time he suspected some supernatural agent at work. He muttered a prayer of gratitude to the Divine Author for sending him such an unlikely and efficient guardian angel.

The sun disappeared. After exchanging anxious glances they tugged at the horse's halter and moved out of the shelter of the trees. Stumbling forwards onto the escarpment, dragging the agitated horse behind him, Small found that he could hardly feel his limbs. Before long only the pain assured him that they were still attached to his body. As the travellers crossed the escarpment, the eddying wind buffeted them and seemed to want to pluck them off into the void. The horse wanted to turn away from the wind and so continuously shied and slithered sending showers of flat shale skittering down the steep slope. The snow began to settle on every exposed surface. Small realised that this escarpment was the point of no return. The snow was laying so fast that by the time they reached the rocky defile at the far end it would be too dangerous to attempt to return. Nor was that all; once they had crossed over this rocky knife edge they would be fully committed to going all the way over the pass. Looking ahead at the inhospitable alpine upland where not even a tree could find a place to grow, he realised that even if they chanced upon a sheltered spot it could only become an icy tomb as winter took hold.

They still did not know how far they had to climb before the path began to descend, but with the snow deepening at every step, to pause might prove fatal. This sudden realisation stiffened his flagging resolve. The instinct for self-preservation overcame his extreme discomfort and instead of being a drag on his will, the pain became a spur to greater effort. He tugged firmly on the horse's halter and strove against the blizzard with a new determination. Domina fell back into the shelter of the horse's body, taking advantage of the respite from her task of providing willpower for two. Both of them prepared themselves inwardly for the ultimate struggle. The rocky defile at the end of the escarpment provided a brief shelter from the cutting wind, but after about half a league they found themselves on an exposed plateau. There they were caught in a gale of such hysterical fury as to stop them in their tracks. They clung to the horse in terror and turned their faces into its sodden pelt. Small stole a despairing glance back to the way they had come. Through a thinning of the swirling atmosphere he could see that the snow had reshaped the very contours of the escarpment out of all recognition. Just before a new onset blotted out the whole vista he glimpsed a flurry of movement and colour at the edge of the trees. It could only be Puttfark and the Warholl. Even as he watched, the coloured specks merged back into the treeline and vanished. He turned in triumph to Domina. Her eyes too were bright with hope as she waved her arm expansively at the way ahead. From here all paths led down to the plain!

Their elation was premature. They had evaded their pursuers. They had topped the pass. They had even managed to leave the shrieking wind behind them on the plateau. But the snow was still falling. Indeed without the scouring effect of the wind it laid more deeply and evenly. Before long they were floundering up to their thighs in a tilted white desert where sky and earth seemed to conspire in suffocating silence. The light had not been good since the clouds had first hid the sun, but now it was failing as early dusk began to fall. Small was exhausted and as his fatigue increased so the cold began to strike ever deeper into the muscles of his limbs. With a jolt he realised that without warmth and shelter they would both die. In these conditions it would be days before they got below the snowline, and they had no idea where the nearest human habitation might be. He turned to Domina but she was nowhere to be seen. He called her name but his voice was stifled by his frozen face and the muffling snow. For one heart-stopping moment he thought that he had lost her. Then there was an eruption of snow behind the horse and the girl was there. She had taken several turns of the horse's tail around her wrist and was letting the animal drag her in its wake.

"Don't stop," she mumbled. "Go on or we die."

Small saw that she was in serious trouble. Her skill and willpower had brought them this far but now they were down to a basic animal level where his larger body bulk gave him an advantage. He knew that a Murgan would have simply cut the horses tail and walked on. She seemed small and pitiful; a mere bundle of rags. With fingers that he could neither feel nor move he unwound the horse's tail from her arm. With his forearms under her shoulders he lifted her up and stood her against the side of the horse.

"Get on the horse," he said, and fell on his knees.

She put her foot on his shoulder and with great effort struggled onto the horse's back, where she lay with her head on the beast's neck. Small wound the halter around his wrist and tugged the horse onwards.

In silence and darkness he floundered on through waist-high drifts, blinded by the swirling snowflakes. There was no sign of any path or track amongst the inscrutable humps and billows of snow. They were completely lost. Small knew that they were freezing to death. He looked around in desperation but everywhere the snow lay like parchment from which all writing had been erased. Between panic and despair he began to mumble a prayer to the Divine Author, but could not remember the second line. The cold seemed to be slowing his thinking. He wanted to lay down in the soft snow and sleep. Was it that strange soporific odour of fallen snow? Why did it remind him of wood smoke? The snow smelled of the Murgan campfires. He thought of the fireside in the inn. With a dull jolt he realised that that it *was* wood smoke he could smell. It was being blown up the mountainside with the blizzard. Smoke meant fire. Fire meant people. People meant shelter. Shelter meant life. He turned the horse into the wind and stumbled down the slope.

A band of fir trees opened onto a steeply descending clearing. The smell of wood smoke was very strong. Small peered into the darkness trying to discover its source. Although it was dark the snow seemed to give off a faint luminescence. At the foot of the hillside a tiny black speck darker than its forest backdrop caught his eye. Through the falling snow he was sure he could also see a dim light. Hardly able to feel his limbs he stumbled onwards. With every agonising step towards the light in the darkness Small gave thanks to the Great Author for the miracle which had directed their steps to the one refuge in this freezing wilderness. As they approached the dwelling the hump of snow on Lucifer's back cracked and fell away. Domina raised herself up unsteadily.

"Wait. Get me down," she said.

He held up his arms but could not catch her as she fell out of the saddle onto him. He pulled her out of the snow and with arms that he could no longer feel, he half carried her towards the source of the smoke. Domina clutched at his clothing with one hand. The other hand still instinctively gripped the knife inside her tunic, as if the weather was some drunken marauder who could be stabbed in the heart if he came within reach. They came up to a low cabin of split logs with a squat chimney of stones at one end. The smoke billowing from the lip of the chimney was tinted by the bright flames on the hearth inside.

Domina pushed him stiffly away from her and stood unsteadily on the threshold. When she spoke her voice was stilted by her frozen face.

"Keep clear...out of the way... I'll kill whoever opens the door...can't take chance that they won't let us in...we'll die out here." She stared stupidly at the door, swaying slightly. "Knock and move out of the way," she grunted. With his hands gripped in his armpits, Small kicked the door with a numb foot, but not as numb as he

268

thought. The pain made him sob out loud as he rolled himself down the rough side of the cabin and clear of the door. For several dreadful moments he thought that the door would not be opened, but then he saw the slight figure of Domina, swaddled in clothing; shrouded in snow; suddenly suffused with a dull rose light. In an instant she had disappeared through the open doorway. Small levered himself away from the wall and tumbled himself stiffly and agonizingly after her. He sprawled helplessly over her body inert and prostrate on the cabin floor. It was hopeless for him even to try to get up. Through thawing eyelashes he saw that Domina was completely insensible, her knife still frozen in its sheath, her arm encased in the ice that bound it to her breast. Behind him the door slammed and he heard the bar drop into its keeps.

The only occupant of the cabin was a stoutly built woman well past her prime. Her iron grey hair glinted in the firelight. The arrival of frost-bitten travellers in the middle of the night could not have been a frequent occurrence, but the woman did not waste time on introductions or explanations. With an ease which belied her age she hoisted the insensible Domina onto the sleeping platform which occupied the wall opposite the fire. She began to pull the girl's limbs out of her frozen clothing and to massage them vigorously. Small she ignored completely until he rolled instinctively towards the fire.

"Hey you! Don't go too near the fire or you will get the hot aches. Come here and rub this girl's feet. It will help get the colour back into your own limbs."

The last thing Small wanted to do was to move, but the cold had frozen his will as well as slowing his limbs. He did as he was told and dragged himself over to the bed. The cabin woman was prising the dagger from Domina's deadly white fingers. She looked up at Small suspiciously as if trying to surprise him into some guilty reaction. Small was too far gone to respond at all. This seemed to satisfy her. She grunted softly and continued to work on the frozen limbs.

All this time Domina had not regained her senses or moved or responded in any way. Small saw the cabin woman's brow had tensed with concern and he too began to feel anxious. The woman walked quickly to the fireplace. "Keep rubbing," she said, "but not too hard now or you'll take the skin off."

Small watched her lift two large round stones from the fireplace. There was a strong smell of singeing hair as she dropped them into bags made from coney skins. These she tucked into the furs close to Domina's inert body.

"I think the cold has slowed her heart. We must make her warmer." she said.

By now the girl's clothing had thawed into a sodden, clinging bondage. The cabin woman began to peel off garment after garment, rubbing any exposed skin with a warm dry cloth. Small stared stupidly as the lissom figure began to emerge.

The cabin woman gave him an old fashioned look and nodded towards the fire. "Tend the fire." She said. Small stumbled gratefully towards the hearth. When he glanced back she had drawn a deer-hide curtain across the end of the room. It was almost as important to preserve modesty as life. Her voice came from behind the curtain. "Get your wet clothes off and hang them to dry. Wrap this around you." The pelt of some large hairy animal appeared around the edge of the curtain and slumped to the floor.

Small poked clumsily at the embers and added several logs. His life in the library had given him a superstitious fear of the consequences of flames and sparks but, faced with cold that could kill, his only worry was his own ineptness at fire tending. Wisps of rank-smelling steam rose from his leggings as he struggled out of his wet and clinging clothes. His limbs were still stiff and numb with the cold and when he had finally managed to rub himself dry with the bear skin he sat exhausted by the effort and warmed himself by the fire.

When the cabin woman drew back the curtain she discovered Small still sitting on the window seat swathed in the fur and fast asleep. She picked up his wet clothes and hung them up to dry. She looked down on his face, open and innocent in its unconsciousness. Sleep had wiped all concern and fatigue from the boy's countenance. The lines of hard experience were not yet engraved upon it. The soft down of adolescence was just beginning to darken on lip and cheek. Unbearably poignant memories stirred inside her as she looked upon the damp tousled hair drying in tufts and spikes. She reached out to smooth it down with an instinctive motherly gesture. Deep in his sleep Small felt the touch of the warm smooth hand as it passed across his brow. He had no conscious memories of motherly or even womanly care, but somewhere deep inside him there had always been a place made ready, like a refuge in a bare wilderness. The simple caress changed him forever. It was the touch which tells you that you did not enter the world alone. From that moment onwards he was in thrall to the care of women and could no longer contemplate a life wholly without them.

Small awoke suddenly. He did not know what had awoken him. Something sudden, something loud; his mind wrestled with echoes and dreams. It was well past sunrise but dawn had scarcely broken. Inside the cabin it was as black as the inside of an ink pot; shutters sealed every opening; frozen snow sealed every crack and knothole. The cheerful blaze of the fire had been reduced to grey ash but the cabin was still mercifully warm. By his shoulder was a tiny shutter. He forced it open and put his eye to the crack. An atmosphere leaden with snow stifled the light and crushed the landscape. The same icy wind which moaned in the chimney roared through the trees of the forest. Snow like frozen sand came out of the sky but was scoured from every hummock and drift by the force of the gale. It smoked away down the hillside till it merged with the grey murk at the forest fringes.

He slammed the shutter to and latched it. Nobody could have survived a night in such conditions. They had indeed been lucky to find the cabin. He murmured a prayer of thanks for his supernatural good fortune. "Great Author may my life be a volume worthy of many more chapters before the plot is finally untied"

"Ah! You are awake." The old woman's voice came from the other side of the hearth. "The snow is early this year. It will keep you here for some time. So I will have some company for this winter. That makes me very glad. These cold dark days and nights can be burdensome for one living alone."

Small nodded politely, not sure if she had finished speaking.

"Put on your dry clothes," she continued, "and I will give you some broth, then…" she smiled in anticipation, "… you can tell me who you are and how you came to be on the mountain so late in the year."

Small thought that her firm tone of voice was pleasant and soothing. It was the confidence of the matriarch accustomed to having her young men do her bidding without demur. Small did as he was told, not just because he was still in a dreamy and exhausted state and could not resist, but also because some deeply lodged and newly awakened intuitive sense made him aware that the woman's demands and his unquestioned obedience were part of the mysterious ritual of maternal care so long denied to him. Small drank the broth greedily and gratefully whilst watching the cabin woman re-kindle the fire.

"Goddinhell!"

Both Small and the cabin woman jumped at the loud shriek from behind the curtain. A torrent of language followed; by turns incoherent, blasphemous, and infantile; shouted, mumbled and whispered. Small rushed over to the curtain and pulled it aside. On the bed Domina thrashed and writhed amongst the furs and hides. Flecks

271

of foam had gathered at the corners of her mouth and her skin was damp and clammy. Her hair clung wet and dark to the skin of her face like the tails of black lizards feasting on her brain. Her eyes were open but unseeing. Small took her by the shoulders. "Look! Look! It's me! What is the matter?"

The cabin woman touched his arm. "She cannot see or hear you. Some form of delirium has gripped her mind. She has been like this all night." Here a new and violent outburst of shouting and movement interrupted her. Domina tore away the bedclothes from her naked midriff and clawed at her own belly until it was cris-crossed by raised red weals.

"She is searching for her weapon," Small said.

"Then thank God she will not find it."

Domina shrieked despairingly and fell back into a restless half sleep. The cabin woman was clearly alarmed by what was happening, but caring was the stronger instinct. She held down the flailing arms and wiped the girl's face, stroked her forehead and rearranged the bed clothes around her.

"What is wrong with her?" asked Small, "She was fine and healthy before the snow."

The cabin woman shook her head. "I have never seen anything like it. It is as if she is in the grip of a fever and yet she is ice-cold. She sweats but there is no heat. She cries out in terror but will not be comforted. This is like no disease I have seen before."

"Then what is it?"

"I cannot say. I am just a simple herbal healer. Beyond bumps and breaks, fevers and chills, fluxes and blockages, I am in an unknown land. If it was not winter we could take her down the mountain to the town doctors, but now the snow will hold us here till spring."

Small listened to the melancholy moaning of the wind in the chimney. The fire so newly re-kindled almost blew out. "Is there nothing we can do?" he said.

"Of course there is something. She lives. We can care for her. Keep her strong. But I fear that the struggle must be hers alone. So, tell me, who are you, where are you from and where are you going?"

"I am …," he began but had to stop while he decided whether he should be Small, or Sharp or even Rider. Suddenly he remembered and leapt from his seat "… Lucifer!"

The cabin woman sat bolt upright. "What?"

"The horse! I forgot about the horse. It's out there."

"Oh, so that's Lucifer is it?" she said relaxing again, "Don't worry. He is a strong animal. He will need some water in a while but for now he is taken care of. You were just going to tell me your name."

"Small. It's Small," he said.

The old woman waited expectantly for the small name. "Oh, I see," she said at last, "Small is your name. I am Kara. Now tell me where have you come from?"

"We met on the road. We were both heading East. We decided to travel together." Small grinned and nodded vigorously. A long silence ensued.

"Is that it? Is that all I get? I save your limbs if not your lives and you have no tale for me? I can see there is much more to you than meets the eye, but I will not press you for it. It is a long time to spring and perhaps you will be glad enough to talk to me before the snow melts. But if you have secrets to keep, beware, thoughts are like mice, they have a way of coming out when you aren't looking. And the girl? Who is she?"

"Her name is Domina. She is from Murga."

"Murga!" The woman whispered the word as if she feared that it might conjure up evil spirits.

"You have heard of it?" said Small.

"Many travellers pass my door in summer. There are rumours. Now here is a girl who travels armed, blasphemes God and names her horse after the Enemy. Perhaps the rumours are true. Have you been there?"

"No! Not me." Small bit his lip. His reply had been a little too forceful, a little too revealing of his mind. He would have to be more careful in future.

"Perhaps Murga has visited you?"

Small did not reply. The less she knew, the less she could reveal. All their lives might depend on that.

"All right, all right!" she said. "I'm a nosey old woman. You won't be the first traveller to pass by here who doesn't want to tell his life story."

As day followed day and the weeks crept by, life in the cabin was only made bearable by the knowledge of what lay outside. The cold held the landscape in a grip of iron. The wind passed over the mountain like a rasp. Every activity of life was gradually reduced until all their waking hours were filled only with what was essential for survival. The cabin woman prepared the food and busied herself with keeping the cabin and its occupants clean and tidy. Small earned his keep by tugging pieces of wood from a frozen heap in the yard and feeding them into the fire. He would also fetch snow for the pot and for scouring the dirty cooking gear. But all this the cabin woman could have done for herself. She left him in no doubt that his real task was to keep the fires of the mind well stoked. "No good having fire and food if you lose your mind." She had said on that first day. "It happens all the time. People alone up here on the mountain in the winter lose their grip on reality. They become melancholy and inward. Then the black humours drive them out into the snow. But now I've got you to brighten up those long dark winter days. So Small related all his stories and in return she gave him her dead husband's winter clothing. While she listened she affirmed her belief in Domina's eventual recovery by making all kinds of beautiful clothing especially for her. Hour upon hour she worked at joining skins with tiny neat stitches and embroidering intricate designs on any plain surface. One day as she worked she had told him the story of her life.

"I did not always live here in the mountains. As a young girl I was married to a carpet merchant in a town far away to the east of here. My husband was a good man but much older than I. Before my husband died God blessed me with one child, a son. My husband left me well provided for and I was able to bring up my son in comfort and ease. So long as I had my son to care for I did not need to take another man. Perhaps he missed a father's hand, perhaps I indulged the child too much, perhaps I told him too many stories of the caravans which brought his father's carpets, whatever, as soon as he could walk he dragged me to the city gate to watch the caravans of camels come and go. When he was older he could always be found sitting late into the night by the campfires of the camel drivers, listening to their tall tales of faraway lands and distant peoples. I think I knew even then that he had the wander-fever, and that one day I would lose him to the spice road.

'Then one day in his eighteenth year my son went to market and never returned. I searched everywhere, asked everyone, he was nowhere to be found. There was talk of a woman, a grand and powerful woman who had passed through the town with many camels and horses. She had made some sign or gesture to my boy, but I could find no-one who had actually seen such a thing. I did not know where he was or if he was dead or alive and I had no means of finding out. I could not believe that he would leave without telling me. Time passed and he did not come home. I met every caravan and asked about him but no-one had seen him. Years passed and still I could not forget. It was if my life was a river held back by a dam. What could I do? I was only a woman. I could not travel the roads searching for him. Then one day a respectable caravan captain told me of this high pass through the mountains. All travellers between east and west must come this way or go hundreds of leagues round to the south. If I lived here I could ask them all to look out for my son. The caravan captain offered to bring me here if I cooked for him on the way. I agreed. I told my relatives where I could be found and joined the caravan.

'I had never travelled before so you can imagine what an adventure it all was. When I first arrived I took lodgings in the town in the valley, but not all the caravans entered the town. Before long my money was running out. There was an old hunter who came to town to sell game and skins. He was called 'Bear'. He had no other name. He lived in this cabin by the mountain road. I offered to keep house for him so that I could talk to every traveller who passed by. The cabin stank of rotting meat, the whole place was heaving with vermin, but this was the only dwelling on the pass road. I moved in and started cleaning right away. I even cleaned the hunter. Of course he shouted and raged and waved his knives about, but he was very old and secretly delighted to have someone to keep him company and look after him. He was a good hunter and put meat on the table until the very day he died. By then I had all the caravans and mule trains stopping at the cabin for food, drink and gossip. I am sure that by now every trader in the land knows about my son. But still there is no news."

Small found Kara's story disturbing. All the stories he knew had a beginning, a middle and an end, but here was a story of which only the Great Author knew the ending. Why would the Divine Author want to keep this young man's ending to himself? What had the young mother done to deserve such a fate? No-one knew whether to mourn, curse or pity him. Had he sent a message? Was the message lost? Was the messenger waylaid? Was the son imprisoned, or ill, or dead and buried by the roadside. Perhaps the story wasn't yet ended and the son would return to tell it himself. The real world was very cruel.

Twenty-four

Months passed in the cabin. Libraries, books, Murgans and innkeepers became occasional memories, and hardly as vivid as the stories he told the old woman. Domina remained in her restless coma. Kara lifted her to feed her, to clean her and to dress her. She talked constantly and encouragingly to the girl whilst flexing her limbs and rubbing life into the girl's wasting muscles. Small had ample time to observe this woman's world in which he found himself. He discovered that women were quite different from librarians. They seemed more intuitive and more manipulative. He suspected that all their relations with men were designed to effect the willing transfer of power. He began to feel trapped. Noises from the byre interrupted his reverie.

Lucifer had not enjoyed his enforced idleness. The horse moved restlessly in the foetid warmth of its stall. Its coat, grown long and shaggy, was caked with filth. The reek of urine and droppings was overpowering. Small knew that the animal needed clean straw but there was very little left. He threw out as much solid matter as he could and then re-arranged the sodden bedding. The last of the clean dry straw did not make a very great difference to the horse's comfort but it was the best he could do. He filled the manger and broke the ice on his water. Later on he would walk the animal around the yard.

Outside a pale sun rose on a frozen silent world. Icy mist wreathed trees heavy with palls of snow. The whole landscape was entombed in white. There was no wind. Mysterious and invisible forces caused the mist to swirl among the trees like a passage of wraiths. His face tightened in the cold, still atmosphere. He inhaled deeply. The crystal air was like a drug. Nothing broke the silence.

Inside the cabin the fire roared softly in the gloom. The old woman worked at her weaving, singing the while in a low hypnotic murmur. The fire crackled and spat. The horse stamped in its stall. In the shadows Domina tossed and heaved in her unquiet half-sleep. She lay amongst heaped skins of wolves and bears complete with their masks and claws. It was as if she was being devoured by wild beasts. By the light of the fire he could see her hair was matted and wet. Her skin shone with sweat as she struggled with the demons which possessed her.

Small sat on his favourite seat by the fire and drew his knees up to his chin. By his shoulder was a wooden shutter. He unlatched it and swung it open. Strong white light slanted in. In the square of sunlight by his foot he saw the ancient leather book bag he had carried all the way from Alligor. It had lain neglected on the floor ever since he arrived. Age and wear had almost worn away the hide. Any structure which its maker might originally have given to it had long since sagged into amorphousness. Its shape was now determined by whatever it contained. Small thought of the ancient beast whose skin it was made from; of the long-dead craftsman who had fashioned it with skill and care; of the book-city which had been dedicated to its service. He thought of the strange thread of destiny which had brought it to this frozen mountain top, then, murmuring a prayer to the Great Author, he loosed its thongs and pulled out the manuscript.

What had appeared to be a book was in fact a leather covered box, plain, untooled apart from the name, and held shut by leather straps much like the harness of horses. Small wondered if Gropius had asked his saddler to make it for him whilst he was on campaign. The straps fell apart in his fingers as he struggled to untie them. There was a faint smell of cedar wood as he opened the lid. The manuscript roll had been cut into leaves so that it would lay flat in its container. The leaves were bound in faded purple ribbons and sealed with seven unbroken seals. He was the first.

In plain view between the ribbons was an inscription. The language was that of Babylon in the young days of first empire. Impure and mongrel in its grammar and phraseology, the written form still displayed its origins in the stabbing marks of the sharpened stylus in tablets made from the yielding and fecund clay of the river plain. Small began to read, slowly at first and with many returns. Before long his experience with the Murgan dialect eased his way and the text began to unravel.

This was not the customary curse laid upon all last testaments. These were the words which had been written.

Gentle reader, if you have come upon this book by chance
If it is not the goal of long seeking
and hard thought, then quickly lay it down and walk away.
Forget you ever held it in your hand.
It is not for you. Do not break these crimson seals out of idle curiosity
For in this packet are demons enough
to bring the whole world down on its knees
To turn all men and women back to beasts.
Once read this book cannot be unread
This is a book of power
Not power which men possess

But power which possesses men.

Such warnings were not to be ignored even if they were written in ages past. Who could tell what spells might have been laid on those seals? Small hesitated. If only the One had come to collect the manuscript. But now the library was in chaos and the book was his responsibility. What if the Murgans got hold of it? He could not even be certain that anybody else would be able to read the ancient script. He had a duty to read it. Somebody had to know what it said. He broke the first seal.

He waited for some time for something terrible to happen; then he cracked the remaining seals and lifted off the cover sheet. On the next leaf the calligraphy was tiny, insistent, restless and alien, like the tracks of a spider that had fallen into an inkpot and was blindly seeking safety in shadows. He began to read:

"Be it known that this is the testament of Gropius the archimage.
Who by his art and skill has forged a sword against which no-one can prevail.
Know that you have in your hands that sword.
Beware! If you unsheathe this weapon then you must be prepared to wield it without mercy and against every man, woman or child who thwarts you. If because of weakness you once hold back where you should have struck then the sword will turn against you. Never let this sword fall into the hands of your enemies."

Underneath was a title writ large:

"THE MASKS OF TYRANNY"

Small began to read:

"It is given to very few mortal men to have the government of the world within their grasp. Know that I was one such. I tried to take the world by force and almost succeeded. I gambled and I lost. The fickle goddess played her part. But I do not blame ill-fortune for my failure. I failed because I depended solely on force of arms. My armies conquered lands but they did not conquer peoples, their weapons broke bodies but they did not break minds. Even had I succeeded in my military conquest I would have had to spend my life putting down one rebellion after another. I would never have been safe from the

assassin's hand. If you would rule the world in peace and safety then learn from this my book as I learned from the wreck of my armies.

The successful head of state is known as a ruler, as if ruling was his only function. But if his true activity was better known he would be known as a divider, for just as the power of the state must be undivided and entire, so all its potential enemies must be divided each from each and amongst themselves. This principle of 'divide and rule' is the weapon of real power in a state. This much is well known, but the true reach of this weapon has never yet been tried. In assimilating any peoples into your Imperium you will need to push this principle of division to the utmost. To unite your subjects under your rule you will need to divide them utterly, each from each. I call my imaginary Empire Murga for reasons which the subtle will descry. This then is how it will be made.

Divide the states from each other lest they combine against you. If a state resists you then set one of its rival states warring against it. Fund first one side and then the other, till both are exhausted. Always try to wage war by proxy.

Divide the ruling hierarchies of opposing or independent states by the same means. An important tool is the Murgan dictator. In every state there can be found an impotent man or woman with a grudge whose rise to power can be secretly financed. Once in power they can either be pressed into dismantling all opposition to Murgan infiltration, or goaded into a war which results in their defeat at the hands of Murgan allies. The way is then clear for the introduction of the finest agent of the destruction of potent ruling hierarchies - democracy. Under this system the uneducated masses are deluded into thinking that they are their own rulers. Manipulated in reality by the hidden ruler they will become an army dedicated to bringing down that experienced and educated elite, their leaders, who alone would be able to mobilize resistance to Murgan rule. The masses will be told that they have been oppressed and exploited for centuries by their betters, but that now all men and women are free and equal. Therefore they will no longer listen to their traditional leaders. But more than this: a majority of ignorant citizens will now have the power to veto policies which affect them adversely, therefore no elected representative opposed to the Imperium who tries to impose unpopular but necessary measures will be able to sustain himself in power for long. Only those who can appeal to the mob will survive. Consequently the visible rule of the country will pass into the hands of actors and demagogues. The draught horse of the cart of state becomes an ass, for which the cart is too heavy and it eventually runs back down the hill dragging the animal behind it. This state of internal ungovernability is fertile ground for the Imperial takeover.

Divide the nation states. National identity is a potent obstacle to incorporation into the empire. All national identity and differences must be eradicated if the empire is to become stable. National pride must be presented as an unmitigated evil leading inevitably to wars. Which is true since all true nations will invariably resist Murgan domination and incorporation into the empire. The duties and obligations which patriotism imposes upon citizens, and particularly that of defence, can be shown to infringe on personal freedom. Where nations need to be fragmented and weakened, ever smaller ethnic identities within the state can be promoted and supported until nationhood is completely degraded. It is relatively simple to convince minorities that they are victims, and the more they complain, the more they will feel inferior and thus the more they will be resented by the majority. Thus is the unity of the nation state undermined. As the saying goes: a divided nation has no defenders. No national differences however small should be allowed. Even local food preferences should be replaced by Murgan fare.

Divide and fragment the culture itself. Any long-standing tradition, custom or ritual is a social adhesive which can form a potential rallying point for a revival of national identity. All such should be ridiculed as irrelevant, outmoded and old fashioned. The young should be encouraged not to take part. In this context, history is particularly dangerous to Murgan rule. All history should be taught as the story of the exploitation and oppression of ordinary people by their rulers and thus as a source of shame rather than pride or interest. Great leaders of the past should be ridiculed and their reputations undermined. Pointing out the immorality of individual rulers and their lack of progress towards freedom and equality is very effective. Only Murgan history should be seen as an object lesson in progressive policy.

Divide and degrade Religion. Religious leaders and prophets can be potent focusers of opposition not to say rebellion. Moral codes and religious taboos can be explicitly critical of the Imperium and its values. Any moral code is inimical to the functioning of the Murgan state which must be free to pursue any policy which is in its interest. Local religions can initially be undermined by insisting on the equality of all religions - toleration is fatal to organised religious belief. Where all are equal, none are credible. Stress the authoritarian and arbitrary nature of organised religion and how it restricts individual freedom. Eventually all organised religion should be replaced by individual belief. Aim also towards the eventual secularisation of all that is held sacred. As with culture the young should be encouraged to see all ritual and taboo as ridiculous and old-fashioned; its perpetrators as insane or deluded. By demokratisation of the temple any intellectual elite capable of resistance can also be marginalised. Ideally the religion will be assimilated into the worship of the Empire and its aspirations. Any genuine attempt at religious revival can be suppressed as the work of a mad and dangerous cult attempting to inspire a moral dictatorship.

Divide the family. What we know as aristocracy is merely the ascendancy of the most consistent and successful families. Families with the strength, wisdom, virtue and tenacity to marshal their wealth and maintain their family bonds over centuries will inevitably rise to power. The population should be encouraged to see this kind of success as unfair privilege based on a mere accident of birth. In reality the family is the building block of the nation state. In fact the family is almost the state in microcosm. The family is also the ultimate focus of all moral behaviour. As with all other aspects of national and ethnic identity, the family can be easily undermined and destroyed by showing how its very existence is inimical to the fundamental tenets of individual freedom and equality. Convince women that their husbands are tyrants, abusers and exploiters, that their children are millstones around their necks; convince children that their parents are bullies who not only restrict their freedom of activity but who also view them as inferior and incompetent beings; convince men that marriage undermines their happiness and status by restricting their freedom to lie with as many woman as they wish and you have begun the disintegration of the state. Nothing is as effective as sexual promiscuity in breaking up cultures and religion. The children from these disaffected and divided families will become the main agents of social subversion. They will be lacking in moral direction, education, and civic values. In turn their ignorance and criminal tendencies will form their own children's minds. Within two or three generations their lack of moral discipline and the resistance to authority will lead to the fragmentation of society, the break-up of its cultural core, the

281

undermining of its religion and the overthrow of its moral architecture.

Divide and confound the language. Ancient languages are like ancient fortresses. Nothing divides empires or unites their enemies more effectively than speech. All the nation's historical, cultural and ethical values are embedded in their native tongue. In the name of freedom of expression and equality of all citizens, the authoritarian nature of linguistic discipline must be at all times condemned. Correct grammar and syntax should be a particular target since this is often what makes the educated and the uneducated unequal. Freedom of expression leads directly to imprecision of language and therefore to a lack of true communication. Debased language means debased thought. Is not logic a function of grammar? Debased rhetoric cannot inspire opposition to the Imperium. The eventual aim should be an Imperial argot, a universal pidgin tongue in which all meanings wander and blur, and into which all individual tongues and dialects will eventually subsume themselves. The stable Imperium will consist of an undisciplined and uneducated mass with an inbuilt ideological suspicion of clever speakers and writers whom eventually they will be unable to understand.

Divide the society into individuals. The safest situation is that in which society is atomised into individuals. There can be no effective opposition where there is no cohesion or organization. Where there is no recognition of rank or privilege, or nobility of mind or intellect, there can be no concept of respect, mutual loyalty, fealty, duty or responsibility. In order to prevent social bonding only one form of human relationship can be permitted to exist in the Imperium and that is the cash-nexus. All human impulses must be subject to the law of the bargain. The use of money must be the only form of social organisation. Nor must any man or woman ever be allowed to feel secure in their material wealth. It is normal to want to secure oneself against future need, but in the Imperium, citizens must constantly strive to secure themselves against all possible future wants and contingencies. Greed and fear are the engines of prosperity a state of war should exist between individual citizens for the fruits of that prosperity.

Divide the individual. Not only will each man or woman be at war with their neighbour but neither shall any man or woman know peace in themselves. War may have been abolished but aggression will have

282

been internalised. No man will trust any other. The carrying of concealed weapons must thus be made an inalienable right. The normal state of every man's soul will be that of constant civil war with individual freedom as its goal. Total freedom is only possible in the absence of authority or control, which on the level of the individual person results in lack of discipline. No man will impose upon himself that which he will resist others imposing upon him. The resulting lack of self-discipline makes a weak and ineffectual individual, unable to motivate himself or carry through any consistent policy, unable to resist the promptings of the appetites and unwilling to defer their gratification for any high purpose. When your empire is peopled with such as these, your rule will be unchallenged.

Divide ideas one from the other. The keeping apart of people is nothing without the keeping apart of ideas; therefore exert yourself to the utmost to control libraries, schools and academies. You must rule the whole commerce of ideas with an iron hand. Ideas can spread like plague through whole continents. They are the only real danger to the Imperium. Nothing is as dangerous as an idea whose time has come. Luckily the democratic system of political control which you have installed promotes a social tyranny of the ignorant majority which is in effect an irresistible power of censorship. Once the Imperium has been established any individual who attempts to champion his family, his nation, his culture, his religion, his ideas or his art against the Imperial norms, will be torn to shreds by his fellow citizens who will feel their own freedoms threatened thereby. If that individual is also an outstanding or talented individual he will be doubly persecuted since talent will be seen as an affront to equality and thus it is said that envy is the peculiar vice of demokracies.

You will ask how all these changes are to be brought about. Put away your spears and shields! Call for your musicians and your poets. Summon your painters and carvers. Your artists will be your army in the conquest of the public mind. Remember that he who pays the piper calls the tune. A wise man once said "You can have the men who make the laws if you give me the music makers." Truly it is written, "When the mode of the music changes, the walls of the city shake." A room full of dancers can keep in step so long as they follow the music. See how even an untrained army can move in good array whilst it follows the beat of the drum. Choose your music carefully and you can move the rabble however you wish. Do you want to inflame them, or quieten them down, make firm their courage, or send them into battle? As a wise ruler you will choose your music to suit. Play the Phrygian mode, it is said, and soon even your generals will put down their vittals and reach for their arms. What then, you ask, shall be the Murgan mode if organised warfare is to be avoided? The Phrygian and the Dionysian must be fused together to produce a constant state of unfulfilled excitement. The constant pursuit of sensation which drives trade in the Imperium is itself fuelled by a sense of dissatisfaction and unease brought about by life lived to the military attack beat. Strike the drum at a rate just faster than the normal heart beat and all hearts will try to follow. The goal is to produce such a state of excitement as to make any profound contemplation impossible. Beat the drum loudly! Murgan musicians will sing of the appetites, of intoxication and copulating. As in all the arts the aim should be to stamp out all that is sophisticated, elitist, thoughtful, disciplined or vernacular. One empire must march to one beat. That is best which is most popular. That which is most popular will be of the lowest order.

Drama is the most perfect vehicle for promoting Imperial orthodoxy, but in your theatres there must be no philosophy but your own. Ideas and plot should be replaced by spectacle, violence, sex and sensation. People must not get into the habit of detecting subtle argument or convoluted plots, else they might put together things best kept apart. Then, before long, some of them could be making rival productions which the people might prefer to yours.

The ear is the key to the emotions but the eye is the first doorway to the soul. Painters and sculptors might be mere artisans but they are dangerous as opponents. As with all artists, if you cannot control them then you must destroy them. Paintings are meaning-carriers and all meanings can be subversive. Just being able to write a name is to give the writer a magical power over the person or thing itself. Simply possessing an image of a ruler gives you power over him. Hence your anonymity. Therefore mere abstract patterns and decorations are safer than skilled representations of real things, but you must not at first speak out against such genius and skill as can produce beautiful and lifelike images. Encourage the purchase of the work of mere patterners and colourists for high prices and before long even skilled painters will strive to make similar things, or starve. There is an eastern tribe whose religion forbids the use of representational images; these people would make excellent arbiters of taste in the Imperium. Make them the keepers of your picture galleries and writers of encomia on art.

In the name of freedom of expression all discipline, convention and skill can be broken down. Money is the key. Patronise the worthless

284

naïves, the trivial assemblers and arrangers, the pursuers of mere sensation and within a generation or two Art will be degraded to the level of latrine scratchings. No serious-minded person will have anything to do with it. Once the historical tradition is broken, it will take centuries to rebuild. What is more important though is that a society of a given shape produces only the art according to that shape. When your Empire is properly fashioned it will by its very nature be incapable of producing real art.

The pursuit of Equality in the Imperium cannot countenance nobility, genius or exceptional power of discrimination. The ability to discriminate between peoples, cultures, languages, religions, good and bad art, is especially dangerous. Discrimination must be made a dirty word. A universal unwillingness to discriminate between right and wrong; black and white; art and trash; is one of the touchstones of Imperial success or failure. In a demokracy there can be no elitism. Art must be of such a level that anyone, even an infant can make it.

Artists of genius, just like prophets, demagogues and saints, are the enemies of your Imperium. All charisma, genius, beauty or moral force must be neutralised by subtle or covert means. Be vigilant! Any individual who can move the populace should never be openly assassinated. Make it appear to be an accident or better still the work of enemies of the Empire. Corruption of a talented individual by grotesque wealth is particularly effective where the artist is young. The man who is a slave to his appetites is a slave to the Imperium. Artistic genius cannot survive without freedom of spirit.

For the ruler, fame is not only corrupting but dangerous. If you wish to have your name in every mouth as ruler of the world then put this book away from you. Join the ranks of those crude adventurers who snatch power with bloodstained hands, never sleep easy in their beds and are soon deposed by other adventurers who believe that rule of the world is in a particular chair, or a gilded rod, or a jewelled metal hat. To have and hold absolute power you must never be perceived as the tyrant you are. The difference between an active tyranny and a firm ruler is one of perception only. The exercise of absolute power is in both cases the same. This you would find out instantly if you became a threat to the ruling power. Instead of throne, sceptre or crown you must habitually wear only masks such as actors wear. These are your masks.

The Mask of Government. At all times you must rule behind a mask. To be always secure from blame or risk you must not be perceived as a ruler. The visible government must be your creature secretly promoted, supported and deposed by you. It must only wield power by *proxy. Its Leader will be an elected actor, the visible government itself a mere pantomime of power, which if it becomes unpopular you can replace with another production. By allowing the people the choice of voting for one of your puppet governments or the other they will not only have the illusion of having chosen their own government but also have only themselves to blame for its actions. There is a fine irony in this so-called 'representation of the people' by demokracy.*

The Mask of Freedom. It is another wonderful unperceived irony that the more freedom your subjects have the more they will be enslaved to the Imperium. Therefore you will wear the mask of a lover of freedom. No man will defend with more gusto than you, the right of a citizen to pursue his individual happiness through freedom of action. Every citizen will believe that he is living in an empire whose most precious possession is liberty, and that it is the only fit place for a free spirit to live in. As his society disintegrates into anarchy and impotence, he will resist all attempts to impose corrective authority and discipline as being attacks on his fundamental rights, even to the extent of taking up arms. Politicians will pander to his appetite for liberty. Wives will count being one with their husbands as slavery, children will deny the authority of their parents, students will mock their teachers, and all will soon look on morality as the grossest tyranny possible. Promiscuity in all things will be the mark of the free spirit. Politicians will parade their immorality and the people will cheer them on. Before long even animals will have rights and wild beasts will be freed from their cages for fear of affronting public sensibilities. In short each citizen will be entirely free to devote their individual energies to gratifying his or her appetites. When the citizen has finally shrugged off all the bonds of nation, history, family, and community, this free spirit is left completely defenceless against the organized powers of the Imperium. In short he has been disarmed and enslaved.

The Mask of Equality. In a successful Imperium, equality is a stronger principle even than freedom. Which citizen will admit his inferiority in anything? Its literal meaning is that all shall be reduced to the level of the lowest, since it is obvious that not all are born equal and the worst will never catch up with the best who in fact will steadily pull away from them. Any other definition is meaningless since in law and business the cleverer and stronger will always have the advantage. The political expression of equality is demokracy, rule by manipulation of the lowest and most stupid elements in society. Just as freedom leads to anti-authoritarianism, equality tends to anti-intellectualism. Equality means the reduction from wisdom to ignorance, intelligence to dullness. Education must be of a fragmented and limited nature, and its teachers incompetent and lacking any real wisdom.

If you wear these masks successfully then the mass of your subjects will be proud to be virtually illiterate, slovenly in speech, dull and irrational, unwilling and unable to marshal complex thought processes or to acquire the self-discipline necessary to do so. These are the perfect demokratic electors. They would rather be slaves than unequal. Their greatest pleasure will be to subvert privilege and excellence and to see the noble brought low. Like pigs they will revel in their mud and filth. They will always outvote and neutralise any accidental minority of intelligent citizens. Behind the Mask the real leveller in Murga is money. Cash replaces all other social ties. Everything in the Imperium must have a monetary value. All intercourse must be business; all appetites and needs serviceable by wealth. Every man, woman and child will be economic individuals motivated by selfishness, greed and discontent, all firmly believing that they are equally free to be the Emperor, or the Emperor's horse when in fact the Emperor is a puppet and the people are the dust beneath his feet. Obedience and discipline will be available to those who can both afford and enforce it, but ultimately it will always be for the highest bidder. That will always be the hidden ruler.

The Mask of Peace. All men think that a good ruler should be a great warrior; a conqueror of many lands. But war is risky and unpredictable. Constant war is bad for trade. Every victory creates generations of enemies for the victor. No defeat is ever forgotten by the vanquished. Defeat is always remembered and resented. The Pax Murgana will be another wonderful irony. All warfare is based on deception and Murga will pretend to be an agent of peace. Thus the Imperium will always try to conquer by proxy. The Empire will be extended and subdued by organised proxy warfare between rival ethnic groups, cultures, religions and nations. These rivalries will then slowly disappear as all their differences are suppressed by the Imperium. Eventually Imperial armies will only ever march out on peacekeeping missions: that is, to suppress dissent or assertions of autonomy. This ravaging of unruly countries will be known as spreading liberty and demokracy. No peasant will ever again be conscripted to fight in distant lands. However he will be in permanent conflict with every other citizen. It is the nature of the Imperium to set person against person. Aggression will not be abolished but merely internalised. The price of the citizen's freedom is the lock on the door, the bars on the window, the attack dogs in his yard and the unquiet sleep. All men shall be free from war but none shall know peace. This is the Pax Murgana. The longer it persists the more solid the ruling power shall be in his position. This is because the citizen will regard the 'government' as his only defender against his fellow citizens. In reality the 'government' is his only enemy.

A book in the hands of an ignoramus is like a sword in the hands of a child. I speak in hard words of difficult things. To be the invisible ruler of the world you have to be capable of subtle understandings and disciplined thinking. You will also need to be utterly ruthless and possessed of great strength of will. Your gods must be money and power; your code that of the assassin. Finding this book has been your first task. Using it will be your next. May Sa'than be with you.

Small gripped the manuscript with both hands and stared at it. He was numbed by the implications of what he had read. He could see the physical reality of the book but his sight was turned inwards. This was the triumph of Power without honour; without scruple; and without any purpose other than its own extension and continuation. In his mind's eye, all he had read paraded before him like a circus procession. Words were actors, acrobats and conjurors. Ideas were traps and snares for the unwary. How else could freedom lead to slavery? Metal chains did not of themselves a slave make. The freedom of the fornicator or the glutton shackled him to his appetites. Only bonds made a people free. The bonds of family, of marriage, of identity, of culture, of language, of religion: these were what made a people strong enough to resist enslavement. Equality of people was an untruth. Everyone was so obviously unequal that the only way to make an equal society was to make nobility and excellence a vice, subvert knowledge and learning and thereby degrade every mind to the level of the lowest. The supremacy of the individual was yet another trick to reduce humanity to a disorganized aggregate. As soon ask a man to cut off his limbs to make him stronger, or tell a soldier to step forth from his army to fight. It was not a sign of strength; it was a subterfuge to make him more vulnerable.

All those words: Freedom, Individuality, Equality; they wore masks! How universally used but how little understood they were! How stupid to narrow down their meanings to what you thought they meant or wanted them to mean. How stupid to assume that they only signified absolute virtues. The murderer, the rapist, the infanticide, the whore, the fornicator, the exploiter, the desecrator, the slave master, all rode in the baggage train of the army of 'Freedom'. Whilst eyeing their prey, all cried 'Freedom' as lustily as any virtuous man, who, if

288

he had the slightest inkling of what he was shouting for, would cut out his own tongue.

After some time Small packed the leaves back into their leather case and slipped it back into the book bag. Almost at once he had a strange feeling that something was changed. The cabin looked the same. The sun still warmed his lap. The fire smouldered. But there was a new quality in the quietness, a stillness almost tangible. He looked over to where Domina lay in her bed of furs. For the first time since they had arrived she lay cool, peaceful and relaxed. For an instant he felt panic. Then he became aware of her breathing: regular, deep and low. She was sleeping like a baby. The old woman looked up at him with a knowing smile. The battle between the young girl and the demons that possessed her was over. Small was not yet sure which side had won.

Outside the cabin a series of muffled thuds attracted his attention. He looked out of the window at a blinding white landscape. The veils of mist had vanished revealing a sky of infinite blue. More snow slid down the roof and thudded onto the ground. The icicles ran with melted water which burned deep holes into the snow beneath them. A foraging bird dislodged a crystal cloud from a branch. The thaw had begun.

That night he lay awake listening to the rumbling of avalanches. It was as if the mountains themselves were crumbling. Through the window, ranks of stars burned with cold fire. Brilliant meteors slashed the velvet heavens. The moon rose huge and yellow from behind the peaks; lifting, silvering, shrinking until its dazzling orb ruled the celestial vault. How wise those first librarians had been to make the night sky the key to their mystery. Everything else could be changed, hidden, disguised, perverted; but not that. It was ever-present, immortal, endlessly fascinating, beautiful unspeakably. There for every wondering being who could lift his eyes from the ground was the pattern of the Maker.

Small woke to the sound of water trickling, dripping and dropping. The morning sun was melting the snow. He did not know how long it would be before the pass through the mountains was open again. What he did know was that Puttfark and the others would be waiting for it to happen. If he knew anything about Murgans it was that they didn't give up: ever. Half the world had been unable to stop the Murgans and their new world order. They seemed to covet want as much as wealth. Difference and autonomy frightened them. No nation was too poor or desolate to escape their ambition and envy; no nation so rich as to be able to sate their greed; no nation so moral as to escape being debauched by their friendship. But now he knew that they were only secure in their power so long as no-one could see behind their masks. In his book bag he, Small, had the power, perhaps the only power, which could stop them corrupting the world. He had the power to make the blind see. And with that realisation came the knowledge of what he must do.

Small approached the bed where Domina lay sleeping. Though she was pale as death, her expression was calm. Her breathing was almost undetectable. He looked down at her ravaged face. Her eyes were dark shadowed and closed. Her cheeks had sunken and her lips were livid and wasted. Yet in the gloom her pale skin appeared luminous with a kind of ethereal beauty. He reached out his hand and gently shook her shoulder.

"Domina," he said. "You must wake up. The snow is melting and I have to go before the Warholl arrive. I am sorry but I have to leave. I have an important task. It is a matter of duty and honour."

He turned to find Kara watching him.

"I just don't understand it. Why does she not wake?" he said.

"When she is ready to wake, she will wake."

"But when will that be?"

"I wish I knew, but this is no ordinary illness. She has no ulcers, boils or blemishes; no rashes, lesions or swellings; she has no fluxes or issues; her breathing is not impaired. She takes nourishment with her eyes closed like a babe. She seems to have no bodily pain and even her mental anguish has finally abated. I have thought long and hard these months about your companion. I think that it is not her body but her mind that is dis-eased. Tell me, is she a sensitive soul?"

"Sensitive ...?" Small was about to dismiss this idea out of hand, but paused. On the surface Domina looked for all the world like an innocent slip of a girl. Underneath she was as dangerous and mercenary as a soldier for hire, but was there something deeper, something concealed inside, something buried deep out of sheer necessity?

Kara took his silence for uncertainty, "Might she have experienced some kind of shock then? Sometimes a great shock can cause fainting and unconsciousness. The sway of reason is often overwhelmed by something tragic and unforeseen."

Small shook his head slowly. "She was not a person who would be easily shocked by anything she saw. I believe she had been brought up in a society in which horror and violence were mundane."

"If it was not something she saw then it was perhaps something she felt. Something that crept upon her; something she could no longer resist when she was weak and at the end of her strength. Did you say anything to her that might have caused such a thing to happen?"

Small thought back to those precious moments with Domina on the mountain. "We spoke only of love ... and survival, but I don't think she believed in love. They don't, you know, the Murgans ..."

"Only of love! Boy, you speak of the only power that tyrants fear; a power that makes fools of kings and kings of fools. Love can be the elixir of youth or a fatal poison. Only of love! It is a powerful drug, but I must confess I never heard of it having such an effect: but then again I never heard of a people who didn't believe in it either"

Small walked over to Kara and took her hand in his. "Kara, I must leave. Please, I beg you, take care of her for me. If ... I mean when she wakes tell her I had to go but I will come back as soon as I can. I thank you with all my heart for saving our lives. I just wish I had something to give in return."

"You still haven't told me your story."

"No." Small covered his face with his hands and screwed up his eyes. "Listen, very bad people are following us. As soon as the pass is open they will come here. It is very, very important that they do not catch me. If they think Domina has helped me they will kill her. I am sorry to have brought all this trouble upon you. It was not intended. I cannot ask you to lie to them. They would torture you if they didn't believe you. Even if you tricked them they would come back and have their revenge. Really the less you know the safer you will be, and even that isn't very safe. If they see Domina's silk clothes or the horse they will be suspicious. The clothes can be hidden: the horse is a problem. Perhaps just turn it loose?"

"It would just come back here. Horses are like that. But don't worry I know a place. I will take it when the snow has thawed. It needs grass anyway. Just one thing," Kara gripped his hand and looked in his eyes, "Tell me, have you done something very bad?"

"I swear by the Great Author of all things that anything I have done I had to do to or I would not have escaped these evil people who most certainly would have killed me."

"Then go with my blessing. Wrap up warmly and take some dried meat with you to eat on the way."

She kissed him on both cheeks, then hugged him and ruffled his hair, now grown long and shaggy.

Small went back over to Domina and bent his mouth close to her ear.

"If I stay we will all be killed. I can't take you with me, you are much too weakened, but I promise I will come back for you. When my task is done I will come back to you. I promise. I will do this for love. I cannot help it. I have to take care of you."

He could not be sure but he thought he saw a movement behind the closed eyelids, but it was momentary and was not repeated. Domina did not move. The almost imperceptible rhythm of her breathing did not falter. He bent down and kissed her forehead.

Twenty minutes later he was stumbling and slipping down the mountain towards the town. Suddenly he felt bereft, unmanned, close to panic. What was he doing? He must go back to the cabin. He felt as if his heart had been torn out of his chest. The intensity of his feelings alarmed him. It was only with the utmost effort of will that he was able to master his emotions and press on.

In the cabin Domina sat up and opened her eyes. "Where is Small?" she demanded. "And who are you?"

Twenty-five

Descending the mountain was like walking from winter to summer. Before he reached the plain he had to take off several layers of clothing. The road became wider and more and more crowded as he approached the gates of the little town of Zimbola. Scores of heavily laden vehicles and hundreds of people were coming in from every nook in the foothills. Small had never seen so many people in one place. He felt both exhilarated and intimidated. His head ached with the sheer quantity of novel impressions which flooded his senses. Before long he was stumbling along in the press of the crowd in a kind of trance. It seemed impossible that all these people could squeeze themselves through the narrow gateway of the town. Wagon wheels made out of rough planks locked into the elegant spokes of chariots. Fights broke out. Camels reared and plunged. Horses tried to mount each other. Several fierce looking young men apprehended a thief and administered summary justice by holding the man's hand under the wheels of the wagon he had pilfered from. The crowd made such a din that the thief's shriek was only just audible as the heavy wagon passed over his hand.

Among the beggars and cripples working the throng was a diminutive man with no legs who sat in a tiny wood and wicker cart drawn by a large shaggy dog. The hound snarled and snapped at the legs of any living thing which stood in its way. The crowd parted to let the ferocious animal and its frail vehicle pass through. It darted beneath plunging and rearing beasts and passed under the wheels and chassis of the big market wagons. Small saw his opportunity and sprinted in its wake as it passed through the dense traffic. Twice the little dog-cart stopped whilst its occupant solicited alms from wealthy market-goers in elegant carriages. Small stood as close as he could to the dog-cart whilst these ritual exchanges took place. The legless man flattered the donor shamelessly whilst bewailing his own misfortune and lowly state. Small knew that in a poor country, giving is a great luxury. The giving of alms was a public display of beneficence and advertised the donor's reputation to bystanders. The passing over of the coins was thus payment for services rendered.

As the third almsgiver handed over his coins, he spotted Small standing close behind the legless man. "Here," he said delving into his purse a second time, "here is another coin for your fine-looking son." The crippled man darted a surprised look over his shoulder at Small and gave him a conspiratorial wink. Then the wicker cart was off again, moving rapidly through the crowd. Small followed.

The press was greatest at the gate itself where two massive ox carts were contesting for precedence. Both were accompanied by a dozen or more supporters of all sexes and ages, all shouting at the same time that the others should back up so as to unlock the wheels. Travellers on foot were having to duck underneath the carts to enter the town. As a consequence, the air was rich with their cursing which, besides comprehensively covering most of the cart owners' bodily functions, also involved every aspect of their family history, present circumstances and future prospects. The dog cart slipped under the chassis of the largest wagon. Small ducked after it and passed through the gateway. He was immediately grabbed by two soldiers and pinned against the stonework.

"Who are you?" one of them asked, "I've not seen you before."

Small was so shocked that he could not answer right away

"He's with me," the legless man called out from the other side of the arch, "he's all right."

A woman screamed. The wagoneers had come to blows. The soldiers glanced at each other. For a moment they hesitated, then they stood away from Small.

"Remember!" the soldier called out as they moved off to settle the fight, "Any trouble at all and neither of you get in again."

"Why did they do that?" Small asked the legless man as the dog pulled his cart off down the street.

"This is a fine and respectable town: no bars on the windows, no bolts on the doors and the women can go to market on their own. If everybody was free to come and go as they pleased, the town would soon fill with riff-raff and ne'er do wells, and then where would we all be? You could be a pickpocket, or a spy, or a fire starter, even a ravisher of women. But I don't think you are any of those, are you? So why are you here?"

"I have to speak with the ruler of this place. I have something very important to show him."

"Ha! Old Kaspar? You won't get anywhere near him. This is market day. He will have scores of petitions to hear. Some of the petitioners will have been waiting for weeks. They may yet have to wait for months."

"But I have to speak with him on an urgent matter. Is there no way I can get him to hear me?"

The cripple called the dog to a halt and gave Small a sideways look as if trying to size him up. "There might be. Perhaps if you were to tell me what this urgent matter is …."

"I cannot do that. What I have to say is of such a secret and dangerous nature that it is for the ears of the ruler alone. If I cannot tell him what I know, then something truly terrible will come to pass. Your nice respectable town will be flooded with a tide of evil."

"It is usually men who bring evil. May I know who they are?"

"They are called Murgans."

"Ah, that is indeed interesting. I see you wear the clothes of a hunter from the mountains, but you do not use the words of a country boy. When you speak it is as if I hear the voice of a councillor. I think perhaps you should tell your story to another councillor. But beware, here in Zimbola those who spread false rumours are severely punished. Come."

The dog cart sped off down the street and into a maze of back alleys. Small sprinted after it. Before long they came to a quiet street of dust and bright sunshine which had high walls down either side. Here and there the foliage of fruit trees and vines appeared above them. Doglegs stopped at a gate and beat upon it with his metal begging bowl. After a long wait the door was opened just enough for a face to appear.

"I want to talk with your Master" said the cripple.

The door closed and there was another longer wait before it opened once again.

A tall bony man with a long grey wispy beard peered out with eyes squinted against the bright sunlight.

"Ah, Doglegs! Are times so hard that you come begging at the door now?" he said.

"No, no honoured sir councillor Mr. Melchior. The wealthy and beneficent citizens still visit the market place as always. I have a young man here who claims to have something very important to tell our esteemed though somewhat senile ruler. He will not tell me nor anyone else what this vital something is. I thought you might be better able to advise him than I." Doglegs lowered his voice to a whisper, "It seems to involve Murgans."

The councillor scrutinised Small. "What is your name and where are you from?" he asked.

"My name is Small and I come from Alligor…"

"Hush!" Melchior gripped his arm violently, and glanced nervously up and down the street. "Say no more! Doglegs, I have a piece of silver here for you. Say nothing of the boy or what you have heard."

The cripple smiled broadly as he pocketed the coin. "I have no idea who you are talking about. Come on Dog take us to the butcher's shop. You have earned your bones. Salam sir Mr. Councillor."

The dog barked furiously as it dragged the cart wildly off down the street.

Small was ushered into the courtyard of the councillor's house and then into a private room. Melchior closed the door and turned to him.

"I will not ask how you managed to get into the city. I only say this. You have indeed been fortunate to have had your footsteps directed to this house. Doglegs spoke of important information. I think that for your own safety you should tell me what you have to say. I am a councillor to the ruler of this place and if your tale is worth telling I can inform him immediately. If you insist on telling him yourself, it may be months before your suit is heard."

Small sat in silence whilst he weighed the options. The Murgans might arrive at any moment. They were far more skilled in diplomacy than he was. They might be granted an immediate audience with the ruler. He looked at Melchior's face. It was benign, concerned, intent. He had no alternative but to tell his tale.

"There is a power risen in the world," he said, "without nationality, without race, without religion, without love. It has no morality and is without conscience. It spreads out of control, faster than a plague. No nation or race can withstand its corruption. All the civilised values of honour, nobility, blood and family are replaced by desire for money, and that money is used only for the sating of appetite. This power brooks no rivals. Although it can muster overwhelming military force to its cause when it needs to, it does not conquer through force of arms. Trade, finance and commerce are its deadly weapons. By amassing undreamed of riches and monopolising the essentials of the market place it is able to impose its will on any state. Neither poverty nor probity will protect you from its corrupting influence once you allow its agents into your land. They will steal the souls of your children and debauch them utterly, and end by teaching your women how to kill their unborn babies as a means of avoiding the consequences of their promiscuity. This I have seen with my own eyes. Whilst your ruler sleeps on his throne this power will make a moral and cultural desert of his nation. As far as I know, this land is the only place still beyond their influence. The agents of this power are already at work on the other side of these mountains. Its envoys wait only for the snows to melt before they come over the pass. They are looking for me and for what I carry. It is perhaps the only power which can prevent them corrupting the whole world beyond recovery."

"I fear that I already know what it is you have brought with you, but you must tell me what you carry."

"It is a book."

Melchior's complexion turned ashen. "I knew," he said. "I knew the moment you said where you came from. You must have had a guardian angel at your shoulder when you entered this town. If not then the city guards would have searched your wallet. If they had found your book they would have instantly arrested you. Books are forbidden here by law. The penalty for bringing a book into Zimbola is death."

"What?" Small was stunned. "But that is absurd!"

"You would say so. But this town is well run, orderly, respectable, without discord. We have no religious heresies, no political disputes. People are content. Books carry change with them, and sometimes worse. Our legends say that once upon a time a man came from that book-city of yours. He warned us about a book; a book that could change the world; a book with the sting of a scorpion. His name was Grupio."

"Gropius!"

Melchior glanced sharply at Small. Then he held out his hands to him. "I will read the book now," he said. "You may stroll in the courtyard meanwhile. There is a fountain there."

Small lifted the book from his pouch. "It is written in an antique tongue, you will not be able to understand it."

Melchior squinted at the first leaf. "I know the tongue," he said finally. "I have also drunk from the deep wells of Alligor. It is part of the training of the guardians of this town that in their youth they spend some time travelling the world. I travelled only as far as the book city. I know all about the power of books."

Small sat outside in the sunny courtyard whilst Melchior read the book. A servant brought an apple and some bread for him to eat. He washed it down with the fountain water which bubbled from a pipe placed cunningly in the mouth of a stone child who seemed to be drinking from cupped hands. Small was amazed at this magical device. He could not find out how the fountain worked or even where the water came from. Eventually Melchior came out to him.

"I have read the book. You wanted me to tell the king. I shall tell him."

Small was not sure how to feel. "What do you think he will do?" he asked.

"Do? He will instantly sentence you to death. Then he will listen to what I have to say. He will read the book and call a meeting of his councillors. They will be told that despite all our precautions the most fearful of our legends has apparently come true, and that you are the one responsible. We will then decide whether we should act upon a thousand-year old legend, well known to every citizen or believe a ragged youth who no-one has ever seen before."

"The way you tell it makes me afraid for my life."

"And do you still want your story to be told? Even if it might cost you your life?"

Small hesitated, and then spoke. "I have risked my life to bring this book to you. The Murgans may arrive at any time. Without your protection I will be murdered and the book lost for ever. This town sits with its back to the mountains and faces the limitless Zahar desert. You sit at the uttermost edge of the civilised world. There is nowhere left for me to run, nowhere to hide. If the Murgans cannot be stopped here then they will not be stopped anywhere."

"So. You will back your story with your life?"

"Yes."

"Then I will tell the king your story. My servants will feed you whilst I am away. Do not attempt to leave the house and you will be quite safe until I return."

By the time the councillor returned, the sun had passed its zenith and the gathering clouds were turning the afternoon grey and dull. Small's heart pounded as he heard the hubbub at the door, then Melchior entered the room.

"What happened? What did he say?"

"I told your story and showed him the book. You were of course sentenced to death … by public beheading if I remember rightly."

Small was aghast. "No! That cannot be."

"Oh, don't worry. I immediately appealed on your behalf to the Court of Common Sense."

"What?" This was all too bewildering for Small.

"There have to be laws and laws must be strictly enforced. But even experts in the making of laws cannot foresee every circumstance. In such cases we convene a special court of twelve intelligent burghers who must decide whether common sense should prevail over common law."

"And they have decided …"

"They have decided that your trial and execution should be postponed until after your accusers have been heard. You see, a large delegation of Murgans has just arrived. They wish to negotiate trading rights with us. They are talking about huge sums of money and reciprocal privileges which they have at their disposal. They say that they are also seeking a young man, a thief, who has made off with a book which belongs to the Murgan nation. They have already offered a very large reward to anyone who finds you."

"They are liars! The book belongs to Alligor. I brought it away with me only to stop them taking it."

"I must attend the discussions. You will come with me. Don't worry; you will be quite safe from the Murgans."

"And the book ...?"

"I think it best if I keep it for the time being. It would be safer. The Murgan party is large and well-armed. If they saw you carrying the book then they might attempt some rash action. Possession in such circumstances would be a very good argument for ownership."

Two soldiers were waiting at the door of the house to escort them to the Royal palace. Small had never before seen a Royal palace. From what he had read he expected luxury, wealth and riches beyond his imagining. What he found was a building which spoke overwhelmingly of age and of continuity. Just like Alligor, the central building of Zimbola had been constructed with the best of materials and the greatest of skill so that it would speak of the stability of rule and not the vanity of rulers.

Each door had its own guardians, and each set of guardians had their own unique ritual of admittance. Any interloper would have been detected instantly by his inability to give the correct addresses and responses. Melchior spoke the words, genuflected, bowed and counter-challenged in a manner honed by a lifetime at Court. Eventually they came to a set of doors which remained closed to them. Melchior spoke in a low voice with the men who guarded it and then turned to Small.

"The Council sits with the Murgans. I must join them. You may listen from the gallery."

Small had a sick feeling in his belly and a slight dizziness in his head as he climbed the narrow stairs which ascended to the gallery. When he parted the curtain at the head of the stair he heard the low murmur of voices in the Council Chamber. He advanced cautiously to where he could see over the balustrade into the Chamber.

It was Puttfark. On his right hand sat Imperia. Facing them were five large thrones on a dais. On each throne sat an old and tired looking man; their expressions impassive and unreadable. Small recognised Melchior. He too looked listless and apathetic. Small's heart sank. It was Alligor all over again.

Puttfark was immaculately groomed and dressed in spotless white silk. With his strong features and impressive body language he managed to neutralise any sense of inferiority arising from the arrangement of the Chamber. His words were deference itself, but in his manner he asserted his position as an equal. His entire performance was the epitome of consummate diplomatic craft. Imperia had never seemed so stunningly attractive. She cast a glamour over the whole room.

Small sat where he could least be seen. The opening pleasantries had already been exchanged and Puttfark was putting forward his trading proposals. It would seem that a golden age was about to begin in Zimbola: if the Murgans were allowed in, of course. When he had finished speaking one of the councillors thanked him gravely. There was a short pause. Then Melchior began to speak.

"Mr. Puttfark, we have heard what you have to say and we will give your proposal the time and attention it deserves. If you return in three months you will have our answer. Now, does your attractive companion also have a petition to press? We are rather intrigued as to why you have brought her before us. Do you allow women into your Councils in Murga?"

Puttfark adopted a noble and benevolent expression. "Our women are free to enter wherever their talents lead them."

Melchior turned towards Imperia, whose voluptuous pose had imperceptibly stiffened into an almost convincing representation of the Goddess of Wisdom herself. An avuncular smile appeared on Melchior's face.

"You are a comely woman, well into your child bearing years. Have you no children to care for?"

Imperia smiled demurely. "No, Excellency," she replied.

"Has God then cursed you with barrenness?" said Melchior.

"No of course not!" Imperia gave a seductive chuckle, confident that she had made a conquest of the old fool.

"But if you have not had any children, how can you know that?"

Melchior's expression was ingenuousness itself. Imperia froze as if she had received a slap.

"Why ... I ..." she looked despairingly at Puttfark.

For an instant Puttfark's genial mask slipped and he cast a glance of unutterable fury at her. But then he was all smiles.

"We in Murga do not believe that the Gods interfere in the lives of ordinary people," he said, and began to explain that neither would the Murgan Gods curse their chosen people. But it was already too late. The councillors nodded their understanding of his point of view, but they had seen the Murgan mask slip. So far was Puttfark habituated to the libertinism of his state that he did not even realise the scope of

Imperia's mistake. Here in Zimbola there were only two honourable childless states for a woman. She was either unmarried and chaste or married and barren. There was nothing in between. Denying that the Gods interfered in the everyday lives of ordinary people was merely an admission of atheism.

Small cowered behind the pillar as the Murgans rose to leave. He gave them ample time to quit the room and clear the corridor. When he thought that they were far enough away he skipped down the stairs to meet Melchior who had by that time descended from the dais and was conversing with the other councillors underneath the gallery. He burst out of the door at the foot of the stairs and found himself face to face with Puttfark. The man in white instinctively grasped at his dagger, but then saw the Zimbolan soldiers guarding the Council Chamber door. He fixed Small with a fierce gaze.

"You! We had a special relationship. That was genuine. I treated you as a partner. I would have given you the life of a prince. We could have travelled anywhere. You could have had anything, or anybody you wished. You could have been free and yet you betrayed me and tried to run away - as if you could! Don't you understand yet? Murga rules the whole world."

"Murga is evil and immoral. You destroy everything you touch."

"Moral, immoral; they are just the words of spells cast upon small people by their keepers. Whilst you struggle with your morality those who rule over you drink the oldest wines, lay with the finest women … To be moral is to be a slave. I am proud to be immoral."

"No! Your freedom is only a mask for your tyranny. It is the freedom of the powerful to exploit the powerless. You present yourselves as the champions of the people you are debauching. The poor deluded beings conspire at their own corruption. But you are all slaves together, Puttfark; slaves to your own appetites. What freedom can there be for those with their snouts always in the trough?"

Puttfark snorted with angry derision. "What deal did you strike with these buffoons? I hope it involved protection."

"There was no deal."

"You fool. Don't you understand? Whatever happens they will still rule as kings and you will remain a ragged foreigner. But in Murga there are no kings. We pull kings down like rotten tenements!"

"There must always be kings. I do not envy them their position."

Puttfark's features had been slowly darkening as he struggled to contain his frustrated anger. Suddenly he brought his face close up to Small's and lowered his voice to a hiss.

"You think you have beaten us you stillborn rat. In fact you haven't even delayed us. Did you not see the young princes drooling over our Murgan women? Even whilst we are speaking Imperia will be lulling their senses into slavery. They don't care about your books or their fine points of moral philosophy. Freedom to them is what Imperia will let them do to her. The more evil you show her to be, the more irresistible she will be to them. Your 'wise councillors' are old and crumbling. Just like your librarians they will soon turn to dust. The moment we are driven out of Zimbola the young princes will begin to plot the overthrow of their elders. The present may be yours, but the future is ours. Murga is irresistible. Soon the whole world will belong to us. Hear me say this boy; Sa'than is the ruler of this world. He rules through his chosen people, the Murgans. We are the sword of his will. We unlock the lusts of the world, the dark forces in every soul so that Sa'than can rule his kingdom!"

Puttfark's face was dark and contorted with hatred but his eyes were fiercely bright and triumphant. Small was terrified. His voice shook when he replied.

"For every crime against nature there is a price to be paid. You will never be happy. Do you think that when you have corrupted the whole world you will be at ease? Do you believe that when the whole world shares your guilt you will be beyond guilt? Not true! The knowledge of good and evil is inbred in all of us as is the need for the love of other people."

Puttfark struggled to contain his rage. "*Love*? I know that word. It is from a fairy tale. For us love is a vile disease, only lust is normal and healthy."

"Lust is a predatory animal. Put a wild beast in your heart and it will always need to be fed: eventually it will devour you. *Freedom, equality*: those are the real fairy tales because they are things which can never be. They are evil masked words which mean the opposite of what they seem."

Puttfark opened his mouth to answer but a cough from his bodyguard alerted him to the Zimbolan dignitaries coming out of the Council chamber. His finger stabbed the air in front of Small's face. "You dare speak to me of evil? You don't know the meaning of the word. I will do evil to you for your treachery. Our business is not yet concluded young man. Our contract is amended. From this day onwards you will never more know peace until, that is, I take your life as final payment on our deal."

Twenty-six

Small found the following weeks frustrating and agonizing. After the Council meeting with the Murgans, it had been decided that Small should be placed under guard. Melchior explained that this was as much for Small's own protection as anything else, but given that the Court of Common Sense had not yet decided on his case, he was still officially in custody. Melchior's house became his place of confinement. There were weeks of inactivity. Small did not understand the intricacy and subtlety of government and diplomacy. He just felt that the ruling Council was taking far too long to decide what to do. They were giving the Murgans too much time to re-organize their strategy. For the Murgans, time was a valuable commodity, not to be idly or carelessly spent. It would already be earning interest for them in the Big Market Place.

All this was frustrating enough, but Small had a far more potent source of anxiety. The view from the window of his room was half filled by the mountains which blocked the horizon and seemed to hang over the town. Clouds boiled and swirled amongst the peaks, threatening the town but never actually arriving. It was as if the mountains were holding back a world of foul weather. Somewhere amongst those iron-grey cliffs and dark veils of forest, Domina lay in her strange limbo between life and death. Had she awakened yet, or had she slipped deeper into the silent world of shadows and phantasms? It was the vulnerability of the girl which had attached him to her in the first place, but now she was not just vulnerable, she was completely helpless. It made the not knowing unbearable. Somewhere up there amongst the melting snows the Warholl would be encamped. Nothing would escape their attentions. Had they found the cabin? He drove the thought from his mind. It was too horrible to think about it.

Constantly looking out of the window, Small realized something else. The Mountains had been the last bulwark against Murgan influence. Now the Murgans controlled the pass. They could close it at any time they chose, and then the little town of Zimbola would be cut off from all trade. Puttfark was right. The Councillors would be forced to accept the Murgan terms or watch their town stagnate. No matter how attractive the proposition, behind every piece of Murgan 'business' lay the threat of physical force.

Melchior's house was not a hive of social activity. Apart from the regular changes of the guards, only one other person ever came in from the street. Doglegs, the crippled dwarf, seemed to have access to the courtyard at any time of day or night. For a mere beggar he seemed to have a lot to say to the Councillor. Small found this rather strange. Eventually Melchior announced to Small that the Council was to meet in order to decide 'the Murgan matter'. Small was summoned to attend.

The Council in session was no more inspiring of confidence this time than it had been the last. King Kaspar himself, with his wild white halo of disturbed hair, looked as if he had just awoken after a broken night. His eyes sparkled maniacally as he compulsively clenched and unclenched his bony hands. The subdued murmuring tailed off into silence and the King began to speak.

"We have assembled as much knowledge of the Murgans and their ways as we were able. This young man's account was not the first we had heard about these people. We had been warned many times of them and what they did to those who came under their influence. We thought we would be safe here behind our mountains. Who could possibly covet such a small, insignificant outpost? Well, now they are here. Though we could not find anyone who has ever seen a Murgan army take to the field, there can be no doubt that they have unlimited force at their disposal. When thwarted they seem to be able to provoke others into violence on their behalf. In any case our population is far too small for us to muster an army with which to conduct an aggressive campaign. We cannot even keep these individuals out of our town. They are a people of no consistent race, language or skin colour, and anyway they are able to conduct their 'business' wholly through agents or third parties.

'My information is that since the high pass opened, these people have been moving numbers of their supporters through it. Merchants and travellers report that these Murgans are already in a position to close the pass at any moment they choose. They are secure and impregnable until winter comes again. The judgement of my Council is that Zimbola cannot resist the strangers by force or by decree. We must be passive and allow the Murgan wave to pass over us and then hope it will recede somewhat. That way we will sustain the least amount of damage and suffering."

Small was so horrified that he could not stop himself interrupting the old ruler. "Are you just going to give up without a fight?"

Melchior, wincing at the breach of decorum, answered for the Council. "The battle cannot be fought here. Alone we can do nothing. How can we succeed when so many mighty nations have succumbed?"

Kaspar nodded in approval. Melchior shot an admonitory glance at Small as the old ruler continued.

"I have thought very deeply about this matter. Hear me when I say this. If Murga is to be resisted, it must be resisted everywhere, and by everyone. We cannot assault their people and we cannot compete with their wealth, but that is not where their true strength lies. Their strength is in their storytelling."

Baffled amazement rippled through the council chamber. Kaspar enjoyed the moment. A ghost of a smile lit his face like pale winter sunshine.

"Let me explain," he continued, "The overwhelming majority of ordinary people are good and honest by nature, but they can be made perverted and vicious if they are told the wrong stories. The Murgans tell a simple story which is easy for ordinary folk to understand. It is this story which is the secret of their power: not their wealth or even their aggressive military. It is a story full of words such as 'freedom', equality, 'individuality' and the like. Ordinary folk do not understand that these fine-sounding words are in fact masked words. They are words which everyone uses but no-one fully understands. The story tells of a dream not of reality. Thus they say everyone can become wealthy, but do not mention that this can only be at the expense of everybody else. They say that everyone can set himself free; of religion, of social responsibilities, even of morality; but not that this can only be at the expense of their culture, their families, their friends and their communities. They say that everyone is equal but not that this can only be at the expense of those superior individuals gifted by the Gods to inspire loyalty, honour and a love of beauty and nobility, who must everywhere be dragged down by their inferiors. The Murgan story is in fact a conspiracy to render the mass of ordinary people politically impotent, whilst allowing total liberty and license to those who prey on them. A philosopher could easily show how false these Murgan stories are, but ordinary people do not want to listen to philosophy.

'The answer is to make sure the people hear a better story. Only in that way will they come to see how thin and insubstantial is the Murgan dream, and what it really costs to dream it. Our story must be more true and more useful. It must be a story about real people and actual events. It must be a true dream not a false one. It must capture the people's imagination."

There was a short silence before one of the other Councillors spoke.

"A dream that is true? That would be like a prophecy. Is that what you mean?"

"Yes! That is exactly what I mean. We must make a prophecy come true."

"But how would that be possible?"

Melchior cleared his throat to gain the attention of the Council, "We have here with us a living example of such an event. Our young friend from Alligor has made our ancient legends live merely by arriving with a book under his arm. There must be thousands of legends waiting to be fulfilled. All we have to do is find the right one."

"There is a tribe far to the south-west of the mountains," said Kaspar, "They are already under the Murgan shadow, but they are a very ancient and proud people. The Abiru were once a great nation but are now reduced almost to beggary by war and invasion. Even now they will not mingle their seed with any who are not of their faith and lineage because they believe themselves chosen for some Divine purpose. They are a race of religious zealots and terrible when roused. They have a prophecy of a baby born of a spotless virgin belonging to the royal house. This child will grow to be a great warrior-king. He will cleanse their lands of godless foreign culture and then go on to conquer the world. This person will usher in an age of peace and prosperity in the world."

There were several snorts and hisses which indicated incredulity and other less complimentary opinions. Kaspar waited for silence and then continued.

"All we need is a young pregnant woman with or without husband or family. If we transport her to the right place and create enough hullabaloo …"

Kaspar's words tailed off. A depressed silence hung in the air. Small did not know what to think. His plans for saving the world had only gone as far as bringing the manuscript to Zimbola. He had naively thought that it would only be a matter of closing the town gates against the Murgans, but everything was suddenly so complicated and distant. A baby! That meant twenty years to wait.

"It would be a very expensive enterprise, with many risks and no guarantee of success," said Melchior.

Kaspar shrugged, "It's all we have. At my age I have no intention of buckling on my armour and making futile gestures. But if any of you has a better idea …?"

Another long silence followed before Melchior spoke again.

"I am not sure how much hullabaloo you would need to convince those suspicious tribesmen, but it would have to be something special.

306

If they believe themselves to be a chosen people then it would take something extraordinary: something supernatural. Might there be something auspicious, something astrological coming up?"

"Yes!" Eyebrows lifted all around the chamber as Small leaped from his seat. "I know something. This year, this very year, there will be a new star in the sky, a hairy star. It will arrive when the sun rises in the Ram."

Kaspar looked at Melchior. Melchior looked at Kaspar. They both looked at Small.

"A comet? Are you sure of this?"

"My friend Velik told me this and he is very learned in these things. He showed me mountains on the Moon and the horns of Venus. These things I have seen with my own eyes. In Alligor he has found books of calculations and observations taken over thousands of years. Some hairy stars return over and over. This one will return this year bright enough to be seen in daylight. The baby can be born with a new star in the sky."

"Such a prodigy would certainly open the minds of these people," said Kaspar to Melchior. "But can we take the word of a mere boy?"

"We have no choice. We will only have time for one throw of the dice before the Murgans return. It is this or nothing."

Kaspar struck the floor with his staff of office, "It is decided. Employ agents who can be trusted. We need a comely young woman who is about to give birth in the next month or two. We will also need a good midwife. The fee is a hundred gold apiece for complete obedience and perpetual silence. Assemble a caravan of camels. We must skirt the Zahar. Only myself and Melchior will go. We will take fifty men as a bodyguard: pick the best. Make haste: we leave as soon as the woman is found."

Small was escorted back to Melchior's house. He felt disappointed at the strategy which the Zimbolans had chosen to adopt, but he was relieved that a decision had finally been taken. He had done his duty as far as he had been able. Now he must get himself back to Domina and the manuscript back to Alligor. He tugged at the councillor's sleeve.

"Melchior, I have to leave now. I must go back up the mountain. I have promised someone that I would return. She is ill and I must care for her until she recovers. I must also take the book back to the Library."

Melchior looked fixedly ahead as he spoke. "You would never reach the mountains. You might not even get as far as the city gate.

The Murgans have agents everywhere, here in Zimbola, perhaps even in the Council Chamber. Such is the power of money."

Small had a depressing intuition that it was his destiny to be always thwarted by cautious old men. "Can you be certain of that?" he asked.

"We also have our agents," Melchior replied in a quiet voice.

"Doglegs!"

"It is indeed odd how people avoid looking at cripples and assume that they are as crippled in their minds as they are in their bodies, and yet one does not require legs to be able to see, and even the blind may hear."

"Even so I must try to reach the mountains."

"That cannot be. If the Murgans suspect that you are still in Zimbola they will need to keep their people in the town. If they catch you they will make you tell them our plan and they will also be able to use the whole of their forces to thwart us."

"So I must remain here?"

"No. You will be smuggled out with the caravan. It will be large. We will have most of the camels on this side of the mountains. Without camels no-one can pursue us. Your book will be returned to you the moment we leave the city."

"The Murgans will not need to pursue us across the desert if they know where we are going. Can all your councillors be trusted?"

"That is a risk we will have to take, but we shall have a substantial number of guards to protect us. In any case it is difficult to imagine how the Murgans could act to thwart our purpose."

Small walked over to the window and stared at the distant mountains and the troubled atmosphere around their peaks, "If I have learned anything at all from my time with the Murgans," he said, "it is never to underestimate their determination and resource. If there is a way to stop us, they will find it."

Twenty-seven

The desert.

Nothing could have prepared him for this land stripped bare.

The endless space; the overwhelming silence. The bizarre paradox of nothingness and beauty. It was a place where the emptying of minds became a spiritual experience. It was an uplifting; a connecting with the divinity within. It was like slipping out of time.

The desert imposed its own rhythms. The sudden splendour of sunrise, the fell descent of dark: the furnace heat of the day, the icy chill of night: all left an indelible impression of the absolute power of the sun and the multitudinous if remote beauties of the stars. The infinite blue of the sky and the vivid hues of the sand had their allure but the desert was not a place for wandering or exploring. To survive it was necessary to know exactly where you were and exactly where you were heading. Such roads as existed were named not according to their destinations but according to the number of days it took to get there. Survival was more important than arrival. The desert was the domain of those with deep intuition of the waters underground: the diviners of secret springs, the discoverers of lost oases, the makers of wells.

The caravan of camels had seemed impressive in the market square, but in the immensity of the Zahar it was as insignificant as a dry weed tumbled along by the wind. The padding footsteps of the beasts; the tinkling of their harness; the echo-less voices of their riders; these sounds only served to emphasize the insignificance and vulnerability of the travellers. Words tended to be spoken more quietly in the desert; the spaces between them extended, their meanings more considered. Sensible people approached the sand ocean with respect: in the wise it inspired a feeling more akin to reverence.

For the first time since the Murgans had come to Alligor, Small was able to gather his thoughts and contemplate the situation in which he found himself. To his amazement he decided that he was engaged in an adventure, a real adventure. Moreover, this whole expedition was because of him. He had taken risks, horrible things had happened, but it had not been entirely for nothing. People had trusted his words; they had believed in the story he had told them. For the first time in his life he had real allies. He was in the company of men who would fight to defend him; and in all the wide world there were no men embarked upon a mission so important as this one. Unfortunately he did not have much confidence in its success. It had not been easy to find a woman about to give birth and who was willing to make the long journey. In the end the choice had been forced upon them. There was only one woman, and she came with a dubious pedigree. Kaspar had argued her case. She did not need to hold polite conversations; she did not need to walk about with a regal demeanour; she only had to arrive, give birth and leave, in that order. The Zimbolans would do the rest.

As far as anyone in Zimbola knew, their ruler was merely embarking on a long-planned diplomatic visit to the King of the South, a flamboyant if impoverished neighbour who ruled over a tiny portion of the desert which no-one else wanted. There was nothing out of the ordinary about the caravan save for a curtained palanquin slung between two camels. This gave rise to a certain amount of ribald speculation in the market place, but wherever such talk arose, there was Doglegs to talk sense, 'Kaspar was a very old man, and who could blame him for wanting to travel in comfort?'

Small had shared the palanquin with the pregnant woman and the midwife for the first day's journey. He was glad to escape from the woman's company. He found her coarse and sensual. She drank wine incessantly and complained loudly and profanely if it was kept from her. Her conversation was limited and frequently lewd. Even if the Abiru did not understand what she was saying, her behaviour was so degraded that they would have to be fools to believe that she was of a royal house. Whatever faint hopes Small had managed to retain that the mission might be a success, quickly drained away from him. The moment the curtains of the palanquin were opened, her raucous laughter and crude flirting with the camel drivers profaned the air. The soldiers exchanged wry glances and Melchior adopted a permanently pained expression. Only Kaspar seemed unaffected; his eyes always on the horizon and that same faint smile always on his lips.

The King of the South's capital was called M'Tafa. It had been built using large quantities of small flat stones laid dry without mortar in irregular courses. High-walled streets undulated their way between houses without right angles or sharp corners. M'Tafa was not a place of vistas or prospects. Its only open space was at the heart of the town. This was the place where water was drawn from a complex of wells, cisterns and reservoirs. Water was the wealth and power of the town. In order to cross the desert, caravans had to stop here to trade goods for water.

The Zimbolan caravan was met by an impressive display of military force. A large contingent of camel cavalry emerged from behind the town and manoeuvred aggressively around them. The riders all wore robes and turbans made from a cloth dyed deep indigo. Only their eyes were left uncovered. Kaspar and Melchior sat patiently immobile until the cavalry had raised the dust of the plain into a choking, obscuring cloud. Out of the swirling chaos of dust, animals and indigo cloth came a man on a pure white camel. His deep blue robe billowed and rippled like water in the wind. He rode towards the head of the caravan and unwound his turban from his face. To Small's amazement the man's skin was black as ebony wood. He touched the centre of his chest in greeting. His white teeth flashed in a broad smile.

"Kaspar, my brother," he said, "welcome!"

Small smiled too. The man's demeanour was so easy and benign that it was difficult not to. Kaspar returned the gesture of greeting and addressed the man.

"Greetings from Kaspar of Zimbola to Balthasar, King of the South."

The slight informality which had existed whilst the caravan was crossing the desert, evaporated as they entered M'Tafa. Whilst King Balthasar entertained his noble guests everyone else was shown into tiny cell-like rooms and left to their own devices. It was the hottest part of the day. The streets of the town were empty. Everybody sought the shade and dozed. Small tried this too but felt restless. After an hour had passed he went out and explored the town. The buildings baked in the sunlight. The dusty streets burnt his feet and the stone walls gave off waves of shimmering heat. The light was blinding: the shade impenetrable. Just walking made him exhausted and breathless. He came to an archway. Through the opening he could see a shady courtyard overhung with trees and vines. At its centre was a large stone basin filled with water. It looked a cool, restful and inviting place to be. He entered under the arch. He trailed his hand in the water and wiped his face with it. There was a stone bench set against a wall. He sat down. After a few minutes he lifted his legs up onto it. Not long after this he laid back and rested his head on the warm stone. Seconds later he was asleep.

He awoke to the sound of spattering water. He opened his eyes slowly. A man with black skin stood by the basin tipping cupped handfuls of water on his naked upper body. In this desert land it was an act of almost reckless profligacy; a squandering of riches; the perquisite of a king. The man turned. It was Balthasar.

Small jumped up from the bench, "I'm sorry," he said, "I did not know where I was. It looked so cool. I fell asleep. I did not mean to trespass on the royal precinct."

311

The king smiled. "Don't worry," he replied, "you haven't trespassed anywhere. This is where I come when I'm off duty. It is not good for a man always to be the king. It can be exhausting and irritating. Here I can be myself."

"But surely if you are born to rule you are the king wherever you are?"

"That may be so, but I was not always a king. Sit down and I will tell you my story."

Small sat on the warm lip of the stone basin. Balthasar fastened his sandals and then sat beside him.

"I was not always the ruler of this desert kingdom. When I was a young man like you, I belonged to a tribe who lived far away in a dark green forest south of the sand sea. The forest provided everything we needed: our food, our tools, our clothes and our houses. We were all very happy. We had our own king and we were all certain that he was the best of men. We were very loyal.

'One day strange men arrived. Their faces were much paler brown than ours and they wore bright coloured clothes. We did not fear them. We were many and they were few. The strangers wanted to barter. They offered our king beads of coloured glass threaded onto a string. We of course had nothing to trade since everything we possessed came from the forest. The strangers could gather everything they needed for free. Our king wanted the beads very badly. Imagine my surprise and horror when he agreed to exchange some of his own people for these trinkets. I found myself given as a slave to the strangers so that the king could wear shiny beads on his ankles. I protested strongly but my relatives and friends were afraid that if I didn't go then one of them might have to go in my place. When the strangers had chosen all the slaves they wanted, we were tied together and marched away from our forest and across the sand sea. It was my first lesson in politics.

'I was sold in the market place to a merchant who traded with ships' cargoes. He lived by the sea which I did not know existed before I saw it for the first time. You must understand that although I was now a slave, I was not constantly thinking of returning to the green forest. I was very angry with my king, and disappointed with my relatives and friends. If I went back what was to stop them giving me to some other strangers? My new master was not unkind, but more than this, I now saw how things were in this land of the north. I began to think about the condition of my tribe. My people had lived in the green forest since time began, and yet we did not seem to have progressed at all. We had no iron tools, we did not have the wheel, we had never learned to ride on animals, our houses were made from straw and leaves, none of us had ever made buildings of stone.

'At first I was ashamed at my own ignorance of such things, and I believed that those of us with black skins might not be so clever as other peoples, but then I realised that not all the northerners were so clever either. I had noticed that the cleverest people amongst them had a habit of making marks on pieces of parchment or tablets of wax. When I had learned the common language, I asked what this meant. I was told that this was called 'writing' and that you could use it to make a record of what someone else had said or done, or even what you yourself had thought about. This was a miracle indeed! Imagine that something as fleeting and insubstantial as a human thought could be made into a something so solid. With such writing in your hands you could know what a man had thought even after he had been dead a thousand years. I set myself the task of learning to read and write. My master encouraged me. His eyes were failing. He taught me how to tally the cargoes and estimate their value. I wrote contracts and agreements for him. I even wrote out his will. He wanted to leave me a large amount of money and give me my freedom. This worried me. Life as a freed slave was not secure. Anybody could kidnap me and put me back to work. I was only safe when I could prove that I belonged to someone powerful enough to defend their property. I insisted that he also provided me with a paper proving I belonged to such a person and was about his business.

'Even though I was a rich man after my master died, I was not comfortable amongst the northerners. I was not of their kind. Nor did I want to return to my own people. I was in between two countries. Perhaps that is why I decided to come here to this oasis in the sand sea. In those days it was just a pool of mud with a few date palms. But all the caravans had to stop here to fill their water skins. I had a dream of building a house of stone and planting some fruit trees. I bought some of my people from the slavers to help me do the work. To each one of them I gave a piece of paper on which it was written that they belonged to the Master of M'Tafa. Then I taught them to read and write. We put up more buildings, planted more gardens. I bought more people. I acquired camels. I taught my people to ride them. In the end I gave them arms. M'Tafa was then a power. Travellers had to trade goods for water or be turned away. The oasis had become a kingdom and I was its ruler. So you see I am the only king in the world who rules over a nation entirely made up of people he has bought and paid for. I purchased my kingdom."

Small thought about this. "I do not understand. Your people are educated, armed and provided with transport. Yet they are slaves. Why do they not simply ride away and live lives on their own? By what power do you hold them here?"

Balthasar smiled. "Let me show you," he said and then called out in a loud voice for his Captain. A large figure dressed in blue and carrying a long curved sword jogged into the courtyard.

"Captain, if you caught one of our people committing a crime, let us say polluting the water, or stealing from a caravan, or causing trouble with someone else's marriage, what would be a fitting punishment?"

"That person would have to surrender the paper proving he was a slave of the King of the South. He would not then belong here in M'Tafa. This criminal would then be set entirely free to wander wherever in the world he wanted except here."

Small was baffled. According to all the authors, the penalty for committing a crime was always to be locked up in a jail or sold into slavery. Here the punishment was to be entirely free to go anywhere and do anything. "But Captain, you live here as a slave. Would you not prefer to be a free agent and ride to the ends of the earth?"

"I have visited other lands and yet I am still proud to be a slave of M'Tafa. This is my place, these are my people. With our own hands we have built our kingdom from nothing. Wandering the earth is for goats, sheep and wild animals. To belong; to serve; to be loyal: these are things of real value. I would die for my people and they for me. My belly is not empty and my soul is full. I am content. Who else in this world of trouble can say such a thing?"

Small was not entirely convinced. He turned back to Balthasar. "This is all well and good because you are a kind and benevolent ruler, but what if you were cruel and tyrannical?"

"That is a problem with any form of government. No matter what type of government you employ, a good ruler will make life pleasant and a bad ruler will make life unpleasant. A bad ruler does not understand the nature of rule. The relationship between the king and his subjects is reciprocal. Here in M'Tafa the slaves are the property of their master but the contract which makes them so is given into their hands. They can simply tear it to pieces if they want. The ruler of M'Tafa is also a bound man. If he neglects his responsibilities then he too can be set free. There are two hundred armed men here to do the job."

Small indicated his understanding by nodding. King Balthasar lifted his blue robe from around his hips and shrugged it onto his shoulders. "If I am not mistaken you are the young man from Alligor. King Kaspar has told me about you. Your mission intrigues me. I have already heard about these Murgans. It is rumoured that they despise kings and they have promised to set everybody free. You can understand that this worries my people. That is why I have decided to accompany your caravan to the land of the Abiru. I want to see for myself what the Murgans are like before we receive them in M'Tafa."

When the Zimbolans set out next day, their numbers had been swollen by twenty camels each with its blue-swathed rider. The caravan was now a formidable power. It would be immune from attacks by irregular forces. They took the twenty-day road heading east across the sand sea. The men of M'Tafa led the way. They knew every oasis, every water camp, every dry river bed, every nook where moisture lurked in this hostile landscape.

It was an anxious time for Small. Velik had said that the hairy star would appear in the sky when the sun entered the house of the Ram. They were already in the third month. Night followed night without any sign of the prodigy. No-one mentioned the star, but he felt all eyes upon him. Velik had seemed so certain about it, but ancient books were not always trustworthy. Prophecies too were notoriously unreliable. Might he have been too gullible? The thought that he might let everybody down caused Small to writhe in embarrassment. At the end of each day he waited anxiously for the stars to come out. Night after night he stared at the jewels scattered on the velvet of the cosmos until he fell asleep. A week went by. The uncertainty tormented his waking hours and disturbed his sleep. When finally he was wakened by someone shaking his arm he thought at first it was another dream.

"Look! Look! It has come!"

The star and its tail hung immobile and awesome across a quarter of the sky. It gave out an eerie spectral light. How sudden it was. Small had wished so hard for it to appear that he felt that he had somehow conjured it into existence. He was almost too terrified by it to feel relief. It was deeply disturbing to see something so prodigious disturb the permanence of the heavens. They passed over the remaining desert with a renewed sense of purpose. Even though the comet had been long predicted, it was difficult not to feel the sense of supernatural coincidence which it lent to the mission. If this did not impress the Abiru then nothing would.

The land of the Abiru was under the Murgan shadow. The influence of the strangers manifested itself in a restless and aggressive way of life. Everyone was busy. Everything was in flux. The roads were crowded with harassed people who did not seem used to travel. No-one smiled and no-one sang. In every town they passed through, groups of rough men with heavy accents would offer their services as bodyguards. Everywhere old and beautiful buildings were being demolished. In their place huge, high square monoliths were being built. They were exactly as Velik had described Murgan architecture: without ornament of any kind and with a myriad of identical window openings. This and their inhuman scale made them look alien and forbidding. They occupied the land and stole the sky. No matter where they lived in the town, at the same time each day, the inhabitants felt the sudden chill as the dark shadow of Murga blotted out the bright sunshine. An atmosphere of anxiety and oppression hung over the whole country like the stench of the Murgans' greasy meat and pungent vegetables. The yellow M of Murga was everywhere daubed on their buildings.

The Zimbolan caravan was forced to camp in the open fields outside the towns because there never seemed to be enough room for them at inns and hostelries. Some kind of government order had put half the population on the roads. At first the Zimbolans told anyone who would listen that they were following the hairy star, but this seemed to make the locals even more wary. They suspected Kaspar and Melchior of being necromancers or hellraisers. When Small asked Melchior where they were going he explained to him that they were heading for a small town up country and not far from the capital. This town was associated with a famous royal dynasty from the time of the prophecy. They would stay in the town until the woman gave birth. If all went smoothly, the woman and child would immediately be taken out of the country by the M'Tafans. The Zimbolans would then travel on to the capital to pay the obligatory courtesy visit to the current King of the Abiru.

Small could only think positively about the plan when they were on the road. Inside the towns he saw the *ulvis* on too many faces. With each town they passed through he felt more and more that the question was not if, but when the Murgans would act against them. He began to carry his book bag inside his clothes where it could not be seen.

316

Twenty-eight

After a heavy day's travelling, the Zimbolan caravan entered the town just after dusk. Because it was on a steep hill the space within the walls was extremely cramped. Jumbled buildings overhung narrow winding streets seething with people. It was only with the greatest of difficulty that they could force their way through to the centre of the town. Balthasar shouted the order to halt and dismount. Small was dismayed by the tide of humanity which surrounded him. He felt his camel being jostled and pushed. This town was even more full of people than the others had been, but at least now they had reached their goal. The woman was very near her time. The midwife had said so. Surely nothing could go wrong now?

Almost before the Zimbolans had knelt their camels, the Warholl were sealing off the town. Puttfark appointed men to blockade the roads and then galloped his horse back to the old byre which was to be his headquarters. He dismounted and pushed his way in through the door. A smoky lamp was burning. By its yellow light he could see that Okni, his bizarre cosmetics streaked by sweat and tinted dark by the dust of the road, was waiting for him.

Puttfark drank deeply from a skin of water which hung against the wall before he spoke. "We don't know what they are up to yet but they are definitely looking for lodgings in the town. This looks like their final destination. Before they get too settled I will go into the town and grab the boy."

"I think not."

Puttfark spun round. He had not noticed the dark figure leaning casually against the wall by the door. It was Rottko.

"You are no longer in control of this operation," he said, "I am."

The assassin put his hand inside his robe. Puttfark went for his dagger. Rottko smiled as he withdrew his hand. He held a small slip of parchment in his fingertips.

"This is a contract signed by the Paymaster himself. It seems that our rich Uncle back in Murga has taken a personal interest in this particular operation. Perhaps he has been hearing some disturbing things about you. Thinks you might have been too long in the field. Thinks you might be letting things slip - getting involved - going native. Thinks you might even have caught … *morality*."

Puttfark turned pale with anger. "Our Uncle can think what he likes. The Paymaster can deal with whoever he wants. I am still going to get that boy. This is personal business."

"No," Rottko pushed himself away from the wall. "The Warholl are going into town to get the boy."

"How can that be? They don't even know what he looks like."

Rottko waved the slip of parchment at him. "You haven't read the contract. It is between the Paymaster and Okni here. The town is to be sealed off. At daybreak the Warholl will go in and kill every male child of whatever age who has not yet managed to grow a beard."

"That is insane! You will provoke the whole province into revolt. People will never forget a massacre of children. Trade will collapse. Business will suffer."

"Our employer seems to think that the situation is very serious." Rottko held the contract to the lamp and began to read:

"All male children of whatever age lodging in the aforementioned town to be killed. The book if found to be destroyed as soon as possible. Extreme measures to be taken against any foreigner or foreigners who have read the book, seen the book, or who know of the existence of the book. All expenses of whatever nature will be covered. All personnel are indemnified for any act. All personnel are expendable. No other collateral considerations to be taken into account."

Puttfark recognized the phrasing. Such contracts were only ever issued to counter a clear and present threat to the Murgan state itself. There must be more to this than just the book. There was something happening here which was far bigger than he had realised. The whole operation had spiralled in importance. Too stunned to react, his gaze shifted from Rottko's triumphal smirk to Okni, eyes glittering, jaw slack, drugged with expectation. Puttfark realised that he had been outmanoeuvred. He would never again be given a government contract. He was finished. Unless ..."

Rottko read his mind. "Just in case you were thinking of saving your skin by a little private enterprise," he said, "I have had your horse requisitioned. 'All acts will be indemnified' remember?"

Puttfark also remembered that 'All personnel were expendable'. He wrestled down his anger and strode quickly out of the building, scarcely believing that Rottko was foolish enough to let him go. Outside, the twilight was alive with noise and movement. Wherever he looked there were crowds of armed men: on horseback, on foot, with bows and with spears. More were arriving. This was a serious force; almost an army. It must have cost a fortune. His horse was not where he had left it. Rottko was not a man to make idle threats, he was however a lone entrepreneur. The assassin had no experience of management. This job was too complex, too important for him. He had already made a mistake in thinking that it would be enough merely to take the horse: letting him walk out of the byre had been another.

He recognised a familiar face in the throng. "Kunig!" he shouted, "What the God is going on?"

Kunig seemed embarrassed to be seen with him. "Big business," he murmured. "Big, big business."

Puttfark grabbed Kunig by the front of his robe. "Tell," he said.

"It's been going on for months. The people have problems adjusting to the new order. There has been a lot of talk recently. It seems the locals have a prophecy that some leaderman will be born who will chuck out all foreigners and bring back the old ways. The Paymaster had the idea of getting all the families to go back to their home towns - for tax purposes."

"Tax purposes? If you want to collect taxes you need to know where people are living, not where their fathers come from."

"Right! Right. But the Paymaster was only interested in having all the possible candidates for fulfilling the prophecy in one place at the same time. Now with that great comet hanging up there and everybody getting excited, Uncle wants this story stifled once and for all - just in case. Our orders are to make sure the prophecy ends here and ends now. It's going to be a bloodbath."

Kunig scurried away into the darkness. Puttfark was appalled. A bloodbath would mean resentment, enemies, disruption of trade. The business of Murga had always been business. Now it seemed that stupid stories were even bigger business. Could the great Murgan world order really be overthrown by stories? If Murgans had to read or listen to every story in the world - just in case - how much time would they have left for making money?

He strolled around the camp for some time until he found what he was looking for: a young man of slight build on a fine strong horse: a young man who was not with a group: a young man who seemed unsure of where he was supposed to be or what he was supposed to be doing.

"You there!" he bellowed, "Come with me."

The figure swathed in burnoose and turban turned towards him.

"Are you deaf?"

The rider hesitated, then lifted the rein and pulled the horse's head round. The horse stopped frustratingly out of reach. Puttfark could not reach the bridle.

"We need more people to blockade the road. Follow me."

The nearest road block was several hundred paces distant. Puttfark hoped the young rider would not be too suspicious of an officer without a horse. When they reached the makeshift barrier the men he had stationed there earlier were still at their posts. To his relief they saluted him. Rottko was an incompetent. No eye for detail.

"This man has to patrol inside the perimeter. I shall show him where."

The men at the barrier exchanged glances, then stepped aside.

Puttfark called back over his shoulder, "Remember, nobody goes in nobody comes out - especially young boys - understand?"

Over the next ridge the ground fell away into a rocky depression. The little town sat on the opposite side of the valley.

"Get off the horse and come over here," he said to the rider. The slim youth slipped from the saddle and landed lightly on the ground. He bent down and trapped the reins under a boulder. The horse dropped its nose to the grass. The youth walked over to the roadside. Infuriatingly he kept just out of reach of a sudden dagger blow.

"Can you see that road where it drops down from the gate? There are two small trees ..." As he spoke he backed slowly away from the youth, "... just to the right of it." The young rider had his back to the man in white and was staring into the darkness. Puttfark turned quickly and bent down to free the reins. A sharp piercing pain in his back blotted out the whole world. Instinctively he straightened and turned, dagger in hand, but the youth had danced back out of reach. Warm blood coursed down Puttfark's back. He knew that the wound was fatal even before his legs buckled and he fell to his knees. He could not understand what had happened. He had picked the youth at random. He was only a boy. Why? How had he known? He fell forward onto his face. The last thing he heard was the soft voice of the young rider calling the horse.

"Come Lucifer, come."

Overhead the clouds parted to reveal the night sky. The great comet hung over the land like a curved sword.

In the town it was bedlam itself. Hundreds of people had returned from the capital to their ancestral home. The Zimbolan caravan was besieged in the main street by the press of the crowds. The soldiers stood guard with their backs against the camels. They were irritable and angry at being constantly jostled and buffeted by the passing multitude. It was almost like being in a deep and turbulent river. It did not take long to discover that the inns were full, the houses crammed to their rooftops, and that even outbuildings and animal shelters had all been taken over and occupied by the throng. Tents had been pitched on every patch of open ground and every thoroughfare was jammed with mules, donkeys, camels and horses. After nearly an hour of searching, the men given the task of finding accommodation had all reported back. There was nothing.

"Everywhere is taken."

"That is impossible!" Melchior shouted, having to make himself heard above the cacophony of beasts and men.

Kaspar seemed to be the only one not affected by the tumult around him. "It is only important that the woman has lodgings here in the town whilst she gives birth. We can camp outside in the fields. Bring her here and we shall see if we cannot melt the hard heart of an innkeeper. The combination of sympathy and a large amount of gold should do the trick, especially if there are soldiers to support our request."

Small found the press of the crowd alarming and unsettling. Being used to the silence of Libraries there was a limit to the amount of random noise and movement he could tolerate. It seemed to be taking a very long time to fetch the woman. Perhaps she was drunk again. Finally a small and nervous delegation arrived in front of the King and his councillor.

"She is gone."

"Gone!" Melchior shouted irritably, "What do you mean 'gone'"

"It seems she has run off with the handsome camel driver."

"How can that be? She was about to give birth! She cannot have gone. She will need the midwife at any time now."

"Highness, she is gone: the camel driver is gone, and a camel is missing."

Kaspar shook his head in disbelief, "Women with child are strange creatures but I don't think that even I would choose to give birth amidst all this chaos and noise. Perhaps she has merely persuaded this man to take her somewhere quieter. Balthasar can you and your riders comb the countryside? We will continue to search the town."

Small could hardly believe that having come this far the mission might after all be in vain. He fought back a sick feeling of disappointment and frustration. Then, unable to sit doing nothing he slid off his camel and thrust his way into the turbulent tide of humanity which surged in the streets.

It seemed that everybody he met was too busy with their own problems to listen to a stranger. "Have you seen a woman big with child?" he asked them, "She may have a man with her." Mostly he was ignored, or else given a distracted shake of the head. They were all too busy finding somewhere, something, someone; jostling each other in their haste to be settled. He worked his way down the main street until there were no more houses. The last building was an inn. It was rowdy and loud. A woman sang, a dulcimer played, men clapped and stamped. Inside it was hot and smoky from the lamps. Small pushed his way through the people. A man, harassed and sweating, was serving drinks across a trestle. "I'm looking for a woman," Small said to him, "She is about to have a child. Have you seen her?"

"What? Oh, yes. Through the back: with the animals."

Small was elated. He ran through into the dark backyard of the inn. At first he saw nothing; then a slight glimmer in the corner caught his eye. There was a cave of some sort. It stank of animals. Inside he saw a man and a young woman. The man was not the camel driver. The woman was not the woman he was looking for, but she held a tiny baby at her breast to suck. A baby was a baby. Perhaps she would need the midwife. Kaspar must be told right away.

"There is a sort of cave. It is used for animals. A young girl has just had a baby - a little boy. Our midwife is with her now."

"What is she like?"

"Very young. A decent girl - the husband looks respectable too - but he is much older than she."

"Perhaps …" Kaspar paused for a moment whilst he stroked his cheek then, "She might have to do." He turned to his captain, "Light up braziers and torches. Sound the trumpets. Assemble the men. Make a big show of it. Make sure the locals notice what is happening. Melchior and I will speak with her. When Balthazar returns tell him where we are."

Small led the two old men to the cave behind the inn. Kaspar spoke briefly to the husband then, with Melchior's help, he knelt down beside the girl. He held her hand for some time while he spoke to her in a gentle voice.

When Balthasar eventually returned from his mission, he was anxious and disturbed.

"I almost could not get in - all the locals are outside wanting to know what is going on. Your soldiers can hardly hold them back."

Melchior drew him to one side and signalled for him to lower his voice. Balthasar continued in urgent undertones, "My men could not find the pregnant woman anywhere, but they did discover that this whole town is being surrounded by armed men. The Murgans are in charge and they have many soldiers, cut-throats and mercenaries, even the local king's army is there. They have not pitched their tents. For this reason I think they will attack soon. I do not know what they intend to do, but if they have bought soldiers then it will involve killing. We do not have men enough to fight them, especially in such streets as these. I think that we should get away now, as quickly as possible, whilst it is still dark and before they have deployed all their men."

Melchior tugged nervously at his beard. Balthasar became aware for the first time of the girl and her baby. Melchior replied to his puzzled expression with a smile and a shrug, "Bend your knee your Highness, at the very least you are in the presence of the goddess Fortuna."

Kaspar received the bad news calmly. "Balthasar is a wise man. He knows his troops. A soldier who would rather march off into the night than sleep warm in his tent is indeed a frightened man. Our mission here is perhaps concluded. We should go whilst we still can. Let me talk to the husband."

Kaspar drew the man off into the darkness whilst Melchior and Balthasar knelt by the mother and baby. The two men murmured wonderingly as they lifted the tiny hands of the baby with their big rough fingers. Small felt strangely moved by the sight of these two serious grown-up men chuckling over the tiny infant. In fact there was something disorienting about the whole atmosphere in the cave. The day and the night had been long and stressful; perhaps that was why he felt so strangely light-headed.

Kaspar emerged from the darkness. "The husband will accept the gold and the other gifts. He is quite alarmed by the crowds and the fuss. I have told him about the soldiers around the town. He thinks it will be safer for his family to leave with us. He will accept our protection. His wife will be more comfortable in the palanquin than here, and the midwife will be able to tend her until she is strong again."

The ancient ruler's face was suddenly grey and drawn with fatigue. He was old; it had been a long day; it was late. He wanted nothing more than to lie down and sleep. He clutched at Balthasar's sleeve, "My friend," he said, "give the order."

Balthasar ran to the entrance, "Captain!" he shouted, "Call in the pickets, load the camels, assemble the men, we leave within the half hour."

Rottko sat brooding over the events of the day. He was disturbed by a feeling that he was not completely in control of what was happening. He had not been told that the forces would be so large. Organising them all in the darkness had meant confusion and delay. No-one had thought to tell the early arrivals that the leadership had changed. He should have had Puttfark killed, but now the man in white was nowhere to be found. What if the Warholl weren't up to the job? What if they took too long? What if the townspeople realised what was going on?

There was a rustle of silk and a clink of weaponry. Okni entered.

"Our agent with the caravan is here. He wants his payment."

"Is the Zimbolan whore dead?"

"Yes."

"And the baby?"

"Both."

"Send someone to check the bodies and then pay the man off...Okni?"

"Mr. Rottko?"

"Tomorrow will be no ordinary operation. The Paymaster thinks you and your men should get out of the country as soon as the job is done. Take a ship to New Adam. Disappear."

"I hadn't planned on hanging around."

"Are you sure your people will do what is required?"

"It is nothing new for them. It is what they do best."

"Just make sure they do this job thoroughly. No stopping to enjoy yourselves. You understand me?"

"Perfectly."

"Go."

Despite the lateness of the hour the streets of the town were still crowded. All was dark and confusion. Even after weeks of travelling, Small was not an expert rider of camels. In the open desert the beasts had simply followed each other's tails. The only skill he had needed was to avoid falling off. Here in the heart of the town he was having trouble making his mount do anything at all. He tried desperately to make the camel turn and follow the rest of the Zimbolan caravan. The beast was tired. It bellowed, spat and tried to bite anyone within reach of its long neck. This provoked the inevitable retaliation. A passer-by whacked it on the neck with a stick. The camel plunged and reared amongst the tormenting multitude. Small sat low and clung to the saddle to avoid being thrown.

The violent motion stopped abruptly. Small sat up. The camel was moving purposefully forward. A man had grabbed the halter, turned the beast around and was leading the beast up the main street. The rest of the caravan was almost out of sight. In the darkness and confusion no-one seemed to have noticed that Small had been left behind. Small attempted to urge the camel onwards. The man cast a worried look over his shoulder. Small did not recognise him but did not have time to think about it. The next moment the camel turned abruptly. The man was leading him into a dark and almost deserted side alley. Small felt an instant premonition of danger. This was no short-cut to avoid the crowds.

"Hey! You! Stop! Where are taking me?" he shouted.

The man did not even turn but began to pull harder at the camel's halter. Small was alarmed. There were figures moving down at the dark end of the alley. Alarm turned to terror. He slipped from the saddle onto the ground and sprinted back towards the main street. Just as he was about to force his way into the crowds, a large white horse blocked the exit from the alley. He tried to duck under its belly but the rider reached down and grabbed him by the hair. The pain blinded him. He felt his head lifted and twisted. He blinked away tears of agony. He found himself staring uncomprehendingly into the rider's face.

"I thought so," Domina said, "... still no idea of how to look after yourself."

The horse was moving forward even as she pulled him up and across her lap. He struggled awkwardly till he was sitting astride the beast and in front of the girl. He caught a last glimpse of the alley. The men and the camel had vanished. Domina urged the horse onwards faster and faster through the crowds. The horse was like a ship cutting through an angry sea. People screamed as they threw themselves out of the way. Many were knocked to the ground. Small remembered just how ruthless Murgans could be. As the horse reached a canter the crowds parted to let them pass. By the time they were galloping towards the town gate, the terrified pedestrians had cleared a path for them. The town guards shouted and brandished their swords but wisely did not attempt to stop the horse. Lucifer careered through the gate and down into the darkness. Domina did not attempt to slow the horse.

"You can slow down now," Small shouted over his shoulder, "I'm with the caravan that just left the town. We will easily overtake it now."

"We aren't joining any caravan," Domina replied, "This whole town is surrounded by Murgan mercenaries. The caravan will be lucky to fight its way out. We are going cross-country."

"Surrounded? What are they after?"

"You - and your book - amongst other things. Just shut up and trust me on this."

The clouds broke. The landscape was again bathed in the eerie light of the comet. On the road ahead Small could see a ghostly dust cloud. Metal flashed in the moonlight. It was the Zimbolan caravan. The Zimbolans and their outriders were riding at full tilt with weapons drawn towards the cordon. Balthasar's cavalry experience would take them through. There was no chance of catching up with them. He felt Domina move in the saddle. Lucifer veered off the road and cantered over the broken ground.

"This is where I came in," she said, "There's a small sheep track and no guard. A few more minutes and we will be out of danger."

"I'm so happy to see you well again. I would have come back to you but ..."

"You might have tried but you would never have made it." Her voice was weak and husky. "Sath'an only knows what you have been up to, but my countrymen have marked you as an enemy of the Murgan state. I have never seen so much money and resources put together, and all just to get you."

"Well I won't be doing anything else now, so after I've put the books back in the Library we ... that is, I ... can go anywhere."

"You have no idea what it means to be an enemy of Murga. They will never, ever stop looking for you. We must get as far away as possible from here and then lie as low as we can for as long as we can."

"Domina, the deal we had. I think you have done enough. You are not well yet. You don't have to help me if it will be so dangerous. So many people have been hurt because of me ..."

"It's not the deal. I'll do it anyway."

Small thought about this, then asked simply, "Why?"

Domina said nothing, but then Small felt her body melt against his back and her head laid against his neck. She gave him the briefest of hugs, then before he could react she sat back in the saddle and kicked Lucifer on.

Baco led his horse feeling angry and humiliated. He was not used to being treated like a common soldier. He had not had time to change his dress in four days and his hairdo had fallen over. What his face looked like he could only guess. He swatted angrily at the bedraggled ribbon which hung down in front of his face. For the hundredth time his ankle went over on the uneven ground. This time the pointed heel of his shoe broke. Curse that horse for going lame! He took off the broken shoe and examined it forlornly in the comet light. He looked around him. He had absolutely no idea where he was. Then he saw

326

another horse approaching. He peered into the night. Perhaps it was one of his companions coming to look for him. He could not quite make out the rider, but the horse looked like a Murgan thoroughbred. He lifted his arm in greeting as the horse came closer, then, seeing that it was not going to stop, Baco reached for the double-curved horn and hardwood bow which hung from his saddle. He strung it and nocked an arrow into place almost before the horse had passed him. It was a difficult shot through a dust cloud in starlight; the target was receding fast. He did not see where the arrow went. The horse galloped on: the rider did not fall. He watched it out of sight before he tugged at his lame horse and limped on. He wondered if the cupid's bow of rouge which he had traced around his lips was smudged. War was hell.

"We did it! We broke through!" Small was elated. Domina made a kind of snorting noise. The horse galloped on for some distance before he felt the reins tighten against his thighs. The horse slowed to a standstill as it was held back. Small felt Domina lay her head gently on his shoulder again. He could smell her hair. She leant her whole body against him. Something hard pressed into his back. He turned and was just in time to stop her slipping from the saddle. A sharp black point stuck obscenely from beneath her breast. It glistened in the comet light.

"No! Oh no," he murmured. The shock had numbed and disoriented him. He felt as if his mind and body had drifted slightly apart. He acted as if in a dream. It was like falling into the water cistern, but this time he was drowning in horror and disbelief.

He lifted her down from the horse as gently as he could, but it was difficult to make her comfortable on the ground. The long shaft of the arrow slanted out from between her shoulders at an awkward angle. He cradled her tenderly in his arms. With every movement she made little gasping noises. He wiped the hair from her face. The months of illness had almost stolen her beauty. Her face was deathly pale. Her cheeks were hollow; her eyes had dark rings under them, but the irises were still bright and lovely. A tiny image of the comet hung in each dark pupil.

"What can I do?" he said, "Tell me what to do. Should I take the arrow out?"

The girl did not speak. She stared straight ahead mouth slightly open as if startled and eyes wide as if concentrating hard upon something far off. Small realised that the wound was very, very bad.

"Don't die," he sobbed, "Please don't die."

The gasping noises had become irregular and less frequent. Small felt completely and utterly helpless and impotent. He looked round at the empty midnight landscape and then up at the night sky. He was in desperate need. He opened his soul to the universe.

"O Divine Author of all things here in this tangled world, please do not let this girl's story end here. Heal her I beseech you."

The stars flew on through the clouds in their mystic formations. They had never seemed so cold and distant. They were the very image of inevitability. There was no help to be had. 'We all die alone', the philosopher had said, but Domina was not alone. He was suddenly overwhelmed with caring and protective feelings towards the girl. Perhaps it was all he could do to help her. To tell her. To ease her way out of this horrible world. He sought for the words and in the end they came.

"I love you." he said.

He thought that her eyes focused for a second. He felt for her hand and held it in his. He thought he felt her respond with a feeble pressure on his fingers. He wanted to hug her to him but was afraid of hurting her. The little gasps had been replaced by strange wet noises. He was paralysed with fear.

Her body convulsed in a spasm which almost lifted her out of his arms.

"God ..." she said. But whether it was a curse or a prayer only the Divine Author would ever know. Her body went limp: her head lolled against his shoulder. The landscape went dark.

Epilogue

The empty plain of Alligor stretched away to every horizon. It had been poor and infertile before, but now the people had gone, it looked windswept and deeply depressing. It seemed that the desert was reclaiming its own. An advancing tide of drought and dust had submerged all the roads and tracks. The exhausted soil had neither weight nor texture enough to withstand even the slightest of breezes. It lay in thick drifts across his path and dragged at the horse's hooves. A few pale unhealthy-looking plants pocked the surface of the ground.

Small was perplexed. Alligor was a substantial landmark. On such a featureless plain it should have been visible from far away, and yet he could not see it anywhere. In the far distance there was a low, dark hill. It looked as if there might once have been some sort of rough structure on it. If he climbed to the top he would be able to scan the horizon. He tried to urge Lucifer into a trot, but the animal was exhausted and plodded monotonously onwards. The hill as he approached it was much larger than he had supposed. It seemed to be a great ruin buried in dunes of drifted sand. As he urged Lucifer up the slope the wind roused itself. The air around him filled with strange whirling, tumbling leaves. One caught in the horse's mane. Without thinking he twitched it loose with thumb and forefinger. In the moment before the wind snatched it away again, he saw the exquisite ancient calligraphy merging into the charred edges of the fragment of manuscript. He had found Alligor.

For many hours Small sat atop the mound of debris and rubbish which had once been the Book-city. Fire had been the main agent of the catastrophe. Great charred beams jutted from the tumbled stones. Each gust of wind lifted scorched and blackened fragments of parchment and vellum which swarmed like angry bees from the moraines of rubble. In his mind's eye he saw each gallery take light; every book on every shelf curling layer by layer, igniting leaf by leaf; rolls spewing flames like dragons. He saw the fire leaping from shelf to shelf and finally to the wooden ceilings and the upper levels. He saw the floors collapse one by one, sending showers of burning fragments of knowledge out of the windows and into the sky. Finally his beloved roof world returned to its primal matter; the lead and copper melting, bubbling, flowing in volcanic streams; avalanches of roof tiles sliding into the inferno as the standing water exploded into gouts of steam.

Fire alone had not wrought the utter devastation around him. The outer walls of Alligor had been thick enough to withstand any conflagration and yet their stones lay tumbled onto the ashes. The masonry must have been levered out of its beds or else mined with strong iron tools. The Murgans were always thorough in what they did. He sat holding his head in his hands. He had lost all his bearings. He could neither think nor act. He was too numbed even to weep for what was lost. He felt as if it was the end of the world.

After some time had passed he became aware of sounds: stones rattled against stones. Then he felt a warm furry feeling on his leg.

"Sardanapalus!" The cat rubbed itself on him. It purred with pleasure.

"Small?"

He jerked upright, "Old?"

The ancient librarian was standing over him with a quizzical smile on his dirty face. "It *is* you!" he said wonderingly, "It's Small come back to Alligor!"

There was more scuffling amongst the ruins. Other scarecrow figures appeared, picking their way amongst the rubble. Sly was one; haggard, sunken-cheeked, eyes ringed with dark shadows. Then, unbelievably, Velik, only recognizable from the remains of his moustache. Tentpole brought up the rear, cursing not a little and pausing often to grip his knees.

Sly started to tell him the story of the end of Alligor. When Puttfark returned without his men he had been in a terrible fury. He had straightaway stabbed Spoon through the heart for poisoning the food. The menials fled into the night and never returned. The next day strange soldiers had arrived. Men who dressed as women. Puttfark rode off with them. Not all the Murgans had eaten from the pot. Those who were still healthy stood guard at the Gate to stop anyone else leaving. Even the women buckled on weapons and took their turn. Puttfark returned several days later without the strange soldiers and the Murgans who had been left behind began to pack up their things right away. It seemed that it had always been their intention to burn the library. They had put the pots of Meton where there was lots of timber construction. When they set light to them they burned fiercely. There were too many strong fires for the librarians to fight. The Murgans had also locked every door they could. Some librarians had been unable to escape. Dim had never been found.

Velik interrupted Sly's tale, "They intended to burn us too! After they set the fires, they even fastened the Great Gate to prevent anyone escaping. I was almost burnt. I only survived by descending the rope into the well. Can you imagine it - at my age and with a cat in a bag?"

Old tugged at Small's sleeve, "We were all locked in the refectory whilst they fired the library. They did not know about the cellars you see! When the fire came in through the roof we went down into the dark." He jerked his hand at the devastated city, "It took us weeks to dig ourselves out. This is what we found when we emerged. Everyone else had died or left Alligor, only we four remained behind. They must have brought in hundreds of workers to pull down the walls. They left their filth everywhere."

Small listened with mounting despair in his heart. "It's all my fault. I'm so sorry Old. I tried my best but I did everything wrong. I failed in everything. Dim was killed because of me. Spoon was stabbed for something I did. Domina died saving me. I led the Murgans to Zimbola and now they rule the whole world. Even Alligor is destroyed."

"No! No! You mustn't think so. It was the Murgans who caused all that. It had always been their plan to destroy this place utterly. It was they who murdered Dim, and Spoon and your friend. And hear this, not everything was lost my boy." Old gripped him by the shoulders, "You see the Murgans never knew how much of Alligor lay beneath the plain. They only saw what was on the surface. They never saw the granaries. They did not know about the well springs. Nor did they ever explore the catacombs and underground tunnels. They did not know that for over a thousand years every librarian who died was interred with a copy of his favourite book. The fire was unable to penetrate the living rock under the book city. So you see there is still a substantial library under the ground. The task of prising the books from the fingers of the dead may be unpleasant, even macabre, but it would be a small price to pay for such treasures as we might find."

Small shook his head, "You don't understand. The whole world belongs to the Murgans. The plain of Alligor is now a desert. All the people have fled. There is no food anymore. How can the library survive?"

"We have survived!" said Old.

"We have fresh water," added Velik, "and lots of old grain left. Where there is water, plants will grow."

"And there is a little food left," this from Sly, "we took it from the kitchen - and there is plenty of charcoal for cooking it. We do not have so many mouths to feed now."

"The birds still come to drink and when they do, Velik catches them," said Tentpole, who had clearly been impressed by the achievement.

331

Old belied the obvious optimism of the librarians by pointing at the horse, "Have you perhaps brought any food with you?"

Small shook his head regretfully.

"Is that food you have in your book bag?"

"No, I only have what I took with me: the manuscript and another book."

"What! You have the manuscript!" Old was amazed. A murmur of puzzlement passed among the others.

"Yes of course, that's why I left Alligor. I had to keep it from the Murgans." Small reached down into his book bag and pulled out first *The Mirror of Almeira* and then the brown leather box containing the manuscript. Old shrank back in horror. Small told his story in as few words as he could. He did not attempt to explain what the manuscript was about, only that it was both poison and antidote, spell and counter-spell, and very, very dangerous to possess.

After he had finished, Old raised his eyes to the heavens opened his hands bookwise and said a prayer to the Divine Author. "Alligor will be preserved and this manuscript shall be our talisman. Evil rises like a tide in the world, but tides always ebb. Perhaps one day someone will come searching for such a book. The library must be waiting for them."

There was a general pause whilst everyone thought about this. It was Velik who broke the silence, "Perhaps we will not have to wait. Perhaps we can set our own wind racing across the plain; a divine wind made from the breath of poets and story tellers; a wind which will lift the Murgan rubbish which is blighting the earth and carry it back whence it came. You say that we are living in a desert. If so then what we can draw up from our deep wells will be worth more than gold. Although now we are only a water camp in an arid waste, one day this could be a caravanserai again. Then the merchants who pass by can carry our stories to the ends of the earth. Perhaps we can even earn our crusts by telling our stories."

Sly narrowed his eyes in the familiar way, "I will begin by writing down the story of our young friend's adventures. Such a tale needs to be told. The people will hear about the Abiru prophecy coming true and understand what has happened here."

Small shook his head sadly, "We were only in the town for a few hours. There was so much going on that night that the people would have forgotten all about us and the baby by the time they woke up. Why would anybody remember what happened? It was probably all a waste of time."

"But that's what books are for; to stop people forgetting."

He looked at each of the old men in turn. They would be lucky if they had ten years left between the lot of them. Then he would be the only one left. He was trapped here. But where else was there for him to go? The Murgans would always be looking for him. Perhaps there might be a way to make a M'tafa out of Alligor: but alone ...?

Old smiled and put his arm around Small's shoulder. "So young man, it seems that the first thing you will have to do is to get used to your new name."

"What new name is that?"

"Why, '*Hero*' of course.

Small was too heartsick to care. These days he only went over and over the events of his recent life; torturing himself for what might have been. "But I made so many mistakes," he said.

"That may well be. Nobody is perfect. But you lived to tell the tale, and that is sometimes the most important thing of all."

Small said nothing and looked down at the two books in his hands. What had he learned? That the love of women was a beautiful but dangerous thing, a cruel sword that could turn in your hand and pierce your heart; that the struggle for power was fatal for innocents; that words had many meanings; that stories were weapons of war. Books had once seemed so safe; so comforting; but no longer. People fought and died over them. He had tried his best to fight evil in the world but had been utterly defeated. And now there was nothing left for him to do but lie low whilst the shadow passed over the land; hide beneath the plain like a serpent under a rock.

Just over the northern horizon a large Murgan caravan stood waiting in the heat. The white clad outriders of their escort of horse cavalry swept back in from reconnoitring the dusty plain. The caravan captain shaded his eyes and called out, "Jayin! Do we turn south or continue? I have a city marked here on my map. It's called Alligor."

The leader woman of the horse cavalry pulled the white silk scarf of her turban away from her mouth. "Alligor! It's just a word on a piece of paper. The map is out of date. There is nothing there but a heap of ruins and a couple of beggars. No market. Nothing of commercial value. Ride on."

ACKNOWLEDGEMENTS

The author is grateful to the current Old for permission to quote from books held by the Library of Alligor in Great Britain. He would also like to thank his family for maintaining his and their enthusiasm, Rob for computer paramedicine, Richard and Jenny for their expert help and encouragement, Thomas for permission to use part of his wonderful name, and of course the author would not wish to forget all those literary agents and publishers' gatekeepers without whose help this book was produced. May the Great Author write them the plots they so richly deserve.